Praise for Sherrilyn Kenyon

"Kenyon's writing is brisk, ironic, sexy, and relentlessly imaginative." —*Boston Globe*

"[A] publishing phenomenon . . . [Sherrilyn Kenyon is] the reigning queen of the wildly successful paranormal scene . . . Just one example of arguably the most in-demand and prolific authors in America these days."
—*Publishers Weekly*

"[Kenyon] sucks you into [her] world and keeps you there from the first page until the last."
—*Midwest Book Review*

"Kenyon delivers the goods readers have come to expect, and more." —*Booklist*

"A master storyteller." —*RT Book Reviews*

ALSO BY
SHERRILYN KENYON

THE LEAGUE

Born of Night
Born of Fire
Born of Ice

THE DARK-HUNTERS

BORN OF
FURY

SHERRILYN KENYON

St. Martin's Paperbacks

This is a work of fiction. All of the characters, organizations, and events portrayed in this novel are either products of the author's imagination or are used fictitiously.

BORN OF FURY

Copyright © 2014 by Sherrilyn Kenyon.

All rights reserved.

For information address St. Martin's Press, 175 Fifth Avenue, New York, NY 10010.

ISBN: 978-1-250-06126-3

Printed in the United States of America

St. Martin's Press hardcover edition / July 2014
St. Martin's Paperbacks edition / February 2015

St. Martin's Paperbacks are published by St. Martin's Press, 175 Fifth Avenue, New York, NY 10010.

10 9 8 7 6 5 4 3 2 1

To my family and friends who put up with my flighty ways while I live in other worlds. And especially my husband and sons, who help search for everything I misplace while writing. To my editor for her endless patience and willingness to never say, "It's too long, Sherri, cut it in half!" To everyone at SMP for their wonderful support and all the hard work they do on all our behalves (and especially you, Alex and John, for keeping up with everything).

And last, but never least, to you, the reader, for all the wonderful notes you send and smiles you give. I know there was a little wait for the next League book. Thanks for your patience, understanding, and support. You guys rock!!

PROLOGUE

Kill or be killed.

That was the single law of a League assassin, and it was the reminder that had been branded onto Sumi Antaxas's arm when the devil had taken her soul in exchange for the life of the only family she had left. The only family that had ever really mattered to her.

Now . . .

As good as I am, I'm going to be slaughtered with extreme and utter prejudice. She had no doubt as she watched the video playback of the attack on a League prison from a few months ago. An attack led by the Caronese emperor and a joint Sentella-Tavali strike force.

Sumi suppressed a low, appreciative whistle as she watched them battling against an overwhelming League force. Heroic was one thing. Moronic was quite another. And in a move that was as brazen as it was stupid, Emperor Darling Cruel had led a group of rebels in to free his captured people—that included his wife—from League custody.

Then, right as he would have escaped clean-free, in a fit of rage, he'd revealed his identity to the prime commander of The League. Not only that Darling was the Caronese emperor making this strike, but that he was also a founding member of the High Command of The Sentella—the one organization that truly threatened the reign and control of The League on the planets that made up their universe.

And it didn't help that The League's prime commander, Kyr Zemin, had a personal grudge against the emperor from years ago. *That* only fueled the war that was now being fought between The League and The Sentella. A war that was quickly forcing all known governments to take sides.

"Right there! That's the bastard!"

She forced herself not to cringe as Prime Commander Zemin pointed to the monitor in front of her and froze the scene of two men blowing the door on the prison.

Well over six feet in height, Commander Zemin had the same intensity as a homicidal psych patient. His right eye was covered with a black leather patch that didn't conceal the scars of the wound that had taken it. Rumors claimed that eye had been lost in a furious fight with the legendary League assassin Nemesis—a man who was one of Emperor Cruel's best friends, and one of the men who'd been in on that prison attack.

The identity of Nemesis was also known for a fact, since he'd ripped his helmet off during that historic raid, and had publicly backed the Caronese emperor in this insane war. But like Darling, Nemesis came with his own army and was completely untouchable.

The rest of their friends were not so fortunate.

She glanced up at the commander, who was so angry as he watched the playback that it was a miracle steam really didn't roll out of his ears.

Or his nose, for that matter.

Cursing, he paced the room around her, making her even more nervous that he might use her as a scapegoat for the men he couldn't touch. He wore his brown hair long and braided down his back—a holdover from the days when he'd been one of the top League assassins, before he'd executed his predecessor and had claimed his place as head badass.

Kyr narrowed his left, silvery blue eye on her. "Pay attention and note the taller of the two men."

It was hard not to notice the ferocious warrior he spoke of. He dwarfed the man he was with by a good eight inches. For that matter, he towered over everyone except Nemesis, who was only two to three inches shorter. But Nemesis was only about half the man's muscle mass.

She sucked her breath in sharply. That warrior was the biggest man Sumi had ever laid eyes on.

It was terrifying, really. Especially the way he expertly cut through the highly trained League soldiers as if they were mannequins. There was a brutal grace to the way he fought. He showed no hesitation or mercy as he literally plowed his way through her compadres and freed the Caronese political prisoners. The warrior didn't even flinch when he was shot or stabbed. The wounds only made him fight harder. More determined.

Deadlier.

Damn.

A furious tic worked in Commander Zemin's jaw as he watched over her shoulder. "I know that hulking monster is Dancer Hauk. *I know it.* I can tell by the way the mutant bastard moves. There aren't that many beings of his size. Period. Not even among Andarions. And no one else that faggot emperor would trust at his back. Not like that."

But the commander had no real proof. Only his gut feeling and the obvious, condemning size of the Andarion male.

He glared at her. "I want you to bring me the evidence I need to convict Hauk and issue the warrant for his execution. If I can't have Cruel's head, I want that of his best friend and main protector. Understood?"

Evidence that would have to be beyond contestation. Dancer Hauk was the last of a very long and prestigious line of military heroes. A line the Andarion people would die to protect from extinction. In fact, it'd been his direct ancestor who had founded The League centuries ago and served as its first prime commander. Hauk's family had literally written the military laws that governed all of them.

And while the Andarion warrior had a kill bounty on his head from many governments, none were from The League directly. Rather, The League wanted him captured for questioning, or—more along Kyr's style—torturing, so that Hauk could indict every member of The Sentella High Command. Until they had a full confession and hard factual evidence directly from Hauk himself, The League didn't dare issue a kill bounty on a member of a family the Andarion people viewed as a national treasure.

That would be suicide. In fact, they'd be better off assassinating the entire Andarion royal family than giving a paper cut to a great War Hauk.

The only way for The League to legally execute Dancer Hauk was if they could get his birth mother to disown him first. And for that to happen, Commander Zemin would have to prove to Hauk's mother that her son had committed treason against his Andarion heritage or acted cowardly in battle.

She glanced back at his unprecedented fighting prowess.

Um, yeah . . .

In short, given his intrepid nature in a fight, an act of God.

And all because Zemin couldn't reach the emperor directly, so he was going after those closest to him. What a callous bastard.

Biting her lip, she glanced up at the commander and

forced herself to speak. "Excellency? May I have permission to ask a question?"

He sneered at her. "If you must."

She took a deep breath and braced herself for what might be a bad reaction from him. "Why me?"

"You're one of the best I have, agent. I've never sent you after a target you didn't take down immediately and effectively." His euphemism for *as bloody as possible* to make her COs happy.

His gaze darkening, he leaned over to pin her between him and the desk where she sat. "And because you look enough like your sister that it should rattle that freakish bastard into making a mistake."

Or, much more likely, get her killed for a relationship she couldn't help. Andarions weren't exactly known for their compassion or forgiveness. One of the fiercest warring cultures in the Nine Worlds, they lived for violence and bloodshed.

Especially *human* blood. For centuries, the Andarions had viewed humanity as cattle and food. A delicacy meat.

Most still did.

The commander grabbed her jaw in a fierce grip and forced her to meet his insane gaze. "You want your daughter spared, agent? *This* is the price of it. Deliver Dancer Hauk to me and I will see to it that she's removed from League training and given to a real family to raise. . . . Betray me or fail and I will have her head delivered to you and mounted to your cell wall."

CHAPTER 1

"C'mon, Darling. You can't do this to me. I'm desperate for you, man. You've got to give it to me. Right here. Right now. I need you like I've never needed you before."

In the hallway of the Caronese Winter Palace, Maris froze as he heard the deeply masculine, pleading Andarion accent through the door speaking with his male best friend.

No . . .

There was no way the two of them were talking about what it sounded like. Unlike him, they were both straight. He knew that for a fact, and yet, as they continued arguing, it definitely sounded like two lovers squabbling.

Completely confounded, Maris met Nykyrian's stunned expression as the royal prince caught up to him in the hallway outside Darling's office. Tall, blond, and lethal, Nykyrian—or Nemesis, as he was better known—was a former League assassin who had an intensity that let you know in an instant he saw you first as a target and then, only if you were lucky, a sentient creature he might not want to kill.

Being half Andarion, Nykyrian's hearing was even more astute than Maris's. Not that anyone needed supersonic hearing to miss this exchange. Their decibel level carried quite plainly through the heavy door of the emperor's office.

And how Darling's two imperial guards remained stone-faced while it went on was a testament to their training.

"Hell. No. Hauk," Darling snapped, enunciating each word with rage. "As much as I love and owe you, I'm not doing *that* for you. *Ever.* Forget it. . . . And even if we did, *you* couldn't handle it. Besides, you've never wanted it before. Not like this, and definitely not from *me*."

Maris's jaw dropped in synchronicity with Nykyrian's.

"Ah, come on, Darling." Hauk continued to plead in a tender, needful tone Maris had never heard him use before. "After everything I've done over the years to protect your sorry ass, I can't believe you won't share it with me. Don't be like this. This isn't a want. It's a need. A major one. If you really loved me, you'd do this for me without question. Now give it to me! Please!"

"No! Not if we were the last two beings in the universe. Not even if you were down on your knees in front of me, buck naked and begging me for it."

His expression horrified, Nykyrian opened the door to show Darling and Hauk standing on opposite sides of Darling's desk, glaring at each other as if they were about to come to blows.

With his short red hair brushed back from his face and his royal harone hanging to his left shoulder, Darling was dressed in dark blue and maroon emperor robes while Hauk was swathed in a red-tinged black blast-resistant Sentella battlesuit that hugged every inch of his huge, well-muscled body. His black hair fell to his shoulders in small, extremely attractive braids that were common for the warriors on his home planet to designate them as the fiercest of their breed. The stark darkness of his warrior's uniform made his skin glow a rich tawny-caramel that would make anyone's mouth water for a taste.

Obviously annoyed, Hauk turned toward them and pinned them with his red-and-white Andarion eyes.

Even though Nykyrian shared many Andarion traits with Hauk, such as fangs, sensitive hearing, and extreme height, he had green human eyes. Ones that showed no fear as he locked gazes with Hauk. "Thank the gods you're both still dressed and not entwined naked on the floor. . . . Now tell me, what exactly are we interrupting?"

Hauk scowled at the comment and question as if replaying their exchange in his head while Darling burst into laughter.

"Damn, Nyk . . . my wife's not *that* pregnant." Darling's tone was filled with utter indignation.

Maris scoffed. "Oh please, honey. Zarya's so pregnant, one good sneeze could launch your son into this world in a matter of seconds."

Darling gave him a droll stare, but he knew it was true. Due any minute now, the poor girl was almost as huge as a shuttle craft.

And crankier than a Gondarion were-beast.

Moving closer to Hauk, Nykyrian looked back and forth between them. "And neither of you has answered my question. What had the two of you shouting lewd come-ons at each other?"

Now it was Maris's turn to burst into laughter, as a smile toyed at the edges of Nykyrian's lips.

With a nonchalance Maris knew he didn't feel, Darling crossed his arms over his chest. "It's something truly horrific, Nyk. We're talking the stuff of *haunting* nightmares. . . ."

Maris arched a brow at that dire statement. Given what each of them had survived, he could only imagine what would make the intrepid Andarion warrior flinch.

Darling jerked his chin toward Hauk. "He's facing six weeks alone with a creature so terrifying that he's actually in here begging me for explosive devices that can temporarily maim him so that he won't have to go near it."

The gape returned to Nykyrian as he faced Hauk. "Seriously? It's a child, Hauk, not a rabid animal you're about to be caged with."

Hauk scoffed at his nonchalance. "I beg to differ, and need I remind you how *you* felt the first time you learned you had a half-grown daughter and a baby on the way? As I recall, you weren't exactly let's-all-go-to-the-park-and-have-fun, buddy. But six kids later, you're fine with it all, while I'm sick to my stomach at the prospect. What do you feed them? What if he has to go to the bathroom? Huh? What do I do then?"

Darling rolled his eyes. "Your nephew's fourteen, Hauk. I promise you, you won't have to burp him or change his nappies."

"Oh, how do you know?" Hauk scoffed.

"True, Darling," Nykyrian said drily. "We still have to change Hauk's anytime you set off an explosion too close to him."

Maris and Darling laughed while Hauk glared viciously at Nykyrian. That alone spoke volumes about Nykyrian's courage.

Anyone else who received such a look from Hauk would run screaming for the door.

Including Maris.

"Go ahead," Hauk growled. "All of you. Laugh at me. Sure. Why not? But none of you have ever had to survive alone with a child, in the wilderness, for six minutes, never mind six weeks. Endurance is the hardest thing *any* Andarion goes through. Both the adult *and* the child."

Instantly, Nykyrian sobered as if he had sudden clarity over this uncharacteristic outburst. A deep sadness darkened his green eyes before he looked at Darling, then Maris. "Would you two mind giving us the room for a minute?"

"Sure." Darling stepped out from behind his desk and followed Maris to the door.

Hauk visibly cringed at the sound of their exit as he realized what Nykyrian really wanted to talk about. It was something he'd been trying to bury for weeks now as this date thundered closer.

And it was the last thing he wanted to discuss with anyone.

Even Nyk.

"This isn't about Darice. . . . I've known you almost the whole of your life, Dancer, and I've seen you roll around the floor with my boys, Jayne's kids, and Devyn enough to know that you're not really afraid of children. This is about you and Keris, isn't it?"

Hauk turned away from his best friend, unable to face the truth Nykyrian spoke. Out of his small handful of friends, only Nyk knew about his eldest brother, Keris—because Nyk, alone, had been in Hauk's life when it'd happened. And since the day Keris had died during Hauk's Endurance, Hauk had barely been able to say his brother's name aloud.

To anyone.

Gods, even now it was enough to bring him to his knees. Every fucking day of his life had been spent with guilt and grief over an unnecessary loss that no one in his family had ever forgiven him for.

Especially not himself.

And now he was supposed to take Keris's son on the same expedition that had scarred them both for life and cost Keris his.

It was so unfair.

"Darice is the spitting image of his father, did you know that?" Hauk whispered. "I love my nephew with every part of me, but there are times I can't even bear to look at him. Even their speech inflections are the same."

"I know." Nykyrian moved to stand by his side so that

they could keep their voices low. "I really *do* know, Hauk. My daughter has some of Aksel's and Arast's mannerisms and expressions. And when she cops their condescending tones and snotty attitudes, it takes every bit of will I possess not to put her through a wall. It's not her fault she takes after them. They were in her life longer than I've been. Hell, she doesn't even know she does it. But even so, it feels like they're back from the grave to torment me."

Flexing his jaw, Hauk winced at the pain in Nykyrian's voice. A pain he understood better than anyone since he'd been there to see firsthand what Nyk's adoptive brothers had done to him. It was a hell no child should ever endure.

And he'd seen the exact tones and expressions Thia used that were identical to those of her long-dead stepfather and uncle. It had to be grueling for Nyk to deal with that all over again.

Fate was a bitch, and that whore mocked them both daily.

His anger mounting, he met Nykyrian's gaze. For once, he didn't see the war-hardened face of an assassin wingman who'd stood by his side for countless battles and protected his ass like a true blood brother. He saw the horrifically scarred face of the boy Nyk had been when they'd first met as children.

A boy who'd once saved Hauk's life while everyone else had stood back to watch him burn.

Literally.

There was a lot to be said for a friendship that spanned double-digit years. But right now, it seriously rankled him that Nyk knew what was really bothering him.

And it made him wonder something about his friend that he hadn't considered before. "Is that why you didn't take Thia on her Endurance?"

Nykyrian shook his head. "Thia's only a quarter Andarion, and by the time her mother got around to telling me I had a daughter, Thia was past the age of it."

Not to mention, the first two years of their living together, Nykyrian had been going through extensive operations and physical therapy for the almost fatal injuries Aksel had given him the day Nyk had finally put the bastard in his grave. Even now, eight years later, Nykyrian still walked with a pronounced limp, and only had limited use of his right hand and arm.

Hauk ground his teeth as other painful childhood memories surged. "It's a *stupid* tradition. It chafes my ass that I have to do this."

Nykyrian snorted at his outburst. "Everything chafes your ass, my brother."

True, but still . . .

Hauk let out an elongated growl. Even if his father hadn't lost his legs in battle or been too disabled to be exposed to the harsh conditions of Endurance, his father was too old to do it now. And his brother Fain had been disinherited even before Hauk had gone through his. There was no other male in their family lineage who could take Darice.

Like it or not, Hauk was honor bound and family obligated to see this through.

But honestly, he'd rather sacrifice a testicle than go. Every time Darice looked at him, he saw the accusation and anger in his nephew that blamed him for Keris's death.

Nykyrian stepped away from him. "Have you mentioned to your father the staggering bounties on your head? Or that you have enough assassins after you that you could start your own army?"

Hauk made a rude noise at the mere suggestion. "My father's an Andarion war hero. Do you really think that would deter him?" He'd think Hauk weak and cowardly for even mentioning it.

Nykyrian sighed. "No. He'd say it adds to the challenge of it all."

"Exactly. You've no idea how many times I've cursed my parents for their blind adherence to the old ways."

Nykyrian clapped a hand on Hauk's shoulder. "Again, brother, I do know. You never bitch about it, but I can read your expressions better than your words." He went to pour them both a shot of Tondarion Fire—a potent alcohol—from the small table beside Darling's desk. "You know, you could take Thia with you as a distraction. It might help you get through this."

A taunting grin spread across his lips as he took the shot glass from Nykyrian's gloved hand. "You would really turn your beautiful daughter loose, alone with two Andarion males, for six weeks?"

"Never. But I would trust her with my family."

And that they definitely were.

Hauk knocked back the drink in one gulp and pinned his gaze on Nyk. "And I can read you as well as you read me. Why do you want her gone so badly?"

"I don't. But . . ." Nyk let his words trail off as he gulped his own drink then poured another. "She's been acting out since Zarina was born. It's almost like she thinks that now that we have another daughter, she's not wanted anymore. Truthfully, I don't know what to do. She stays out all night. Drags home the kind of dregs we're paid to kill, and then dares me to lay a hand on them." He growled low in his throat. "I'm a trained assassin, Hauk, and they're dating my precious little girl. Putting body parts on her . . . and that's just their hands, that I know of. Any idea how hard it is for me to let them leave my house upright and in one piece? She won't even let me give them a damn bloody nose. Gah, it's more than I can bear."

He scoffed at Nykyrian's irritation. "And now you

know why your father-in-law had you shot . . . multiple times."

Nykyrian glared at him. "I curse you, Hauk . . . may you live to raise a beautiful daughter. And I hope you have more than one, you son of a bitch." He slung his shot back even faster than Hauk had. "Thia's been way too serious with this latest *veriton*. I'm thinking if she's gone for six weeks, he'll get bored and move on to someone safer."

"If he doesn't?"

"I still have a few places left to hide bodies no one knows about."

Hauk laughed then sobered as he seriously considered the offer. In all honesty, Thia would be a welcome distraction. While she didn't care for roughing it, she could cook better than either of them. And the additional body might keep the memories of Keris at bay. It wouldn't be the same as it'd been when he and his brother had gone alone to Oksana for Endurance.

Best of all, Thia actually liked him.

He inclined his head to Nykyrian. "I'll be more than happy to spend a few weeks with my first love. Besides, as an Andarion princess, she needs to have this on her résumé."

"Just don't let her think for one instant that I'm doing this to get rid of her."

"Trust me, I know. You're doing this to get rid of her boyfriend."

"Exactly." Nykyrian headed to the door to readmit Darling to his office.

Before he could open it, Hauk pulled him to a stop. "Thank you."

Nykyrian held his hand up to him. *"Estra, mi drey-stin."*

Taking his proffered hand, Hauk pulled him into a rare familial hug and repeated the Andarion words of loyalty that literally translated to *anytime, my brother*. But the Andarion connotation was much deeper than that. It was an oath of absolute kinship. One that bound them closer than blood.

No Andarion said those words lightly. It meant that they would die back-to-back, fighting any and all attackers.

And it was one they'd both proven to each other repeatedly.

Nykyrian stepped away from him. "Just remember, Hauk, I know Andarion urges, and if any male, including you, lays a finger on my girl while she's in your custody, I will cut you into pieces and feast on your entrails."

Laughing, Hauk knew Nykyrian meant *those* words most of all.

CHAPTER 2

"Nyk," Hauk breathed. "If you really loved me, *drey*, you'd take that blaster at your hip and shoot me right between the eyes. Right here. Right now. *This* instant."

Nykyrian came as close to laughter as the somber warrior could.

As if on cue, Darice stormed off the shuttle and slung his pack to the ground in front of Hauk's feet. At fourteen, he was as tall as most full-grown human males, but he only reached the middle of Hauk's and Nykyrian's chests. Even so, he was still just a boy with the very lean build and temperament that marked the young.

And as he moved to glare up at Hauk with his fists clenched at his sides, Hauk understood why some species chose to eat said young rather than raise them to adulthood.

It was *so* tempting.

Furious, the boy gestured toward the shuttle. "I'm not going anywhere with *that*—"

"Bite it," Hauk growled before his nephew let loose a word that would have him disciplined.

Or worse, hunting on the ground for his teeth.

Darice hissed and exposed his long canines in protest.

"Oh my God, did he just fang you?" Thia gasped as

she joined them in the landing bay. With an exaggerated gape, she blinked at her father. "Dad, he just fanged Uncle Hauk and Uncle Hauk didn't kill him. Is the world coming to an end and I missed the e-mail?"

His features turning even darker, Darice snapped toward her with obvious intent.

Hauk caught his nephew's arm in a gentle, yet firm grip. "Fang her, boy, and you will feel the pain of my displeasure to such an extent our ancestors will curse you for it."

Darice jerked away from him. "You're *not* my father. And that—" He gestured angrily toward the shuttle. "Is *not* my family. I will not dishonor our blood or ancestors, or dishonor my blood father's memory by being in a shuttle or on a planet with *him*! You know our laws! How dare you bring *him* here!"

Hauk glanced past his nephew to see the look on Fain's face as he heard those cruel words. The pain his brother felt nauseated him and increased his need to tan the backside of Darice's buttocks until the boy limped.

For all eternity.

His features guarded, Fain stepped down from the shuttle's ramp. "I've got Chayden coming in to do the drop. He'll be here in five minutes."

"A human?" Darice sneered as if that was the only thing worse than Fain.

"Careful who you insult, boy." Hauk jerked his chin toward Nykyrian, who was the crowned prince and heir for their native Andaria.

He was also half human.

To impugn the honor or prestige of the Andarion royal house was to defame your own Andarion family and ancestors. It was also viewed as a blatant act of treason.

That alone made Darice calm himself.

Satisfied the boy was subdued, Hauk released his arm. "And while you might not claim kinship with Fain, *I* do."

Darice rolled his eyes. "*You* would," he mumbled under his breath.

Ignoring him, Hauk went over to his older brother, who was one of the very few beings taller than him. And not by much. "I'm sorry. I should have known how he'd react. I was only thinking of tradition. Not selfish pubescent stupidity."

Fain clapped him on the arm. "It's all right, *drey*. I knew what I was giving up the day I walked out your mother's door. I have no regrets."

That wasn't true and they both knew it. The deep sadness that never left Fain's eyes called him a liar for the choice he'd made all those years ago. But it wasn't Andarion to admit you acted rashly, or that you made a mistake.

Especially not when you chose one family member over another.

Too bad most humans lacked the loyalty and honor of the Andarions. But then, they were a different species. And not just in coloring and dental needs.

"Thanks for coming, Fain."

Fain dutifully inclined his head to his beloved younger brother as hurt and anger tangled inside him. Though his brother was one of the fiercest warriors he'd ever fought alongside, he still saw Dancer as the boy he'd been. The one who used to run after him with worshipful stars in his eyes, begging for any attention from him.

A brother who'd recklessly and courageously defied their parents to maintain a relationship with him that could cost Dancer dearly. For any Andarion male to do such was an incredible testament of loyalty and love.

For Dancer, that risk was so much higher.

He already had a mark against him. One more, and he would be relegated to an Andarion class even worse than the one Fain was in. Fain knew of no other who would risk that.

Not even for a full-blooded brother.

But then Dancer was the bravest male he'd ever known. He lived his life with reckless disregard for the fact that he was mortal. And there was absolutely nothing he wouldn't do or risk for those he loved.

Smiling, Fain clapped Dancer on his back. "For *you*, anything. Any time."

Hauk watched Fain leave with a heavy heart. At his departure, Darice started to shout something to him, but the sight of a guard carrying Thia's pink floral rucksack for her distracted him. His jaw gaped even wider than Thia's had a moment ago. "Seriously?" he said to Hauk. He gestured after the guard who was headed for the shuttle to deposit his cargo. "She can't even carry her own pack?"

Thia flashed him a sweet, adorable grin. "That's what I have *you* for, punkin'. Didn't you know?"

Hauk heard Fain's insidious laughter as his brother vanished. "Just like his arrogant father . . . Not enough Tondarion Fire in existence to make me take that brat across the street, never mind do an Endurance with him. Good luck not choking the little bastard, Dancer."

Hauk actually whimpered as he heard his brother's mumbled words. *Thanks a lot, Fain.* If his brother really loved him, he'd do this for him.

"Are you listening to me, Dancer?" Darice tugged at Hauk's sleeve. "Why is *she* going with us?"

He pulled his arm out of Darice's grip. "Because she's Andarion."

Again with the eye rolling that, since puberty, had become Darice's automatic response to most stimuli and any words uttered by an adult. But the eye rolling stopped as a group of men brought in a large covered crate and took it on board.

"What is that?" Darice gestured toward the men. "Her wardrobe?" He put his fists up to his temples and growled fiercely. "This is a disaster. I want to go home. Now, Dancer! I don't want to be here. With her or with *you*!"

Hauk knew the feeling intimately. "Get on board, Darice."

"But—"

"Now, boy!" It was his turn to fang his nephew.

Screwing his face up, Darice appeared to have the same degree of intestinal woe that currently plagued Hauk. "You're not my father," he mumbled between clenched teeth as he snatched his pack up from the ground. "You'll *never* be my father."

Thia moved to rub him gently on the back. "It'll be all right, Uncle Hauk."

No, it wouldn't. His family, and in particular Darice and Dariana, would *never* forgive him for what had happened to Keris. But it wasn't Thia's fault they were assholes.

Smiling, he cupped Thia's gentle face and started to thank her, but before he could say a word, two excited voices rang out.

"Thia! Thia! Thia! Thia! Thia!" The last one was punctuated with a screech so high, he was amazed his ears weren't bleeding.

He barely had time to step away from her before Adron and Jayce all but tackled their older sister to the ground. To her credit, Thia stayed upright and hugged them against each side while laughing at their enthusiasm. At six and eight, the blond boys had blue eyes and were almost identical in looks. The only way to really tell them apart was the difference in height. Adron, being older, had a good three inches on his brother.

For now. Hauk remembered well when his older brothers and Nykyrian had towered over him, too, and that definitely wasn't the case these days. He was a good three inches taller than Nyk, and had Keris lived, he'd have barely reached Hauk's shoulders.

The boys were talking so fast and furiously that Hauk got a headache trying to figure out what they were saying. With the patience of a saint, Thia nodded and listened attentively.

Except for the difference in their ages, no one would ever guess she wasn't their full-blooded sister.

Freakishly tiny, and graceful in everything she did, Nykyrian's wife Kiara approached them with her golden-amber eyes twinkling. "Boys, slow down. Take a breath. Give your sister a minute to catch up."

Jayce immediately started in on a round of "buts" and ended with a simple "Mama!"

Still laughing, Thia patted his back. "It's okay, Kiara. I can strangely follow their gibberish." Kneeling down, she took both of Jayce's arms in her hands and smiled at him. "And yes, I'll bring you back a rock for your collection. Two, even."

Adron sighed heavily. "I wish I could go with you."

With an exaggerated pout for him, she cupped his cheek in her hand. "Me, too, sprout. Maybe next time."

Nodding, he stepped away then pulled his brother with him. She stood.

Kiara held out a black sweater toward Thia. "Stay warm, sweetie. Don't get hurt."

"I will and I won't." Thia took her sweater and gave Kiara a light hug. She looked expectantly at her father, who had the same what-did-I-do-now look Hauk was sure he'd worn when his parents told him he had to do this with Darice.

Facing her intense husband, Kiara motioned toward Thia with her hands. "What do we say to our daughter before she leaves us for six weeks?"

Nykyrian recovered himself and unstrapped his blaster from his hips. He checked the charge level before handing it to Thia. "Remember what I taught you. Check your perimeter every night and never sleep with your head-phones on."

With a patient sigh, Thia took the blaster from his hands. "Thanks, Dad," she said drily.

Arms akimbo, Kiara approached her husband. "Sweetie? Are you out of your mind? You don't give a loaded weapon to your little girl right before she leaves. What are you thinking?"

"That she might need it."

"A blaster?" Kiara asked incredulously.

He frowned as if he had no idea why she was upset at him. "I'd rather she have it and not need it than need it and not have it."

"And what if she accidentally shoots Darice?"

Thia snorted. "Trust me. If I shoot Darice, it won't be an accident."

Hauk bit back a laugh at something that really shouldn't amuse him.

"You see!" Kiara said to Nykyrian as she indicated Thia. "You see what could happen?"

Nykyrian shrugged. "She's a Quiakides. She'll have to make a first kill at some point. Why not keep it in the family? Hell, it might even make Hauk's day if she shoots Darice."

Sighing in surrender, Kiara shook her head. "You're awful." She turned her pleading eyes toward Hauk. "Would you help me out here?"

He met Nykyrian's gaze. "Is she trained?"

"Fully."

Hauk duplicated Nykyrian's earlier shrug. "Then I'm glad to have the backup."

The boys stared bug-eyed while their mother sputtered at the men's lack of concern.

Adron flashed a big grin to Jayce. "When I'm big, I'm going to be an assassin, just like Daddy and Uncle Hauk!"

Jayce shoved him. "Hah! I'll be an even better one than you."

"Nuh-uh!" Adron dove at his brother. The two of them hit the deck, pounding on each other.

Kiara's face flushed bright red as she pulled them apart. "Stop it! Both of you. None of my children are going to be assassins. None of you! I mean it!"

"Mom!" they whined.

She made that imperious maternal gesture that never failed to quell squabbling children, and reminded Hauk of how his own mother used to break him and his brothers up from fights.

Hauk let out a tired "heh" as he faced Nykyrian. "Remember when it was just the five of us and the only kids you had to break apart from fighting were me and Darling? Oh, for the blessed peace of those days."

Nykyrian swept Adron up in his arms to keep him from punching at his brother. A rare devilish grin curved his lips as he held his son against his chest, and Adron laid his head on his father's shoulder. "I will gladly take one minute of this chaos over an eternity of that peace."

A tender, heated glance passed between Nykyrian and Kiara. The love they bore for each other never failed to amaze Hauk. The gods knew, he didn't understand it. He'd never felt that way about anyone. And he still couldn't believe Nykyrian did. Battle-hardened and battered by life, Nyk had every reason to kill. No reason whatsoever to understand, never mind show, any kind of love or compassion.

For anyone.

Nykyrian pulled Thia against him with his free arm and placed a kiss on the top of her head. "Let no harm come to you, *mu tina*."

Adron launched himself from his father into his big sister's arms with such unexpected force that she stumbled back. "Love you, Thia! Don't be gone long."

Closing her eyes, she squeezed him until he protested it. "Love you, too, Addy. Be a good boy and I'll bring you back a souvenir."

"Like what?"

She cast a speculative glance toward Hauk. "Darice's head on a pike if his manners don't improve."

Adron laughed as she set him down on his feet. Thia opened her arms for Jayce to get just as warm a hug from her. She released him before ruffling the hair on both their heads. "Keep Tiernan and Taryn out of trouble, and don't let them steal Zarina's bottle from her while I'm gone."

They gave her sharp, military salutes. "It will be done, Captain."

"Captain?"

Hauk turned at Chayden Aniwaya's teasing tone as their longtime ally joined them. Almost as tall as Nykyrian, Chayden had the lethal swagger that marked most of the Tavali pirates who brazenly preyed on League ships and flouted the laws of any organized nation or empire. But his laughing hazel eyes and mass of short curly dark hair stole the bad-ass from his gait and demeanor, and gave him a boyish, carefree appearance. It was why he kept his face and hair covered whenever he had to deal with people he needed to intimidate.

Only those who called him friend got to see this relaxed, playful side of the fierce pirate captain who never took prisoners.

Or showed mercy to his numerous enemies.

"Guys," Chayden said to the boys, "she's at least a commander. Can't you tell?"

The boys whooped as they ran to Chayden and jumped into his arms while rattling off their rapid-fire words. The bewildered look on the pirate's face was hysterical as he met Nykyrian's gaze. "Help! I don't speak small-human Andarion. I need a translator."

Kiara took Jayce from Chayden's arms while Nykyrian

retrieved Adron. "They're wishing you a safe trip," she said with a smile.

"Ah, 'cause I could have sworn the bigger one just asked me for my pilot's license and the launch code to the shuttle."

Kiara laughed. "Actually, that's exactly what Adron did. See, Chay, you do speak small-human Andarion."

Chayden grinned, exposing a deep set of dimples.

Hauk didn't miss the sudden blush on Thia's face as she averted her gaze from Chayden then quickly ran into the shuttle without greeting him.

Shit. A sick dread clenched his stomach as he realized she had a crush on their friend.

And he wasn't the only one who noticed it.

Nykyrian's features turned to stone.

As soon as Chayden saw that dark expression, he stepped back and held his hands up. "Sacred embryo, Nyk. Got it. Have no fear." He lowered his hands to cover his crotch. "I value my body parts highly and none of them will breech the no-fly zone for the most precious fruit of your loins. Not even my eyes. I won't so much as glance in her general direction. I'm just here to fly the shuttle and leave. Immediately."

"Good. Remember all that."

Chayden took another step back. "Um, Hauk. I'm going to need you to lead me in since my eyes will be clenched tight, like my sphincter, until I hit the pilot's seat."

Nykyrian set Jayce down beside Kiara. "No need. *I'll* lead you in."

His expression terrified, Chayden turned toward Hauk, out of Nykyrian's line of sight, and mouthed the words, "Help me," to him as Nyk grabbed the front of his dark gray battlesuit and hauled him inside.

Kiara laughed. "You better go make sure he doesn't hurt poor Chay."

"Yeah, let's get this fiasco started." Hauk gave a quick kiss to her cheek and a hug to the boys before he ran inside to make sure Chayden was still breathing and not bleeding.

Thia was belted in across from Darice, who had his bright orange earbuds in while he played a handheld game and blatantly ignored her.

True to his words, Nykyrian had the door to the flight deck blocked as Chayden ran through the preflight checks.

Hauk snorted. "You know, Nyk, Chayden really is good at this. You and I have put our lives in his hands, many times."

Nykyrian gave him a harsh, dry stare. "What I do with my life is one thing. What I do with my daughter's . . ."

"Copy that," Chayden said, without looking up. "I will fly like I'm hauling eggs."

"Unless you run into League ships. Then you better fly like your life depends on it."

"'Cause it does," Chayden fearlessly finished for Nykyrian. "Again, copy that, Commander. Now, let me concentrate so I don't miscalculate and wind up in the wrong galaxy or splattered against an asteroid." He flashed a devilish grin.

One Nykyrian returned with a look that promised a painful death would be Chayden's if he spoke another annoying word.

Hauk wedged himself between them and gently nudged Nykyrian back. "We're all good here. You might want to go help the mother ship with your unruly spawn."

Nykyrian hesitated before he inclined his head to them. Turning around, he went back to where Thia and Darice were now both absorbed by their electronics. He paused to stare at his daughter, but Hauk knew what he was really doing. He was mentally assuring himself that she had everything she needed, and that she was properly fastened in.

Something Nykyrian verified for himself an instant later by tugging at her harness and double-checking the buckles before he left them.

Amused as hell, Hauk retracted the loading ramp behind him and closed the door.

Thia let out a tired sigh as she pulled her headphones from her ears to glare at the ramp her father had just used. "He really doesn't think I can do anything for myself, does he?"

Hauk tsked at her as he double-checked the seal on the door. "Ah, Thee, this isn't about *your* competence. It's about his fear over his own."

"How do you mean?"

Hauk glanced to Darice, who had them all completely tuned out. "It's something you won't understand until you have kids yourself. But don't take it to heart, *kisa*. All of us still want to cut up your uncle Darling's food before he eats it, and he runs his own empire."

That succeeded in making her laugh. "Does he know this?"

"Yeah. And like you, he hates that we mother him."

She fidgeted with the small MVM in her lap as she looked past Hauk, toward the flight deck. "You think I could sit up front for the launch? I'd like to learn to fly."

Yeah, right.

"Uh . . . no."

She curled her lip at him. "You're just as horrible as *he* is. I'm not a child anymore, you know?"

"Trust me, we know. Why do you think I'm not letting you ride up front?"

Rolling her eyes in a way that would make Darice proud, she put the headphones back in her ears and turned the music up so loud that even a human would be able to hear it clearly across the room.

Satisfied the two of them were safe and occupied, Hauk

returned to the flight deck, where Chayden was firing the engines. "Are they secured?"

"Yeah. Nyk tucked Thia in before he left."

"Of course he did." Chayden passed a wicked grin to Hauk. "I'd be just as bad, if not worse if I had a daughter that age. That pretty. She's what? Twenty-two now?"

Hauk didn't answer. "She's too young for you."

Chayden laughed. "No. She's too *connected* for me. But don't worry. Meant what I said about my fondness for my protruding body parts. I can keep my hands to myself. I never violate my oaths or my codes. . . . Only international laws." He pulled the mic closer to his lips and turned on the intercom. "All right, kids, hang tight. Last time I tried this, it didn't work out so well. But that's okay. I can learn from my near-fatal mistakes, and I have the fire extinguishers ready this time. There was only minimal superficial scarring, and my innards healed up quite nicely, after a while. Oh hey . . . I wonder what this button over here does. Never seen one like that before. Maybe I should have checked the shuttle's model number. Hope I'm licensed for it."

Buckling himself into the copilot's seat, Hauk laughed at the expressions on Darice's and Thia's faces as they heard that over their music. "You're so wrong."

"That's why all of you love me . . . I always fuck things up and make it interesting."

"Isn't that an old Gondarion curse?"

"What?"

"May you live an interesting life?"

Laughing, Chayden hit the boosters and lifted the craft with such skill that Hauk barely felt it move.

As soon as they cleared the port, Hauk saw a small ship on their starboard aft monitor. "We have company."

"Relax. It's just your large, hairy mother tailing us in a fighter in case we need him to beat up some bad guys."

"Why didn't he say something to me about it?"

Chayden shrugged. "Hell if I know. He's *your* mother. Maybe he didn't want to upset Darice any worse. Or, knowing my second-favorite Tavali, he wanted to piss him off more."

"Second favorite?"

Chayden flashed a grin. "Yeah. I like me best . . . most days."

Hauk snorted at his old friend.

"So what's the deal, anyway? What heinous crime did Fain commit to be blacklisted by the entire War Hauk clan? I mean, damn, you're an outlaw to most governments, you've kicked in the front door of a League prison, been tossed out of League military service, and started a rebel organization, yet your family still claims you. What could be worse than all that?"

Hauk stared into the darkness of space as he considered everything Chayden was asking and how best to answer it. "Acts of political defiance are forgivable, according to Andarion tradition. But Fain . . . he foolishly besmirched our family's honor and tainted our lineage."

"How so?"

"Married a human."

Gaping, Chayden turned his head toward him. "Seriously? That's *it*?"

He passed a dark glower to the Tavali for his hypocritical contempt and outrage over their customs. "Your mother? Your father? They were both humans, and how were you and your sister treated because Mom was Qillaq and Dad Gondarion?"

While Andarions and humans were close enough genetically to procreate, they were two *vastly* different species. Two species that voraciously hated each other and had spent centuries at war. Human-on-human prejudice had never made sense to Hauk.

"Valid point."

Yes, it was. Chayden's treatment over the fact that his parents were from two different human cultures had been so foul that Chayden had run away from his homeworld at fourteen, and had grown up on the backstreets of other planets, alone. It said a lot that the hell he'd known on his own was better than the one he'd left behind.

Chayden leaned back in his chair to check their headings. "So where's Mrs. Fain now? I've never seen or heard of him being with any female. Or male either, for that matter."

Hauk winced at the tragedy that had been his big brother's life. "Sadly, he's never been with anyone except Omira. She was everything to him. And when she left him, he never got over it. I don't think he's gone near a female since."

"Left him? Why?" he asked incredulously. "What's not to love about Fain?"

Hauk sighed as he remembered the harsh betrayal Fain had never recovered from. "Bitch didn't care that he'd given up everything for her. His education, his military career, his future . . . his entire blood family. Less than two years into their marriage, she packed her things and went back to her human family."

"Damn," Chayden breathed. "That's so cold. How old was he when it happened? Five?"

Hauk frowned. "When she left him?"

He nodded.

"Eighteen."

"Damn," Chayden repeated. "He *was* an infant."

"Yeah." He'd been way too young to have his heart carved out and handed to him. "Fain was completely wrecked by it. He tried to come home, but my parents wouldn't have anything to do with him. My mother told him that he'd died to them the day he chose to walk out the door to be with a human *harita*. That the last thing she wanted was the stench of a human-lover in her house."

"And yet you two are still close."

Hauk glanced to the monitor, where Fain followed at a discreet distance. Just like he always had. He was the only blood family Hauk had who had proven to him, time and again, that he would always stand at his back and not judge him. That was too rare a gift to take for granted. "Like my brother, I don't give up on my family. For *any* reason."

Chayden brushed his hand against the small religious medallion his sister had given him. "I know the feeling." He glanced over to Hauk. "And that includes all my brothers who get on my nerves."

Snorting, Hauk playfully turned Chayden's head back toward the instrument panel. "Don't be cutting them eyes at me, human." But in his heart, he knew what Chayden did.

They *were* family.

And every bit as screwed up and dysfunctional as one related by blood.

Still, he hated what Fain had been through because his brother had given his heart to an unworthy bitch. Omira Antaxas had been the sorriest excuse for a supposed sentient being as Hauk had ever met. Devoted love like Fain held for her was so incredibly rare. Even for Andarions. How could anyone walk away from that?

For any reason.

He glanced back to Thia and Darice. Thia had been the by-product of her mother's curiosity about what it would be like to sleep with an Andarion. Because Dariana had been young, and she and Nykyrian were different species, it'd never dawned on her that she could actually conceive a child by him.

But Darice . . .

His parents had loved each other in that mythical way that Fain had deluded himself into believing he'd shared with Omira. To this day, Darice's mother elevated Keris to a godlike status that no mere mortal could touch. No one was allowed to besmirch his memory in any way, and she would die before she allowed another male to claim her.

At the time Hauk had gone on his Endurance, he'd envied the hell out of both of his brothers for the women they had in their lives. Back then, he'd naively assumed he would have it, too, one day.

Decades later, he knew what an idiot he'd been for that assumption. Both relationships had ended tragically.

And once this was done, his parents expected him to go home and marry Keris's widow, who hated him for the part he'd played in his brother's death.

It was something they should have done years ago, but Dariana had *violently* refused him at every turn. She couldn't even look at him without baring her fangs, and she hadn't called him by name since the day his brother had died.

Yet she was Andarion and their custom was for an unpledged male relative to marry the widow to keep her safe and provide for her.

Especially when there were kids involved.

Duty. Honor. Obligation. Loyalty. That was the life-blood of all Andarions. It flowed thick in their veins and ruled their entire existence. Like it or not, hatred or not, Dariana would marry him and keep her family's honor, and protect her son's prestigious lineage.

And make his life a living hell over something that hurt him as much as it did her. Sick to his stomach, Hauk sighed at the bleak future that awaited him.

Maybe I'll get lucky and Darice will throw me down a mountainside, too. And this time it would succeed in killing him.

One could only hope.

CHAPTER 3

"I wouldn't do that, if I were you."

Darice curled his lip at Thia before he went out of his way to kick her crate. "I'm not carrying this off the ship. You can carry your own clothes, *human*."

Hauk cuffed him on the back of his head. "She's your princess, *tarsen*. Respect her as such."

Rubbing his head, Darice screwed his face up. "Why did we have to bring someone along who's so high maintenance?"

Thia tsked at him. "I'm not high maintenance, punkin'. Rather, I'm precious cargo that comes with lavish instructions for upkeep."

Darice curled his lip. "I'm not carrying *your* clothes." He kicked the crate again.

This time, the crate growled and hissed in response.

Darice jumped back three feet. "What is *that*?"

Thia passed an amused smirk to Hauk and Chayden. "Not my clothes." With a grand harumph, she threw the switch on the crate and opened it.

A giant black cat leapt out, ready to attack as it skimmed them for a target. Darice squealed and jumped up on the seat behind Hauk.

Chayden tsked. "Damn, bud. Your nephew just callously threw you to the lorina he pissed off."

Hauk glanced at Darice over his shoulder. "I noticed that." Clicking his tongue, he called the vicious predator over to him. "Hey, Illyse." He patted the huge cat on her head and allowed her to lick his chin, then stepped aside and pointed to Darice. "Eat my nephew!"

Darice glared at him as the cat moved to lick Hauk's fingers and nuzzle his hand, instead of attacking on command. "You're not funny. Why is that thing here, anyway?"

Thia sighed heavily. "Because my father's overprotective, and lacks any semblance of a sense of humor. It was either bring his cat or half his army. I personally told him I wanted the army, so long as they were young, cute, male, and virile . . . which is why the cat was sent."

Chayden draped his arm over Hauk's shoulders. "Brother, I don't envy you the next six weeks."

"Brother, I don't envy me the next six minutes."

Chayden laughed. "You sure you want me to leave you alone with them?"

"Don't tempt me." Hauk went to grab his survival pack and gear. When he picked up Thia's too, Darice hissed. He glared at his nephew.

"How is this an Endurance test when she doesn't even carry her own pack? Huh?"

Hauk leveled a cool stare at Darice. "Trust me, son. This is definitely a test of my endurance."

Chayden and Thia burst out laughing while Darice stormed off the shuttle, cursing them all and their ancestors under his breath.

When Hauk started for the large haul bag, Thia rushed in to grab her rucksack from his shoulders. "I'm not really helpless, Uncle Hauk. I'm only going along with this to watch the smoke come out of Darice's ears." She slung the large bag over her shoulders and buckled it, then called for Illyse to follow her off the shuttle.

Hauk met Chayden's amused look and whimpered. "Please don't leave me here . . . alone . . . with *them*."

Chayden grinned without sympathy. "You'll have communications for three more days. After that . . ."

"We're on our own for the next month," he finished for him.

He inclined his head to Hauk. "If you have to eat one of the young to survive, or to salvage your sanity, I would suggest Darice. He'll give you more indigestion going down, but the ensuing torture that comes afterward will be a lot less painful, I think."

"Again, don't tempt me." Hauk took a deep breath for mental strength. "You know, I would rather walk naked, with my hands cuffed behind my back, into League headquarters and tell Kyr that I was one of the raiders on his prison than do this."

Chayden sucked his breath in between his teeth. "That says it all."

"Yes, it does. . . . See you in six weeks."

Chayden inclined his head to him and offered him an arm. "Walk with peace, *drey*."

Hauk shook Chayden's arm before he disembarked on his voyage to hell. And as bad as it was, the moment he stepped onto the stark, barren landscape, it worsened as old memories assailed him.

In the back of his mind, he could see himself as a boy, filled with excitement, jumping onto the surface near this very spot. Then, it'd been his father's best friend who had dropped them off. Hauk had run ahead to start exploring while the sound of Keris's laughter had filled his ears.

"Don't get lost on day one, Dancer!"

"Yeah, yeah! You're getting old, Kerry. Otherwise you could keep up with me!"

"I'll show you who's old. . . ."

Dropping his pack, Keris had effortlessly closed the distance and tackled him to the ground. They'd wrestled for dominance, until his much older and better-trained brother had pinned him then tickled him until he'd pissed his pants. Angry, Keris had beaten him for peeing on him, and left Hauk sore for days afterward.

A sad smile curved his lips as bitter tears choked him. He'd give anything if he could go back and forego his test. Go back and exchange his life for Keris's. He should have died that day. Not his war-hero brother who could do no wrong where their parents and Dariana were concerned.

Unlike him.

Since the hour of his birth, Hauk had been nothing but a disappointment to them.

Why did I live?

Honestly, he shouldn't have, and he still couldn't remember anything about those three weeks after he'd been injured, other than the intensity of that feral instinct not to die.

Broken and bleeding, he'd somehow crawled his way to their rendezvous point.

In the back of his mind and in every nightmare since, Hauk saw Keris's wry grin as his brother had relegated himself to death. *"Take care of Dari for me. Tell her I'll always love her."*

Hauk involuntarily flinched as he saw Keris's death flash through his mind. Heard the sound of his brother's body falling and slamming as it made its way to the jagged, unforgiving ground.

There had been nothing he could do to stop it. No way to save Keris. His brother had given him his life at the expense of his own.

Now the best he could do was safeguard his brother's child. No matter what, even with Darice's attitude and mouth, he'd keep him safe. And the same for Thia. But for Nykyrian, he'd have died a dozen times over. Nyk had believed in him when no one else had. And he had seen Hauk through the grief of losing both Fain and Keris from his life.

As soon as Chayden was gone and the sounds of the engines had faded, he heard Thia and Darice fighting again.

Looking up at the sky, Hauk shook his head and let out an aggravated sigh. He'd keep them safe from others, all right, but before this was over, he might end up killing one of them himself.

CHAPTER 4

Hauk checked his calendar and cursed before he tossed it aside. Cruel effing bastard thing. It'd only been a week since Chayden had abandoned him here.

With *them*.

It was the longest week of his life, and made him grateful as hell that he would never have any kids of his own.

"Dancer!"

He winced at Darice's high-pitched shout. *Gods, give me strength not to kill one of them.* . . . He'd sent them out after breakfast to wash and dress for the day, and look for something they could use for lunch before he strung them up by their intestines.

"Dancer!"

What had Thia done now? Dunked his head?

Again.

I swear, if the two of them don't stop trying to murder each other. . . .

"Uncle Hauk!"

Now they were calling him in unison, only it wasn't the same tone they used whenever they were fighting.

This one was more . . .

Scared.

He ducked out of his tent to find them running toward

camp like they were being chased by something other than Illyse, who was hard on their heels.

His heartbeat quickened. Hand on his blaster, he ran at them as fast as he could to cover their flight.

Thia was the first to reach him. She grabbed his arm to tug him in the direction they'd just run from, while Illyse circled all three of them protectively. "Come quick! We found someone."

He pulled her to a stop, and kept her at his side until he had more information. "Who?"

"A woman. She's hurt. Bad."

Still, he hesitated. This northernmost part of Oksana hadn't been legitimately inhabited in well over three hundred years. Not since The League had punished the citizens of this world for a revolt, and had bombed their entire civilization back to a stone age. What little part of it that held a human population was under a dome on the other side of the planet. Three continents and two huge oceans away.

No one should be here.

"Is she in uniform?"

"No," Thia said breathlessly. "She's unconscious. Just over that rise. Barely breathing."

"It looks like a *tourah* got her and tried to eat her. It's really gross, but totally awesome."

He ignored Darice's commentary. "Is she human or Andarion?" Each species had colonies set up here on separate continents in the south.

They both shrugged.

Thia tugged at his arm. "She has black hair and is really tall, so she could be either. But does it matter? She's hurt and needs help."

"All right. Both of you take Illyse back to camp, and wait for me."

"But—"

"No buts," Hauk said sharply, cutting off Thia's protest. "Get the blaster your father gave you, and wait for me in my tent. If I don't come back, you two are to return to our meeting spot, and wait until your comm comes back on, and you can signal Chayden for retrieval, understood?"

Still, she hesitated.

"C'mon, Thee." Darice pulled her toward the camp. "He'll never let us go with him. You know that."

Reluctantly, she grabbed Illyse's collar and followed after Darice.

Taking inventory of his weapons and their charge levels, Hauk waited until they were halfway to his tent. If this was a trap, he didn't want the kids anywhere near it.

He prepared for the worst, and strapped his short Andarion battle sword across his back. While it wasn't his primary weapon, which was why it was worn over the back and not at the waist with his blasters, it was the one that wouldn't run out of ammunition.

Extremely wary, he made his way toward the rise Thia had mentioned. A rise that would make a great spot for a sniper to set up surveillance. . . .

His senses on high alert, he saw the body as soon as he came up the slight hill. She lay on her side, facing the opposite direction. He skimmed the horizon in all directions, but detected no obvious threats. Even her rifle was several feet away, out of her reach.

Not that it mattered. He knew the tricks his kind implemented. He hadn't lived this long by being a *total* idiot.

That being said, partial ones apparently lived to fight another day.

Crouched and ready, he secured her weapon first. A standard laser rifle, it had no markings of any kind. Military or civ. Nothing he could use to ID her with. However, these were the weapons of choice for many assassins, since they made very little sound when they were fired.

It appeared she'd squeezed off two shots at whatever had attacked her. Other than that, it didn't tell him much. Still unsure if it was a trick or not, he made his way over to her.

She didn't move.

Looking around again for any friends she might have, he carefully rolled her to her back. There was a gash above her right brow and another along her ribs. Something had tried to rip out her throat, but she must have fought it off.

Thia had been right, the woman was dressed as a civ, in dark brown desert clothes and a dirty poncho. She might be a native or raider.

She might yet be an assassin after him. Given the rifle and the specialized scope on it, that was definitely not off the table.

He hesitated as he took in her exotic features. Not classically beautiful by any means—he knew that face well. For one full minute, he couldn't breathe as old memories surged. Except for the black hair and height, she was a dead ringer for Fain's ex-wife.

But that wasn't possible. Omira would be older than this woman. And as Thia had noted, with the short black hair, light caramel skin, and height, she might not be human at all. Andarion was still a possibility.

Even so, the similarity in looks was striking and unnerving.

As gently as he could, he parted her lips to check her species. Her teeth were small and well shaped. Clean and white. Given that, and the rest of her appearance, it was doubtful she lived in this hellhole full time. Way too much attention to personal hygiene for a desert raider who scavenged for sustenance. Though why she'd be out here alone, unless she was hunting him, he couldn't fathom.

"Okay, you're human." And she was definitely not faking her injuries, otherwise she'd bite him for his rude intrusion of personal space. He holstered his blaster and slung her rifle over his back.

Gathering her into his arms, he rose with her. As he did so, her hair caught against the thorny bush under her and the black wig was pulled free to expose a flesh-colored skullcap. Curious, he removed it to find a wealth of long blond hair that was almost as pale as Nykyrian's.

Damn. She *really* favored Omira. Thank the gods Fain wasn't here. His brother would have a stroke.

And probably cut her throat.

Hauk cradled her against his chest, amazed at how little she weighed. Especially given her height. She was a *lot* taller than the average human woman. Andarion females were normally well muscled and stout. They had a nice heft when you picked them up, and like the other males of his species, Hauk preferred a female he didn't fear crushing. One who would be physically able to enjoy and return the fierce passions of an Andarion male. Underneath her poncho and loose pants, she must be as scrawny as Kiara or Thia.

Careful not to hurt her more, he carried her back to camp, where the kids were waiting.

And fighting.

While it was the Andarion way to argue over any little thing, he'd spent enough time among humans or alone that he now craved a modicum of peace once in a while.

Silence would be even better.

As soon as he entered his tent, Thia opened his pallet so that he could lay the woman down. "I already got the medical pack and water."

"I told her not to waste supplies on someone so pathetic they couldn't protect themselves. But she didn't listen."

Thia shoved at Darice.

He shoved back.

"Stop it!" Hauk snapped at them.

The scent of blood, combined with that of their anger, had the lorina growling and unsettled. Hauk held Illyse off the woman by her red collar. "Take her outside and tie her up."

Thia immediately obeyed.

Hauk pulled the medical pack to him so that he could go through it, and see if they had something that could help their unknown "guest." How he wished Syn was here. His friend and ally was a doctor well versed in human medicine. Him, not so much. What little he knew about human anatomy was how to apply tourniquets to those injured in battle until a medic could relieve him.

And what vital organs he needed to disable or puncture to kill them.

"She's human?" Darice curled his lip at the sight of her blond hair.

"Don't start, D. Like Thia said, she needs our help."

Darice scoffed. "She's human," he repeated. "She wouldn't help us if we were the ones hurt."

"You don't know that." Hauk pulled out an antiseptic cloth. "Go start lunch."

Sheepish, Darice glanced away.

Dread consumed Hauk over that look. "What?"

"We didn't catch anything, after we dressed. In case the woman wasn't alone, Thia wouldn't let me keep hunting while she came back here for you."

"Good for her."

Darice curled his lip in defiance. "What could *humans* do to me?"

Oh to be that naive and stupid again.

He cupped the back of his nephew's head and forced him to meet his gaze so that he could see how serious he was. "They could make you wish you were dead. *Never* underestimate an enemy. No matter who or what they are. That is a special kind of stupid arrogance no one can afford."

Darice inclined his head.

"Now, go. I have emergency rations in my pack near the water. You can rehydrate it and warm it."

Darice scooted away and left Hauk alone to tend the woman.

He cleaned the obvious wounds first then looked for more torn clothing to show him others. As he pushed the sleeve back on her arm to wipe off a scratch there, he froze at the words that had been viciously branded into her flesh.

Kill or be killed.

Shit. He knew that mark. Intimately.

Clenching his teeth, he pulled at the neck of her poncho until he had her left shoulder blade exposed. Sure enough, there was her League dagger tattoo. He cursed again.

The harita *is an assassin.*

Fury darkened his mood. She must have been caught unawares by a wild animal while sighting him. But for a freak accident, she'd have killed him, and left Thia and Darice alone to fend for themselves in the harsh wilderness.

What kind of woman could do such a thing?

An assassin, dumbass.

So much for human compassion. Darice had been right. They should have left her out to die.

Just kill her and get it over with.

It was so tempting. But he'd never murdered anyone. Killing a fully armed soldier who was fighting him was one thing. Cutting the throat of an injured, unconscious woman, even an assassin, was another. *That*, he couldn't quite manage.

His mother would be so disappointed in him for that mercy, especially given that the spared female was human.

Nothing new about that. He'd been disappointing her

since he popped out of her womb as an underweight pree-mie and almost killed her.

If he wasn't the last of his prestigious military line, his parents would have disinherited him when he'd been dishonorably discharged from The League during training.

Hauk winced as he remembered his father's sneer the day he'd found out. He'd slammed his fist straight into Hauk's chest and spat in his face. *You disgust me, and you dishonor your noble ancestors. It should have been* you *who died on Oksana. Not my one, true son* you *killed with your incompetence. How dare you humiliate our bloodlines so!*

Even now those words cut him soul deep. Neither of his parents, Darice, nor Dariana ever let him forget the fact that he, the lesser son, had survived by a miracle of twisted fate, and not by any skill he possessed. They used every opportunity to throw it in his face.

But it wasn't his fault Keris had died. He'd done his best to prevent it, and had almost been killed himself trying to save his brother's life.

Shaking his head to silence their condemnation and the memories that tore him apart, Hauk forced his thoughts away from the past. No need to dwell there. He couldn't change it.

And right now, he had something a lot more impor-tant to focus on. This was a trained assassin who had been sent to kill him. One who'd almost succeeded, and she wouldn't stop coming for him so long as he breathed. While assassins usually worked alone, they didn't always. If there were more League assassins behind her, he needed to know. They still had four more weeks before they were in satellite range again and he could call for a pickup.

The whole point of Endurance was to survive as if they'd crashed on the planet and had nothing save one survival pack of minimal supplies to sustain them. There was no one to call for help. No backup.

Completely alone, they were supposed to climb to the top of Mount Grenalyn, pluck a feather or bone from the nest of a sparn, and return to their drop site. It was a bonding experience that was usually shared between parent and child. A once-in-a-lifetime adventure designed to teach the teen confidence, self-reliance, and everything he or she needed to know in the event they should ever be on their own in a hostile environment.

And it didn't get any more hostile than to have an assassin on your ass.

How had she found him? No one knew where they were. That, too, was part of the training. The only one who was supposed to have their coordinates was the pilot who dropped them off—the primary reason why it was always a trusted family member.

Chayden would die before he gave them up. As would Fain.

It made no sense.

And that, too, concerned him.

Hauk narrowed his gaze on the woman. "You better live." He had to have answers from her. And if she was here to kill him, she had a ship nearby. One he might be able to use to get the kids to safety before anyone else came after him.

"Are you all right?"

He looked up as Thia returned to the tent. "What?"

"That expression on your face . . . it's terrifying, Uncle Hauk. I'm used to my dad looking like he's about to kill someone all the time, but not you."

He softened his features for her and smiled. "Better?"

"Kind of. But I think I've been emotionally scarred. For life."

He lovingly scoffed at her words. "I hope it takes more than my grimace to emotionally scar you, little one."

"Says the male who has no idea just how bloodthirsty and cruel he appeared a minute ago. It's one thing to be told your beloved uncle is a fierce warrior, it's another one to see it firsthand."

That was true. Because of his massive size, especially compared to Thia, he'd always gone out of his way to smile and be gentle and soft-spoken around her. When she'd first moved in with her father, she'd been absolutely traumatized by her violent stepfather, and the lunatic animals who'd worked for him. Animals Aksel had had around Thia since the moment of her birth. Not to mention the fact that the sadistic bastard had beaten Thia to the brink of death, and then brutally murdered her mother in a fit of rage.

Back then, understandably, the girl had been terrified of her own shadow.

The first time she'd officially met Hauk, Thia had burst into tears and run off to a closet to hide. It'd been a good three months before she'd finally stopped trembling in his presence. Almost a year before he could hug her.

And he'd sworn to her that he would die for her protection.

He held his hand out toward her to reassure her that his anger was under control, and would never be directed at her. "You know I'd never hurt you, baby."

She moved to hug him. "I know." She gave him a fierce squeeze. "Love you, Uncle Hauk."

"Love you, too, precious." He kissed her cheek. "Why don't you go oversee Darice while he attempts to poison us?"

She laughed. "I've never seen anyone more inept at food preparation. It's really quite impressive . . . in a very sad sort of way."

"Yes, it is." He watched as she left him alone with his hostage.

And while he would never say or do anything to hurt

or scare Thia, this assassin didn't fall under his protection. Wounded or not, she would answer his questions or feel the full wrath of the warrior who wouldn't hesitate to make her bleed until she spilled her guts to him, or he spilled them at her feet.

CHAPTER 5

Sumi came awake to the sound of female laughter. For a mere instant, she was again a girl at home with her sister, lying on her bed while they traded stories of hopes and dreams.

But as her gaze focused on a tan cloth wall, she realized that she wasn't at home. She was in a strange tent. And that wasn't the sound of her older sister's voice.

Omira was long dead, and she . . .

Her eyes widened as the pain in her body hit her and she remembered what she'd been ordered to do. Why she was here.

She'd been assigned a target, and had been attacked by something huge.

The laughter outside ended in a fierce curse. "I swear, Darice, if you don't learn to pick up your dirty underwear and stow it properly, I'm going to choke you with it! I mean it! You're so disgusting! Ugh!"

What in the Nine Worlds?

Sumi ground her teeth against the pain and rolled over. But as soon as she realized she wasn't alone in the tent and her gaze focused on the other occupant, she froze in stark terror.

Holy gods. He was absolutely huge! While she'd seen

that on the monitors, seeing it and being close enough to be dwarfed by him was an entirely different experience. He practically took up the entire tent.

No male should ever have shoulders so broad. Nor a scowl so fierce. For that matter, one of those beefy biceps had to be bigger around than her entire waist . . . and she wasn't skinny. Dressed in the black and brown leather of an Andarion desert nomad, he made a ferocious sight with his braids pulled back from his face and secured by a leather tie at the nape of his neck. From the short leather epaulettes of his shirt, thick leather straps were wound around both arms and held more weapons than she'd ever seen on a dozen soldiers, never mind one male. His large hands were covered with black leather fingerless gloves, and an ancient Andarion battle sword was sheathed and strapped across his back.

I am so dead. . . .

Another thing the commander had failed to warn her about was how much Dancer Hauk favored his brother Fain.

Every bit as muscled and fierce as Fain, Hauk took second to no one. His dark brows arched over a pair of eerie, piercing white-and-red eyes that glared a hole straight through her. There was no doubt she was on his menu, and he was already barbecuing her butt in his mind.

I am so dead, she repeated again.

Trembling uncontrollably, she did her best not to show her fear. But she was pretty sure he saw it. He'd have to be blind not to.

His gaze followed every move her hands made as if he was waiting for a reason to kill her. And still he didn't speak. He just watched with a deeply unsettling intensity. If she didn't win him over fast with guile, she would be a stain on the ground at his feet.

With perfectly sculpted features, he'd be pretty if not for the lethal aura and well-trimmed goatee and mustache.

But there was nothing feminine about this gorgeous warrior.

He was simply horrifying and bloodthirsty.

"Before you lie to me," he finally growled in a low, feral tone that was thickly accented. "I know who and what you are, assassin. Why you're here."

She swallowed hard at the underlying threat. "Then why am I still alive?"

"Uncle Hauk? Can you please tell your monkey that—" The female's voice broke off as she entered the tent with a plate, and saw them. A friendly smile spread across her beautiful, innocent face as she met Sumi's gaze. "You're awake! I'm so glad you're not dead."

She handed the metal plate to Hauk, who made it look more like a saucer in comparison to the size of his gigantic hands, before she knelt down beside Sumi and felt her forehead. The girl's concerned kindness stunned her. "Do you remember being injured? Do you know where you are?"

Completely confused, Sumi couldn't answer at first. She'd been told that Hauk would be alone on some Andarion spiritual quest. No one had mentioned he'd have companions, never mind family with him. This girl, who appeared in her late teens or early twenties, had called him "uncle." But she was quite human while Hauk was definitely not.

The girl glanced over her shoulder at Hauk, whose gaze threatened Sumi's life. "Uncle Hauk, stop scowling like that. You're terrifying the poor woman. She thinks you're going to eat her."

She turned back to Sumi with another bright, dimpled smile. "I know he's huge and scary and a full Andarion, but he won't hurt you. I promise. I tend to think of him as just a big attack dog, who's actually quite cuddly once you learn to ignore his growls."

Arching a brow, Hauk pinned a look of utter disbelief on the back of his niece's head.

Unaware of his ire, she continued talking. "I'm Thia and he's Hauk. We found you wounded and brought you back to our camp. Uncle Hauk patched you up. Can I get you something to eat or drink?"

Thia's tenderness was as startling as it was unexpected. "W-water?"

Thia patted her hand. "Be right back." She passed a glower to Hauk. "Try not to scare her to death until I return, okay?"

How could she be so brazen with him? Did she lack all sense? That tone she used with him was tantamount to popping a ravenous, rabid beast on the nose and telling it to shush.

To Sumi's shock, he actually appeared charmingly sweet as he smiled at the girl and spoke to her in a calm, gentle tone. "Thee? Can you give us a few?"

That seemed to unsettle the girl a bit. "Sure." Biting her lip, Thia glanced to Sumi as if she realized there was more to Sumi's appearance in their camp than mere happenstance.

As soon as she was gone, Hauk set his plate aside, and stood to tower over Sumi's pallet.

She fought the urge to run. While he'd been huge before, up close and in her space, he was gargantuan. And there was no missing the bloodlust in his white-and-red eyes. Something made even more ominous when he opened his lips and ran his tongue down his long canines as if savoring the taste of her blood and bones. "What's your name and rank?"

"M-m-my what?"

"I saw your League markings, assassin. . . . Name. Rank. Now!" That had to be the fiercest, deadliest bark she'd ever heard.

"Agent Sumi—" She answered immediately, barely catching herself before she spoke a surname that would guarantee her a slow painful death at his humongous hands.

"Sumi, what?"

"Just Sumi."

Crouching in front of her, he grabbed her arm and pushed her sleeve back to expose the branded words that mocked her every day of her miserable life. "I know you were conscripted into League service. What felony did you commit?"

Sumi stared into the intensity of his cold glare as old memories returned to torment her. Like Hauk, the bastard she'd killed had been merciless and cold. Unyielding. Unforgiving. And his attack on her had been completely unwarranted.

"Murder."

"Premeditated?"

Without thinking, she shook her head. Then she cursed her stupidity. It was never a good thing to admit to your enemy that you were anything other than ruthless. But then, as now, she'd acted out of fear.

"Who did you kill?"

Trying her best not to return to that horrid night with her thoughts, she snarled the answer. "My boyfriend."

He arched a brow at that. "For?"

"Breathing."

One corner of his mouth twitched as if her sarcasm amused him. Then he sobered into a terrifying countenance. "I can well understand the urge to kill someone for breathing. Been known to succumb to it myself from time to time." He glanced to the opening of the tent. When he looked back at her, she had no doubt that she was only one wrong answer from death. "I also know you're a mother."

Stunned at what she thought was a well-kept secret, she sucked her breath in sharply. "How?"

He pulled the covers back to show the bandage over her abdomen where she'd been gored by the *tourah's* horns. "I saw the stretch marks when I cleaned your wound. Given the location, there's only one thing that could have caused them. And by their number and depth, I know you carried to term."

Damn, he was good. And he was right. Tears filled her eyes as she tried her best not to remember the baby that had been stolen from her before she'd ever had a chance to hold her.

"Where's your child now?"

A single tear fled past her control. It always did whenever she thought about her daughter. "She was taken from me."

"By The League?"

She started to lie, but why bother? He obviously wasn't stupid. And it was standard League procedure to seize custody of any child born to their soldiers. "Yes."

Hauk sat back on his haunches as she bravely blinked away her tears, and stiffened her spine in spite of the pain she had to be in. He admired her courage, and there was no way for her to fake the agony he saw in those hazel green eyes. He'd been around assassins and soldiers the whole of his life. And he knew more than his share of ruthless liars and grifters.

She was none of those. While she was trying to be fierce and tough, she was failing miserably at it.

In the dark, with the element of surprise on her side, he was sure she was extremely accomplished at killing someone. But right now, she knew what he did. Up close, face-to-face, she couldn't go a single round against him and win. She just wasn't large or strong enough to take him in an open fight. Nor was she some psychopathic assassin who had gleefully chosen her occupation and relished it.

No, that role had been forced on her. And those hazel eyes and scared demeanor betrayed the deep vulnerability he'd just laid bare. This woman had a soul.

Unlike him.

"Is your daughter why you agreed to be an assassin?"

She drew a ragged breath. "Does it matter?"

Yes, it did. Greatly. "Answer me!"

She flinched at his growl, making him wish he'd chosen a softer tone. "Yes. They would have executed me during my pregnancy with no regard for the fact that she would have died with me."

Yet she would never be allowed to see her child. That was the law of The League.

Hauk forced himself to bite back a scoff at her blind ignorance. She wasn't doing her baby any favors by allowing The League to raise it and train it to kill. Nyk was living proof of that.

But Hauk didn't want to spit on her sacrifice or maternal love. Not when she was doing what she thought was best for the child. She'd sold her soul to the devil to save her daughter's life.

That gave him hope for her humanity.

He placed the covers over her again. "There are two children outside this tent. My niece and nephew. Neither of them can survive here on their own. If you kill me, you will be consigning them to death, too. And just like your daughter with your actions, they don't deserve to die for *my* crimes. Let me get them to safety, then I will surrender myself to you. I swear it on my ancestral blood."

Sumi scowled at his offer, which was essentially suicide and they both knew it. "Why don't you just kill me?"

"Is that what you want?"

"Not really. But I don't understand why you would do this when my death would be a much easier solution."

Hauk wasn't sure either. His emotions were all over the place. Yet the one thing he kept coming back to was the futures of Thia and Darice.

Keris had been cut down before he had a chance to live. To see his own son born. Hauk didn't want to deprive them of that. They had a lot more to live for than he did.

Honestly, the only future he had was hellacious and cold. Even a tortured death at Kyr's hands would be better than what awaited him at home. He'd already had more than his fair share of Dariana's "compassion." He really didn't want any more of it.

Sooner or later, we all die. And he'd rather go out for a good reason than a bad one.

Clearing his throat, he lowered his tone so that neither child could overhear him. "Two reasons. One, but for whatever accident befell you, I'd be dead already. You had the drop on me and we both know it. And two, if *you* found me here, someone else might. In the event I go down, I want to know that they'll make it home alive and unharmed."

Sumi wasn't sure what to think of him. The one thing she'd never expected from him, especially given the way he fought in battle, was this degree of humanity and love.

Not from an Andarion male who had plenty of reasons to want her dead, and more than an easy opportunity to do it. It defied everything her sister had told her about their species.

But there was no missing the dark torment in his eyes. The relegation to die in order to save his family that stung her with its remorse. He was so unexpected.

And yet . . .

"There's only one problem with your noble offer."

He quirked a brow at her.

"I'm no longer a League assassin."

His other brow shot north.

Sumi fell into the role Kyr had demanded she play so

that she could gather intel on him. "I escaped them. It's why I'm here. I'm in hiding. I didn't find *you*. You found me."

Oh yeah, *that* was a scary look. But beneath his fierce scowl was doubt as he tried to ascertain whether or not she was lying to him.

And she was a terrible liar. The only thing that might save her was the fact that he didn't know her well enough to guess the truth.

"You expect me to believe that?" he asked.

"Why else would I be here?"

"To kill me."

Now it was her turn to arch a brow at his simple, unemotional statement. Granted, there was truth to it, but still . . . "My goodness, that's some ego you have there. Does everything in the universe revolve around you?"

"When it involves death and treachery, it tends to." He glanced at the opening of the tent. "And this isn't just about me. It's about *them*." He jerked his chin toward the arguing voices.

"You really do love them."

He nodded without hesitation. "Thia has already had her mother brutally murdered by her stepfather. Her father and stepmother would be devastated if something happened to her. Darice lost his father before he was born. His mother is an honorable female who doesn't deserve to lose her son, too. He's all she has in this world that's keeping her sane and in it. She barely survived the death of my brother. She'd never survive the death of their son. If you have any decency at all, I . . ." He clenched his teeth before he finished with a word she was sure choked his pride. "Beg you, for all their sakes, not to add any more tragedy to their lives. They love their children as much as you love your daughter. This trip is supposed to be a happy memory for them. Please, don't taint it."

Tears choked her over his sacrifice. He didn't ask to spare his own life.

Just theirs.

She wanted to hate him for what his brother had done to her sister. Needed to hate him so that she could complete this mission that would end with his capture and eventual death.

But having had her own innocence slaughtered when she'd been too young to deal with it, she had no desire to pay that forward to anyone. She would have given anything to have had a protector like this, guarding her.

No matter what, she wouldn't see someone else's children hurt. For any reason. "I swear to you, as a mother, that I will not harm them."

"Or cause them to be harmed," he added.

"Or cause them to be harmed."

He inclined his head to her.

"Uh, Darice! I can't believe you did that! Really? You suck so much! Your mother ought to rent you out for birth control. Five minutes with you and any fertile female would beg for sterilization!"

As Hauk stood, a pained expression crossed his face. Sighing heavily, he stuck his head outside the tent to check on his family. "What'd he do now?"

"He farted, belched, then spilled all the food onto the fire."

"I didn't mean to. It was an accident."

"Accident, my blessed buttocks! You burped with me telling you not to!"

"For the love of all gods, don't kill him!" Hauk snapped at Thia. "His mom would really miss him. And I might, too. Maybe. Just . . . grab some water and bring it in for our guest. I'll help clean up the mess in a second." He growled low in his throat before he returned to his plate and held it out to Sumi.

Stunned by his kindness, she stared at it.

"Go on," he said with a tenderness that shocked her even more. "I ate earlier today and you need your strength to heal."

As she took it, Thia came in with the water. She was still highly agitated as she faced her uncle. "Can I please make him lick up the mess?"

"I'd rather you not since I'd have to listen to him bitch about it all night."

"Then can I kill him?"

"Please don't. I want to do it myself. I think I've earned it more since I've had to tolerate him longer."

Finally laughing, Thia handed the water to Sumi.

When Hauk started to leave, he tugged gently at Thia's arm. "C'mon, sweetie. Let's give her time to rest." He held the tent open for Thia, who quickly made her exit.

He hesitated as he pinned a sharp glare on Sumi. "Do we need to move camp tonight?"

She shook her head. "I'm here alone. I told you. I'm on the run from The League. Unless someone hunting me stumbles on us, we're safe."

Suspicion darkened his glower. "Truth?"

"I swear. Had someone else been with me, I wouldn't have been left for dead out there, and you'd be dead already."

That finally succeeded in getting him to relax. "All right. Just remember, whatever your intentions, Thia and Darice both have parents who love them as much as you love your daughter."

And then he was gone.

Sumi didn't miss the fact that he said nothing of his own parents and how they'd feel about losing their son. Both of whom, she knew from her research, were very much alive.

Fascinating . . .

Nor had anyone ever attempted to surrender to her before. In the past, her targets had gone out kicking and screaming, trying to take her with them.

Hauk's actions were more akin to a parent guarding his young than an uncle. And it said a lot about the male's integrity and decency.

How can I convict him now?

What choice do I have?

Sickened by her cowardly assignment, she dropped her gaze to the plate and water. How long had it been since anyone had been nice to her, never mind kind?

Honestly, she couldn't remember.

No, that wasn't true. Her sister had always been kind to her. But Omira had died a long time ago.

Unshed tears constricted her throat as she thought about Thia, who was obviously part human. Omira's worst fear had been having a hybrid baby. Half human. Half Andarion.

Too bad her sister hadn't known how beautiful her child could have been. In Omira's mind, she'd pictured a monster that would devour her should she try to feed it. But Thia wasn't a monster.

Never had Sumi seen a prettier young woman.

In a weird way, Thia reminded her of her sister. They both had that inner fire that warmed you and drew you close to them. She only hoped Thia didn't lose her spark the way Omira had.

And all because of a Hauk. Brother to the one outside, which made her wonder if one of the kids was Fain's.

Thia was too old. But the boy . . .

Dancer had said his father was dead. Could Fain have met the same fate as her sister?

She didn't know why, but that brought another wave of tears to her eyes. Even though she hated Fain now, she'd loved him as her brother-in-law. She'd been just a kid when her sister had married him. And he had treated her with the same respect and regard that Dancer had shown her thus far.

"Sumi! Come here and meet the male I've been telling you about!"

Closing her eyes, she remembered the smile on Omira's face as her sister and Fain had picked her up from school the first time. Because Andarions weren't human, they couldn't stand being referred to as men, women, or people. They were male or female.

And scary as all get-out.

Sumi's eyes had widened as she looked up and up and up at her sister's boyfriend. Barely sixteen, Fain had been huge for any human male, and given her much smaller size, he'd seemed even larger.

But as soon as he'd seen Sumi's fear, he'd knelt down and given her a sweet, tight-lipped smile to hide his fangs so that he wouldn't frighten her any worse. "Hi, Sumi. I'm Fain. It's nice to finally meet you."

She'd swallowed in terror. "Are you going to eat me?"

He'd narrowed his eyes on her with a frightening intensity. "Are you made of chocolate?"

She'd shaken her head.

"Then you're safe from me." Smiling tenderly, he'd taken her hand in his and led it to his warm cheek so that she could see that though he wasn't human, he was humane. "I promise I don't bite without an invitation." With the kindest touch, he'd picked her up and carried her home.

In that instant, she'd fallen in love with him as a big brother.

Even though Fain had been forced to work three jobs to pay for her sister's school and their living expenses, he had always made time for Sumi. Whenever she'd stayed with them, he'd gone out of his way to make her feel like she was his blood sister, too.

And all the love she had for him had died when her sister had taken her own life because no human would have her once they found out her ex-husband was Andarion.

None of them.

Either their prejudice got in the way, or their fear that Fain would stalk and kill them for being with her. Omira had been a total anathema to everyone. Male and female.

Unable to deal with it and her own fear that Fain would hunt her down and kill her, she'd overdosed on painkillers.

And left Sumi with no one and nothing . . . only the remnants of a shattered heart that refused to heal. Something Fain had promised her would never happen. He had said he would always be there for them both. But instead of protecting her like he'd promised, he'd done more harm to her and her sister than anyone else.

All because Omira had told him that she didn't want any children in their marriage. For that single reason, he'd walked out on his vows and left Omira to fend for herself.

After that selfish breach of trust, Sumi's love for him had turned to pure hatred. If Fain had never come into their lives, she'd still have her sister, and none of these last few horrid years would have happened.

Everything would have been different.

She would have been different.

Fain had lied to her and Omira, and no doubt his brother was lying to her as well. No male of any species could be trusted. They were violent and selfish. Both of her live-in boyfriends had taught her that with the back of their hands.

Whatever else happened, she couldn't let herself forget that she was alone in this world. And regardless of what others said, they didn't care. They were too busy with their own lives to waste time or energy on someone else.

She looked down at her wrist where she'd been branded.

Kill or be killed. That was the way of this harsh world. And she would much rather be a killer than a victim.

At the end of the day, no Hauk was worth her life or her daughter's well-being. She would complete this mission, get her daughter free of League custody, and then she'd find some way to join Kalea, and raise her daughter so that no one would ever be able to harm her baby the way they'd harmed Sumi.

No lies. No feeling lost and alone. Adrift.

Kalea was all she had in this universe, and she wouldn't fail her child.

Not again.

CHAPTER 6

Sumi came awake with a start. She'd been trying to stay up and listen for Hauk and the others. But her pain had proven too much, and she'd dozed at some point in the night.

Now that pain was back, and it'd brought friends to join in and sing a symphony of agony through her entire being. Every inch of her body throbbed in protest. But unfortunately, her bladder took no pity on her. And it couldn't care less how much she hurt. It wanted attention, and it wasn't taking *no* for an answer.

Stupid, crappy, inconsiderate body.

Grinding her teeth, she forced herself to her feet. She whimpered as the urge to sit back down overwhelmed her. *I've got to go. . . .*

It really was *not* a choice. Not unless she wanted to embarrass herself.

She made her way slowly to the flap, and brushed it aside to find it early morning outside. But that wasn't what held her attention.

With his back to her tent, Hauk stood near a small fire, holding a towel to his face. Stripped to the waist, he was absolute male perfection. Every bit of him . . . and she could see quite a percentage of that lush, rippling body.

Never in her life had she seen so many highly defined muscles on one person. Muscles that were covered by a wealth of scarred caramel-colored flesh.

She frowned as she realized just how many scars marred his body. From his left shoulder down across his back were vicious burn scars. Those would be bad enough, but over them were a large number of claw marks, as if he'd been held down by a wild animal and brutally mauled. Numerous times. For a human, those scars would be bad.

For an Andarion, they were shameful. Their species valued beauty and strength above all things. Any kind of physical imperfection, except scars sustained in honorable battle, or tattoos designating military service or family lineage, could result in their being abandoned by their family and sterilized.

Even killed.

Was that why Hauk had never married? He was long past the age when most Andarions took mates. But with those scars, no female of his species would consider him desirable or handsome.

Nor would an Andarion female's family give permission for a joining of bloodlines to someone who would be considered deformed on their world.

Lowering the towel, Hauk turned as if he sensed her presence. As he moved, she saw even more scars on his chest and arms. Some from knives and blasters, and others she could only guess at. But the one that really stood out appeared to be a diagonal claw mark over his left biceps and shoulder and down across his pectorals. From the depth and pattern, it looked as if it'd been done intentionally.

Maybe as a punishment?

The moment their gazes met, she saw clearly the shame he felt at having been caught undressed like this. He immediately dropped the towel and retrieved his leather shirt so that he could cover himself.

Completely mesmerized, she watched as he fastened the front and wound the intricate straps and buckles down his arms, leaving parts of his skin exposed while covering enough to give him protection without inhibiting his movements or holding body heat. In fact, the leather cloth was a strange mesh-like texture that gave as much protection as battle armor while venting the wearer so as not to overheat them while fighting.

Andarions certainly knew how to battle and design clothes for it.

In an almost bashful manner, Hauk stepped over his damp shaving implements to approach her. "I didn't know you were conscious."

She gestured toward the small copse of bushes. "I . . . um . . . you know." As she started for them, she stumbled slightly and winced.

Suddenly, Hauk was by her side to help her.

"I can do it."

He snorted at her bravado. "You've lost a lot of blood, and while I'm not a human medic, I'm pretty sure it takes more than a day for those kinds of injuries to heal." He swept her up in his arms and carried her to the bushes, where he deposited her. "The kids are off, probably trying to kill each other, but in theory they're supposed to be hunting breakfast. So you can take your time and not worry they'll return soon. Experience has shown me that the whole concept of *hurry* has eluded them." He indicated the camp over his shoulder. "I'll get you some supplies and when you're finished, if you want, I can help you wash."

Again, she was mystified by him. "Why are you being so nice to me?"

"You're injured."

"But you think I tried to kill you. I can see it in your eyes that you still don't trust me."

Hauk shrugged nonchalantly. "Don't take it personally. I trust no one. Not even me." He gave her a charming, lopsided grin that was completely at odds with his massive size and intense stare. "Besides, you haven't killed me yet."

Cocking her head, she scowled at him. "That makes no sense. In *any* universe or capacity."

He laughed deep in his throat. "To a human, probably not. In my culture, we tend to let overt attempted murder slide."

And still it made no sense to her. "Andarions are supposed to be vicious warriors. I thought you killed over *any* insult."

"Insults, yes, but we're not Partinie, humans, or Phrixians. There's no honor in attacking women or children, or anyone who's weaker. That isn't our way. Trying to kill me would be thought of as a challenge to my species—meaning you consider me a worthy opponent. So it's not an insult. It's actually a high compliment."

As he walked away, she suddenly remembered Fain telling her something very similar when she'd been a child. *"Andarions intimidate. We verbally and physically test everyone we meet. And we live to fight. But never against lesser opponents. There's no glory in winning a fight when you know the other person is unequal to your challenge. Victory is only sweet when it's properly earned. And that is when you're either equally matched or your opponent has an advantage over you."*

For such a violent culture, there was also a strange beauty to their philosophy.

Hauk returned with a small pack that he left with her before he gave her privacy.

Once she was through, true to his words, he carried her back to the tent. He placed her on the ground beside the small bucket he'd been using to shave with when she'd first seen him. "The water's fresh and warm."

"Is this what you used to bathe?"

He shook his head. "There's a river nearby, but the current is rather strong. You don't need to be in it until you're better." He reached for the bandage over her stomach.

Sumi flinched instinctively, causing him to pull back. "Sorry," she said quickly. "It's not you." That wasn't entirely true. It was a lot him, but for some reason she couldn't even begin to fathom, she didn't want to hurt his feelings.

"I'm just checking your wound and the dressing. Don't worry, I kept your honor while you were unconscious. The only part of you I've seen is what was exposed by the torn clothing during your fight and the assassin's tattoo on your shoulder. I've looked no further."

She gave him a stern, teasing glare. "What? You really didn't cop a feel?"

"No." His expression lightened as if he realized she wasn't entirely serious. "But I was tempted."

She bit her lip at his uncharacteristic admission. "I tempted you?"

His cheeks mottled with color as he looked away.

"Oh my God, Hauk, are you blushing?"

He scoffed. "Andarions don't blush."

"Oh, okay," she said sarcastically. "I guess Andarions just have spontaneous cheek colorations that resemble human blushes."

He snorted. "No, we don't."

Yeah, right. He was definitely embarrassed over his admission. "Good to know."

Without a word, he carefully laid her down so that he could open her bandage and examine her wound. Sumi did her best not to think about the fact that no man had touched her this intimately in years. And never had one done so who was this handsome or this gentle. No wonder her sister had fallen so hard for Fain.

Andarions were exceptional beings.

In spite of Hauk's immense size and innate ferocity, his touch was featherlight and tender. Almost loving. The kind of caring touch she'd spent her entire life craving.

The kind that had always eluded her.

Before she realized what she was doing, she reached out to touch the hollow of his cheek. Freshly shaven, it was every bit as smooth and soft as it appeared. Until she reached his prickly, well-trimmed goatee and mustache that framed his handsome lips to perfection.

He locked gazes with her. His eyes were so strange compared to the human eyes she was used to. But even so, they were every bit as sexy as the rest of him. And for some reason she couldn't even begin to fathom, the intelligence and compassion in those eyes made her blood race. She was so attracted to him that it was more frightening than he was.

I am losing it.

She was here to frame him, not screw him.

Damn, the legends were true. There was something innately alluring about Andarions. Almost like they put off some kind of ferocious *do-me* pheromone.

"Sorry." She withdrew her hand.

Hauk couldn't speak as a strange fire simmered in his body. He had no reason to trust her. She was human, and with the exception of the handful of humans he called family, he hated all things human. Never had one of their females ever held even a passing curiosity for him.

And yet . . .

He wanted to kiss this one so badly that he could already taste her lips. Her scent filled his senses, and the softness of her skin made his mouth water.

Think of Dariana.

Exquisitely beautiful and completely Andarion, she

was to be his wife. He was pledged to her and had been since Keris's death. No matter how tempting this woman was, he couldn't dishonor his vows to his brother's widow. He must take care of Dariana first.

Even if she hated him and begrudged him every breath he took.

Hauk forced himself to examine Sumi's wound then cover it before he looked over the smaller cuts on her leg and arm. "They seem to be healing without infection."

"Thank you."

He inclined his head to her. As he started to withdraw, she caught his hand. That small contact sent a strange wave through him. One he'd never experienced before.

"Why does Thia call you Hauk, while your nephew uses Dancer?"

He released her hand. A smile twitched at the edges of his lips. "Thia likes me more."

Sumi frowned at his unexpected answer that made no sense whatsoever. "I don't understand."

The humor faded from his gaze. He took a deep breath before he explained. "Since Darice's last name is also Hauk, he uses my given name. As do all members of my immediate family."

"But you don't like it?"

He gave her a droll stare. "If you were named Dancer, would you?"

She smiled. "I guess not. But it strangely suits you."

He stiffened at something she'd intended as a compliment. "Now, *mu tara,* you insult me."

Did he just insult her in turn? *"Mu tara?"*

"My lady." And with that he left her alone.

"I didn't mean it as an insult," she called after him. But he didn't respond or come back.

Grimacing, she pushed herself up and reached for the water and cloth he'd left behind. She washed as best she could, but it wasn't easy.

She'd just finished when Thia entered the tent with a small bowl of fruit. The young woman sat down beside her and placed the bowl on the ground between them.

Thia screwed her face up at the bowl's contents. "I know it's not much. Darice spilled what he had and that's all that's left. Uncle Hauk and Darice are now foraging for more and better. But he wanted me to bring this to you to tide you over until their return."

"Thank you." Her gaze dropped to the blaster strapped to Thia's hips. "Is there trouble?"

"Not yet."

"Meaning?"

Thia rose to her feet and stepped back to eye her warily. "I'm thinking you must be an assassin who was sent after my uncle."

She froze at the girl's assumption. "Why do you think that?"

"Because of the way Uncle Hauk's been acting since he brought you here. While he's always cautious, he's even more so now. Instead of sleeping last night, he walked the perimeter, heavily armed."

That was impressive, especially given how alert he was without sleep.

Sumi dropped her gaze to Thia's weapon, and wondered how proficient she was at its use. "Yet he let the two of you hunt this morning. Alone."

"And insisted I be armed and extra vigilant while we did so." Thia glared angrily at Sumi. "Just so you know. You hurt him and I *will* kill you. Without mercy or hesitation."

There was a sincere ferocity in her tone that belied the girl's years and innocent appearance.

Sumi remembered what Hauk had told her about Thia's mother. "Were you there when your mother died?"

Thia stiffened. "How do you know about my mother?"

"Your uncle told me."

Her eyes shimmered from unshed tears. "No. I wasn't there. Had I been, I would have killed my stepfather myself."

Sumi felt for the poor girl and the fate of her mother that had almost been Sumi's. No one should have such a tragedy in their life, and definitely not when they were so young. "I'm sorry, Thia. I lost my mother when I was young, too. I know how hard it is to grow up without one."

"Then I'm sorry for you as well. How did *your* mother die?"

Sumi looked down at the fruit as her own tears choked her. "She didn't. She ran off with a boyfriend and left us behind with my father."

"Us?"

"Me and my sister."

Thia glanced away as she digested that. "Is that what made you become an assassin?"

Was every member of their family so astute? It was actually unnerving. "No one said I was an assassin."

"Then why were you in the middle of a desert, alone, with a sniper rifle?"

Damn. Was it training or genetics that made the whole family so paranoid? "Sabbatical?"

She gave her an unamused glare. "Is that really your answer?"

Sumi sighed as she picked through the fruit. "No. You're right. I am a trained assassin. But I'm not here to kill your uncle." Which was actually the truth. She was here to get evidence for Kyr to do it, instead.

Thia jerked her chin toward the bandage on Sumi's stomach. "How did you get hurt?"

"Target fixation." She met Thia's bloodthirsty gaze levelly. "I was so worried about the fire I saw from your camp, I missed the *tourah* that came up on me and tried to make me its lunch." Again, that was the truth. She'd been trying to get bearings on Hauk before she made her presence known.

"So what are your intentions now?" Thia still eyed her suspiciously.

"Trying not to die."

That did not placate the young woman at all. "You know what I mean."

"Yeah, I do. And I promise, I'm just passing through." Which was also the truth. She had no intention of staying here, with these beings, a moment longer than she had to.

Thia drew her blaster and angled it at Sumi. "I want the truth and I want it now. I mean it."

Faster than Sumi could blink, Hauk entered the tent and grabbed Thia's hand.

He wrenched the weapon free. "What are you doing?"

Thia threw herself against him then started sobbing uncontrollably.

Holding her to his chest, he glanced helplessly at Sumi. "What did you say to her?"

Before she could answer, Thia pulled back and cupped his face in her hands. "Don't you leave me, Uncle Hauk. Don't you dare!"

"I'm not leaving you, baby," he said gently as he rocked her against him. "Your father would kill me in a most painful way."

"No. I mean don't die on me. You can't! You hear me?"

His jaw slackened. Then he pinned a murderous glare on Sumi. "What did you say to her?"

"Nothing. I swear."

Suddenly, a younger version of Hauk stuck his head into the tent to check on what was happening. Instead of Andarion warrior's braids, he wore his black hair pulled back into a ponytail. But other than that and his size, he looked enough like Hauk to be his clone. It was adorable.

Until he spoke.

"Ah gah," Darice groaned. "Human emotional females. What has her stirred up now? Is she ragging?"

That succeeded in drying Thia's tears as she lunged at him.

Hauk held her fast against his chest. "Don't. He has to live, too."

"Oh please, Uncle. It's a moral imperative that I kill him!"

Darice rolled his eyes before he gave Sumi a gimlet stare that was eerily similar to the one Hauk often used. "Are you fully human?"

"Yes."

"Shit," he breathed.

"Darice!" Hauk snapped. "Watch your tongue."

He bared his fangs at Hauk. "How much worse is this trip going to blow, huh?" He gestured angrily at Hauk. "First, I'm stuck with *you,* then . . ." His voice trailed off as if he realized what he'd just said.

Hauk looked as if he'd been slapped. When he recovered, it was with a furious glower that made Darice step back and Thia suck her breath in sharply.

Without a word, Hauk brushed roughly past his nephew and went outside.

Thia glared at her cousin. "You're such an ungrateful bastard, Darice."

"You know nothing about it, *human.*"

Thia grabbed the front of his shirt and snatched him to stand in front of her so that they were nose to nose. "Do not make the mistake of thinking I don't have enough Andarion in me to spill your entrails, little worm. I do. And you better well remember exactly who my father is. *His* is the blood that flows thickest through my veins. Much more so than any human gene I *might* carry."

Darice's eyes widened at her threat.

"And you know *nothing* of your uncle's skills," Thia continued. "Instead of insulting him, you should consider this. *Your* father was twice Uncle Hauk's age and size when he died. Yet Hauk survived. Alone and injured. For *three* weeks."

"Because he killed my father!"

"You don't know that."

He lifted his chin defiantly. "My mother told me so. It's why he has yet to marry her when he should have married her long ago. He's a coward who shirks his responsibilities. Rather than save my father, he saved himself. If he were really Andarion, he'd have killed himself, instead of returning home in shame."

Thia shoved him away so forcefully, he stumbled and fell to the ground. "You know *nothing* about being Andarion. You shame your ancestors and taint both your parents' bloodlines." She kicked at the dirt next to him before making an angry exit.

"At least I'm not the one tainted with *human* blood!" he snarled after her. He cast a feral lip curl at Sumi before he pushed himself up and stormed out.

Okay then.

Sumi released a slow, steady breath. She didn't know why, but she felt bad for all of them. And honestly, rather intimidated by Thia. For a little thing, she was ferocious and highly unpredictable.

Who *was* her father?

To her knowledge, Hauk only had Fain and Keris as brothers. But then she hadn't done that extensive a dig into his family. Only enough to get the parameters of this mission straight in her mind. And Fain had never said much of anything about his family. Since he'd been disowned by them, he'd told everyone, even her, that he was an orphan with no blood lineage whatsoever.

"What do you mean, we're staying here another day?" Darice whined outside. "Gah! It's not fair! This is supposed to be *my* Endurance, not an exercise in learning to tolerate humans!"

"And it's not supposed to be an exercise in my learning to tolerate *you*," Hauk shot back. "Now do what I told you."

"You're *not* my father! I don't have to do what you tell me." There was no missing the hatred beneath those words.

Thia let out a tired sigh. "And all this *wondrous joy* because *my* father can't stand the thought that I'm a grown woman and he can't rule my entire life anymore."

"Not a word against your father, Thee. That's my brother you're talking about, and I will not have you disparage him in my presence."

"Disparage him? Excuse me? Have you *met* my father, Uncle Hauk? The man who smiles with a grimace and has perpetual PMS and an itchy trigger finger? Try dating with *that* . . ." When she spoke again, it was in a falsetto. "Why yes, hon, my father is the legendary killer with a higher body count than the top three League assassins combined. No, he's not planning to eat you or hide your body, dear. That's his version of a smile, and yes, we're all well aware of the fact that he looks like he's in extreme pain when he does it. Just don't make any sudden moves and you *might* live long enough to get to the front door. . . ." She made a shriek of indignation. "Really, I should just go ahead and join a convent now."

Hauk snorted at her tirade. "Be glad you have a father who loves you."

"I am delirious that he loves me. I just wish he'd loosen the noose once in a while so that I can breathe around the choke hold."

Sumi swallowed hard as she realized who Thia's father was. Given that tirade, there was only one male it could be. Nykyrian Quiakides. Crowned prince of both the Andarion and Triosan empires.

And the most wanted being in the history of The League.

Holy gods . . .

Nykyrian was the assassin who'd taken the eye of the prime commander. The one creature Kyr Zemin would sell his soul to have in custody.

And his prized daughter was standing just outside this tent. A daughter Nykyrian would do anything to protect.

Even die for her.

If Sumi handed Thia over with Hauk, Kyr would give her anything she wanted. Not only would she be able to negotiate Kalea's freedom from League custody, Sumi might be able to bargain for her own.

Her conscience balked at the idea of making such a trade. But Kyr wouldn't hurt Thia . . . and as Thia had pointed out, she was full grown.

Unlike *her* baby.

Kalea was barely three. Still young enough that she would have no memory of being in League custody. If Sumi could get her back now, they could finally be a family. It was the only thing she'd ever wanted. The only thing she'd ever craved.

Closing her eyes, she cherished the thought of finally knowing what her baby girl looked like. Of being able to hold and rock her to sleep at night.

Those strangers outside were her key to that dream.

She was going to get her baby back. No matter who or what she had to betray. Nothing and no one came before her Kalea.

CHAPTER 7

Sumi froze as she uncovered the only personal item of Hauk's, other than clothes, she'd found during her thorough search of his meager belongings. It was a palm-sized device that held his rowdy native Andarion music, a few videos and photos, and files written in the strangest alphabet she'd ever seen. It might be from encryption, but she'd lay money that was what the Andarion language looked like. She'd never seen their written language before, however it only made sense that he'd keep files in his native tongue. And if it contained anything so sensitive that it needed encrypting, she was sure Hauk wouldn't have left it where she might find it. Rather he'd have it on him.

Curious, she opened the file marked *Family* in the Universal alphabet so that she could flip through his images.

She'd expected it to contain mostly photos of Darice and Hauk's brothers, the rest of his blood family. Yet oddly enough, the majority of images were human children and infants of varying ages, including one of Hauk playfully sparring with a much younger Thia. The girl was even skinnier than now, with braces and short, dyed red hair. Even so, it appeared she was giving Hauk a good run as they laughed and fought.

And as Sumi flipped through more, she couldn't help smiling at the pictures of Hauk holding the human babies and children. They were so tiny in comparison to him. He looked awkward and scared in some, and in others—later ones—he was much more confident. One of the most adorable was a more recent image of him with a girl around a year old. She was dressed in a frilly tulle gown that filled Hauk's muscular arms with pink fluff. Laughing, the girl had her hands tangled in his braids while she laid her little head against his massive shoulder.

Tears filled Sumi's eyes as she thought about her own daughter, and wished Kalea could grow up with a doting father who would cradle and protect her so adoringly. Unlike Sumi's own callous bastard progenitor who had donated his sperm to her and her sister, and begrudged them everything else. Never mind the rank dog who'd tried to murder her when he found out she was pregnant with his child.

She flinched at the memory of Avin's violent reaction when she'd given him what she'd stupidly thought was happy news. *"You got pregnant on purpose just to trap me in this godforsaken job I despise, didn't you, you bitch! I hate you!"*

Part of her didn't believe that any man could be a decent parent, or person for that matter. It just wasn't in their genetic makeup.

And yet . . .

She wanted to believe that there really were decent and kind men in the universe. Somewhere . . . probably microbial fathers, living under a rock on some remote backwater planet.

She drew a ragged breath, hoping she was wrong. Surely, statistically, they couldn't all be assholes. Could they?

Maybe I am nothing more than an asshole magnet,

after all. It certainly made sense, given her dating record. *Yeah, I take perfectly nice guys and ruin them.*

Forcing her thoughts away from that uselessness, Sumi paused as she discovered a picture of Hauk around the age of five with his brothers. She hadn't realized Keris was that much older until she saw them together. Fain, however, didn't appear more than two, maybe three years ahead of Hauk. With their arms slung over each other's shoulders, and bright smiles, they were the epitome of loving siblings . . . until she flipped to the next one that was time-stamped a few seconds later. Then, they were in an entwined heap on the floor, viciously fighting.

She laughed in spite of herself. How very Andarion.

For that matter, how very male.

The next was of Hauk in his late teens or early twenties in an Andarion government IT contractor uniform standing back-to-back with Nykyrian Quiakides, who was wearing a League assassin's battlesuit that held the command assassin rank on the sleeve. Arms folded across their chests, they appeared ready to take on the entire universe.

No wonder Hauk considered the Andarion prince his brother. They appeared to have been good friends for a *very* long time.

It was so strange to see these glimpses into Hauk's past. Like seeing his underwear—which he apparently didn't have—or being able to read his thoughts. Each photo betrayed the heart of a fierce beast she knew would kill her without flinching if he ever learned why she was really here.

For all the humanity in these pictures, she'd seen the warrior who had brazenly stormed a League prison to back his friends, and fought against overwhelming odds to emerge victorious.

He was terrifying as a soldier. Like her, a brutal killer.

And that hadn't been the only time he'd participated

in such an assault. The Sentella was forever making those kinds of raids against The League. Never had they retreated. Never had they been defeated.

By anyone.

Frowning, she hesitated at an image of Hauk pretending to choke the Caronese emperor, who was barely more than a scrawny teenager at the time it was taken. It was obvious the two of them were clowning for the photographer. And while she knew the Caronese emperor wasn't a small man, he appeared tiny next to Hauk. But more than that, the next series of pictures with the two of them over the years showed that Hauk viewed the emperor more as a pesky little brother than an untouchable, elite aristo.

And that the two of them were extremely close. There was even one where they were both wounded from battle. Dressed in unmarked black battlesuits, Darling lay with his head uncovered on Hauk's stomach while they were either passed out or asleep. His helmet clenched in his left hand, Hauk had his right arm slung across the emperor's chest as if, even half dead, he'd fight to protect him. As a goof, someone named Syn had handwritten the word "blackmail" across the photo before he'd e-mailed it to Hauk.

Completely charmed and amused, she laughed at the warped humor, and wondered if Hauk had beaten the sender for it. But then he must have taken it in stride, or he would have deleted the photo long ago and not kept a copy.

And there were many more of him and the emperor and Nykyrian, as well as several other men, climbing in various terrains and climates. But the ones that fascinated her most were where he and his friends were free solo climbing. There were numerous pictures of them hanging from boulders and rocks by nothing more than their fingertips.

Ye gods, that was a dangerous combination of brave and stupid.

Yet the sight of Hauk's bulging muscles while he dangled precariously fascinated her and made her breathless. The male was fearless and ripped in a way that had to be illegal in most galaxies. And it left her with fantasies that would have Kyr cutting her throat if he ever learned of them.

How could anyone be so lickably delicious?

When she got to one of Hauk on top of a picturesque mountain, with his arm around a Hyshian female, she froze. The woman was beautiful. Exquisitely so. There was no missing the admiration and love in their eyes as they stared at each other. A weird, inexplicable fissure of jealousy went through her. Though why she would care who Hauk loved was beyond her.

Disturbed by that thought, she quickly moved on past additional photos of them together that did nothing to improve her ire.

Until she came to a photo of *five* people. Her heart leapt into her throat as a bitter chill consumed her. Hauk, Nykyrian, Darling, the Hyshian woman, and another handsome man with dark hair and dark eyes, who'd been in several of the earlier pictures.

All five wore unmarked red-tinged black battle-suits. . . .

The same suits that were used by Sentella members.

Holy shit.

These were the five members of The Sentella High Command. They had to be. She'd meticulously studied the footage of their mission into The League prison enough to know their heights and builds as well as her own. With them clustered together, there was no mistaking those tough I-will-kill-you-where-you-stand stances.

Oh my God, this is it. She had what she'd been sent for.

Swallowing hard, she shivered. With this one, condemning picture, she could destroy The Sentella once and for all. This, right here in her hand, was the intel Kyr would sell his other eye to possess. . . .

"Uncle Hauk?"

Sumi quickly turned the device off and stowed it as she heard Hauk and Thia outside, preparing dinner. Terrified of being caught and killed, she scrambled back to her pallet while her heart continued to hammer in her chest.

But the images were burned in her mind. Worse, they made Hauk a real person to her. Not a target. And that was so dangerous it wasn't even remotely amusing.

I cannot allow myself to feel anything for him.

He must remain the enemy and nothing more personal than that. It was the only way for this to work. The only way she could survive and do what she had to do. For her sake and for Kalea's. She'd already made the mistake of putting her life and faith into a man and his integrity.

Sumi had barely lived to regret that stupidity. There was no way she'd ever do that again.

She refused to be a victim. It was that stubborn determination that made her such a lethal killer. Why she was one of the best assassins in her division.

When she went on the hunt, it was to the end. Nothing ever distracted her or got in her way. Especially not her own feelings.

And while Hauk might show loyalty to his friends, his brother had coldly turned his back on her sister, for no other reason than because Omira was afraid of having his child. Never once had Fain tried to contact them and, to the day she died, Omira had been terrified that their paths would cross, or that Fain would hunt her down and kill her for divorcing him. Her pacifist sister had even carried a small blaster wherever she went.

Just in case he found her.

Sumi would assume that callousness ran in their blood. That Hauk would be every bit as vicious as his brother. Especially if he was betrayed.

For now, she'd play her part and do what Kyr had demanded. But when the time came, she wouldn't hesitate to do whatever she must to get out of this alive and unscathed.

No one's life was worth more to her than Kalea's.

CHAPTER 8

Waking with a start, Sumi cocked her head as she heard the most incredible music of her life. Low and haunting. Soulful. At first, she thought it was something the kids had on a player, until she left the tent and found Hauk sitting on the ground, with a beautiful violin tucked under his chin while he played with his eyes closed. He was so large and it so tiny in comparison, that it looked more like a toy than a real instrument. But there was no mistaking the skill he possessed as his fingers flew through an extremely complicated melody.

Now there was the last thing she'd ever expected to find. An Andarion who played a delicate instrument with the expertise of a virtuoso. Unbelievable.

Damn you, Hauk. You need to stop being so unpredictable. So unexpected.

So damn alluring. It was wreaking too much havoc with her convictions and sanity. He made it way too easy to see the beauty that was him, and not the cold-blooded killer she knew him to be.

She took a step. He immediately stopped and rose as if expecting an attack. And she had no doubt he could easily impale or even decapitate someone with the flimsy bow in his hand.

When he saw her, he relaxed into the sexiest, most masculine stance she'd ever beheld. It exuded confidence and lethal grace, yet simultaneously managed to be adorable and hot. "Do you need something?"

Yeah, against all sanity, she needed a taste of that hard, ripped body, but she wasn't about to say *those* thoughts out loud . . . and *never* to him. "A change of scenery."

And all that wealth of tawny male was definitely the most interesting thing to look at on this godforsaken rock.

"Ah." He set his instrument aside then came to help her. Before she could protest, he swept her up in his arms and carried her over to the small fire pit, where he set her down on the air cushion he'd been using. The ease with which he could do that given *her* height was extremely disconcerting. Standing just over six feet in shoes, she was used to being taller than the average man by quite a few inches. By the time she'd turned five, her own father had refused to pick her up at all, claiming she was too big for him to manage.

Yet Hauk carried her about as if she weighed no more than his boots.

It was *very* unsettling.

Without a word, he went to return his violin to its case. "You don't have to stop."

He closed the case and set it aside. "I don't like to play in front of others. It's something I do alone."

She could understand that if he played badly. But his skill level said that he'd been playing for a very long time. It also seemed like an odd hobby for an Andarion warrior. Far too peaceful.

And speaking of peace . . . she suddenly realized it was eerily quiet.

Concerned, she glanced around the darkening camp and saw no trace of Thia or Darice. Only the remnants of Hauk's dinner. "Did you get so irritated at them that you finally ate the kids?"

At first, he scoffed at the question, then he appeared to seriously consider it. He gestured at the vibrant pink tent that was to the left of his. "Thia's off, drawing." He pointed to the black one on the right. "Darice is tied up in his."

"Tied up with what?"

"Rope," he said simply. "I considered using the violin strings, but didn't want to get blood on them. Given the amount of venom flowing in his veins, it might damage the wood."

Aghast, she stared at him. "You're serious?"

The innocent, almost childlike expression on his face was comical. "It was that, or kill him. It seemed the lesser evil, if not the better good."

She pressed her lips together to keep from laughing. "How long has he been tied up?"

He shrugged nonchalantly. "How long has it been quiet?"

Eyes wide, she covered her mouth with her hand. She was appalled at what he'd done, and by the fact that she actually found it charming. And probably warranted. "You're so bad. . . . Aren't you worried about him?"

"I'd be more worried about his continued well-being if he were untied and still running his mouth around me."

Lowering her hand, she shook her head at him and his cavalier demeanor. "I wish I could be more on Darice's side, but given his attitude . . ."

He handed her a bottle of water as he sat down beside her and opened a bag of dried fruit. "He is his father's son. Stubborn. Hot-tempered. Rash. And he never knows when to shut up for his own good."

"Why do I have a feeling that someone has rattled that list off for you as well?"

He licked his fingers. "Probably because they have. Many times."

Grimacing, she tried her best to unscrew the cap from her water. Had someone hermetically sealed it?

Hauk took it from her hands and effortlessly opened it. As he returned the bottle to her, she hesitated. Before she even realized what she was doing, she placed her hand over his, marveling at the strength and size of it. Unlike humans, Andarions had fingernails that were more akin to claws. Another natural weapon they were born with, like their fangs and heightened hearing and eyesight—they were a true predator race. Things that had terrified her sister whenever she thought of birthing such an alien creature with Fain. Omira had even feared that a hybrid fetus would claw its way out of her stomach while she carried it.

Andarions were extremely dangerous to humans. And still, against all rationale, she was attracted to him, while she considered the differences between an Andarion male and a human man. Hauk's hands were more beautiful than she would have thought, especially given the stories she'd heard about Andarion savagery and battle skill.

"Your hands are massive."

He stroked her knuckles with his thumb. That single sensation sent chills all over her body and made her hormones sit up and pant. "And yours are incredibly delicate. How is it a woman with hands so soft and tiny has managed to take a man's life?"

"With great regret." As soon as the words left her lips, she cringed at the slip. For some reason, her guard evaporated every time they spoke. It was way too easy to forget what she was supposed to be doing.

Hunting him—the predator.

But it wasn't her fault. He reminded her too much of Fain, and in spite of her hatred for Fain Hauk, the little girl inside her wanted to feel safe again, like she'd done whenever Fain had rocked her to sleep while she'd stayed with her sister at their flat. It was easy to silence that stupid, needy voice when she was alone. Easy to tell herself that this was how life was supposed to be. Brutal and lonely.

Yet now that she was with Hauk, and saw how he protected his niece and nephew . . .

That whiny little bitch was back with a vengeance.

Appalled by her own train of thought, she glanced away.

Hauk reluctantly let go of her hand. "That bastard beat you, didn't he?"

She stiffened as his unexpected question jerked her back to the days when Avin had felt threatened by her height and intelligence. Jealous of the job she had that she loved and the one he did that he hated. Back to when she hadn't been a trained assassin, and had lived her life in stark terror of her boyfriend's bipolar mood swings. "Excuse me?"

"Your boyfriend. It's why you killed him." It wasn't a question. It was a statement of fact.

Sumi wanted to deny it, but how could she? He spoke the truth. And while she'd learned how easy it was to physically kill a man, even one who was a lot larger and stronger than her, it was never easy to live with the guilt that forever remained afterward. "Yes."

Hauk saw the horror and shame in her hazel green eyes before she glanced away again. It was a mannerism so similar to one Omira had once used that it sent a chill over him.

Nor did he miss the way her hands trembled as she noticed how much room he took up on the ground beside her.

"It's why my size unsettles you."

She nodded as more awful memories surged. "You've no idea what it's like to be trapped and helpless. To be held down with no way to fight back, no matter how hard you try."

"That's not true. You've seen the scars on my back. I

know exactly how it feels to have my life in the hands of someone else, and to hate it with every part of my being."

She scowled at his angry tone. "What happened?"

Hauk ground his teeth. Her question knotted his gut and took him straight back to that day he would rather forget. A day that had forever changed his life, in more ways than one, and set him on a path he'd never foreseen. While it'd destroyed his destiny and cost him the respect of his parents, it'd compensated him with a battle brother he was grateful for every day of this existence.

Sipping his water, he narrowed his gaze as visions from the past haunted him. He'd been in a training pod at the academy with what he'd stupidly assumed were two Andarion friends. Unfortunately, all of them had been schooled with humans long enough that some of humanity's *finer* traits had infected them. When Nykyrian had been sent to their academy, the full-blooded Andarions had declared it open season on the hybrid.

Something that was *not* in their culture. Fighting an equal or answering a challenge was Andarion. Picking on the weak was human. But Prince Jullien had insisted that they attack the hybrid, and drive him from their school so that they wouldn't have to look at him.

Unaware at that time that Jullien and Nykyrian were fraternal twins, Hauk had assumed the animosity came from Jullien's fear that the full-bloods would remember that he was a hybrid himself and turn on him. Jullien appeared mostly Andarion and usually passed without much comment as one of them.

Nykyrian had never been so fortunate. One look, and it was woefully obvious he was born of both species.

Now, Hauk knew Jullien had done it to protect his grandmother, who had abandoned Nykyrian to a human orphanage, hoping that the humans, in their hatred of Andarions, would kill the boy. Jullien had pushed them all hard to attack Nykyrian, and keep him in trouble so that he'd be kicked out of school.

Or die from their hazing.

In those days, Nykyrian hadn't been the invincible warrior his extensive League training and adoptive family's brutality had turned him into. He'd been a skinny, skittish boy. Unable to defend himself. All he'd wanted was to be ignored by everyone. Especially since the humans in his past had left him horrifically scarred, defanged, and declawed.

Instead of following the ways of their ancestors and teachings, the Andarions had banded together to traumatize Nykyrian, as if they were afraid he was infectious and would destroy them all.

On that particular day, Jullien had intended to run Nykyrian down with the pod.

Hauk had taken issue with their plans. And they had taken issue with him. While fighting each other over it, they'd caused the pod to malfunction and crash.

Jullien and Chrisen had abandoned Hauk. Left him in the wreckage to burn alive. Even now, he could swear that Chrisen had intentionally shoved him into the panel that had fallen on his leg and trapped him inside the pod. That the bastard's eyes had gleamed in satisfaction.

While the flames had singed his flesh and the smoke had closed in on his lungs, he'd heard them outside, blaming his "incompetence" for the crash. Along with them and the other students, their teachers had made excuses as to why they couldn't do anything for Hauk. Why it was acceptable to let a kid burn to death.

Knowing they had no intention of helping him, Hauk had held his breath as best he could, while he tried desperately to free his damaged leg from the searing hot metal. He knew he was completely alone. That no one would ever put their ass on the line for his.

At least that had been his thought until a shadow fell over him.

Nyk, well aware of the fact that they'd been trying to hurt him when they'd crashed, had run inside the craft, oblivious to the danger. For all he knew, Hauk had been as determined to hurt him as the others. But Nyk hadn't let that stop him. And as he struggled to free Hauk, he'd been burned and wounded to his bones.

Still, Nyk had fought to save his life when no one else could be bothered, and then, wounded himself, he'd lifted Hauk up and carried him to safety right before the craft had exploded and sent debris raining down all over the two of them.

Out of a crowd of people and Andarions, it'd been Nyk who'd jerked his jacket off and used it to put out the flames on Hauk's back.

To this day, Hauk didn't understand Nykyrian's mercy.

And every time he saw one of those scars on Nyk's body caused by that crash, he knew the debt he owed to a boy who should have let him burn for his part in making Nyk feel unwelcome at their school.

But that was a long time ago. And it was something he'd never spoken of to anyone.

Not even Nykyrian.

Clearing his throat, he picked through the fruit in his bag until he found a friggle. "It was a training exercise when I was a boy. My pod crashed and I was trapped in the burning wreckage." He offered her the fruit.

She declined it with a shake of her head. "It must have been awful."

He ate the friggle before he spoke again. "It isn't one of my happier memories. Sadly, it's not one of my worst, either."

"Were you scared?"

He wiped his hand on his pants. "No."

"Really?" she asked incredulously.

He gave her a pointed stare. "Really."

Sumi couldn't fathom what he was telling her. Not given the wealth and brutality of the scars on his back. He'd been burned severely enough that she was sure it'd taken him years of physical therapy to be whole again. And probably a number of skin grafts. "How old were you?"

"Thirteen Andarion years."

She gaped at his answer. "You were a baby."

"I was bigger than most."

Typical Andarion answer, and it was one that brought to her mind that image of him as an adorable child with bright eyes who'd been holding on to his older brothers. She bit her lip as she tried to imagine the nightmare it must have been for him to be so young and so close to death. "How is it possible that at that age, you weren't scared even a little?"

"I was too pissed."

"At?"

He cut a feral look in her direction. "Acting like a bunch of scared human schoolgirls, Andarions I thought were friends had run out to save their own asses without trying to help me save mine."

"Then how did you escape?"

"Thia's father. Even though he was just a kid, too, he ran in and dragged my bleeding hide out."

She didn't miss the fact that he had yet to mention Nykyrian by name. "Is that why you're so loyal to him?"

"I'm loyal to him for *many* reasons." He rose to tower over her. "I should check on Darice now."

She watched as he made his way to the small, black tent. Dang, that surly male had the most predatorial walk of any creature she'd ever met. Loose limbed and sexier than it ever should be. And she knew the minute he ungagged his nephew. Darice let loose with a string of foul curses for his uncle.

"Stop, or I'll gag you again."

"Why? Does my truth offend you?"

"No," Hauk snarled. "Your tongue offends me. Now bite it or lose it."

"I vote he cuts it out for all our sanities. What do you think?"

Sumi started to smile at Thia's words until she saw the huge black cat by the girl's side. Gasping, she scooted away from it.

"Don't panic," Thia said quickly, stroking the cat's head. "It's just Illyse. She only attacks when I tell her to, or whenever someone attacks me."

Her heart still pounding, Sumi returned to her seat. "You are a scary woman, Thia."

A slow grin spread across her face. "You should meet my father sometime."

"Only if I'm heavily armed."

Thia laughed. "Trust me. It won't matter if you are. In fact, you're more likely to survive if you're not. Then, he *might* take pity on you and show mercy. Armed, you're on your own, and that's a very terrifying place to be with him on your tail."

"I think you enjoy scaring people."

Thia shrugged. "We all need a hobby."

"I hear crocheting is the most therapeutic and calming."

Sitting down by her side, Thia wrinkled her nose. "I strangely like you."

Sumi opened her mouth to respond in kind then froze as she saw Hauk coming out of the tent, holding Darice by the belt of his pants while his nephew squirmed and insulted him more. "What the . . . ?"

"Oh Lord," Thia breathed before she ran to head Hauk off. She held her arms out to block his path. "Don't do it."

A tic beat a furious rhythm in Hauk's jaw. "Thia, get out of my way. I'm going to drown him. I mean it this time."

"Please, Uncle. Don't. Let me do it, I've earned the right after this last week with him."

Trying not to laugh, Sumi rubbed at her brow as Hauk and Thia argued over who had more reasons to kill Darice while Darice continued to shout obscenities at them both. Confused, the fierce lorina circled around their small group like it was trying to figure out which one it should bite.

Since it'd been just her and her sister at home, and there had been a large age gap between them, they'd never really fought.

Not like *this*.

Sumi blew a loud whistle to get their attention. "Guys?"

They paused to stare at her as if *she* was the crazy one.

"Is this normal? Do all families fight this way?"

Thia sighed. "I don't know about *all* families, but it's the norm for my little brothers. I'm pretty sure they're all going to grow up to be terrorists."

Without warning, Hauk dropped Darice. He hit the ground with an audible groan. Stepping over his nephew, the huge Andarion approached Sumi. "Are you sure you don't have a ship?"

"Quite positive. Sorry. I did have a rifle, but you confiscated it."

That ferocious tic returned to Hauk's jaw.

Glaring at his uncle, Darice pushed himself up from the ground. "When we get back, I'm telling Yaya how you have shamed us all with your *human* behavior!"

Hauk turned toward him with a fierce grimace that would make anyone with a brain back down. "Like I give a *minsid* fuck. Trust me, boy, my mother did a lot worse to discipline us than tie us in a tent. She'd only be appalled that I have yet to put you in a ring."

Darice lifted his chin defiantly. "You're not Andarion enough to face me there!"

Hauk gaped at Darice as if the boy was shy a few charges on his blaster. Snapping his jaw shut, he went to grab a bottle of water before he paused next to Thia. "I'm going hunting. Keep your blaster close and your eyes and ears open."

As Hauk left, Darice threw dirt in his direction. "That's it, you coward! Keep walking. That's all—" His words ended in a grunt of pain as Thia shot him.

Sumi gasped at her cold-blooded actions.

"Relax. I set it to stun first." She holstered her blaster, and passed an unrepentant smirk to Sumi. "Though I shouldn't have. It would serve him right to have a giant scar in the center of his chest, or better yet, on his arrogant, entitled ass." She sat down next to Sumi and called the lorina over to her so that she could calm the beast.

Biting her lip, Sumi was confused by everything that had happened in the last few minutes. "Shouldn't we take Darice back to his tent?"

Thia gave her a dry stare. "Ever tried to pick up an Andarion male? Even a small one?"

"No."

"Don't." She jutted her chin out for the lorina to nibble on it. "Trust me, that prick's not worth the hernia. I say we leave him out in the open and hope something foul eats him. Slowly . . . and with relish."

Unsure of what to think, Sumi glanced after Hauk, who had vanished into the night. He hadn't even looked back as Thia had blasted Darice. That degree of callousness for his family seemed out of character for him, and said a lot about their relationship. "So what's the deal with them, anyway? Why does Darice hate him?"

Thia paused as she took a minute to consider her words. "Most of the sniping is just being Andarion. We're a snarky, warring bunch."

"But . . ."

"As you have heard, repeatedly. They blame Hauk for the death of Darice's father."

"Was he?"

Thia shook her head. "From the snatches of conversations I've heard over the years between my father and Fain—Keris, Darice's father, in spite of being an Andarion war hero, had some serious problems with drugs and alcohol."

Sumi sucked her breath in sharply at that. While those weren't good things for humans, Andarions had a very harsh penalty system for it, especially for those who wore a military uniform. Some drinking was allowed.

Excess was not.

As for the other, drugs could be a death sentence if used by a civilian who was caught, and was always such for those in uniform. "Why would he risk drug use?"

"Again, I'm speculating, but as you've heard Uncle Hauk say, their mother isn't exactly a beacon of maternal instinct. Even though she's a brilliant negotiator, she has little patience for her sons' misbehavior."

"Negotiator?" There was something his dossier hadn't revealed. "I didn't know Andarions had such in their world. I thought they just slugged out all their problems until someone gave up or died."

"Not always." Thia ran her hand over Illyse's ears. "And his mother is one of the best ever trained. Like Hauk's father, his mother is a military veteran who expected a lot from her three blood sons." She paused to pour water for the lorina to drink. "Darice's mother is also a veteran and was Keris's wingman. I've heard that when Uncle Hauk told her what had happened to Keris on his Endurance, she buried a knife in Hauk's stomach and gave him a gut wound so deep they had to remove part of his stomach to save his life."

Sumi sucked her breath in sharply at that. What an

awful thing to do, but it went along with the stories she'd been told about Andarion savagery. "You're serious?"

Thia nodded.

"How old was he?"

"Fifteen."

And she'd stabbed him? How could anyone do such a thing? Sumi understood grief, but that . . . She looked over at his nephew. "Darice's age."

"No, he's fourteen. Uncle Hauk had to delay his Endurance because of an accident at school. He was still having skin grafts when he should have gone originally."

Sumi's jaw went slack. So she'd been right about his injuries from the pod. What the hell had he been doing out here after all that? "Was he fit for Endurance?"

"According to my father, not really. It should have been delayed longer, at least another year, but their mother insisted Uncle Hauk go and that Keris not take mercy on him."

Shocked, Sumi tried to grasp how any mother could be like that. But then, her own mother had abandoned her and Omira to an angry alcoholic who hated them, so she was well versed with women who had no business birthing children. "Why would she do that?"

Thia ran her hand down the lorina's spine, ruffling its fur as it arched its back against her touch. "She was furious that Uncle Hauk had allowed himself to be scarred during the accident. Apparently, he was already pledged at the time it happened, and when his betrothed's family saw the damage to his body, they withdrew their daughter from the Hauk lineage, and embarrassed his mother greatly and publicly. My father thinks his mother sent him so that Uncle Hauk wouldn't return. In her mind, his death during Endurance would have restored their family honor."

That was so cold and cruel. "Is that also why he's never married?"

She shook her head. "That's *all* Dariana's fault."

"Dariana?"

"Darice's mother."

Sumi scowled as she tried to follow this nonsensical logic. "How is it *her* fault that he never married? Is it because she stabbed him and gave him a scar?"

"No. Andarion law and custom stipulates that if a female is widowed and there's an unpledged male in the lineage, he is to marry her and provide for her in the absence of his fallen brother."

Sumi remembered hearing Darice yell at him for that. "Then why hasn't he married her already?" Keris had been dead for quite some time. The gods knew, Sumi wouldn't have waited five minutes to drag that lush piece of malehood into her bed and ride him until he begged her for mercy.

What an idiot.

Thia ground her teeth before she answered. "Dariana hates his guts and refuses to accept him as her mate."

Sumi's scowl deepened. "Then why are they still pledged?"

"You're thinking like a human," Thia chided. "It doesn't work that way on Andaria. Pledges are negotiated and drafted by the females. The male cannot back out of one. Ever. He is honor bound to see it through."

"The woman, too?"

"They're not women, they're females. And a female's primary duty to her family is to protect her lineage and ancestry, and to build the best possible alliance for her children. They do this by picking the best male lineage they can legally tie into. As the undisputed holders of the blood lineage, females are sacred. They can be thrown out of their homes, but they will never lose their lineage. However, if a male does something unworthy, he can be thrown out of his family's lineage. Forever. And the last thing any male wants is to be thrown out of his family."

"Why?"

"Andarions have a very stringent and rigid caste system. When you lose lineage, you are totally outcast from your blood family, and it cannot be undone. No Andarion is ever supposed to speak to such a being again. They are considered worse than dead. And if found in Andarion territory, the Outcast can be imprisoned or killed, without trial. It's why all their paperwork requires a dual lineage to be listed. And why they methodically check it."

That was so harsh. Not to mention the fact that the rest of the universe hated and feared Andarions, passionately. Even in times of peace, Andarions weren't welcomed into the populations of other worlds. In some worlds, they were killed on sight or instantly enslaved.

The prejudice against them was extremely severe, and since they stood out, there was no way for them to hide or blend among the other known races.

"So how does an Andarion know if another has been disinherited without the paperwork?"

Thia rubbed noses with her lorina. When she met Sumi's gaze, rage burned bright in those green eyes. "Their fathers hold them while their mothers slash them across both their left and right biceps and pectorals in a specific pattern so that everyone who sees it will know they've been disinherited and are Outcast. When they say 'present arms' they're not talking about weaponry. They mean for their males to literally bare their arms for public inspection and scrutiny."

Sumi vaguely recalled seeing those scars on Fain's arms and chest when she'd been a girl, but she'd had no idea that was what had caused them. She'd assumed it was from some kind of accident. Never would she have dreamed his own parents had injured him so. "Is that why so many of the Andarion male fashions and formal military uniforms show their upper arms and pecs?"

Thia nodded. "It's done to prove they're legitimate

sons. Fully lineaged. And those who have tattoos are either paying homage to their noble or heroic bloodlines, or to those they married into . . . it's considered bragging when it's their blood lineage. Noble when it's the wife's."

Sumi sat back as she remembered all the scars that bisected Hauk's flesh. He'd had something similar to what Thia described on the left side of his body. "What about the claw marks on Hauk's arm? Is that—"

"No. The single claw marks, like he has, are a public chastisement from his mother for Keris's death. . . . One set of claw marks just means he's displeased his matriarch. And it was done to eternally embarrass him in front of other Andarions whenever he has to make a formal public appearance, or go to temple on holy days. Should he displease his mother again, the next marks will be those of lost lineage, and he will be cast from his family." Thia sighed. "The worst part though, is that those scars kept him from his obligatory military service that's required of all nonroyal Andarion males and females after graduation. His mother should have just killed him. It would have been far kinder than marking him like that and leaving him for the rest of his breed to sneer at."

Sumi didn't know why, but that made her ache for him. Whether he'd been responsible or not, he must have been traumatized by his brother's death. What kind of mother would further injure him, especially given how young he'd been at the time it'd happened?

"How did Keris die?"

"He fell during their climb. Uncle Hauk tried to save him, and ended up falling himself. He survived his own fall by crashing into a ledge and broke about a dozen bones. Even so, he managed to climb down and make it back to the pickup spot."

Sumi gaped. "How in the Nine Worlds can they blame him for *that*?"

Thia rolled her eyes. "I know, right? They claim Uncle

Hauk slipped first and slammed into Keris. My father says that had Uncle Hauk not been recovering from his last surgery, he would have probably been able to hold them both. As it was . . ." She sighed heavily.

None of this made sense. "It was an accident. Why blame him for it?"

"Because Keris's rope had been cut with a knife. Deliberately."

"What?" Sumi breathed.

Tears welled in Thia's eyes. "I've heard different things, but from what I understand, the belay and anchors weren't set properly, and weren't capable of holding their combined weight. Even so, Uncle Hauk continued to hold on to Keris and was trying to pull or swing him to safety before the anchors gave way. Since it was obvious they would both die if something wasn't done fast, Keris cut the rope, hoping to save Uncle Hauk. But neither Dariana nor his mother believes it. They think Hauk cut the line to save himself, and let his brother die, then lied about the events to save face."

Her stomach constricted to the point she feared she'd be ill. The horror Hauk must feel over that day. She couldn't imagine watching her sister die so horribly. Right in front of her . . .

And then to be blamed for it?

No wonder people called the Andarions barbarians.

In that moment, she wanted to go over there and kick Darice for his cruel words against Hauk. How could he be so mean? So unfeeling?

Gods, it was so hard to live with the death of a loved one. Especially when they died young. It was something she struggled with every single day of her life. She missed Omira so much that it still burned like a fire in her gut. She could only imagine how much worse that had to be for Hauk, who probably blamed himself even more than they did for it.

How many times had he relived that event and had no one to turn to for comfort?

Deep inside, she needed to soothe him, and she didn't know why. Other than she understood the lonely pain of coping with the fear that maybe you could have done something to save your sibling. That you were to blame for it, even though you weren't.

Bastards!

And unlike his family, she believed Thia's version of Keris's death. Hauk's loyalty to his family and friends went too deep for him to have killed his brother to save himself. That wasn't the warrior who'd thrown himself into the thick of League fire to cover his friends in the prison raid.

Hauk did *not* value his own life. Anyone who'd ever seen him fight would know that beyond a doubt. Fearless, he battled like he had a death wish. Not to mention the photos she'd seen.

No, he hadn't hurt Keris. He would have fought to save his brother with the same ferocity and determination she'd seen him use against her League brethren.

"Have you ever talked to him about it?"

Thia shook her head. "My father told me that I should never mention it to him. That it's too painful for Uncle Hauk. And I would never do anything to bring him hurt. He's been too good to me."

Sumi remembered the pictures of Thia playing and sparring with her uncle. He did love and adore her like a proud father.

But that also made her wonder about Thia's Andarion family lineage. "So your father . . . was he disinherited for being with your mother?"

Thia snorted at the question. "My dad is only half Andarion, through his mother's blood. Again, females are the keepers of the lineage, so in theory, they can bolster it with the blood of other species they deem worthy, either through marriage or adoption. The males cannot."

"That's not right."

"No, it isn't. And while my father has the predatory nature and lethal skills of an Andarion warrior, he wasn't raised in their culture, so his beliefs and customs are more human than Andarion. And what he knows of their culture, he learned later in life. Mostly from Uncle Hauk and Fain."

Sumi wasn't sure if that was a blessing or a curse. Given the horrors her sister had been subjected to, she couldn't imagine what life must be like for Thia and her father. "Do you ever take flack for being Andarion?"

"Nah. Until eight years ago, no one, except my mother, knew I had any Andarion blood at all. I just thought I had some unique quirks." An odd half smile toyed at the edges of Thia's lips. "Since I moved in with my father, no one, Andarion or human, has dared to say a word to me over it. He'd spill their entrails if they did. But he wasn't so fortunate, especially when he was a kid. Since he has some very obvious Andarion and human features, people tend to give him a wide berth, and they're not always polite or pleasant about it. Even now."

"Yeah. My sister was with an Andarion male for a while, and it was extremely harsh for her after they broke up. Once a guy found out about her ex, he hit the door running."

Thia inclined her head to Sumi. "And that's why my mother never told my father she was pregnant with me from their affair. . . . Humans are brutal."

Sumi glanced over to Darice, who had yet to stir. "Andarions have their moments, too."

Thia stretched her legs out so that her cat could lay her head in her lap. "Yes, they do. Every time Darice snarls to Uncle Hauk that he's not his father, I want to cut his treacherous throat."

"Why?"

"To you, it sounds like he's being a snotty brat. Which he is. But what he's really saying to Uncle Hauk is that his mother finds Uncle Hauk unworthy of adding his DNA to her bloodline. It's the worst sort of insult an Andarion youth can say to an elder."

"Then why's he allowed to say it?"

"Dariana taught him to use it against Uncle Hauk to hurt him."

Okay . . .

"But why?"

"I told you, she's a bitch." Thia kept saying that like it explained everything.

Sumi scratched at her cheek. "Could you elaborate on the concept of bitch as you see it? It's a vague, insulting noun that covers a lot of territory."

"Yes, and the head queen of all bitchery's only child lies over there." Thia cut her gaze toward Darice before she looked back at Sumi. "While normally a female can withdraw from an unwanted pledge with no drama, Dariana's is a special case. There are only two original and completely pristine Andarion bloodlines that females and their families will sell their souls to tie into. One is the direct royal bloodline of the ruling house."

"The Most Sovereign Blood Clan of eton Anatole."

Thia smiled at Sumi's knowledge of their world. "Very good. The other bloodline belongs to the family of the first thirteen Andarion heroes. The Warring Blood Clan of . . . Hauk."

Legendary warriors who'd been regaled since the beginning of interplanetary travel. Before there had been a single noble bloodline established on Andaria, the Hauks had stood united as a family to defend their race from the offworlders who'd come to conquer, kill, and enslave them.

It was a story of raw grit, patriotism, and exceptional sacrifice that everyone learned in school, no matter what species they belonged to. Seven Andarion males and five Andarion females. Brothers and sisters, along with their father, who was a retired veteran and shaman. When the first offworlders had come to Andaria to conquer them, their father had led their family out to stall the enemy's advance, while their mother ran to spread word of the invaders and warn their people.

Single-handedly for three days, the Hauks had battled the tech-superior army, and held the invaders back from their capital city walls, until the Andarion chief could mount a counterattack. But the cost to their family had been a high one.

When that battle ended, only two Hauks remained. Father and son. The father died just days later of his injuries, leaving his son to found what was considered the first true blood lineage of Andaria. A hero who would later refuse to be the chieftain of his homeworld when they'd offered him the first united crown of Andaria.

"A Hauk is not a politician. There is no room in our hearts to sit in peace with those who would do any Andarion harm. We are, and will forever be, protectors of our brethren, family, and homeworld. So long as a single War Hauk lives, no nation will defeat us. No race will dare to invade our air, lands, or sea. We will stand and we will defend.

"For we are not bred of mercy and we are not bred for peace.

"We are born of fury.

"Forever Andaria!

"And forever fear the Warring Blood Clan of Hauk."

Sumi had learned to recite that speech as a class project to honor Fain's Andarion heritage. He'd never once said a word about it being his direct ancestor who'd originally given it.

She looked at Thia. "I didn't realize that was his lineage." Because of the legend of the Thirteen War Hauks, Hauk was the most common surname on Andaria—taken to honor the family that had given so much to protect their freedom and planet, and to remind their people that it only took a handful of brave Andarions willing to fight and die for their brethren to hold back a superior army.

Thia nodded. "Dancer is the name of that first War Hauk who founded their lineage. His brother Fain is named for the War Hauks' father and the eldest brother, who was the first to die in action while protecting his father's back. Uncle Hauk and Darice are the last two members of that most prestigious bloodline, and are the only two in all of Andaria who can legally be styled as the Warring Blood Clan of Hauk. If Dariana releases Uncle Hauk from his pledge—"

"Another female could tie into his lineage."

Thia nodded. "One with a higher-caste bloodline than hers. Should Uncle Hauk do that, Darice would no longer be styled as Darice of the Warring Blood Clan of Hauk—only the children of the two strongest unified lineages can use that title. Darice would be downgraded to Darice of the War Hauk Blood Clan. And Dariana would fall back a level in the Andarion caste system. Forever."

But there was one thing that still didn't make sense to Sumi. "Then why not marry Hauk and breed children with him herself? Would that not ensure her lineage and theirs?"

The darkness returned to Thia's gaze at that question. "To begin with, that would still downgrade Darice's title. Unless she's willing to allow Uncle Hauk to be listed as his father and remove Keris from Darice's lineage—something she has said repeatedly that she would never do . . . as I said, she hates Uncle Hauk and really doesn't believe he's worthy of *her* bloodline. So much so, that to preserve her right to keep Keris's lineage as her own and to block Uncle Hauk from his, she had Darice more than a decade after his father's death."

Sumi gaped at something she should have figured out by their ages. But honestly, it hadn't dawned on her. "How did she do that?"

Had she exhumed his body for DNA?

Ew!

Thia raked her hand through Illyse's coat. "Whenever the males of prestigious bloodlines enter their obligatory military service, their sperm is taken and frozen so that if they die before they procreate, a female who has a legitimate claim to that bloodline, such as a pledged or married female, can be artificially inseminated with it."

To carry on their lineage and DNA. Man, Andarions were weird.

Sumi was still aghast at their customs. "Pardon the pun, but that is so cold."

"No, the coldest part is keeping Uncle Hauk tied to her and not going through with unification. It's selfish and wrong on every level." There was a lot of hatred and venom in those words.

"How so?"

Thia cursed Dariana under her breath before she spoke. "How much do you know about Andarion male anatomy?"

"They're huge compared to humans."

She snorted at that statement of the obvious. "Anything else?"

"No. Not really. Other than the fangs, claws, and eyes. Why?"

Thia lowered her tone before she spoke again. "They are creatures *with* very strong passions and urges."

"Yeah, the whole I-would-rather-kill-you-than-look-at-you kind of gives that away."

"Yes, but that's not the only thing they're aggressive about. Unlike humans, Andarion males have to . . ." Thia's face turned absolutely red in the darkness.

"You okay?"

Fanning her face, Thia glanced to Sumi. "No idea why I'm telling you this, other than to illustrate what a bitch Dariana is, but . . . the males have to be . . . drained, for lack of a better word. Kind of like a lactating woman. If they don't get regular release, it's extremely painful for them and causes all kinds of problems and even severe illnesses for them. It's why they mate early and tend to have extremely," she dragged out the word, "large families."

"Oh." Now her face was as red as Thia's. "So why's that a problem? I'm sure any female would be more than willing to . . ." she cleared her throat, "drain Hauk."

Including her.

Thia snorted. "He can't. Ever. *That's* why she's a whoring, conniving Queen Bitchtress."

Sumi arched a brow. Why not? Was there something physically wrong with Hauk? "You've lost me again."

Thia released an irritated breath. "Long ago, to protect the purity of the lineages, the Andarions set down stringent laws. Adultery, which covers both married and pledged males, is punished severely and publicly. And . . ." Thia held her index finger up for emphasis. "Adultery by their laws means an Andarion male can't touch *any* female, except his wife or pledged, without being removed from his lineage."

Whoa. Wait a minute. Was Thia implying . . .

"Are you telling me Hauk's a virgin?"

Thia visibly cringed. "Well . . . this is really awkward suddenly. Given that he's my beloved uncle, my thoughts never went to *that* particular conclusion. I was speaking of celibacy, generic Andarion customs, and total bitches. But . . . now that you've mentioned it . . . considering his age when he was first pledged, and that the only time he wasn't pledged, he was undergoing surgeries and physical therapy . . ." She bit her lip and nodded. "Yeah. That would be a safe bet. One that makes me want to hurt Dariana even more now that I know. What a *minsid* whore!"

Wow. Sumi sat back in total stupor. So no one had ever climbed aboard that giant piece of sexy male and taken him for a ride.

Unbelievable. Who in their right mind would by-pass *that* opportunity? She didn't know who this Dariana was, but the female had to be the dumbest cow ever bred.

It explained a lot about Darice. So much for superior genetic material. Brains were a nice component to have with all that brawn.

Not to mention, her opinion of her own sister bottomed if Omira had been told any of this. And surely she'd known what her marriage to Fain would do to him. That it would cost him his extremely prestigious family name. Forever.

Why would Fain have given up all of that for Omira? Surely not even love would be worth that degree of stupid.

"What about his brother Fain? What happened to him?"

Thia curled her lip in distaste. "Fain made the mistake of marrying a human who decided too late that the last thing she wanted was to be tied to an Andarion male who had no lineage."

Not exactly, but Sumi couldn't argue that with her . . . not without outing herself. "I notice you're not insulting her. Not like you do Dariana."

Thia turned toward Sumi with an expression that was riddled with seething hatred. "Believe me, it's hard not to, given what he's been through because of what she did. But I love Uncle Fain and I would never dishonor the woman he gave his heart to. He'd beat my butt if I did. No one's allowed to say a word against her. Ever. Being

Andarion, his philosophy is that had he been worthy of her, she wouldn't have left him. He takes all responsibility for his failed marriage, and still holds her on a pedestal. For that matter, he wears her wedding ring, she threw in his face, on his pinkie and has never removed it."

Tears filled her eyes at the last thing she'd expected to hear. All this time, she'd assumed, from what Omira had said, that Fain hated her sister. That he'd been the one who'd left their marriage first.

"I should never have married an Andarion, Sumi. What was I thinking? They're not human. They don't act human. They're terrifying creatures who will tear you apart. I know Fain's going to come for me one day, and rip out my heart and eat it. I know it."

Omira had lived in absolute fear of him finding her. But she'd never really said why she was so scared of him. Other than he was an Andarion barbarian.

"How do you know he didn't leave her first?"

"Because I know Uncle Fain. Why would he still have her ring on his hand? Not to mention, all he'll ever say about it is that he wasn't what she really wanted." Thia shook her head. "No, he feels too much grief to have left *her.*"

Sumi's throat tightened as she remembered how heartbroken and terrified Omira had been when she came home after Fain had supposedly left. For three days, she'd locked herself in the bathroom, and had refused to come out. Barely nine, Sumi had been scared that Omira would kill herself.

"Father . . . we have to do something to help her."

"Let the tainted whore die. Better for all of us if she's gone."

She still didn't know how their own father could be so callous and unfeeling. When Omira had finally emerged, he'd refused to even look at her. While he hadn't thrown her out of their house, he'd treated her like a ghost. Never would speak to her or acknowledge her presence.

Omira had accepted it as best she could. But it was the reactions from other people who'd learned about her husband and her ongoing terror that Fain would hunt her down that had finally done her in.

Sumi had just turned eighteen when Omira had decided she couldn't handle it anymore—that life, and the condemnation of others, wasn't worth the struggle to get through it.

All Omira's suicide had done was worsen their father's alcoholism and his hatred of the only family he had left. He'd turned on Sumi like some bastard stepchild he wanted out of his sight.

"You're a whore, just like your worthless mother and sister. You'll find some cock to suck and then leave me, too. Just wait and see. You bitches are all the same."

As he'd predicted in his drunken stupors, she'd moved in with the first man to invite her, during her first year in college. She'd have done anything to get away from her father's insults.

Little had she known, it wouldn't be long before she'd wish herself back to her father's hell over that of her first boyfriend's. And even that disaster hadn't been nearly as bad as the one that would arrive with Avin.

Old enough to have known better, she'd somehow allowed that bastard to deceive her completely. And she still wasn't sure how she'd missed the warning signs of his insanity before she'd allowed Avin to move in with her.

At least with her father, she'd been able to gauge what would send him off into a rage and avoid most. Avin's triggers could be as simple as asking if it was raining outside. They were so arbitrary and capricious. . . .

She'd make a stew and it would be too salty. Then she'd make it again and it wasn't salty enough. *Don't wear heels and tower over me! Why aren't you wearing heels? Huh?*

You've wasted money on a closet full of them, and yet you never wear them!

"Closet full" by his definition was three pair. But that was another argument.

Gods, he'd been such a bastard. How had she ever allowed herself to think for one minute that she loved him? Who could ever love such a selfish prick?

A tear slid down her cheek as the pain of her past sank its claws into her heart. Sumi wiped it away before Thia saw it. There was no need in thinking about the life she'd had before. She was an assassin now. Her marriage was to The League alone. And at least it wouldn't be too many more years of torture. She was already over the average life expectancy of an assassin. Sooner more likely than later, someone, probably Hauk, would kill her before she got them.

That was her life. The best she could hope for was to save her daughter from the same fate.

Clearing her throat, she brought the topic back to Fain. "Where's Hauk's brother now?"

Thia stroked the lorina's head as it napped on her leg. "He lives as an Outcast and nomad. Sometimes in human zones. Sometimes Andarion, even though it's dangerous. He never stays in one place too long."

"So he's healthy?"

Pausing her hand midstroke, Thia pinned her with a gimlet stare. "You're showing a lot of interest in Fain. Should I ask why?"

There was no missing the underlying threat in those words. She better assuage the girl's suspicions or she'd be meeting with a bad accident soon. "Curious is all. Sorry. I ask questions when I'm nervous. I rather stumbled into all of your lives. I'm just trying to get my bearings."

Thia seemed to accept that. "I know the feeling. It took me awhile to acclimate to all of them myself. Especially Uncle Hauk." A nostalgic smile tugged at her lips. "The first time I met him, I thought he was going to cut my heart out and eat it, and I ran screaming down the hallway."

"Why would you think that?"

She raked a less-than-flattering look over Sumi's body. "*You* do that now and you're a trained assassin who's a lot closer to his height than I was or am. Not to mention that whole wide-as-a-house thing he has going for him. . . . It's extremely off-putting, especially when you're a kid. That male can palm a twenty-pound bowling ball. Seriously. I've seen him do it."

Illyse rose suddenly and hissed.

Before either of them could move, the lorina launched herself into the darkness. Thia shot to her feet and pulled her blaster out.

"Relax, Thee, it's just me." With Illyse by his side, Hauk slowly made his way into the circle of firelight, carrying a giant beast over his shoulder.

Sumi's eyes widened at the size of the creature while Thia holstered her weapon. "When you hunt, you don't play around, do you?"

"Not really." He scowled as he dropped the beast and then noticed Darice, facedown on the ground. Arching a brow, he turned toward Thia. "You kill him?"

"No. Just a good stunning."

A slow, boyish grin curved his lips. He rubbed at his goatee with his thumb. "Would it be wrong if I left him there until morning?"

Thia shrugged. "It's an Endurance. You tell me, oh great uncle."

"Maybe I'll just throw a blanket over him and leave him there for a while."

Thia scoffed. "It's more than he deserves."

As Hauk prepped his prey, Sumi noticed that he was much more relaxed than he'd been when he left. He was almost peaceful now.

"So killing things is how you unwind?"

He looked up with a wicked smile that flashed a bit of his fangs. "Indeed. Want to help me skin it?"

She screwed her face up as he pulled out a huge knife from the sheath on his thigh that also holstered his blaster. "I'd really rather not."

Pausing, he arched a brow. "A squeamish assassin? Really?"

"Conscripted," she reminded him. The last thing she needed was for a trained killer, holding a knife, to see her as the threat she knew she could be. "Before that, I was a botanist."

He sharpened his knife against the bracer on his forearm that contained a whetstone. Sumi wasn't sure what part of that disturbed her more. The fact he was so nonchalant about it, or the fact he felt compelled to wear a whetstone for such occasions.

Hauk tested the edge of the blade with the pad of his thumb. "So slaughtering innocent plants doesn't bother you?"

"I never slaughtered any plants. I only studied and catalogued them." She turned away and grimaced as he . . .

Shivering, she couldn't even think about it. It brought back too many awful memories for her.

Suddenly, she felt his warmth at her back. He was close enough to touch her, yet he didn't breach that little distance between them. "How did The League train you?"

She trembled even more. "Death matches and hunts."

He turned her to face him. In spite of the darkness, she saw the sympathy in his eyes as he stared at her. "Botanist, huh?"

Sumi nodded.

Hauk watched as she nervously bit her bottom lip. That single act sent a ferocious wave of desire through him and set his heart pounding again. Because he wasn't allowed to touch a female, he'd never spent much time around any who weren't bound to a male. Not that it mattered. Andarion females considered him disgusting and hideous. One look at his scarred flesh, and they curled their lips and insulted him before they scurried away to their mothers.

None of them would ever accept him in her bed.

The one and only time he'd tried to kiss Dariana, she'd stabbed him and warned him that if he ever offended her like that again, her next attack would be against his groin.

As for human women, they'd never appealed to him, especially since their reactions to his presence made the Andarion females seem kind. Not until this one. He couldn't explain it or understand it, especially given how much she reminded him of Fain's wife.

A woman he'd vowed to kill should their paths ever cross again.

And yet there was no denying what he felt anytime he caught the sweet floral scent of Sumi's hair. All he wanted was to bury his face in those pale strands and breathe her in.

To feel her body pressed against his. Skin to skin.

Damn it. He was even harder now than he'd been when he left to take care of . . . things and hunt. He wanted her so badly that he wasn't sure how he remained apart from her.

Touch her and Dariana will gut you with glee.

No, his own mother would gut him. Ever since Keris's death, she'd been lying in wait for a chance to honorably end his life and he knew it. And all because of a blood feud that had nothing to do with him.

Rather his mother, desperate to tie her blood to his father's lineage, had seduced his father the day before he was to have been pledged to Nykyrian's mother. The moment the Andarion princess had learned that her champion had sampled another female's body, she'd refused his pledge and sent his father home in disgrace.

But at least Cairistiona hadn't demanded his father's head or his cock, which any other female would have.

His paternal grandmother had never forgiven his mother for that act that had risked his father's life and denied them a royal lineage. Her life's dream had been to live long enough to see the War Hauks tied to the eton Anatoles. Because Keris had been conceived during that night when his mother seduced his father, his grandmother had been forced to allow them to join bloodlines to keep the Hauk lineage pure. But she'd never liked it.

In spite of that, his grandmother had held on to the hope that her great-grandchildren might merge. It was why she'd paid to send Hauk and Fain to school with Prince Jullien, as companions and guardians for him. But that would never happen now. Childless, Prince Jullien had been removed from the royal succession and only Nykyrian remained.

Even if one discounted the age difference, Thia hated Darice and viewed him as a pesky little brother. She would never accept his pledge. And Nyk's youngest daughter was barely three months old. There was no chance in hell that Nyk would allow her to marry someone that much older—provided he *ever* allowed Zarina or Thia to marry at all. And even if by some miracle Nyk did accept Darice, Hauk's grandmother wouldn't live long enough to see Zarina to adulthood. She was already almost two hundred years old.

And so his mother, a former negotiator for the Andarion royal house, had found in his grandmother the one being she couldn't win over with her guile.

No matter what she tried.

To this day, he and Fain were caught between their ongoing war as his mother tried to prove to his grandmother that she was the better mate for his father than the queen would have been. That his mother had conceived the better sons.

Because Hauk loved his mother, he had done everything possible to please her, and show his grandmother that he could be a grandson she could take pride in.

Never once had he asked for anything of his own. Duty. Honor. Family. Obligation. Loyalty. Those were the oaths of an Andarion male. No matter what others or life had thrown at him, he'd done his best to rise above it and adhere to their customs.

Until now.

For the first time ever, he craved the one thing he knew he could never have.

The gentle touch of a woman's hand on his bare skin. It would mean his life to taste those lips that lured him toward suicide. But what truly scared him was the part of himself that really didn't give a shit. The part of him that was willing to die painfully for one night in the arms of a female who didn't loathe him.

Clearing his throat, he stepped back from her before he gave into his supreme stupidity. "You should probably rest in the tent while I do this."

Sumi hesitated. She didn't want to leave him. Strangely, she wanted to walk into his arms and have him hold her. To kiss his lips until she was drunk from passion. That urge was worsened by the knowledge that he'd never taken a lover.

That she would be the first woman to have him inside her body.

If what Thia had said was true, he'd never even been kissed before. How was that possible that no one had sampled such an incredibly sexy beast?

But then she'd seen his photos. He'd spent most of his life around male humans. Probably to avoid temptation.

Which meant he wouldn't be interested in her.

At all.

He's your target, moron! Not your boyfriend.

Oh yeah. There was that.

Yet as she walked away from him, and he returned to skinning his kill, she didn't see a target there. She saw a beautiful Andarion male whose intelligent eyes were tinged with the deepest sadness and pain.

As Sumi neared the tents, Thia arched a brow at her. "What?" she asked the girl.

"I shouldn't have told you any of that."

"What do you mean?"

Thia jerked her chin toward her uncle. "First, Uncle Hauk would kill me if he knew I'd said anything to you about it. Second . . . I've stoked a fire with you that I shouldn't have."

Sumi scoffed. "I have no idea what you're talking about."

"Yeah, you do. You know he's forbidden, and it's irresistible now. But just remember this . . . I'm not the only one who loves him and who considers him family. If any harm comes to him because of your actions, we will hunt you down to the outer edges of the universe, and take turns making you wish you'd never been whelped."

The scariest part of that wasn't the fact that she knew Thia and the others *would* do it.

It was the fact that she knew how much they'd relish her torture.

CHAPTER 9

Sumi came awake with a start. Lying perfectly still, she squinted against the oppressive darkness, trying to discern what had shocked her from her dreams.

Footsteps. Just outside her tent.

It's probably one of the kids going to the bathroom. Had to be. Hauk, despite his hulking size, never made so much as a whisper when he moved. He was like a wraith.

Scary, really. No creature that size should be *that* silent. It was unnatural.

That was her thought until she heard someone grunt. Another person groaned and fell quiet. Three blast shots rang out, each punctuated by a sharp blast of color that was bright even through the fabric walls. Rolling to her feet, she crouched low, and went to the opening so that she could join whatever fight was going on outside.

Her jaw fell slack as she saw Hauk in a similar crouch, only he had a blaster in each hand. Turning in a slow circle, he scanned the area in front of him.

When she moved, he jerked around and brought both weapons to bear on her. She held her hands up to let him know she wasn't currently a threat. The instant he realized it was her and not another attacker gunning for his back, he relaxed and lowered the blasters.

"Kids!" he called in that deep thunderous tone as he rose to his feet and holstered his weapons. No wonder he softened his voice whenever he spoke to her and Thia. That resonating growl was terrifying. "Get out here. Now!"

Not even Darice balked. He left his tent, rubbing his eyes.

"What happened?" Thia gaped at the ten large bodies strewn around their camp. To Hauk's credit, he'd dispatched them quickly and in virtual silence. An impressive feat for anyone.

Hauk moved to the body closest to him so that he could search it. "Big fluffy bunnies paid us a late-night visit. And look, kids, they were kind enough to bring us ammunition and weapons. Could they be any more thoughtful?"

Ignoring his sarcasm, Thia aimed her blaster toward Sumi, who held her hands up again as she feared her imminent death.

"Stand down." Hauk jerked his chin to the body at Thia's feet. "They're not League. Look at them. They're incas."

Sumi frowned. Incas were independent contract assassins who didn't follow League protocols. They were killers for hire, regardless of law or procedure. If you paid their exorbitant fee, they would deliver the head of whomever you named.

Thia toed the body by her feet. "Are you sure?"

He gave her an offended glare.

Without another word, Thia examined the body she'd toed in a way that left Sumi astonished. Most girls Thia's age would be sickened or horrified by the grisly sight, and honestly, she was a little herself. While she wasn't fond of killing, she *really* didn't like handling dead bodies. But Thia acted with the abrupt sternness of a seasoned soldier. "There's nothing on this one. You got any markings over there, Uncle Hauk?"

"No." Standing up, he shot the body again.

Sumi arched a brow at his actions.

"For being so damned inconsiderate," he explained. "And waking me up from a good nap . . . toe-humping bastard."

Still ignoring him, Thia sat back. "Are they all human?"

"No." Darice kicked at the legs of the one closest to him. "This one's Partini . . . Partinai . . . Partiny? Whatever you use for them. They're a screwed-up race when it comes to singular and plural." They were also a race known for their brutal fighting skills. It was hard for anyone not born of their breed to hold their own against them, never mind actually kill one.

Highly impressive.

As Darice skimmed the bodies and he noted their number, he duplicated Sumi's earlier gape. "Gah, Dancer . . . You took them all out without even breathing hard. How?"

Bracing his forearm on his bent knee, Hauk gave his nephew an irritated smirk. "What do you think I do for a living, boy? Bake fucking cookies?" He holstered his newly found weapons and continued to search bodies.

"I thought you did IT for the aristos. Computers and desk stuff."

Thia laughed out loud. "You're so stupid, D. You really think your uncle keeps a body like that from lifting microchips? Yeah . . . Stay delusional. The planet Oblivion needs more occupants." She moved to untie the lorina so that it could patrol for others. "I don't know how they got through my traps and alarms that I set earlier."

"Don't think about it, Thee. I promise, they won't get through me." Hauk confiscated more of the assassins' weapons and tucked them into various places in his clothes. He met Sumi's gaze. "Any of them friends of yours?"

Sumi shook her head. "Never seen them before." When she reached for a blaster, Thia actually shot at her. The blast barely missed her head, and by the look on Thia's face, she knew the girl had expertly placed it, but wouldn't be so considerate next time.

"Uncle Hauk?"

He narrowed his eyes on Sumi as if trying to read her thoughts. "Let her have it. The one at her feet was going for her while she slept. Leads me to believe he wasn't working with her. Or if he was, they had a falling-out."

Thia hesitated. "You sure?"

He nodded. "Besides, she's not much of a killer."

Sumi resented the teasing humor in his deep voice. "I am a chief field assassin, you know? I've never failed a mission or missed a target. I'm damn good at what I do."

"Ooo," he said sarcastically as he rose to his feet. "Someone cue my fear pheromones."

Sumi put her arms on her hips. "What's that supposed to mean?"

"That he's less than impressed by your rank," Thia explained wryly. "By the time my father, his best friend since childhood, was my age, he was top ass."

Sumi tried not to be impressed, but she couldn't help it. Very few made the rank of command assassin of the first order, and only one had ever attained it by Thia's age.

Nemesis was the most brutal of them all.

But then, as she looked over the bodies, Sumi was glad that Hauk wasn't threatened by her skills. It didn't work out well for anyone he perceived as a threat.

And she didn't want to meet the brutal end of the men on the ground around them.

Thia clapped Sumi on the arm. "You got a lot of confirmed kills to go, puddin'." She winked at her. "Not to mention, Uncle Hauk left The League as a teenager with the rank of special agent."

Darice made a rude sound of disagreement. "Lorina shit. Dancer was still in training when he washed out."

Hauk cocked and locked his jaw at his nephew's snotty dismissal. "For your information, punk, I rose to the rank of captain *during* training."

Sumi made an exaggerated gape at him. Yeah, okay, that rankled. Captain was the fourth-highest rank an assassin could aspire to. And it was the one most assassins never rose above before someone violently ended their career and life.

Darice raked his uncle with a scathing glare. "If you were a captain, how did you wash out, huh?"

Hauk didn't answer as he began carrying bodies off to the side of camp.

"Your mother," Thia snarled at Darice. "After Hauk had gone through two years of grueling training where she hoped someone would kill him, she ran to his CO and told him that Hauk couldn't graduate to full assassin because he was pledged to her. The League discharged him immediately."

Sumi winced at what Thia described. That would do it, since assassins were forbidden to marry. But what a callous thing to do, especially if Dariana had no intention of seeing their marriage met. Why not let him have that much in his life, if it was what he wanted?

Not to mention, it would have guaranteed that he'd never marry someone else. For that matter, why would his parents allow him to go through League assassin training, knowing he couldn't graduate? Did they not love him at all?

As a full-grown woman when her courses had started, Sumi had seen firsthand the horrors and degradations of it all. The young boys and girls, Darice's age and only a year or two older, who were ruthlessly put into arenas and forced to fight for their survival. It was why she was so desperate to get her baby out of that system before they forced Kalea into training.

Kill or be killed. The League didn't respect age or pull punches for recruits. It was pass or fail, and failure was a brutal death at the hands of another student or instructor. It was the worst sort of daily beat downs.

Thia was right. Only a first-rank bitch would let a teenager go through all that, and then have him tossed out right before graduation. Why would Dariana be so vicious?

Unless, as Thia had said, she'd wanted him dead.

Darice scowled at Hauk. "Is that true? Is your pledge to my mother the reason you were thrown out?"

With a heavy sigh, Hauk picked up the Partini. "Yes."

"Then why do you tell everyone you washed—"

"What does it matter?" Hauk snapped at Darice, cutting him off. "The end result is the same. I was dishonorably discharged just before graduation for not disclosing the fact I was pledged."

Confused, Darice looked between them for an explanation. "I don't understand why my mother would do such a thing when she has no desire to go through with unification."

Hauk tossed another body over his shoulder. "Doesn't matter."

"It does matter!" Thia stepped forward and gestured toward Darice. "For once, Uncle Hauk, tell him the truth."

"It's his mother. Leave it be, Thia."

"Leave what?" Darice asked. "What happened?"

Thia's eyes flared before she defied her uncle's wishes. "Your mother couldn't stand the fact that Uncle Hauk was a better soldier than your father. That he had more honors, awards, and kills as a recruit than Keris had as the head of the Andarion armada. She knew if Hauk stayed in The League, he'd outshine Keris's glory and—"

"Thia!" That ferocious growl made Sumi's heart leap. "Enough!"

"No, it's not. I'm sick of listening to him attack you all the time when he knows nothing but the lies his selfish mother has told him. If he's old enough for Endurance, he's old enough to know the truth."

Hauk moved faster than Sumi would have thought someone so large could manage. He towered over Thia with enough fury that the girl finally took a step back and swallowed. "The past is done. Leave it where it belongs."

Thia gestured toward Darice again. "But—"

Sucking his breath in audibly, he bared his fangs to her. "There are other things to focus on right now."

Thia held her hands up in surrender. "Fine."

Hauk retrieved another blaster from the ground near Thia's feet then handed it off to Sumi. "We need to break camp. There's nothing on them to say who or what hired them, or how they found us. For safety's sake, let's assume they have friends who might miss their stench."

The kids ran to collapse their tents while Hauk headed for his.

Sumi went over to the bodies to search them herself. True to his words, they had no marks whatsoever.

But that didn't make sense. Kyr wouldn't have sent amateurs when he had an entire army of highly trained assassins at his disposal. Her own tracking device had been temporarily disabled so as not to alarm or alert Hauk to her mission or make him suspicious.

She knew Hauk wouldn't be tagged.

Which left her with another thought.

Sumi headed to the tent that Hauk was quickly stowing in his pack. "Are the kids chipped?"

He shook his head. "Their parents know better. They wouldn't risk an enemy tapping the signal and using it to trace them."

"Do you know who the assassins were targeting?"

He glanced over to make sure the kids weren't in hearing range before he spoke to her in a low, hushed tone. "They were after me. It was my tent they beelined to, and I heard them talking about it."

"But they gave no clue as to who sent them?"

He shook his head. "My enemies are many, and it's really not unusual for me to be attacked." He ran his tongue over his right fang as he glanced back toward the bodies. "I just don't know how they found me *here*. That's what's bugging the shit out of me."

And not the fact they tried to kill him while he slept. Okay . . .

She checked the charge levels on her weapons then hesitated as she realized exactly how skilled Hauk really was at his brutal craft. "Did none of them get a shot off before they died?"

"No," he said simply.

Her heartbeat picked up its pace. If Thia's father was a better assassin than Hauk, she hoped to the gods that she never faced him as an enemy. "Captain, huh? How old were you when you earned that rank?"

"Eighteen."

She let out a low, appreciative breath. Still, it was hard to believe him. "You killed over one hundred targets, half of them trained soldiers, by age eighteen?"

"I'm a War Hauk," he said simply, as if that explained it all. He started for the blankets.

Sumi pulled him to a stop as she tried to digest what he was telling her. "That's more than five kills a month, during training. How did you manage that?"

A tic started in his jaw as a dark anger engulfed him. "I was younger than most of my class. Because of that, I had a lot of challengers."

She winced at what he was really saying. His classmates and instructors had chosen him for the ring more often than the others because he'd been so young and was scarred from the fire. "They thought they could kill you easily and advance."

He gave her a brief nod.

"I'm sorry, Hauk."

"For what?"

"You should have been at home with your mother being a kid, and not forced to fight for every breath you took." Every meal he ate. Every minute he was allowed to sleep . . . Her heart aching, she pulled him into her arms and hugged him close.

He went absolutely rigid. "What are you doing?"

Suddenly, she became aware of just how ripped and hard his body was. Damn, he couldn't have more than two percent body fat. If that. It was like leaning against a stone wall. "Hugging you."

Her answer appeared to baffle him. "Why?"

She clapped him on the back before she reluctantly stepped away. "It's what people do to comfort each other."

He didn't respond.

She looked up to see his attention focused behind her. Turning, she caught the angry glare Darice had pinned on them.

Hauk mumbled something under his breath that had to be Andarion.

With long, angry strides, Darice closed the distance between them. "Have you dishonored my mother?"

For a moment, she thought Hauk might actually strike the boy for his impudence. "No." It was a low, guttural sound in the back of his throat.

"You better not."

Thia pulled Darice away from Hauk. "Son, we need to talk about your inability to sense near-death experiences."

"What are you talking about?"

Thia glanced back to Hauk, who still hadn't moved.

He hadn't even blinked. "Can you not see how pissed off he is?"

"So?"

Rolling her eyes, Thia sighed. "You're an idiot, Darice. I seriously hope you have no intention of entering any kind of military service."

He lifted his chin defiantly. "Of course, I am. I'm Andarion. I'm going to be a fighter pilot like my parents."

"No, punkin'." She patted him on the cheek. "With those well-honed survival instincts, you're going to be a bright stain on someone's blast shield."

Darice curled his lip at Thia's warning. "What do you know?"

"Stop arguing and pack," Hauk growled at them. "We need to move like your lives depend on it."

It was only then that Sumi realized he was already packed up completely.

And within minutes, he had the kids packed, too. When he handed the haul bag to Darice, his nephew balked. Loudly.

Darice jerked his chin toward Thia and Sumi. "Why can't they carry more?"

"They're females."

"So?"

Hauk mumbled in Andarion again. Sumi was beginning to suspect those were foul curses he was spewing. "Thia's right. You're just a walking stain. Stop bitching and soldier up. Take my *minsid* pack and march. You need to build the muscle mass." He grabbed the huge haul bag and slung it over the sword strapped across his back before he led the way. Illyse trotted after him.

Holding on to the straps of her pink floral rucksack, Thia rolled her eyes at Darice, who continued to pout at all of them. "In a fight, as a rule, women are quicker and more nimble than men, moron. We're also much smaller targets."

"So?"

Hauk glanced back over his shoulder to check their pace. "Should we come under fire, they don't need their muscles fatigued from carrying heavy packs and ammunition. It leaves them sharp with the freedom of movement to keep an eye out while we travel. If we're attacked, we need someone to take point and lay down cover fire for us while we scramble."

Thia nodded. "So standard protocol is, one soldier, usually the larger of the pair, plays pack mule so that the other can take that point and defend. It's why Andarions assign male-to-female strike teams. Everyone does their part and everyone goes home."

Darice rubbed at his nose. "I didn't know that's why we do that."

Thia scoffed at him. "Has your mother taught you nothing?"

He cast a sullen sneer at Thia. "Who taught *you*?"

"My father. Uncle Syn. Aunt Shahara. Uncle Hauk. Uncle Darling. Aunt Mari. Uncle Fain. Uncle Caillen. Aunt Desi. Uncle Nero. Aunt Jayne . . . Constantly." She sighed. "Everything is a life lesson that invariably ends with . . . *and then you can die*," she said in a mock masculine tone. "It's rather ridiculous."

"No, it's not." Sumi swallowed as the pain of her past hit her hard. "You should be grateful that your father loves you so, Thia. My father taught me nothing, except how to take an insult without flinching. He sent me out into the world with a blindfold that was brutally ripped from my eyes. I would have given anything to know the things you do at your age. And it would have saved me a universe of hurt."

Hauk paused to frown at her. In his eyes, she saw a kindred spirit, and knew he understood exactly what she was talking about. It brought a tenderness to her heart that was as startling as it was unexpected. And

as they walked, she found her gaze continually stray-
ing to him.

He cut an incredible sight as his muscles bulged from
the load he carried effortlessly. She envied him that ability. Most of all, she envied those pants that cupped an ass
so sweet she ached to take a bite out of it.

Sumi!

Her face heated up instantly, making her grateful for
the darkness. It wasn't like her to have those kinds of
thoughts. After what had happened with Darnell and
Avin, and the ordeal of League training, she'd never
thought to find a man attractive again.

Hauk's not a man.

True, but as an Andarion, he was even more dangerous to her. Stronger. Scarier.

Faster.

And yet, she felt safe with him. *You're insane. If he
ever learned what you're here to do, he'd cut your throat
quicker than he took out the assassins tonight.*

That was definitely true.

"You know what really chaps me?" Thia asked suddenly.

Sumi gave a light laugh as she considered the answer.
"Well, from all the drama and death threats of the last
two days, dare I say, Darice?"

Thia snickered while Darice glared at her in the darkness. "Well yeah, okay. I'll give you that. But no. If I were
at home, my dad would have known the instant my heart
rate went up. Three guards and two drones would have
magically appeared and laid a bead on whatever was annoying me."

Hauk laughed.

Thia tried to shove him, but it didn't alter his stride at
all. "It's not funny."

Hauk tsked at her. "It could be worse, little sister."

"How?"

"Your father has five other children and your mother he also loses sleep over. Imagine poor Devyn. Both his parents are overprotective psychos, and he's got their combined undivided attention on him *all* the time. Not to mention Vik, who *never* sleeps."

Thia made a face of utter pain. "Oooo. You're right. No one hooks me up to a monitor and draws blood from me every time I sneeze."

Sumi arched a brow.

"His dad's a doctor," Thia explained. "If Dev so much as hiccups, his father runs every known test to make sure he hasn't contracted some incurable rare disease. And don't get me started on his mother. Aunt Shahara makes Uncle Syn look like the negligent, uncaring parent."

Hauk passed an amused smirk to Sumi. "She's not kidding. I was playing with Devyn when he was a baby, and I pretended to drop him. His dad snatched him from me, and his mother shot me for it."

Sumi gasped. "No, they didn't!"

He placed his right hand over his heart. "On my honor, they did. I have the scar to prove it."

Thia nodded to back him up. "Saddest part? Uncle Hauk's their designated TAM."

Sumi cocked her head at the unfamiliar term. "TAM?"

"Tactical assault monkey," Hauk answered.

"And that is?"

Thia grinned. "The raw, insane brute force they sic on things that annoy them, and who pulls anchor on missions. I told you. Uncle Hauk's an attack dog. . . . And they *shot* him." She playfully slapped a hand on Hauk's arm. "No one should ever blast the TAM they depend on."

Sumi glanced to Hauk to gauge what he thought of her description of him. Oddly, he seemed to take it in stride. "Doesn't that offend you?"

"No. It's true."

Thia's smile widened. "Uncle Darling refers to calling Uncle Hauk as summoning the beast."

Hauk scoffed. "I thought he just called me Grandma."

"Well, that too. But only when you sit on him like a hatchling."

Sumi fell silent as she listened to their family stories. They had the tight-knit relationships that she'd craved all her life. And while they took jabs and complained about each other, there was an undeniable loyalty and love between them all.

"What about you, Sumi?" Thia asked, intruding on her thoughts.

"What about me, what?"

"Your family? What are they like?"

She glanced to Hauk before she answered. "I don't have any."

Thia stopped so suddenly that Sumi almost collided with her. "No one?"

She shook her head. "My parents and sister are long gone."

"Grandparents?"

"Died before I was born."

Thia gaped at her. "How long have you been alone?"

"Since I was nineteen."

The look in Thia's eyes said that she realized her fate could have easily been the same. She hooked her arm through Sumi's and started forward again. "Then welcome to our family."

That offer stunned her. "Pardon?"

Thia tightened her grip. "My aunt Mari always says that family isn't about the blood you share. It's about the people willing to bleed for you."

Those words brought a lump to her throat and she wasn't sure what to make of them. This wasn't the kind of attitude she was used to. In her world, family was the first to bleed you, and strangers bled you out totally. Honestly, she couldn't imagine the world Thia and the Hauks described.

"Mari sounds like a very wise woman."

Laughing, Thia patted her arm. "*He* is very wise. And our extremely large family is always willing to grow even bigger. So welcome to it."

Thia's naive sweetness confused her. "That's not very Andarion, is it? I thought blood was the only thing that mattered."

Hauk grunted. "It is and it's not."

Sumi sighed at his evasive answer. "I think you two like messing with my head."

Thia wrinkled her nose. "It is fun toying with new people. But back to your question, while it is rare for Andarions to adopt, it's not unheard of. Again, it has to be initiated by a female who is willing to bring the child into her lineage . . . it's why I'm still allowed to be princess even though I'm a bastard."

"Thia!" Hauk snapped. "You would make Kiara cry with that statement, and rile your father."

She rolled her eyes. "It's true and we all know it. While my grandmother has been extremely loving and accepting of me, I see how she looks at Zarina."

"Zarina is an infant," Hauk growled.

"And she looks Andarion. Fully."

Hauk paused. "Is that what's been bothering you?"

Sumi saw the tears in Thia's eyes before she blinked them away.

"Forget I said anything."

Hauk started for her, but Sumi held her hand up to stop him.

"Why don't you two go on ahead and let us catch up in a few?"

Hauk considered it for several minutes before he nodded. "Illyse, stay with Thia." Then he motioned for Darice to follow him.

Sumi gave them a decent head start before they resumed their trek. "Zarina is your sister?"

She nodded. "I love her. But she's so strange-looking with her Andarion eyes and thick black hair and claws. None of my brothers were born like that. They all look human."

"Does it bother you that she's Andarion in appearance?"

"No." She brushed at a tear that fell down her cheek.

"Thia? What is it?"

More tears fell as her lips quivered. "Since she was born, I get so jealous sometimes that I want to lash out and hurt her, and I hate myself for it. She doesn't deserve that from me. Like Hauk said, she's just a baby."

Sumi couldn't follow the girl's logic. "Jealous of what?"

"Everything." Sobbing, Thia held her hands up to her eyes as if she were physically trying to stop her tears. "It was bad watching my father and stepmother with my brothers. Seeing what life was supposed to be like. You know?" She ground her teeth. "It just rams home how wrong my childhood was, and makes me so mad at my mother for her part in it, that I want to go back and confront her for it. Why did she have to sleep with my father and then, knowing she's pregnant with *me*, marry his stepbrother, who hated him? Really! Why would she do that? Aksel was such a sick, demented bastard. I don't understand why she didn't gut him the first year they were married and save us both years of misery."

"Oh, Thia. Pray that you never understand that fear."

"How do you mean?"

Sumi cupped the girl's face in her hands. Gods how she wished she didn't know how easy it was to get sucked into an inescapable nightmare. To feel trapped and lost, and to have no one to help, and no way out. To be so desperate for love that you'd accept insults and blows for any semblance of it.

She still couldn't believe she'd done it, not once.

Twice.

"Thia, you are headed down a bad path. One I walked before you, and I'm here to tell you that it sucks in ways you can't imagine. So long as you keep this anger inside, it will infect you. You have to let it go and move on. Life isn't fair. It's not supposed to be. It's just better than being dead."

"You don't know."

"Girl, I do. I know exactly what it's like to be angry at the gods who put you here. Furious at the ones who were supposed to protect and love you, but instead were focused on their own selfishness and consumed by their own pain to the point they didn't care what happened to you." Sumi swallowed. "From what I've heard, your father and stepmother sound wonderful. They love you."

Her lips trembled. "I know. Kiara has always treated me like a blood daughter. But I just want what they have."

"You do have it, sweetie."

"No. I have the same demons inside me that my father has, and I know it. I've seen humanity for what it is, and I know how tenuous safety can be. How fleeting." She knelt down and buried her face in Illyse's fur. "I always feel like an outsider in my own family. And I know it's not really true, but I can't stop it. It just hurts to know that I could have been their real daughter, instead of the one they were forced to raise. Sometimes I just want to run for the door and not look back. Ever."

"Thia—"

"Sumi, it's not what you're thinking. I was a teenager when my mother died . . . brutally. I'd only met my father one time, just hours before it happened. I didn't know him. At all. He didn't know me. And he died that night, too, protecting Kiara from my stepfather—who my father killed while rescuing her. In the blink of an eye, everything I knew was gone. Violently ripped away. And suddenly, everyone around me was a complete stranger."

Thia swallowed hard. "It was so surreal to be thrown into this giant, unrelated family. And they're not normal. My stepmother notwithstanding, they're *very* scary people. And having been raised with very scary, highly volatile and violent people, I was terrified of them all. And my dad, while he tries, he's so skittish around me. Like he's afraid he'll break me if he touches me, and he never knows what to say. Not that he speaks much to anyone. But still . . ."

She looked up at Sumi. "I'm sorry. I didn't mean to dump this on you. It's just those bodies brought back memories I wish I could burn out of my mind."

"Yeah. I noticed you didn't flinch."

Drawing a ragged breath, Thia stood. "As I said, Aksel was a psycho bastard. It seemed like every other day my mother was cleaning blood out of the carpets because he'd killed one of his men for something . . . like sneezing while he was talking." She laughed bitterly. "I feel as if my entire life has been one poorly written melodrama."

"Sweetie, we all feel that way at times. Trust me."

"I guess so." Thia pulled her sweater tighter around her as they walked. "My father tries so hard to protect me. It's suffocating. And it wouldn't bother me nearly as much if I didn't see the differences between how he treats me and how he is with my siblings."

"What do you mean? Does he love them more?"

"No!" Thia said quickly. "It's not that. Because he's wiped their butts and spoonfed them from birth, he's . . . well, as relaxed as *he* can get. With me, I can tell he feels like he owes me something. I can see the guilt in his eyes every time he looks at me, because he wasn't there when I was little to protect me and keep me safe. And all I really want is to crawl into his lap like my brothers do and have him hold me until it all stops hurting."

Sumi pulled Thia into her arms and held her close. "I know, sweetie. I really do. When I was little, I had a brother-in-law who was my hero. He, alone, would do just what you said. He'd envelop me in those strong arms and tell me that he'd never let anyone hurt me. And I believed him."

"What happened?"

"He divorced my sister and went away, never to return."

"You hate him for it?"

"I call it hatred, but it's not. It's shattered trust. I never had anyone who protected me. Anyone who picked me up when I fell, except him. And I miss him so much that I can't help but hate him. I will never understand why he left me, how he could do it, knowing I had no one else."

Now they were both crying.

Until Thia started laughing. "Thank the gods you sent Darice ahead. I'd have to gut the little booger if he saw us like this."

Sumi joined her laughter as she wiped away her own tears. "Why does life have to be so hard?"

Thia sniffed back her tears. "Aunt Mari says that the assholes in our lives are our biggest blessings."

"How so?"

"Without them, we'd take the ones who aren't for granted. Assholes give us needed perspective to appreciate the people who really love us."

Strange, she'd never thought of that before. "I really need to meet your aunt Mari one day."

Thia hooked her arm in Sumi's and started walking again. "Now that you're family, you will. Just don't wake him too early in the morning or he's a beast. As he says, his maternal instincts don't kick in until midday, and after his first cup of tea."

Sumi laughed at that. "Does he know you call him your aunt?"

"Of course. It's how he introduced himself to me when we met the first time." She pushed playfully against Sumi's side. "To clear your confusion, he's gay. As I said, we're a motley bunch. You'll fit right in."

How she wished that were true. But it would never be. It couldn't be.

And once she turned her intel in to save her daughter, she had no doubt that Thia would be the first one to kill her for it.

CHAPTER 10

Sumi slowed as she saw Hauk and Darice waiting for them. He handed a bottle of water to Thia. Smiling, Thia rose up on her tiptoes and kissed his cheek before she went to sit beside Darice.

Hauk handed a bottle to Sumi. Scowling, he brushed his thumb against her lower lashes. The concern in his eyes was almost enough to get her crying again, but somehow she managed to keep her emotions leashed.

"We're okay. Thia just needed some girl time. We're weird that way."

He grunted in response.

She shook her head at him. "Is that really your idea of an answer?"

He shrugged.

Sumi gave him an irritated stare. "You're not helping yourself, big guy."

"Don't be so hard on him, Sumi," Thia said while she watched them with an amused grin. "He's never spent much time around females so we're all like alien beings to him."

"Really?"

Hauk moved to check supplies. "Just Jayne, and a

female cousin who used to severely kick my ass when I was a kid."

"And Jayne ain't typical," Thia said in an exaggerated tone to illustrate how odd this Jayne was. "She's a fierce Hyshian assassin lunatic. Love her dearly, but she ain't right, and you *never* know what's she's going to say or do."

Sumi let out a low whistle as she remembered the pictures of the tall, dark-haired woman with the men. That explained a lot about the woman. "I understand now what you meant by scary."

"Actually," Thia said, grinning, "scary is the fact that she has children and hasn't eaten one of them yet."

Hauk snorted at her words. "You should ask her about Sway's older brother sometime."

Thia scowled. "Sway doesn't have an older brother."

"Exactly." Hauk's tone was flat and his expression quite serious.

Thia laughed, then sobered. "I know you're joking, Uncle Hauk . . . right?"

His features were still stony and gave nothing away. Though to be honest, he was a bit distracted. "The fact you have to ask says it all."

Darice stretched out on his side. "Can we stay here, Dancer? I'm tired of walking." He yawned like a small child and folded his arms under his head before he closed his eyes.

Hauk looked at Sumi, then Thia. "How are you two holding up?"

Thia stood and did an adorable little dance. "I'm good to go. Always nocturnal. Which might be helpful, if my father wasn't more nocturnal than me."

Smirking, Hauk met Sumi's gaze.

"League trained. Sleep is overrated."

He stroked his goatee with his thumb as he considered their answers. "Thee? Can you carry Darice's gear?"

"Yeah. Why?"

"Grab it." He pulled his blaster out and handed it to Sumi while Thia slung Darice's gear over her back. "Mind the recoil."

Sumi arched a curious brow.

"It's twice the range and blast radius of what you're carrying."

She still didn't understand why he'd given it to her. Not until he picked up Darice and cradled him against his chest. For once, Darice didn't protest. He draped his arms around Hauk's neck and placed his head on his shoulder.

Thia made an exaggerated gape at Sumi. "Well, if I'd known being carried was an option, I'd have called dibs!"

In those arms and against that rock-hard body . . . "Definitely."

Hauk scoffed at them as he led them forward. "I wish one of you had. You weigh a lot less. . . . Now let's get a little more distance from the bodies. There should be a small oasis a few ticks from here. It'll give us cover from exposure and should hide us if another group comes after me."

As they walked, Sumi noticed that Hauk kept visually checking on her and Thia to make sure he wasn't over-taxing their strength. Meanwhile, he said nothing about the load he carried. Darice probably weighed a good 150 to 170 pounds alone.

And judging by the boy's snore, it was deadweight.

Not to mention the fact that Hauk was carrying all the water and the heaviest part of their supplies and his sword. No wonder they called him their TAM.

She frowned at Thia. "Is Hauk good to do this? I'm thinking if he goes down, none of us can carry *him*."

"He won't go down."

She arched a brow at the certainty in Thia's voice.

"I've seen Uncle Hauk spar with my father and his brother. Trust me. Our TAM is stronger than a fortified League cruiser."

Sumi wasn't so sure about that. "Yeah, but that's practice."

Thia scoffed. "Not the way they do it."

Okay then. She would rely on Hauk's knowledge of his own tolerance and limitations. Her senses alert, she dutifully pulled up the rear.

It was almost dawn before they came to the oasis. Yawning, Hauk waited until Thia had pulled out a sleeping bag and unfolded it before he put Darice down and tucked him into it.

When the young woman stumbled away, he swung her up in his arms and carried her to where Sumi had opened Thia's bag. Identical to Darice, Thia snuggled against him like an infant as he carried her.

Her father might be skittish with her, but Hauk wasn't. He treated her just like she was his own as he gently kissed her head and tucked her in. Thia snuggled in just like a contented child.

He rose into that sexy predator pose with all his weight on one leg, while he scanned the landscape around them, and made sure that they were adequately shielded by the clump of shrubs. Without a word, he pulled out his bag and placed it near Thia.

Then he held his hand out for his blaster. Sumi returned it to him, and moved to stretch out to sleep. She'd barely moved before he picked her up and took her to his bag.

Apprehensive and yet strangely excited and aroused, she arched a brow at him. "What are you doing?"

"Putting you to bed."

That made her heart pound faster and sent a wave of frightening heat through her. "*Your* bed?"

He tucked her into his bag . . . then, to her disappointment, stepped back. "I'm not going to sleep tonight."

She gaped at him. But for the circles under his eyes, there was no sign of fatigue. Even so . . . "When was the last time you rested?"

He didn't answer as he called the lorina over to him and had it lie down between her and Thia.

"Hauk?" she chided. "You're not invincible."

He scratched at his jaw in a boyish gesture that made her smile. "I don't need to sleep yet. I'm fine." When he started to withdraw, Sumi caught his arm and gently tugged him closer to her.

Hauk dropped his gaze down to where she held on to his wrist. The heat in his eyes was searing. His breathing turned ragged.

Unable to put into words how grateful she was to him, she leaned in to kiss him for all he'd done for them.

Hauk couldn't move as she laid her soft, gentle hand against his cheek. No female had ever touched him like this.

Like she wanted him.

At home, he was too scarred for an Andarion female to look at him with anything more than a contemptuous sneer. And that was far preferable to the human women, whose hatred, fear, and loathing were palpable. All his life, he'd felt hideous and undesirable.

Disgusting.

Like a mutant, mangy animal no one wanted to touch.

But that wasn't what he saw in Sumi's eyes. She stared at him as if she wanted him as much as he wanted her.

He held his breath, craving her kiss with every part of his being. He opened his lips to receive it, then remembered why he couldn't.

Remembered what one single kiss would cost him.

Damn it to hell.

Grinding his teeth, he pulled back an instant before their lips met. "I'm pledged, Sumi."

Still she kept her hand on his cheek, tormenting him with things he knew he could never have. "Has she ever kissed you?"

He looked away as he remembered the one time he'd

tried. Dariana had moved so fast that he hadn't even felt the knife go into his flesh, until she'd twisted it in his gut. Instead of tasting her lips, he'd tasted his own blood.

"You ever do that again, unworthy, repulsive dog, and it'll be your testicles I slice open." Coldly, she'd wiped her blade off on his sleeve before she'd stepped over his body.

He swallowed hard as he pushed that memory away. "No."

Sumi brushed her delicate fingers over his mouth, raising chills all over him. "You should have a female who kisses you, Dancer. And often."

Before he could stop himself, he ran his hand through those pale tresses that had been tempting him since he'd pulled her skullcap off. They were even softer than he'd imagined. Lifting a lock, he inhaled her sweet scent. "You smell like flowers." And all he wanted to do was bury his face against her neck until he was drunk from it.

But he could never do that. Dariana was trusting in him to keep his vow to her. His body belonged to her and her alone. It was something his father had beaten into them from birth.

"I ever catch you with a female other than your pledged or wife, I'll cut your cock off myself."

And after the nightmare and infighting between his mother and grandmother, the last thing he wanted was to put any more drama into his already fucked-up life.

It just wasn't worth it.

Swallowing hard, he forced himself to leave her and take up a sentry post. It was, after all, the only thing he was good for.

Lying down, Sumi watched as Hauk finally grabbed a bottle of water for himself, and went to sit with his back against a small tree so that he had an unobstructed view of the surrounding terrain. It was weird, but she no longer saw his resemblánce to Fain. He'd established his own identity to her.

While they were physically similar and shared some personality traits, there was a deep sadness to Hauk that Fain had lacked. In many ways, he was even more fierce.

More wounded.

And she wanted to gut Dariana for what she was doing to him. If the bitch was going to force him into a lifetime of celibacy, why not allow him to be an assassin? What would have been the harm?

Was it really so that he wouldn't outshine Darice's father?

It was so unfair that someone like him was tied to an undeserving whore like Dariana while Sumi would have sold her soul to have found a father for her baby with one-half his decency. Loyal and caring males were far too rare in this world to be taken for granted. They should be cherished.

Before she could stop it, the picture of him holding the unknown baby girl went through her mind.

A male so gentle should have his own children to dote on and protect. In spite of his protests and denials, he was amazing with Darice and Thia. Far more patient with Darice than the little snot deserved.

Damn you, Kyr.

And damn her for what she was going to have to do to someone who definitely didn't deserve it. *I have no right to hate Dariana*. Not when she was going to have to do a lot worse to him before all was said and done.

His entire body aching and warm, Hauk came awake slowly. He grimaced at the throbbing, awful pain he felt as he realized he'd fallen asleep, sitting upright.

Then he remembered why.

Fully alert now, he jerked his blaster out and jumped to his feet as he searched for more attackers.

"You always wake up like that?"

His heart racing, he turned toward Sumi, who was sitting a few feet away. She was freshly bathed, her pale hair still damp and coiled into a bun at the nape of her neck. There was an amused glint in those beautiful hazel eyes as she finally watched him without fear.

Damn, she was a beautiful woman. And he hungered for her in a way that should be illegal, and it probably was in most galaxies.

By the sun's position, he knew it was well past midday. Holstering his blaster, he toed the blanket at his feet that someone had placed over him while he slept. "You?"

She nodded. "You were awake when I brought it to you. Don't you remember?"

His thoughts and sensations still fuzzy and dull, he rubbed at his forehead as he vaguely recalled it. Since she hadn't posed a threat, he'd accepted the blanket and thanked her for it.

Sumi smiled as she watched the boyish way he rubbed at his face. He had to be exhausted still. He was much more sluggish now than he'd been the days before, and even last night.

He stifled a yawn. "Where are the kids?"

"Exploring the caves. I'm rather surprised you didn't take us there last night to camp."

"Bad defensive position." Rubbing at his side, he grimaced again. "Too easy to trap us with no way out."

A mistake she would have made on her own. "You know this place well."

"It left an impression on me." He crouched down to where she'd placed some of the meal they'd prepared for breakfast and a bottle of water. It was the first time she'd actually seen him eat anything other than snacks. His slow, studied movements were strangely savage and yet oddly beautiful.

He paused as he caught her staring at him. "Do I offend you?"

"Hardly."

"Then why are you eyeballing me?"

She wrinkled her nose. "I can't seem to help myself. You are an incredibly sexy beast, Dancer Hauk. Full of strange incongruities."

He snorted at her as he swallowed his food. "You sound like Mari."

She laughed. "He come on to you a lot?"

A slow, charming grin spread across his face. "He teases, but I think he'd have run for cover had I ever accepted."

She inclined her head to him. "Another surprise."

"What?"

"That you'd tolerate sexual harassment from a man."

His answering deep, throaty laugh did the strangest things to her stomach. "He's a Phrixian male, not a man, and I take a lot of shite in stride from all my brothers."

She paused to consider that shocking revelation. "Phrixian and he's gay? How did he ever manage to live to adulthood?"

"He's one of the fiercest warriors I've ever had at my back."

He'd have to be. Phrixians were the only race she'd run up against the Andarions for cold-blooded brutality and adherence to some rather savage laws.

Sumi fell silent as she remembered seeing a burgundy Phrixian uniform in the group that had attacked the prison. If that was Mari, Hauk was right. That male could fight. And he could take a beating without flinching.

Yeah, Mari was fierce indeed.

Hauk scowled as he noted the hot salad she'd made for him. "What is this?"

"Botanist, remember? Plants are good for you. You

should try making friends with them sometime. Vary that heavy carnivorous diet of yours."

He made a face similar to the one Darice had when she'd insisted he try it. But unlike his nephew, he sampled it without audible bitching. With an adorable astonished expression, he met her gaze and smiled. "It's good."

"Best of all, it doesn't run or try to kill you when you go after it."

He laughed again. "I like the danger."

"I'm sure you do."

Licking his lips, he finished his food in silence.

Once he was done, Sumi took the plate to wash it off while he went to attend his morning needs. It'd been a strange day so far. She'd awakened unsettled and couldn't figure out why. Just a gut feeling that something wasn't quite right.

Hauk had been barely lucid when she'd approached him earlier with the blanket, but she had no doubt that had she done something he perceived as a threat, he'd have shot up like he did a few minutes ago. Ready and willing to kill.

The poor, exhausted baby had fallen asleep before she'd finished tucking the blanket around him. Knowing he needed the rest, she and the kids had tiptoed around and left him to it.

Rubbing at her neck, she scanned the terrain, looking for the source of her discomfort.

What is wrong with me?

She was anxious and jittery. Unsettled. Like someone was watching her.

Not wanting to be alone, she started for the caves, then changed course to see if Hauk was okay. The kids had the lorina with them and Darice could scream loud enough to be heard for miles if they came under threat.

Hauk should have returned by now.

Sumi made her way to the small pond that was between

the oasis and the caves, where a shirtless Hauk sat sideways to her. He was already washed, with his damp hair pulled back from his face. When he picked up his knife, she thought he was going to shave with it.

Until he used it to cauterize a wound in the side she couldn't see.

"Oh my God," she breathed, rushing forward.

He drew on her, then lowered the blaster as he recognized her.

Aghast, she gaped at him. "You're wounded?"

Grinding his teeth, he returned to cauterizing the vicious knife wound across his lower left rib. "They didn't all miss last night."

"Why didn't you say something?"

He shrugged.

"Dancer!" she snapped at him. "You could have bled out."

The expression on his face said that she was the one overreacting. . . .

As if!

"I stopped the bleeding before we left. It didn't reopen until I carried Darice."

And he hadn't said a word about it. To anyone. She stared at him in total disbelief. "Son, you can't just walk around bleeding and not say something. Hasn't anyone ever told you that?"

"No," he said simply.

Astonished, she shook her head. How hard had everyone leaned on him in his life that he accepted this without flinching? To him, *this* was normal.

Really?

Suddenly, the TAM label wasn't amusing to her. It seriously pissed her off. He wasn't some invincible armored tactical vehicle to carry and cover them. He was a flesh-and-blood male.

One who'd been injured protecting them.

Wanting to help him, she moved closer so that she could examine the wound he'd sealed. Alone. Without even thinking to ask for help. That said it all about how others treated him.

She winced at the sight of his injuries. The raw, jagged flesh was next to another scar from a knife wound where someone had practically gutted him.

Was that the injury from Dariana when he'd told her Keris was dead?

He frowned at her. "Why are you so angry?"

"Because you're wounded!"

"Then shouldn't I be the one who's pissed off?"

She sat back to glare at him. "Yes. Yes, you should."

And still he appeared baffled by her anger on his behalf. "I'm not. So why are you?"

"I don't know." That was the truth. If it didn't bother him, it shouldn't bother her, and yet it did. "Were you injured anywhere else?"

He twisted at the waist to show her the knife wound on his lower back that had narrowly missed his lung and kidney. From the depth and precision, it must have come from the Partini. "I can't quite reach that one."

She pulled his medical pack closer so that she could clean it. "How did you walk so far, like this?"

He shrugged nonchalantly. "It wasn't safe to stop."

Oh. Okay. That made all the sense in the Nine Worlds. . . .

To a *minsid* lunatic.

Sighing, she knew better than to try and talk sense into someone insane. "You know, you really shouldn't say shit like that to me when I have a knife nearby."

His fierce features softened to that adorable expression that made her melt.

"What are you doing!"

She ground her teeth at Darice's outraged snarl as he stormed toward them. Her own fury snapping at his, she glared at him. "Your uncle is badly wounded and I'm trying to tend it."

Coming up behind Darice, Thia gasped at the sight of the jagged, awful cut Sumi was cleaning. "What do you need me to do?"

"Keep Darice back so that I don't kill him."

Darice refused to budge. Instead, he stalked forward to confront his uncle. "She shouldn't be touching you like that, Dancer. It's indecent."

His uncle glared at him as a fierce tic beat in his jaw.

"Can you treat a wound?" Thia asked him.

"No."

"Then shut up, Darice."

He pouted like a toddler. "You should tend him, Thia. It's your place, not *hers*."

Thia's expression called him a complete idiot. "All I know about field medicine is to call Uncle Syn or my dad or look it up . . . none of which I can do here."

"Then he should be left to bleed."

Stunned, Sumi gaped at the little snot. He would really rather leave his uncle here, bleeding, than allow an unrelated woman to tend him?

Unbelievable.

When Darice moved to sit in front of Hauk, he bared his fangs at his nephew. "Do you really think so little of me that you have to document and observe my treatment? You *are* your father's son." He sucked his breath in sharply as Sumi poured antiseptic over the deep wound. His breathing ragged, he glared at Darice. "Get out of my sight before I hurt you."

Darice looked as if Hauk had slapped him. Rising to his feet, he kicked dirt at Hauk in what she was beginning to suspect must be some kind of Andarion insult in and of itself. "You're not my father!"

Hauk let out a ferocious growl that had to have come from the deepest, angriest part of his soul. "You're damn right I'm not your father! If I were, I'd be so high right now I wouldn't feel shit, and I'd have beat you and made you walk naked here last night, after you whined like a little bitch whelp." His entire body trembling in rage and pain, he started to rise.

Darice shot off, back to camp.

Hauk collapsed to the ground with a groan.

Swallowing in fear for him, Thia stepped forward and knelt by his side. "Uncle Hauk?"

"I'm all right, baby," he assured her in a much softer tone as he reached to touch her hand. "I just need a minute . . . please."

In a loving gesture, Thia buried her hand in his braids and nodded before she left them and followed after Darice.

In that moment, Sumi felt for all of them. Thia, who was terrified at the thought of losing another person she loved. Darice, who wanted to protect his mother's honor, and Hauk, who had obviously been hazed by his eldest brother. It made her wonder what nightmares had turned an innocent boy into a warrior so fierce that he could walk for miles in the dead of night with wounds this severe and not even flinch.

Aching at where her thoughts went, she returned to prepping his wound for sutures. "Did Keris ever do that to you?"

He didn't even tense as she pierced his skin with the sterile needle. "I don't want to talk about it."

"Okay. Just hold still and I'll be done in a minute."

Hauk didn't respond as he stared at the mountain range in front of them where he'd once climbed with his brother's insults ringing in his ears. Memories surged with a brutal bite.

Because of the way Keris had been conceived, their father and paternal grandmother had always been lukewarm at best toward him. And their mother had pushed Keris hard to be the ultimate soldier, so that she could show them all that her bloodline was as good as the royal lineage she had denied to the Hauk progeny. It was why she'd named Keris after their Hauk ancestor who'd founded The League.

My sons will be legends, too. . . .

Her constant demands on his brother and incessant bitching had been such that they'd embedded a vicious cruel streak in Keris's heart. Something that had worsened anytime Keris drank or took drugs. Fain, alone, had been able to calm Keris's rages. But after Fain had been disowned, Keris's violence and cruelty had escalated. He'd acted as if he was afraid of meeting the same fate.

And he'd turned all that anger at their parents, whom he couldn't attack, to his youngest brother—as if it was somehow Hauk's fault Fain had chosen to be with a human over them.

But even before that, Keris had resented Hauk for the fact that Hauk had "shamed" them all when he'd been depledged after the pod accident that had left him scarred and humiliated by Jullien's lies.

With the exception of Fain, from that day forward, his entire family had seen him as deformed and lacking.

Useless.

Worthless.

Embarrassing.

So much so, that only Fain had visited him the entire time he'd been in the hospital's burn ward. Dutifully, Fain had watched over him as if he felt responsible for it and for Hauk.

To this day, even though Fain had never mentioned it, Hauk was sure Fain had paid for his surgeries and treatments. Had it been up to their parents, his mother would have left him to die.

Hauk didn't blame her for that. It was, after all, the Andarion way. If you weren't strong enough to survive, you were better off dead.

To this day, Keris's first words to him when he'd finally come home from the hospital were carved in the bitterest part of his heart. *"I hope that hybrid bastard kissed you before he fucked you in the ass. You should have died like a warrior in that crash. Not been dragged to safety like a human bitch by a worthless mutant dog."*

Fain had gone for Keris's throat. But for their mother's quick actions, Fain would have most likely killed Keris for it. But it hadn't erased the scar those words had seared into Hauk's heart.

Whenever Keris had been sober, he was the fun-loving, surly brother Hauk remembered growing up with. But the moment any drug touched his system . . . the stopgap was removed, and out came a monster even Dariana had feared.

Hauk had tried to use the same tactics Fain had to calm him. But that had only pissed him off more.

"You're not Fain! You'll never live to be the warrior he is. You're just a sorry excuse for a brother, and a disgrace to your name, and to every War Hauk who's come before you. It's not right that Fain was cast out while you're left to bear our badge in his stead. You're worthless, Dancer. I hate you!"

Now Sumi was staring at every bit of shame he carried. All of it. His scarred back was a road map of the *minsid* hell he'd survived. Of all the people who'd found him lacking and rejected him for it.

But he didn't see disgust in her eyes as she tended him. Only kindness and concern. Her gentle touch was so different from Dariana's.

Not that Dariana had ever touched him except to publicly humiliate him.

Closing his eyes, he felt Sumi running her fingers over the claw marks that covered his burn scars, and the ones left behind from his Endurance. While her touch soothed him in ways he wouldn't have thought possible, the memory of those wounds tore through him, and left him bleeding even more than the Partini's knife had.

A light frown wrinkled her brow. "What happened to cause all these?" she whispered, fingering the vicious claw scars.

Normally, he'd have never answered. But before he could stop himself, the truth come out. "Dariana."

"I don't understand."

Hauk sighed as she bandaged his sutures. "Every year, on the anniversary of Keris's death, I'm required to go to her and ask if she'll accept me as husband. And every year, she refuses unification with me."

Sumi felt sick as she realized that these scars were Dariana's annual answer to his marriage pledge. "She claws you?"

He gave a single curt nod.

"Why do you keep doing it, then?"

"I'm Andarion and I'm pledged to her," he said nonchalantly as if that explained everything.

Her heart broke over the cruelty his family forced on him. "I don't understand why she doesn't just release you."

He sighed heavily. "It doesn't matter. I won't have to tolerate it again."

"What do you mean?"

"After his Endurance, Darice will be old enough to bond marriage."

He said that as if she should understand its significance. "And?"

"Whenever a hero dies, there are three years of mourning for the spouse, to ensure the sanctity of both bloodlines and pay tribute to his life and service. After that, the widow has nine years to accept the pledge of her husband's brother, provided there are no children. When children are involved, the two are pledged until the youngest goes through Endurance. If they haven't unified by then, he's released from his pledge." He sighed in quiet resignation. "When I picked up Darice to do this, Dariana swore to me that on our return she would finally honor her pledge and accept me as her husband."

Sumi sat back as she digested that vicious little nugget.

Surely the bitch hadn't done what Thia had said. "Are you telling me that the whole reason Dariana had Darice was to keep you tied to her longer, without marriage?"

To continue denying and punishing him for as long as she legally could? Meanwhile, she got to keep the Warring Blood Clan of Hauk as her moniker, and maintain a place in their world that she couldn't have without Hauk's family?

Hauk shook his head. "She loved my brother. I'm sure she only had Darice to carry Keris's line forward and to honor him and his memory."

Then why not conceive him sooner? Why wait until the year she'd have been forced to either free Hauk or birth a child?

No. Sumi didn't believe it was a coincidence for a minute.

Thia was right. Dariana was a conniving Queen Bitch. But she bit her tongue. Let Hauk have his delusion about the honor Dariana obviously lacked.

Wishing she could save him from the whore's clutches, she leaned forward and brushed her lips against those marks of selfish cruelty.

He tensed. "What are you doing?"

She laid her cheek against the assassin's tattoo on his shoulder that had another vicious scar bisecting it from an old blast wound. "I'm giving you something I don't think you've ever had."

"And that is?"

The fact he had to ask said it all. "Tender affection."

Hauk swallowed as he felt a hot tear slide from her eye and onto his skin. She was right. No one had ever touched him like she did.

Inside or out.

For the first time since that pod had crashed, he felt visible to the world.

Desirable.

Sumi brushed her hand through his hair, raising even more chills over him. "I'm done, sweetie."

That single endearment meant more to him than it should have. And it made him wonder what kind of bastard could have ever struck a woman so decent. How could anyone harm the mother of his child? It made no sense to him. But one thing became crystal clear in his mind.

"I will get your daughter back for you, Sumi."

She frowned at him as if she couldn't believe what he was saying to her. "What?"

"I swear to you, on my blood honor. On the blood of my ancestors. I will see your daughter into your arms if it's the last step I take in this life."

"Hauk—"

He placed his hand over her lips to stop her protest. "Trust me. She deserves a mother like you. Not some callous League bitch who views her as a replacement drone."

Sumi swallowed hard at a promise she wished she could see fulfilled. He made it sound so easy. But she knew better. Even if he kept that oath, she'd be hunted by The League.

Forever.

She didn't have the political ties to force amnesty from them like Thia's father had done.

They would be on their own, and The League would track her and Kalea down and execute them both, with cold and extreme prejudice. And knowing her compadres as she did, neither death would be pretty.

And neither would be quick. They would use them both as examples of what happened to anyone dumb enough to cross The League. Still, it meant a lot to her that he would make such a promise.

If only she could allow him to keep it.

CHAPTER 11

"What's going on?"

Her hands trembling in fear, Sumi paused in her quest as she heard the concern in Thia's tone. "I'm looking for Lyris root."

Thia's green eyes turned suspicious. "Isn't that toxic?"

"It can be."

"Then why are you looking for it?"

Sumi sat back on her haunches to give the young woman an irritated smirk. "I'm not trying to kill someone with it, Thia. I'm trying to save your uncle's life."

Thia's face went white. "What happened?"

Sumi glanced past Thia's shoulder to make sure Darice couldn't overhear them. "The Partini's blade was coated in poison. When he stabbed Dancer last night, it—"

"What does it look like?" Thia gasped, cutting her off. She fell to her knees to help search.

Sumi pulled some from her pocket to show her the delicate pink flower that marked the weed's location. "I need at least twice this to even begin treatment."

"Okay." Thia took up position across from her. "He's not dying, is he?"

She started to lie and tell her Hauk would be fine, yet she couldn't bring herself to do it. The bitterest truth was always better than the sweetest lie. "He's stronger than anyone I've ever known. But I could beat him for not telling someone he was wounded last night. Then we could have treated him immediately and he wouldn't be in as much danger as he is now. He pushes himself too hard."

"It's what he does." Thia pulled a handful of it out of the ground and handed it to Sumi. "I've heard Uncle Syn threaten a million times to embed an off switch in him so that when he refuses to rest when he's hurt, Syn can force him. And my father threatens to hold him down while Syn implants it." She gave more to Sumi. "How are your wounds, by the way?"

"I've had worse."

Thia snorted. "You fit in nicely with this bunch. Sound just like them all."

Sumi didn't comment as she dug around for more root.

With Thia's added help, it didn't take long to gather enough and return to their small, mobile camp that Hauk had already packed up and slung over his back.

Aghast at him, Sumi gestured at the gear strapped to his wide shoulders. "What are you doing, sweetie?" she asked in a sarcastic falsetto.

He brushed at the sweat on his forehead. "We need to get going."

"Dancer," she chided. "You're not up to this."

"I'm fine."

Hands on hips, Sumi gave him an oh-really stare. "The sweat beading on your forehead calls you a big fat liar pants. And the pallor of your skin calls you out even more." She tugged at the strap of his haul bag. To her shock, he allowed her to remove it *and* his sword. That alone told her how bad he felt.

Shaking her head at him, she placed the back of her hand against his cheek. "You're burning with fever."

"It's still not safe here."

She pulled more gear from his shoulders. "You

know . . . really hard to protect us when you're dead. So unless you know some kind of mystic Andarion resurrection spell, I think you should sit down now before you fall over and we're stuck dragging you behind us. In spite of what you think, I am a trained soldier, fully capable of defending us from attackers."

He mumbled in Andarion under his breath. The words were beautiful, but she was quite certain their meaning wasn't.

"You keep insulting me like that, and I'm going to have Thia translate it."

Thia laughed. "He called you a bossy little mouse, which is actually not an insult in Andarion. Rather he respects the courage you're showing by telling him what to do when you're too small to physically force it."

Sumi frowned. "What's the Andarion word for mouse?"

"*Mia. Kahrya* is bossy. *Kahrya mia* . . . bossy little mouse." Thia handed her the medical pack. "On Andaria, they see mice as brave, aggressive creatures. Fearless . . . Of course, on Andaria, like everything else, the mice are ferocious, fanged and much scarier than they are on most other planets."

Sumi could just imagine. "Do they suck blood and eat small infants, too?"

Thia pressed her lips together before she answered. "Actually, they do."

"We really should be going," Hauk groused again.

While Sumi continued to deal with the surly, stubborn attack beast, Thia searched through the pack for water and the zip stove and cooking cup so that she could start boiling the root to soften it and release the juices they needed for an antidote.

Hauk was torn between the pain of his body that begged him to lie down and the need he had to keep his family safe. "Where's Darice?"

"He went to the bathroom," Thia answered.

"And Illyse?"

Thia's eyes widened as she set the root into the water, while it warmed. "I haven't seen her in a while. And now that I think about it, Darice should have been back before we were."

That cleared his head immediately. "Sumi?"

She already had her weapon drawn. Thia pulled in to stand on his six.

"Illyse!" he shouted.

Normally, the lorina would have come running immediately. But there was no sign of her.

"Stay together," he said under his breath. "Hands on, flank guard." Which meant they walked backwards with one hand on his body to let him know where they were. It was a tight formation normally used for narrow, low-light situations. But with his senses dulled, it kept him focused on only one thing.

Whatever was in front of them. And it allowed him to know that so long as they touched him, they were all right while they scanned for attackers coming at their rear.

The downside was that it lined them up for easy targeting.

Willing to chance it, he started forward. "Darice!"

No one answered. Hauk cursed under his breath. Why hadn't he noticed Darice's absence sooner?

Because he felt like utter shit. Even now, he feared he'd vomit and fall.

You've been through worse, Hauk... and under heavy fire.

Still, his heart was in his throat as visions of past missions and bodies played through his mind. He'd seen too many teens die over the years in battle. Darice was a major pain in the ass, but if something had happened to him because of his inattention, Hauk would never forgive himself.

And with every step he took, the past slashed into him with vicious claws.

Over and over, his mind tortured him with the sight of Keris laughing at him while they climbed, and Hauk hesitated to put his hands, cams, and feet into crevices because of the hidden charges Keris had set on the mountain to "up the ante" of their mission.

"Stop being a pussy, Dancer. What are you going to do in battle when you find an XD or someone lobs a grenade at you? Deal with it and move forward."

But having already been buried in twisted debris and surrounded by flames, Hauk had been skittish of repeating the experience, especially since his body had still been healing from the last round of skin grafts. He hated the sound of an explosion worse than anything, and it had seemed like Keris had lined the entire mountainside with explosives. Every time he touched something on the mountain, it exploded in his face.

With a disdainful sneer, Keris had allowed himself to hangdog while Hauk ascended to tie in. Keris had shoved at him. "Go on and take lead, belay bitch. I'm tired of waiting on your pansy ass to catch up."

Hauk had glared at him as Keris pulled out a small bottle and inhaled it. Last thing he wanted was their lives in the hands of a stoned belayer. "Give that to me."

Jerking it away from Hauk's reach, Keris had hit him so hard that he'd slipped and lost his hold on the mountain.

Hauk had slammed into the wall and set off another charge. Rocks had rained down all over him as he tried to find something to hold on to that wouldn't explode when he touched it. Worse than that, the percussion of that charge loosened Keris's anchors and belay.

One second Keris had been laughing at Hauk's fear and in the next, he was falling, too.

Cursing, Hauk had somehow managed to catch himself, while he attempted to pull Keris up with his other hand or swing him toward a ledge or crevice. Upside down, he had one anchor still holding, but it was slipping as more rock rained over them. Worse, he hadn't had time to properly tie in.

Keris also felt it. There was no chance the remaining anchors would hold their combined weights and the gear. Hauk's rope was slipping from its belay device. And once those gave way, there was nothing that would stop them from free-falling. He tightened his bleeding hands on the rope.

For a full minute, they'd silently stared at each other, knowing that at this altitude death was imminent. His face grim, Keris had pulled his knife from his sling.

Hauk had stared in horror as he realized what his brother intended. "What the hell are you doing, Kerry?"

"Take care of Dari for me. Tell her I'll always love her."

"No! Stop!"

But it was too late. That fast, that cruelly, Keris had sliced the rope and was gone.

Unable to move or breathe, Hauk had watched as his brother plummeted, and when Keris had finally slammed into the ground, he'd landed on the controls for the charges.

In that instant, it'd seemed as if half the mountain had detonated. The blast had sent him careening down. He'd tried to grab on to any and every thing. Petrified, he'd feared he'd never stop falling.

Until he'd slammed into a ledge so hard, it'd knocked the breath from his bruised body, and broken his arm, collarbone, nose, and ribs. For several minutes, he'd lain there, staring up at the perfectly blue sky, unable to believe what had happened. Unable to believe how much pain a single body could hold and not kill the one who felt it.

The rest of the day was a blur to his memory. He had

no idea how he'd managed to climb down to his brother's broken body.

All he remembered was sitting in the canyon, holding Keris against his chest and screaming out for help while Keris's blood dripped down his arm. It was a nightmare that had haunted him every time he closed his eyes.

One he couldn't escape.

A horror that burned out his blackened soul. And now he might have to bury Keris's son.

Please, Darice, don't be hurt. . . .

He couldn't take seeing someone who looked that much like Keris lying dead again. Nor would he be able to live with the guilt of it. It was hard enough to cope with the past he already had. He couldn't stand more being heaped on his conscience.

As they drew near the caves, Hauk paused and cocked his head to listen.

Thia tightened her grip on his shirt. "Hear something?" she whispered.

Suddenly, Illyse whined and hissed.

Angling his blaster, he rushed forward, into the nearest cave. And what he found there enraged him to a level he wouldn't have thought Andarionly possible.

In that one heartbeat, he could taste the blood he wanted to spill. Could feel its sticky texture on his hands as he choked the life out of the asshole in front of him.

Holstering the blaster, he put his arm out to catch his weight against the rock wall.

"Darice! You selfish asshole!" Thia snarled as she moved forward to confront the spoiled, petulant brat. "What are you doing?"

He jerked his chin toward Hauk. "I'm not going anywhere with him until he apologizes for what he said! He had no right to impugn my father's honor! Unlike him, my father was a hero!"

Sumi put away her blaster before she yielded to the desire to lay open Darice's skull with it. Had she not been so worried about Hauk, Darice's life would have been in even more danger.

As it was . . .

Hauk looked like he was about to collapse and die.

She rushed to Hauk to check his fever. He was shaking to the point his teeth chattered. She forced him to sit with his back against the cave wall. The adrenaline from this had caused the toxin to spread even quicker through his system and infect more organs.

"Thia? I need you to run back and grab the root. Fast as you can!"

She went without hesitation.

Total fear consumed her at the sudden pallor of Hauk's skin. She cupped his face in her hands. "Dancer? Stay with me."

He blinked so slowly that she wasn't sure if he heard her or not.

"What's wrong with him?"

For one, he has you for a nephew. She barely managed to bite those words back. "He's been poisoned."

"What? When?"

"Last night. The Partini was using a knife coated with a very slow-acting poison."

Darice's lips quivered as he finally realized how sick Hauk was.

Hauk's eyes rolled back in his head.

"Dancer?" Darice grabbed his shirt and shook him.

Hauk hissed in pain. "I'm coming, Kerry. I just need a second."

Darice backhanded him. "Get up!"

Sumi shoved at him and discovered the truth of what Thia had said. Andarion males were heavy bastards.

Darice exposed his fangs at her.

She pulled her blaster out and flipped it to stun with

her thumb. "Hit him again and so help me, Darice, I will make your mother weep at what I do to you."

"He's not your family!"

"Funny, between the two of us, I'm the only one acting like he is. Now get away before you do any more damage to him."

Darice curled his lip. "What's that supposed to mean?"

"It means had I been able to get the antidote into him twenty minutes ago, instead of searching for a spoiled, pouting brat, he'd have had a better chance of survival than what he has now. Thanks, by the way."

Darice didn't say anything as he took up post on the other side of Hauk.

Ignoring him, Sumi helped Hauk to lie down as they waited for Thia to return. Minutes dragged by as she began preparing the berries she'd need to mix with the root. Luckily, they had still been in her pocket.

Please, let this cure work for Andarions, too. For that matter, she hoped she'd guessed the right poison the Partini had used. Never in her life had she tasted panic like this. She barely knew him, but she couldn't stand the thought of losing him.

Not like this. Not over something so stupid and wrong.

Hauk hissed as if he was being tortured. He shook all over.

Sumi cupped his face in her hands. "Dancer? Can you hear me?"

"Munatara a la frah."

Darice sucked his breath in sharply.

"What does that mean?"

Thia handed her the small pot of burned root as she rejoined them. "He just called you the most precious lady of his life."

"He has dishonored my mother!"

Thia turned on him with a snarl. "When, Darice? Tell me? When has he been alone with Sumi where one of the two of them wasn't wounded, and us within earshot? Please strain that limited brain capacity you have and think about it."

"Why would he call her that, then, huh?"

"I don't know," Thia snarled. "Maybe because she's been nice to him, which is more than your mother has ever been. Or, brace yourself for this concept. Perhaps the poison has made him so delusional, he doesn't know who he's talking to or what he's saying. Now, if you don't mind, I'd rather try to save his life than deal with the fact you know your mother's a bitch who has treated him like shit, and your fear he'll finally come to his senses and leave you without your father's lineage." She knelt down by Sumi's side. "I salvaged what I could. But it burned while we hunted the knuckle-dragging degenerate."

Sumi added the berries and mixed them together with the root as best she could. "It won't taste good, but hopefully he won't notice."

Once the ingredients were blended into a thick syrup, she had Thia hold his head up to drink it.

Unfortunately, it was too thick to pour.

Thia panicked. "What do we do now?"

Sumi considered her options. With no better thought, and afraid of diluting it with water, she dipped her fingers into it and placed them in his mouth.

Thia held his head as he tried to turn away from the burnt taste. But after a few minutes, he finally licked the antidote from Sumi's fingers.

Bit by bit, Sumi fed it to him and prayed it would still work like this. That they hadn't boiled all the necessary nutrients out of the root while searching.

As soon as it was all dispensed, she wiped her hand off on an antiseptic cloth, then used it to clean his wounds again.

Darice continued to stare a hole through her.

Thia hissed at him over her shoulder. "What is your problem now, Darice?"

"My mother has long suspected that he hasn't upheld his pledge to her. It's why she has yet to accept him."

Thia gave him a mocking stare. "Oh, okay, *that's* the reason, huh?"

"What's that supposed to mean?"

"If your mother really believes that, why not break pledge with him?"

"She doesn't want to see him lose his lineage. She says it would dishonor my father if she allowed that to happen."

"Ah. Glad to know that she cares so much." Thia's sarcasm was even thicker than the paste they'd made.

"What?" Darice asked defensively.

Thia stalked toward where he sat. "So it's not a slap in your father's or uncle's face every time she refuses to honor the pledge, or allow him rights to you?"

He scoffed at her words. "She's never done that. Dancer has full rights to me, he just doesn't want them."

"Bullshit! I've been there, Darice, and seen the number of times your mother has told him he could have time with you, and then he comes back alone with some ridiculous, fabricated reason why she couldn't let you go at the last minute. Honestly, I was stunned she allowed you to come with him for Endurance. But for the fact it would relegate you to perpetual infant status, I'm sure she would have backed out of this, too."

He shook his head in blatant denial. "She's told me how often she's begged him to spend time with me and he refuses. How many times I've invited him, myself, to games and he has never come to one! Not once. He wants nothing to do with me."

"Can't imagine why he'd want to avoid *you*," Thia mumbled, then she let out a rude laugh. "Face the truth, Dare, your mother's a liar. She's manipulative and a bully."

He shot to his feet. "Take that back!"

"I won't take back the truth. Had your mother not fed illegal drugs to your father, *for years,* he wouldn't have died when he did."

Clenching his fists, he glared at her. "What lie is this?"

"No lie. Honest truth. Contrary to your mother's bull-shit, your father's body *was* recovered. Uncle Hauk didn't leave him as scavenger meat as your mother claims. With a dozen broken bones, he dragged Keris's body back, and kept watch over it until they were picked up."

Darice scoffed bitterly. "You don't know that. You weren't there."

Still, Thia gave him no quarter. "Neither were you! And for your information, I do know. Fain has the autopsy, and the order, signed by your mother, to burn Keris's body so that no one would ever discover the truth of what she'd done. Fain was there, alone, when Keris was cremated. She didn't even have the decency to attend his last rites. Then your mother buried all the evidence that showed Keris had enough drugs in his body at the time of death that he would have most likely overdosed had he not fallen first."

"If *any* of that's true, why does she blame Dancer for it?"

"Because he's the only one who was there when Keris died. He alone knows how high Keris was and he knows she's the real culprit."

Darice stood toe-to-toe with Thia. "Then why hasn't he told anyone? Huh?"

She snorted. "Why do you think? He refuses to disparage his brother. By the time he was out of the hospital, your mother had already concocted the lie that Uncle Hauk had saved himself by cutting the rope, and left your father to die, and that no one had found the body. The only person he tried to tell the truth to was his mother, because he didn't want her to hate him for something he didn't do."

"Yaya knows?"

"She knows. It's why she slashed him. It wasn't done as a warning. She attacked Uncle Hauk because she couldn't attack Keris. She was mortified by what your father had done, and she told Uncle Hauk that he better never breathe a word of it to anyone!"

As they continued fighting, Sumi let out a loud whistle. "Please, for the love of the gods, stop it! Both of you! Let him rest in peace without you two going at it like jacked-up snipies. If you need something to occupy yourselves with, go get our supplies and bring them here without killing each other."

Thia untied Illyse and left.

Darice paused by Sumi's side to stare down at his uncle. "Do you believe Thia?"

Why was he asking *her*?

"Does it matter what I think, Darice? I don't know your mother, at all. I barely know your uncle. However, he seems to be extremely kind and devoted. I can't imagine he would dishonor your mother, and I know he hasn't done so with me."

That seemed to calm him. Nodding, he ran after Thia.

Alone with Hauk, Sumi brushed her hand along the whiskers on his cheek. In the chaos of this morning, he hadn't shaved. The added growth made him look wild and untamed.

Even more masculine.

Smiling at the proud image he made even while he slept, she wound one of his thin black braids around her finger to toy with it. Unlike the rest of him, his hair and lips were so incredibly soft. Warmth spread through her at the memory of his tongue licking her fingers while she'd fed him the antidote. The sensation of his fangs brushing against her skin as he took care not to bite her, even though he was barely alert.

You are *an incredibly sexy beast, Dancer Hauk.* And he deserved a lot better than a female who couldn't love and appreciate him.

"Deserving's got nothing to do with anything." Her father's angry voice echoed in her head. *"You think I deserved a whore who ran off in the middle of the night, and left me with two daughters to raise? Show me the Life Manual where it says things are fair and we all get what we deserve!"*

As a girl, she'd thought him a fool for that reasoning. Had virulently disagreed with him.

Too bad the old bastard had been more right than he was wrong. Her heart breaking, she stroked Dancer's goatee with her thumb.

Sighing in his sleep, Dancer nuzzled his head against her hand. The unexpected sweetness touched her. Removing her poncho, she made a pillow for him.

He mumbled something in Andarion.

"Shh," she whispered, trying to soothe him.

"Munatara."

She knew he couldn't be referring to her as such, but she allowed herself to pretend for a moment that she was the one he called out for in his stupor. What would it be like to be loved that way? To have someone, just once, she could turn to for comfort?

Someone who would call her the lady of his life, and not a whore or a bitch?

It was all she'd ever wanted. Someone who could actually love her and not hurt or insult her. An impossible dream that was now lost to her forever. Even if it wasn't, Dancer would be the last person she could ever have a relationship with. Forgetting the fact that they were two different species, their siblings had married and parted as bitter enemies. And he would absolutely kill her if he ever learned that fact.

I should be terrified of you.

He could snap her in half or gut her without even raising his blood pressure.

Vicious memories of Avin surged. She still couldn't believe how easily she'd found herself in such an abusive relationship, especially after the year she'd spent with Darnell, and his insults when she'd been in college. She'd always prided herself on being independent and strong. Yet both men had lured her in with sweet words and acts of kindness. Then something would hit them wrong and they'd turn violent without warning. They'd always apologize later and swear it would never happen again.

Like a fool, she'd believed every lie. In that, she wasn't any different than Darice, who wanted to believe his mother, in spite of the truth that was right in front of his face. But it was easy to believe in lies when all you wanted was to be loved and accepted for who and what you were.

Sometimes it was good enough just to be loved for who they thought you were.

But that wasn't real and she knew it.

"Sumi?"

She met Dancer's suddenly lucid gaze. "I'm right here."

He laid his hand over hers and moved it from his cheek to his lips so that he could place a tender kiss in her palm. Sighing, he slid his head into her lap and held her against him with one powerful arm.

"Are you awake, Dancer?"

His answer was a mumbled something she couldn't make out.

"I guess not." Sumi brushed the braids back from his face as she hummed to him one of the lullabies Omira used to sing to her. She lost herself to this one moment of pretend domesticity. The cave and everything else fell away as she studied Dancer's chiseled features, and wondered what it would be like to make love to someone like him. Someone who still had a soul and a heart.

In the serene quiet of this moment, she allowed her fantasies to run wild as she imagined living with him and Kalea in a small apartment on some planet where no one would pay them any attention, and they could go about their boring lives in total happiness.

You're such an idiot.

She was indeed. It had always been her greatest flaw. As Omira had so often mocked, she was a dreamer. Through and through.

But wanting it to be real, she leaned forward and rubbed her nose to his. Then guilt struck her hard as she remembered her mission and why she was here.

How can I ruin him?

How could she not?

Conflicted and angry at fate for dangling this in front of her when it knew she could never have such a life, she didn't move until she heard the kids returning. Only then did she gently place Dancer's head on her poncho, and put a few feet between them.

Thia came forward with a blanket while Sumi went to set up a few things for the night. As Dancer had pointed out, it wasn't safe here, but they had no choice. They had to make do. At least until morning.

And if more men came for him, she'd make them wish they were facing Dancer and not her.

As they unpacked for camp, she learned why Hauk didn't play the violin around anyone.

While digging through Hauk's bag, Darice found the case, opened it, and curled his lip in supreme disgust. "What kind of human thing is this?"

Thia's eyes narrowed angrily as she snatched the case from his grasp and closed it. "It's mine. Leave it alone." But when Thia met her gaze, she saw the truth. Thia knew it was Hauk's and was trying to save her uncle any more of Darice's contempt.

The girl placed it in her own pack while Darice continued to mumble in Andarion. "Shut up, Darice," Thia said irritably. "I'm as fluent in Andarion as you are."

That set them off into arguing with words that were meaningless to Sumi. But given the nuclear escalation of their gestures and pitch, she knew she needed to break them apart or there'd be blood on the cave walls soon.

"Thia? Can you gather more root and berries for me? We should make additional antidote for your uncle."

Glaring at Darice, she nodded. "Sure, Sumi. I'll be back in a few minutes." She took Illyse with her.

Sumi paused to watch Darice return to digging through Hauk's things. He reminded her of a little kid with a treasure chest. It was actually adorable to watch him try on Hauk's gloves and see just how much more he needed to grow to be the same size.

For the record, it was a lot. Hauk *was* huge.

"I'm going to start a fire, outside. Okay?"

Darice responded with a nod.

"Let me know if your uncle wakes up and needs something."

That got her a heated, furious glare.

Holding her hands up in surrender, she left them alone, even though a part of her wondered if it was the wisest thing to do. Darice held a lot of hatred and resentment toward his uncle.

Sumi sighed. Family was such a pain in the ass. A lifetime of hurt feelings and misunderstandings. Of two very different accounts of the same event that could result in all-out war between siblings and parents, even years later.

Still, it was something she craved with every part of herself. She'd always been envious of her friends who had families they could visit. Siblings and parents they got along with. She just couldn't imagine such a thing.

Trying not to think about it, she started the fire, and when Thia returned, she showed the girl how to make the antitoxin.

As soon as it was finished, she returned to the cave to find the last thing she would have ever thought possible.

Dancer was awake. And nestled up against his chest, in his arms like a little puppy, was Darice. With his chin resting on top of his nephew's head, Dancer was lacing one of his leather bracers onto the boy's arm.

She froze as their low voices reached her.

"So what was my da like as a brother?"

"He was fine, Darice."

"Just fine? Matarra says that he was the most honorable of all. That he always took care of his brothers and watched over you."

Dancer snorted. "She wasn't the one getting her head dunked into toilets by him."

Darice turned to look up at Dancer. "What? Why would he do that?"

Dancer sighed heavily as he checked the laces to make sure they weren't too tight on Darice's arm. "Your father had a temper, Dare. And I seemed to ignite it often. Sometimes by doing nothing more than breathing in the same room with him."

"Really?"

"Really. Fain has always said that I'm a particularly vexing and talented . . . hemorrhoid."

Sumi bit back a laugh at his editing of what she was sure his brother actually called him.

"Mostly," he continued, "because I had two older brothers who took turns bossing me every minute of every day. And because I don't like being told what to do, I always had an issue with them thinking they were my parents." Dancer touched the tip of Darice's nose. "And like you, I'm quite vocal when I don't like something."

"Is that why you never want to spend time with me?

Why you never come to any of my games when I ask you to?"

Sumi's throat tightened at the pain in Darice's voice as he asked that question.

His jaw slack, Dancer lifted his head to stare down at his nephew. "I *never* miss your games, Dare."

Curling his lip, Darice started to rise, but Dancer held him in place. "You're a liar! Let go of me!"

With a fierce grimace, Dancer refused. He forced Darice back and held him with one arm while he turned on the small PD on his wrist. He swiped the screen with his finger. "See for yourself. I was even there at your last match when you scored the winning goal in overtime."

Darice went perfectly still as he saw what must be a photo of him during the game. His lips trembling, he used his index finger to skim through the pictures on Dancer's module. "I don't understand. If you were there, why have you never come to see me after the games?"

"Because I'm not your father and I've never been in the Andarion military. Your mother said it would shame you for your friends and their fathers to see me there. So I always go when you play and then leave afterward before any of them see me."

Sumi choked at the pain in his voice.

His brow furrowed, Darice continued to flick through the photos. "You were at my graduation?"

"I've always been there for you, Dare. And I always will be. Any time you need me, all you have to do is call."

Tears glistened in Darice's eyes as he tried to digest what Dancer showed and told him, against the lies his mother must have filled him with. "Why don't you ever take me for weekends?"

"Whenever I go to pick you up, you're always busy with school, games, practice, and your friends. Your mother says that it's better for your growth that you stay with her, especially given the shame and embarrassment

I would bring to you should any of them see me with you. It's why I've only been allowed to train you for Endurance climbing every few months or so."

Darice swallowed hard as he clutched at his uncle's arm that held the module that catalogued how much Dancer loved him. "You don't shame or embarrass me, Dancer."

"That's not what you've said in the past. I thought I was doing what you wanted . . . what was best for you, by leaving you with your mother and staying in the background."

His gaze troubled and fretting, Darice fell silent as he turned off the module then laid his head on Dancer's biceps.

Sumi moved forward, expecting Darice to say something snotty to her. Or jump up indignantly from Dancer's arms. Instead, he merely watched her approach them from where he lay cradled.

"How are you feeling?"

Dancer licked his lips. "Wrung out. You?"

"I'm fine." She knelt beside them and felt his forehead with the back of her hand. "Your fever's not as bad." Then she handed him the small cup. "It's more of the antidote."

He wrinkled his nose at the smell, but said nothing before he dutifully drank it. "Thank you."

"You're very welcome." She took the cup back then smiled at Darice. "I'm making more salad for your dinner."

Squeezing his eyes shut, he twisted his face into an expression of supreme disgust. "I don't like eating plants."

She widened her smile. "And that's why I made it for you."

Dancer laughed. "Now you know what it's like to have a sibling, Dare. They all treat you that way. The minute they know you don't like something, they're honor bound to torture you with it. For eternity."

"Then I'm glad I'm currently an only child." He closed his eyes again and sighed contentedly.

Dancer caught her hand before she moved away. "What can I do for you?"

Sumi hesitated, wondering if he even realized how he phrased things. He never thought of himself first. Rather, he put everyone's needs above his own. "Rest. Get better for me."

"I feel useless lying here. I should be—"

"You should be resting," she repeated firmly. Then she dropped her gaze to Darice. "Plus, I think he needs some uninterrupted guy time."

Only then did Dancer nod. "If you need anything, let me know."

"Fair enough." Sumi brushed a stray piece of hair back from Darice's cheek before she stood and left them alone.

As she reached the opening, she heard Darice's faint voice. "Are all humans like her, Dancer?"

"How do you mean?"

"Kind and gentle. Caring."

"Sadly, no. Especially not to Andarions. She's very different from most of her kind."

"Ah . . . Is that why you like her?"

"No. It's why I treasure her. Now, shush and give me peace from your questions for a while."

Those words made her heart swell with an inexplicable joy. Dancer treasured her. Was it even possible?

"Are you okay?"

She looked up at Thia's question as she neared the fire. "Fine. Why?"

Thia shrugged. "You have a strange, weepy look on your face."

She set the cup down and checked their dinner. "Do I?"

"Yeah, you kind of look like I do whenever I get a new boyfriend."

Sumi arched her brow at that offhand comment. "How many boyfriends have you had?"

"A ton. I cycle through them faster than socks."

"Really?"

Thia nodded as she fed Illyse. "Not entirely my fault. First, they get pissy that I don't sleep with them within fifteen minutes of meeting them. Then when they find out why, i.e., my father, the psycho-killer let's-gut-people-for-fun, really is an assassin and bigger than most shuttles, and has not one, but *five* major armies at his command, they hit the door screaming."

"I can see where that might be unnerving."

Thia checked the cooking stew. "Did your father ever have issues with your choice of boyfriends?"

"Not really. From the time I turned fifteen, my father assumed I was a slut, so he didn't care who I dated. Best I ever got out of him was that he better not find us naked in his bed."

"I'm sorry, Sumi."

"Nothing to be sorry about. It is what it is."

To her complete shock, Thia hugged her. "I think you're great."

"I think you're great, too." Sumi gave the girl a strong squeeze before she released her and finished making their dinner.

That night, she took sentry duty, and it gave her a whole new appreciation for Dancer's stamina.

Yawning, she stretched then jogged in place, trying to stay alert.

"You look like an adorable little girl when you do that."

She jerked around with a gasp to find Dancer standing behind her. "Dear gods, man, make a sound when you move!"

"Not a man," he reminded her simply.

She took a deep breath to steady her nerves. "Sorry. I

didn't mean to insult you. I just don't understand how someone so huge is so silent. It's not natural."

He gave her a charming, lopsided grin. "Grow up with two parents who have Andarion hearing and nasty tempers, and you'll learn to be silent, too."

"I guess so," she said with a laugh. "Get caught much?"

"Never. But I was often sacrificed."

"Meaning?"

"Whenever *they* got caught, my brothers threw me to the parental units and ran for cover, leaving me behind to face them. Alone. They were both selfish bastards that way."

She cringed at what had to be less-than-pleasant memories for him. "Sorry."

Dancer shrugged nonchalantly. "Curse of being the youngest. I never could get away in time. But it gave me a lot of good survival skills. And a really tough ass. For *that,* I'm eternally grateful." He took the rifle from her shoulder. "You should go rest."

"I'm not the one who was poisoned," she reminded him.

"That wasn't poisoned. Trust me. I've eaten Jayne's cooking. It's far deadlier."

He was so incredibly tempting. More so in that he never really insulted anyone. Not even Dariana. Rather, he had a teasing, fun-loving way of looking at others' shortcomings and actions.

"I still don't feel right leaving you to guard us after what you've been through, and what you've already done for us."

"Then sit with me and keep me company." He sank down in front of the small outcropping of rocks so that he could lean against them.

The sight of him there, like that . . . was more than a mere woman could turn away from. She sat down

beside him and made sure to keep a little distance between them.

Dancer gave her a chiding stare. "I don't bite, Sumi."

"I know." She was more afraid *she* might start nibbling
on some of that lush tawny skin. Especially his jaw. It
was the sexiest thing she'd ever seen on any male.

Against her better judgment, she leaned into his arms
and let him hold her like he'd done Darice earlier. He
rested his chin on the top of her head as his warmth enveloped her. As promised, he kept his hands to himself
while they sat there, listening to the quiet desert breeze.

Hauk smiled as he felt Sumi fall asleep in a matter of
heartbeats. Only then did he adjust her weight slightly so
that she wasn't pressing so much on the part of him that
was most desperate for her. His senses light, he brushed
his face against the softest hair he'd ever felt and inhaled
her unique scent.

She was the sweetest heaven.

And the most torturous hell.

As he held her, he was rock hard and aching for a taste
of her soft, voluptuous body. His back and side throbbed,
but he welcomed the distraction from the heavy need in
his groin that he could do nothing about.

Closing his eyes, he let her scent wash over him as
stupid fantasies tormented him with things he knew he
couldn't have.

Fantasies of her touching him that made no sense. He
was an Andarion, fully pledged. She was a human League
assassin. Both of them were forbidden to have relations
with anyone. Both were hunted by enemies and had a
death sentence hanging over them.

Yet as he felt her breath on his skin, none of that mattered. All he wanted was to offer himself to her.

To have her claim him as her mate before everyone.
Just once he wanted to know what it was like to be inside

a female's body, and have her hold him while they made love.

Every year since he'd turned nineteen, he'd gone to Dariana in his ancestral temple, in full faith and before his family and hers, for unification. And every year, she'd brutally denied him in front of them all. As if he was defective or unworthy of her.

In the beginning, he'd been hopeful that she'd find some way to forgive him for what had happened to Keris. That in time, she might accept his troth. But that hope had died somewhere in his midtwenties when it became crystal clear that she had no intention of ever seeing his pledge met. Rather, she took a perverse pleasure whenever she opened up his back before their families, and abandoned him to their ridicule and scorn.

When he'd turned thirty, he'd gone to his mother on the eve of another humiliation, and had begged her to negotiate a rare severance with Dariana.

She'd answered his request with the back of her hand. "How dare you shame me with such! You're a War Hauk. You will do your duty and you will stand before her like the proud Andarion warrior you're supposed to be, not some sniveling cockless coward! Besides, there is no one else who will have you. Look in a mirror. You're deformed and revolting. You should be grateful that she hasn't already broken pledge with you. At least this way, we can pretend you have some value and desirability."

And as Dariana had done every year before that, when the priest had asked if she found him acceptable for her lineage, she'd sliced open his back and walked out the door. It was the most brutal way for an Andarion female to deny her lineage to a male.

Worse, it'd become a sick sort of ritual for him. One that made him more furious every time he was forced to endure it.

Every year Dariana denied him, he saw more of his mother's love for him die. She could barely stand to look at him now. She blamed him fully for the shame he brought to their family.

In his heart, he knew Sumi would never do that to him. She would be honorable enough to slit his throat and end his hell. A death sentence for them both. Not force him to undergo public humiliation, year after year.

He took her tiny hand into his and smiled. Of course, she'd need a knife to hurt him. Her delicate hands could never rip open his back, or his throat.

And before he could stop himself, he placed her hand on his cheek and nuzzled it. He didn't understand how she'd come to mean so much to him so quickly. He wasn't a trusting soul. Nor did he make friends easily. He expected the worst from others, and seldom was he disappointed.

Yet this tiny assassin had found a place in his heart where very few dwelled. And instead of cutting her out of it, he was allowing her to burrow in even deeper.

What the hell is wrong with me?

Dariana was right. He *was* defective. He had to be to even think the thoughts that were in his head.

No good could ever come of a relationship with her. Andarions and humans didn't mix. They never had.

And sadly, no matter how much he might want otherwise, they never would. Humans weren't welcome in his world and Andarions were voraciously hated everywhere they went outside of their own territories.

When this was over, he'd have to leave Sumi and do his due diligence. Tie his blood to a bitch who hated him. If he was half the Andarion Fain was, he'd say fuck it and be done with all of them.

But he was the last of his mother's sons. If he walked away from his lineage, it would destroy her. She would be honor bound to kill herself. It was acceptable for one son to leave their lineage.

Not two.

While his mother no longer cared much for him, she cared about her lineage and honor. He couldn't buy his happiness for such a cost. The one thing he'd learned in his life was that no one could build a better future over the corpses of others. Better he should suffer for eternity than save himself at the expense of his family.

It was the Andarion way.

And he was an Andarion War Hauk.

It was his duty to serve his family and people. To honor them no matter the personal sacrifice.

But in the back of his mind was an image of Sumi in his family paint. And a burning in his gut to have a female, just once, accept him as mate-worthy and not look at him as if he was a total piece of shit.

CHAPTER 12

Sumi came awake slowly to a deep warmth. When she reached to rub her eyes, her hand brushed against rock-hard skin. Startled, she jumped and slammed her head straight into Dancer's face.

He muffled a curse as he moved his jaw to make sure it still worked. He frowned at her. "Morning, *mia*."

Horrified at what she'd done, she cupped his jaw in her hand. "Oh, Dancer, I'm so sorry. I forgot where I was."

"It's fine. You're not the first one to slap me awake. Doubt you'll be the last."

That didn't make her feel a bit better. Before she could stop herself, she pushed up in his arms to place a chaste kiss on his lips then one on his cheek where she'd inadvertently struck him. "Better?"

He brushed the back of his finger over her face. "For that, *mu tara*, you can hold my head in a grinder."

His offer amused her. "By Andarion standards, is that better or worse than a toilet?"

He arched a surprised brow. "You heard that yesterday?"

She nodded. "So how many times did your brother dunk your head, anyway?"

"Enough that Fain swears the oxygen dep gave me permanent brain damage."

Laughing, she rolled her eyes at him. "You're terrible."

"Fain's words, not mine." He took a deep breath as his eyes teased her playfully. "I wish I could keep you here against me, but the kids are waking."

Which meant Darice would stroke if he caught them like this. She would say screw it, but didn't want Dancer in trouble with Dariana.

Reluctantly, she withdrew from him and stood up just a few heartbeats before Darice came bounding out of the cave as if the little booger knew she was standing too close to his uncle.

I swear that little bastard has radar.

He gave them a suspicious look, but for once kept his mouth shut. "Is there any of that stew left from last night? It was good."

Sumi tsked at him. "The surprise in your voice as you say that almost offends me."

Darice grinned at her. "Yeah, but—"

"I'll have it heated in a few minutes."

Yelping in happy delight, he ran off toward the stream to wash and dress.

"Wow," Sumi breathed at his uncharacteristic enthusiasm. "I had no idea it was that easy to reprogram his attitude. I should have made stew my first night."

Dancer laughed. "They say the quickest way to a man's heart is through his stomach. For Andarions, it's even more true."

"And here The League taught me that the quickest way to a man's heart was through the chest cavity. Shows what they know, huh?"

With the sexiest smile she'd ever seen, Dancer scraped his fangs against his bottom lip. "I love it when you talk assassin to me."

Laughing, she wrinkled her nose at him. "You're so sick. Why am I so attracted to you?"

They both sobered as those words left her lips. For several heartbeats neither of them moved as the words hung heavy between them. And lit a fire in his eyes that made her heart quicken.

Finally, Sumi cleared her throat. "I know you're pledged, Dancer. I didn't mean to trespass."

He looked away, but not before she saw the regret in his eyes. The sad torment. "I should check on Darice. He has all the hygiene of a wild *torna*."

Sumi wanted to kick herself as she watched him walk away. *Why did I say that? What is wrong with me?*

She knew better. But something about Dancer sucked all her common sense out and made her forget everything, except the beauty that was a fierce Andarion male and her desire to make him laugh and smile.

Leaning her head back, she glared up at the sky. *I swear I'm going to keep my hands away from him.*

Her thoughts, too.

She had no choice. Even if she wasn't here to gather evidence against him, she knew that there was no chance in hell for a future with him.

His love for Fain would never allow it. It would kill his brother to see them together, knowing they had divorced because Omira refused to have Fain's children. That would be the cruelest blow of all.

No, come hell or high water, she would stop this before it went any further.

Sumi had almost convinced herself of that when Darice returned to eat the stew she'd warmed for breakfast. Thia had just awakened and was still yawning as she sat next to the fire.

As Sumi went to get some food for herself, she heard the dreaded symphony of a war zone. Both of the kids bolted to their feet beside her. Her heart hammering, she motioned for Thia to cover her, and return to the cave for protection while she headed for the battle.

And a battle it was. Near the stream where he'd gone to bathe, Dancer was pinned down near a short outcropping of rocks by three men. She could tell by the dimness of the blasts that Dancer was almost out of ammunition. It was what the assassins were waiting for.

As soon as he was empty, they'd end him.

What they didn't know was that Dancer had a secret weapon. And she was about to unleash hell on them for daring this. Moving silently and with every bit of League training she'd mastered, Sumi closed the distance between her and Dancer's attackers.

She caught the first one completely unaware. Shooting him in the back, she rolled and dropped a bead on the second one. He dodged her blast and returned fire. Anger pounded through her that she'd missed what should have been an easy mark.

Grinding her teeth, she threw a fully charged blaster to Dancer and then laid down cover fire for him so that he could reach it. As soon as he had the weapon, he took the one on her left and she finished off the third.

Crouching low, he closed the distance between them. "Thank you."

"Any time, big guy." She clapped him on the arm as she skimmed the bodies around them. "Is this all of our party crashers?"

"Think so." Still wary, he went to search the body closest to him. "They're a little more high-tech than our last batch of friends. These came with short-distance radios."

Given the magnetic field here that played havoc with electronics, they'd have to have some serious credit invested in those radios for them to work. "How many?"

"Dozen. I was trying to get them farther away from your position when they cornered me. Told you this place sucks for defense."

"Sorry." Sumi holstered her weapon. "You're a little hard to move when you're unconscious."

Instead of being offended, he actually grinned. "So I've been told. Least you didn't wrench my arm out of its socket trying."

Her gut clenched at the thought of how much that would have to hurt. "Happen to you often?"

"More times than Nyk wants to admit."

"Nyk?"

"Thia's father."

It was the first time he'd used Nykyrian's name with her, and he was way too cautious, even wounded, to let it slip out. Dancer was learning to trust her.

Sumi didn't know why, but that sent a rush of warmth through her. When he turned, she saw the blood on the back of his shirt. Worried about him, she went over and lifted the hem to investigate the blood's source.

He tugged it down, out of her hands. "What are you doing?" he asked in an agitated tone.

She gave him a droll stare. "Oh, I don't know . . . I was considering molesting you on top of these grotesque dead bodies. Ripping your clothes off and running my hands all over that long, hard body until you beg for mercy. What do you say, babe? Want to add something exotic to your diet?"

He gaped so widely, it exposed his fangs.

Laughing, Sumi tsked at him. "Oh my God. So that's what stark terror looks like on that gorgeous face. Who knew?" She winked at him. "Relax, sweetie. I was joking. Just wanted to check your wounds. See if you pulled the stitches out."

"Oh." He finally relaxed as he flipped her rifle up to hold it over his shoulder. "Only a few."

A few?

"Dancer!"

"What?" he asked in an equally irritated tone. "If you'd cauterized it, I wouldn't have done it."

Oh yeah, this was so *her* fault. "I was trying to save you the pain of a burn wound."

"Pain is pain. Does it really matter if it's from a burn or a stitch?"

He had a point, but she didn't want to admit it. "How are you feeling?"

"Hungry."

She arched a brow at the unexpected answer. "Killing humans makes you hungry?"

"Killing, breathing, bathing, basically everything makes me hungry. Syn swears I'm still in my growing phase."

Sumi snorted. One day, she really wanted to meet this Syn. "It's good to have Your Snarky Highness back. I've missed you."

When she started away, he gently caught her arm and held her by his side. Unsure of what he needed, she stared up into those haunting, eerie eyes. He looked as if he wanted to say something to her. Instead, he bit his lip then placed his cheek against hers in the tenderest of gestures.

Hauk closed his eyes and savored the warmth of her skin on his and the scent of her hair as he fought the craving inside to kiss her. It was absolutely searing.

More than that, he wanted to bury himself deep inside her body. To have her do exactly what she'd teased. To ride him until he begged her for mercy.

Stand down, soldier. You belong to another.

Yeah, but Dariana didn't want him. Not for anything other than target practice.

Grinding his teeth, he forced himself to step back. But as he did so, he made the mistake of looking at Sumi. The hunger in her eyes matched his own. More than that, it stoked the heat in his body to a frightening level.

One kiss . . .

He could already taste it.

Don't! Dariana waits for you.

But it wasn't Dariana he wanted. She had been Keris's love, never his. And in this moment, he totally understood why Keris had been willing to slit the throat of any male who glanced at her. Why Fain had denied them all to be with Omira.

He felt the same way for Sumi. A fierce protectiveness to keep her safe from all others.

The memory of the concern on her face when she'd found him pinned down and the way she'd handled herself in the fight . . .

He would kill to have the honor of lying inside her.

Just once.

But he knew better than to let such thoughts tempt him. That path led him straight to death.

Sumi held her breath as she waited for Dancer to deliver the heated kiss his eyes promised her. Never once in her life had she felt this kind of craving for any male. All she wanted was to bury her hands in his braids and straddle him until neither of them could walk without limping.

Kiss me. . . .

Instead, he blinked twice then went to review their attackers. That aggravated her enough that she actually kicked the assassin's body at her feet.

Damn, stupid Andarion customs! It was so unfair that she didn't dare encroach on a male it was obvious Dariana had no intention of accepting. Ever. She didn't believe for one second that the bitch would make good her promise to take him.

She had no doubt that Dariana would find a way to turn him away again.

You're a League assassin, Sumi. Remember that. She was here to hurt him, not straddle him.

Yeah.

Even more frustrated, she kicked the assassin's legs again, just for spite.

Dancer flipped one of the bodies over to search the man's pockets.

"Incas?" she asked.

Nodding, Dancer moved to search another body. "Who are these bastards? Why are they coming for me now?"

"I don't know." She sighed as she scanned their civilian clothes. "But I know The League wouldn't do this."

"They would if I gave them cause." He clicked his tongue teasingly. "But I'm not quite that stupid. At least not yet."

She didn't comment. As she searched the body at her feet, she froze. His armband had a receiver on it.

Was that . . .

Frowning, she pulled it off to study it and see if her suspicions were right. She angled it in different directions to pinpoint what it was tracking.

Sure enough, it went straight to Hauk.

Every time.

"Dancer?"

He faced her with a harsh grimace. "Why are you using a name you know annoys me?"

"Bitch about it later. I have something more important." She handed him the tracker.

He scowled at it as he realized the same thing she had. "Shit."

"Yeah. They're definitely tracking *you*."

And if this one set of assassins had a trace on him, others most likely did too. Or if they didn't, they could hone in on this frequency.

Dancer angled it toward the cave where the kids were hiding, then to her. As before, it only pointed to him. His frown deepened as he shook his head. "This makes no sense. I'm not tagged. I would have known had I been

implanted . . . unless . . ." He handed her the tracker then
began disrobing.

Oh, hello . . .

She definitely liked this new turn of events.

Heat scalded her cheeks at the sight of all that rippling
muscled flesh as he unwound all the leather straps from
his arms and braces and then dropped his shirt to his feet.

Dear gods. Even scarred, he was a fierce, fabulous
male.

His gaze met hers expectantly.

What did that look mean? Was it an invitation? *Oh
yeah, baby. Gimme!*

Her throat suddenly dry, she couldn't think. All she
could do was gape.

"Well?" he asked.

"Well what?"

"Is it in my clothes or my body?"

Ah . . . so *that* was why he'd given her this show. A
slow smile curved her lips as a very naughty thought went
through her mind. "Maybe we should remove your pants
to be sure. What do you think?"

He laughed, flashing a bit of fang at her. "This is serious, Sumi."

"As am I," she mumbled as she moved closer to him.
"We really should be *very* thorough. Just in case."

But he wasn't so accommodating.

Pouting, she scanned him. The signal strengthened.
She aimed it to his clothes and it lessened. "Bad news,
big guy. It's not your clothes."

Using the tracker, she ran it up and down his back to
see where the signal was strongest. "It seems to be right
in the center of your spine." She put her finger on the exact location. "Could it be your League chip reactivated?"

Thanks to his friend Nykyrian, who'd dug his tag out
of his own body the day he quit, The League now embedded them in the spines of their assassins. The only

way to remove them was with a surgeon, and any surgeon who removed a League tag was to be executed without trial.

"No. They pulled it out when I was discharged." He growled in frustration.

"Maybe someone shot you?"

"Maybe. They do do that a lot." A tic worked in his jaw as he bent to retrieve his shirt. He pulled it on, but didn't fasten it. "We've got to get to a subspace transmitter. Did any of them have a link on them?"

She shook her head. "Everything I found was short range."

He pulled a link out of his pocket and tried to use it, then cursed. "We're still blocked from getting a signal. But . . ." He glanced away.

"But what?" she prompted.

He hesitated before he answered. "There is an abandoned base about a day's walk from here. Even with the satellites out of range, it should be able to transmit. And it should have an impressive armory."

She detected a thick note of dread in his voice. "Why don't you want to go there?"

"It's where Thia's mother was murdered."

CHAPTER 13

When Dancer started back for the cave where the kids were hiding, Sumi saw his limp.

"Are you hit?"

"It's fine."

"Dancer!" She pulled him to a stop.

Leaning down, he pressed his forehead to hers. It was an Andarion expression of affection. One made even more tender when he laid his fingers against her cheek. "I am fine, Sumi. Now that I know I'm tagged, I'm a threat to all of you. I need you to get the kids and walk to Aksel's base. Immediately."

Oh yeah, right. Was he out of his mind?

"What if you're hurt worse? What if the poison—"

"If you worry about every *what if* that might befall you, your fears will paralyze you. I assure you, I've been through much worse than this."

"Alone?"

"Alone." Stepping back, he rubbed her on the arm. "Now go. Take Illyse with you. I need the three of you safe to do what I must. Will you do that for me?"

Every instinct she had screamed out against his wishes. Yeah, okay, while she had the physical skills and expertise, she mentally sucked at being an assassin. She always had. Ruthless cruelty had never been part of her personality. She'd killed the first time for self-defense only. And while the Overseer's court had deemed it overkill, it hadn't been. She'd been the one battered. And Avin had been the one to go for her father's old blaster first.

Terrified of his intent, she'd hit him with a lamp, bit his hand, and taken the blaster from him. Had he backed off, she would never have fired it. She'd told him to leave. Begged him to, point of fact.

Curling his lip, he'd laughed at her and her fear. *"I know you're not going to pull that trigger. But bitch, when I get it from you, I promise you, I will. Then I won't have to worry about you or that bastard you're carrying holding me back from my dreams."*

When he'd lunged at her, Sumi had closed her eyes and let the blast fly. Honestly, she hadn't meant to kill him. She'd never shot a blaster before. Her hands shaking, she'd aimed for his shoulder and blasted his head instead.

To this day, she couldn't get the sight of him lying dead in her flat out of her mind. But that was nothing compared to the kills The League had forced her to make after that.

Every time she'd taken a life, she'd lost more of her soul.

She wasn't like the ones Dancer ran with who didn't flinch at death. She couldn't stand it. And the last thing she wanted was to leave Dancer wounded and on his own.

Hauk paused as he saw in her hazel green eyes her reticence to desert him. Her concern for him made his heart ache. No one had ever hesitated to put him in harm's way before. And for the first time in his life, he was beginning to understand his friends and their devotion to their spouses. Why they were so willing to risk everything to make them happy.

That rancid fear in the gut of returning to an existence where you lived without their smiles lighting up the innocuous moments that made up any given day . . .

He totally understood Nykyrian's words to him before he'd left for this hell-bent quest. Why his friend preferred the mad chaos of his current life over the peace in his past.

Gods, how he wanted that with her.

But it could never be.

"I won't be harmed, Sumi. I promise."

She narrowed her eyes on him. "Don't make me have to come back here and kick your hulking ass. I am a trained assassin, you know?"

He smiled at her anger. She was a fierce little mouse, indeed. "I know."

When he started away, she grabbed his shirt and pulled him back toward her. He thought they were under attack again, until she buried her hand in his braids and led his lips to hers.

Fire erupted through his entire body as he tasted her warmth for the first time, and her tongue teased his. His head spun at the sweetest tenderness he'd ever known. Growling in the back of his throat, he deepened the kiss, taking great care not to hurt her with his fangs or strength. His head swam with pleasure that left him ragged and wanting before her. Exposed.

Completely pliant.

Sumi trembled as he enveloped her in his arms and pressed her fully against his hard body. Her breasts were flush to his chest. She ran her hands over his hard, sculpted ribs to his muscular back, taking care not to brush against his wound. He was absolutely humongous. Harder than steel. Fierce. And hotter than hell. For a male who'd never been kissed before, he was incredible at it.

His breathing ragged, he nipped at her lips with his fangs before he finally pulled back to stare down at her. "You shouldn't have done that."

"I know. I'm sorry." But not as sorry as he'd be should Dariana ever find out. Guilt stabbed her hard. *Please don't get hurt because of me.* Horrified over what she might have done to him, she placed her hand over his lips. "Please tell me you won't be harmed for this."

Hauk couldn't answer that without lying. As part of their unification, he would be asked if he'd ever tasted another female during his pledge time. He'd be honor bound and under oath to tell the truth.

Dariana would have a fit when she learned of it. There was no telling what part of his body she'd demand as restitution.

But there was nothing to be done to correct this. He couldn't change it. As with all things, all he could do was deal with the repercussions when they came for him.

Hauk brushed his thumb over Sumi's lips and winked at her. "Don't worry, *mia*." Reluctantly, he pulled her arms from around his bare skin and stepped out of them.

Yet what he really wanted to do was carry her into a secluded corner and taste more of her. To lose himself in the warmth of her body until he was too sore to continue on.

Damn assassins. When he got his hands on more of them, they would feel the full weight of his displeasure over having to separate from his family and Sumi.

"We need to hurry before more are sent."

She nodded. "Any idea who's behind this?"

He laughed at her question as he gathered more weapons and ammunition from the bodies. "I'm on the hit list for more than two dozen nations. Then there's all the assholes who hate me. That list is endless."

Sumi could imagine, given how lethal he could be. Still, the list might give them some idea as to who would pay this kind of money for his life. "Who's at the top of it?"

"Your boss. Kyr Zemin. Psycho cyclops bastard. You can't really miss him in a crowd."

She ignored his acerbic description. "Why is he your number one? What did you do?"

Squinting up at her, he tucked the weapons into a pack. "Showed him multiple times that in a fight between an Andarion and a Phrixian, the Andarion always wins."

She arched her brow at that. Dancer wasn't bragging. He'd said it very matter-of-factly. And it spoke a lot for his skill level. She'd seen the commander spar enough to know that even with no depth perception and a serious handicap on that eye, he was still a lethal opponent. She could only imagine how much more lethal he'd been without his current physical limitations. "Personal grudge?"

"Yeah. He was my League ATA, and he took offense to the number of times I face-planted him on the mat during training. Then once I befriended Mari, it became all-out war."

Her scowl deepened at that. "Why?"

"Mari's his little brother. Whenever Kyr feels the need to lip off about Mari's lifestyle, I'm possessed by the need to beat his ass for it."

That explained a lot.

However, she pointed to the bodies around them and spoke the most obvious fact. "But these aren't League assassins."

"Which puts me back to my overwhelming list of enemies."

"And the first runner-up is?"

"Jullien eton Anatole."

She choked on the last name she'd expected to come out of his mouth. "The Andarion prince and heir?"

"Was. He's still royal, but he's been removed from the line of succession and direct lineage."

"Because of you?"

He rose slowly and in an almost bashful, boyish gesture rubbed at his cheek. "I helped a little."

"Sheez, Dancer," she breathed, "you do not pick your enemies wisely, do you?"

"What can I say? Sometimes you have to put your foot down. Sometimes you have to put it up their asses."

She rolled her eyes at his dry tone.

Darice and Thia poked their heads around the rocks near their cave.

"Dancer? You alive?" Darice called.

Unamused, Hauk stared at him. "No. Much like your common sense, I'm upright and dead."

Sumi shook her head as she tucked surplus ammo into her belt. "I swear you have an advanced degree in sarcasm."

He actually laughed at that while he latched his shirt shut before the kids saw it open.

When they joined them, he handed his primary blaster to Sumi and his secondary to Thia, who scowled up at him.

Hauk cupped her cheek in his massive paw of a hand. "They have me tagged and are coming for me, *kisa*. I need you to lead Sumi and Darice to Aksel's base and call your father. Can you do that?"

Tears welled in her eyes, but to her credit, Thia blinked them away. "How are you tagged?"

"It's embedded in his spine."

Thia winced then nodded. "I will get the whole army here for you, Uncle."

He kissed her brow. "And I will keep them away from you. Tell Fain that I'll be at Canyon Point. He'll know where that is."

Darice stepped forward. "I will come with you."

Hauk pulled him into a tight hug. "You're not a warrior yet, *mi tana*. And I need you to guard the *taras* for me. Since the dawn of our civilization, War Hauks have protected the eton Anatoles. Respect our princess. Let no harm come to her, especially not the poison that drips from your tongue."

Darice made a rude sound before his gaze turned deadly serious. "Take care, Dancer."

"And you." He went to retrieve the packs for them.

Sumi frowned as he only took the haul bag and a small portion of water for himself. "You'll need more than that."

He flashed a fanged grin at her. "I'll be fine. Scrounging supplies is what I do best." He jerked his chin. "Now go. All of you."

Thia hugged him.

By the way he braced himself, Sumi realized that Thia must be pressing on his wounds. But he didn't say a word.

As they started walking forward, she turned back to say one last good-bye.

Dancer had already vanished into the desert.

"He'll be all right," Thia assured her. "My father has always said there's no one he'd rather have at his back than Uncle Hauk. And coming from my dad, that's the highest endorsement and compliment."

"Tactical assault monkey," Sumi breathed, more to remind herself of his fighting skill than them.

Thia nodded before she picked up speed. "All right, soldiers. Double time. We have to get help, and fast."

Hauk had been walking for hours. His side was absolutely killing him. But for wanting to put as much distance between himself and his family as possible, he'd have sat down and let the bastards come for a fight. It'd never been in his nature to dodge any battle. Busting heads was his favorite pastime.

But his family came first.

He opened a bottle of water and sipped at it. Then he took a moment to rummage through the electronics he'd scavenged from the assassins. If he could rig a strong enough booster, he might be able to reach The Sentella.

Or make a jammer to block the transmitter in his back.

As he worked on it, he tried to figure out when and how

he'd been implanted. It defied logic. No one ever touched him that intimately.

No one except Sumi.

It wasn't her, dumbass. He'd have known had she done it. Not to mention, she hadn't touched his back until *after* the first group had attacked.

Mark one suspect off the list. Only a million and two more to go.

Hauk wiped at the sweat on his brow as he continued mulling over his infinite number of enemies. How long had the device been there? Honestly, he might have had it for years.

At home, assassination attempts were so common that he was only surprised when he went a week without someone trying to end him. It was just par for his life.

He raked his hand down his pants before he opened the back of a radio and started rewiring it.

"Why are you messing with those stupid electronics again, Dancer? You should be training and building your muscle mass. That shit won't ever help you as much as fighting strength."

Shaking his head to clear it, he tried to get Keris's disdainful voice out of his mind. There was still enough of the poison in his system that it was playing havoc with his senses.

And he was mad as hell at himself about that. He should have known to check for poison after he'd been stabbed. It was a common practice for the Partinie to taint their blades. Bastards were callous that way.

Andarions viewed such tactics as cheating and cowardly, which was why he hadn't thought about it. If you weren't strong enough to kill with your hands or standard weapons, then you should perish with honor. That was how *his* people lived and died.

But Partinie, for all their knife skills, were basic cowards. They wanted easy kills they didn't have to work for.

Hauk opened his shirt to check his throbbing side. The blisters where he'd cauterized the front wound had opened and were festering from his sweat. Curling his lip at the sight, he tore open an antiseptic pack to clean it.

Something rustled to the north of his position.

He dropped his hand to the blaster he'd confiscated from one of the assassins. A Rit weapon, it had a larger blast radius than anything except his modified Andarion PX8s. Damn, he missed his blasters. A gift from Darling years ago, they were his most cherished belongings. He'd even named them. The fact he let Thia and Sumi take them said it all about his feelings toward the females.

He'd never had those weapons out of his hands before. Death had come quickly to anyone dumb enough to try to take them from him.

Cocking his head, he listened. Someone was crawling on the ground not that far away.

Hauk rose to his feet and lowered his head to scan the area around him. Then he heard it. The distant whine of an airbee engine. Lightweight airbikes, they were the choice for this terrain.

Walking slowly, he headed for a small copse of desert trees to use for cover while he mentally ran through all the weapons he'd kept. For once, he wished he'd taken explosives training from Darling. His friend had begged him countless times to do it. But after what had happened with Keris, Hauk had no use for anything that could blow up in his face and rain debris down around him. All he knew how to do was build the switches and timers. He'd never wanted anything to do with the explosive minerals or compounds themselves.

But that was okay.

He could kill well enough without it. At least that was the thought until he heard more engines approaching.

And more.

Shit. Were they planning a festival? The annual Hunt

Hauk's Head Event? Exactly how many were coming to this little soiree? It sounded like an army mobilizing. *Who the hell hates me* this *much?*

Okay, a lot of beings. Still . . . he would be impressed by their determination and number if it wasn't his life they were here to claim. Damn.

Had Kyr finally figured out he was one of the prison raiders?

The prime commander was the only one he could think of who bore this amount of animosity toward him.

If Kyr had no proof that Hauk was part of The Sentella, but suspected Hauk's ties . . . he *might* resort to this. Maybe.

Too bad he didn't have a working link to check on it.

No, he chided at himself. *It can't be Kyr.* If Kyr put out a contract of this magnitude, even a civ one, one of their spies would have intelled it and Nyk and the others would have beelined here to pick up the kids.

This was much more covert. It had to come from someone who knew of his illegal allies and ties. Someone who didn't dare let anyone know he had assassins after him.

Dariana . . .

As Hauk positioned himself to watch his pursuers regroup to come after him, he paused to let that possibility play through his mind.

No. He was being stupidly paranoid. She wouldn't do that. Well, she *might* do that if he were here alone, but not with Darice in his company. No matter how much she might hate him and not want to marry him or release him, she wouldn't dare endanger her son.

Yet she had been close enough to implant him.

Many times.

Then again, so had countless others he'd fought with and against. For all he knew, it was the bar brawl he'd been in a couple of weeks back. He, Chayden, Ryn, and Fain tended to get rowdy whenever they drank. Fights were their stock-in-trade, especially when they were in some of their "finer" pubs.

Yeah, but these guys after him were seriously motivated. He watched in awe as they unloaded a small ion cannon and headed for his position.

Time to move.

Dropping gear weight, he only kept what he had to. They launched two probes to set eyes on his location. He stood up and batted the first one to reach him with the stock of Sumi's rifle. The other probe shot a laser. He barely ducked it before he returned fire and sent it to the ground.

Not that it mattered. He was now firmly in their sights. No sooner had that thought entered his mind than all hell erupted around him as they rained down everything they had.

CHAPTER 14

"I hear engines." His brow tight with worry, Darice started back toward Hauk's last location.

Thia caught his arm. "Uncle Hauk can handle it."

"What if he doesn't?"

Sumi arched a brow at the sound of tears in Darice's voice. The little booger actually did love his uncle.

Who'd have thought?

Tears glistened in Thia's eyes as well. "Sumi? Tell him we can't fight them. We're better off here."

"As much as I hate to admit it, Darice, she's right. While I'm trained, you two are not ready for a professional strike force. You'd endanger your uncle by getting hurt, and would probably cost him his life as he tried to save yours."

"You're a coward!"

Sumi glared at him as she struggled with a fierce desire to give him exactly what he needed. A takedown he'd never forget. "Darice. I'm not Dancer or Thia. I have no familial love for you. What I am is a trained assassin who is one step away from cutting out your tongue. Think about it before you continue down this path that will lead you to a short lifetime of utter misery."

His breathing ragged, he fanged her. "He better not die!"

Those words caused all semblance of humor to fade from Thia's eyes as she picked up her pace even more.

Sumi ran to catch up and pull her to a stop. "Thia, you won't do Dancer any good if you break something or collapse from exhaustion or heatstroke. You're the only one of us who knows where we're going. We need you with us one hundred percent. Dancer's life depends on it."

Darice snarled at her. "Only family calls him Dancer. He's Hauk to you, *human*!"

He should be on his knees in gratitude that they couldn't afford stunning him. If Dancer wasn't under fire, she'd shoot him just on principal.

Sumi glared at him. "Do you talk to your mother like this?"

"No. She'd beat him till he bled."

Sumi cringed as she heard a cannon's blast. "Is that—"

"Ion cannon fire," Thia finished for her. "I know that sound. Intimately."

The lorina hissed and started toward the battle sounds, but Thia caught her collar. She looked expectantly at Sumi.

It took everything Sumi had not to run back for Dancer. That was her natural instinct. Only the sight of the kids kept her focused on the fact that she needed to protect them more than a trained soldier. Unlike Dancer, the kids wouldn't survive an attack, and he'd never forgive her if they were hurt.

For that matter, she'd never forgive herself. Neither of these kids needed another nightmare added to their memories.

But with every step they made toward the base, terror consumed her more. How could anyone survive the thunderstorm behind them?

Alone.

She made herself remember Dancer attacking the prison as one of their two lead points. The Sentella had been significantly outnumbered, at least twenty to one. By heavily fortified League forces. No one should have survived such a reckless assault. Yet they had taken minimal casualties and put a major hurt on League guards and trained assassins. Dancer and Darling had led the others in. The TAM had paved the way for their troops.

But Dancer hadn't been alone then. She kept returning to the fact that he was fighting this battle today with no one on his six.

Please be all right.

Even Darice was growing paler by the heartbeat as he kept looking back over his shoulder. "Thia," he breathed, his voice cracking. "Tell me a story to give me hope."

Thia had to practically drag the lorina with her. "Um . . . okay. Let me think." She bit her lip before she drew a ragged breath. "Uh, there was this time on Broma, back when Uncle Syn lived there. It wasn't long after he and Uncle Hauk had become good friends. To celebrate the fact that Syn had just finished his first residency, they went out drinking. After they'd been there for a while and were . . . let's say consumed by excess, this really gorgeous woman came up and decided to give Uncle Syn a lap dance."

Sumi arched a brow at where this story was headed. "Thia! They really tell you these things?"

She blushed. "No one in my family knows I have Andarion hearing. I get lots of good stories they don't know I can overhear."

Shaking her head, Sumi laughed. "And will we be getting the adult version of this tale?"

Thia flashed a cheeky dimple. "It's appropriate, I promise. I'm editing as I go." She turned back toward Darice. "Anyway, she hadn't been there long when all of a sudden this shadow falls over them. He grabs her by the arm and snatches her off Syn's lap then goes to slap her. Quicker than anyone can blink, Uncle Hauk catches his fist in his hand and glares a hole through him. In that deep, terrifying growl of his, he snarls to the man, 'Boy, before you kick open the door, you better make sure you have on the right boots.'"

Darice scowled. "What does that mean?"

"It's an old Triosan saying. It means before you start a fight, you better know you can finish it. But like you, the guy didn't know that. Any more than Hauk or Syn knew he was the son of Balur Droug."

Sumi sucked her breath in sharply at the name. Droug was second only to Idirian Wade when it came to cruelty and cold-blooded murders. He was a legendary criminal who had been captured and executed only a few years back. "Oh my God, what did they do?"

"Well, Syn is the son of Idirian Wade."

Stunned, Sumi widened her eyes. That was the last thing she'd expected to hear. Wade had been a serial killer and madman so twisted that even decades after his death, mothers still used his name to frighten their misbehaving children.

Damn, Dancer ran with some extremely dangerous people. No wonder Thia had called them all scary. "What?"

Thia nodded. "But back then, Syn was in hiding under a false identity and was wanted for treason on Ritadaria—which is a whole other long story in and of itself. Anyway, he couldn't afford for anyone to find out who he really was."

Which an arrest for a bar fight and the resulting DNA scan at the Enforcers' headquarters would have certainly exposed.

"Droug pulled a knife and tried to stab Uncle Hauk. Uncle Hauk threw the first punch then realized half the bar's occupants were on Droug's payroll. When Uncle Syn started to help, Hauk shoved him toward the door, and told him to take the girl and run before the Enforcers came and arrested him."

Sumi gasped. "Surely he didn't leave him there."

"Uncle Syn had no choice," Thia said simply. "It would have been a death sentence for him to be caught. But he did shoot and stab a few on his way out. He said his last sight of Uncle Hauk was him standing in the middle of a dozen muscled goons . . . my word substitution. Anyway, Uncle Hauk was barely grown and was surrounded. Right? So what does he do? He holds his hands up," Thia illustrated her words, "and as calm as you please, takes the shot glass from the table where they'd been sitting and pours himself a drink. He knocks it back, and puts the glass down like it ain't no big thing and there aren't a dozen guys waiting to gut him. He sweeps his gaze over the men and smiles. Then faster than lightning, he grabs the bottle and goes on the attack. By the time he was finished, there were twenty-two bodies on the floor and he had Droug by the throat, threatening to rip it open with his fangs if anyone else came near him. And all that completely bare-handed. He walked away with a bruised jaw and ear. A couple of cracked ribs and a broken nose. But he was intact and no one dared to arrest him for it. No one."

Darice frowned. "What happened to Syn?"

"He was waiting outside the bar the whole time, watching the fight. Had he thought for one minute that Uncle Hauk couldn't handle them, he would have run back in, regardless of what it cost him. It was that very fight that led to Uncle Syn dubbing him the Andarion Tactical Assault Monkey, because Uncle Hauk had been laughing and enjoying the fight the whole time. Completely calm and in control. Unfazed. Syn said that at one point during the fight, Uncle Hauk had ripped a piece of pipe from the bar itself to beat down one of his attackers who came after him with a machete."

Darice passed a doubtful look to Thia. "Is that really true?"

She placed her hand over her heart and bowed her head—the Andarion gesture for honesty. "On my ancestors' honor. My father has said repeatedly that no one is better in a fight than Uncle Hauk. Even *he* would think twice before challenging him to a brawl . . . and that he'd never be dumb enough to do it alone, or sober."

Darice shook his head as if he still couldn't believe it. "That is so different from the stories I've heard of him. From what I've seen of him."

Thia gave him an agitated smirk. "That's because you haven't seen his fighting side, Darice. You've only seen Uncle Hauk with elders, family, and females. And you're right, he's very different with your mother and yaya and paran. For that matter, he's very, very different with me and any woman or child. He's respectful of the fact that he's a terrifying individual, with an incredible amount of strength. My stepmother said that the first time she was left alone with him, she almost wet her pants and locked herself in her room for the day."

His eyes widened in anger. "When was she alone with him?"

"Oh shut up!" Thia snapped irritably. "Stop with that Andarion male bullshit. He was guarding her from assassins. He didn't touch her. At all. And the fact that my father left him *alone* with my stepmother tells you just how much faith he has in Uncle Hauk's abilities. Believe me, my daddy is the most paranoid, overprotective lunatic you've ever heard of . . . second only maybe to Shahara. In all honesty, I'm surprised I'm not required to harness myself to the bed at night for his fear I might roll out of it in my sleep and bruise a knee."

Sumi laughed.

"You think I'm kidding. . . . He really is *that* bad."

But in spite of what Thia said, Sumi was terrified for Dancer and what he was facing.

Why do you care? If he survives, Kyr will do a lot worse to him than the assassins with him now. All they'll do is kill him.

Kyr would torture him first.

Her stomach cramping, Sumi flinched as she remembered Kyr showing her what he was doing to Safir Jari. And all because Jari had been taken and used as a hostage by The Sentella during one of their escapes. She still didn't know how Jari could live, given the torture Kyr had heaped on him. It was horrible and wrong.

And Safir Jari was Kyr's own brother.

How can I turn Dancer over to that madman?

What choice did she have? Jari was Kyr's youngest brother. She was nothing to the prime commander, and her daughter even less so. Their torture and deaths would be far more horrific than anything he'd done to Jari, whom he should, in theory, love and be loyal to.

And still the sounds of battle reached them.

Needing a distraction, she turned her thoughts to the way Dancer had looked when she kissed him. The way he'd felt in her arms.

But with that came an even bigger fear.

"Thia?"

She glanced at Sumi over her shoulder.

"I'm still a little fuzzy on Andarion customs. Why is it such a big deal that Hauk was alone with your stepmother?"

Thia let out a sinister laugh. "Because Andarion females are extremely predatorial, like their male counterparts, and they have ferocious appetites in all things. No pledged male is ever supposed to allow himself to be alone with any female he's not pledged or related to.

Case in point, it's why Uncle Hauk's parents are his parents."

"I don't follow."

"Uncle Hauk's father, Ferral, was originally pledged to my yaya. The day before their unification, Endine seduced him. When he admitted to it during Disclosure, my yaya refused his pledge and sent him home in disgrace."

Sumi cocked her head at something that made no sense to her about Andarion weddings. "Wait, Disclosure? I thought all Andarions had to do was admit to a third party that they were husband and wife and they were deemed married by Andarion law."

That was what Fain and Omira had done. Fain had said that by Andarion law, it was completely legal and binding.

"It *can* be that informal . . . in fact, that's how my father and stepmother were married, and most Andarions aren't big on ceremony as a rule. However, that's like eloping and the high-lineaged Andarions frown on it. Greatly. So much so that even my dad and stepmother were later remarried in our Andarion ancestors' temple."

Sumi furrowed her brow as she tried to understand. "Why would it matter?"

"In a traditional, high-lineaged Andarion family, it's considered shameful to marry that way, like there's something wrong with one of the partners, and many times the parents force a divorce from the couple. The tying of pure, high-ranking bloodlines is seen as a very serious matter that isn't taken lightly."

"Really?"

Thia nodded. "It's why my parents remarried—to make sure no one disputed the legitimacy or heritage of their children. Tradition dictates that a pledge be made before a priest and that the parents and immediate families bear witness to it. After that, the couple has to wait a full Andarion year before they meet back at temple. Then before the priest, they disclose if they've allowed another to touch them during the time they've been pledged. If their public Disclosure is accepted by both parties, they go forward with unification, and the next day they have their marriage completed and blessed."

Sumi didn't like the sound of what Thia described. "What exactly do they admit to in this Disclosure?"

"If they've allowed someone of the opposite sex to touch them in any way that could be construed as sexual contact."

Sumi gaped at her. "Wait! Are you telling me that high-lineaged Andarions have to publicly catalogue all the sexual activity of their lives before they can marry?"

"No," she said quickly. "What happens before pledging is inconsequential. Even what happens between the male and female who are pledged is inconsequential. They accept the fact that Andarion passions are fierce, and that many couples don't wait. But once pledged, it becomes a sacred trust, like marriage. To allow any part of your body to be touched by someone other than the one you're pledged to is the same as adultery. And it's treated that way. Darice's paran is extremely lucky that my yaya was already in love with my grandfather, and was more than happy to release him from his pledge. Otherwise, she could have demanded his offending body part be given to her . . . or his head. It's called Restitution, and the dishonored party is allowed to choose what they find acceptable physical payment for a broken pledge."

Was the girl kidding? "Excuse me?"

Thia nodded grimly. "If he's slept with another, a male can be castrated at the command of his pledged. If he's touched another female, he loses his hands. A kiss can cost him his tongue and lips."

She felt sick over what she'd inadvertently done. And Dancer hadn't said a word about it. "Are you serious?"

"Very. Andarions don't take disloyalty or broken

pledges lightly. We are a *fierce* proud race. You do not break an Andarion oath. Ever."

What have I done?

Sumi wished desperately that she could go back and refrain from a kiss that, knowing Dariana, could get Dancer killed. "So what do they do to females, then? They can't castrate them. Right?"

Thia actually flinched. "You don't want to know. Trust me. I don't want to think about it. But if a female has slept with another while pledged, the best she can hope for is death."

"Is that true of who they slept with, too? Do they get the same punishment?"

"No. In fact, it's not uncommon for a pledged to hire someone to try and seduce their betrothed to make sure that they are marrying an honorable Andarion. Especially if the marriage is arranged."

Wow. It made her so glad she wasn't born Andarion. But it also terrified her for Dancer. "So what if you're accidentally kissed? Do you have to disclose that?"

Darice scowled. "How do you get accidentally kissed?"

"Like someone stole a kiss from you when you weren't expecting it. Or you were raped. What then?"

Thia sighed. "In that case, the perpetrator would be severely punished and the pledged would have to undergo another period of purification to make sure no child was conceived. The other beautiful thing about Andarions, they are very fertile little turtles. Even with birth control. Hence the five kids in eight years of my father's marriage . . . and my lovely presence here today."

Sumi didn't comment on that sarcasm. She was too busy processing what Thia was telling her. The punishment made sense for rape, but . . .

"The perpetrator could be killed for a simple stolen kiss? Really?"

"Oh yeah," Thia said, wide-eyed. "Because of their

passionate natures, Andarions are extremely respectful of each other's bodies and protective of their own. *Any* encroachment is seen as a violation of their personal rights. In fact, that's part of the unification ceremony. Each partner asks for permission to touch the other and is granted the right to do so in steps. Unless you're seen as very close family, you don't just walk up to an Andarion and touch them, in any manner. Not even a hug or handshake. They get really upset about that."

Darice nodded in agreement. "It's why we stand like this whenever we meet strangers." He stopped to cross his arms over his chest and stand with his legs braced wide.

She'd seen Andarions do that, including Fain, but had never realized the significance of it.

"Unless they're unconscious and need immediate care, even medical providers have to ask before they can touch a patient," Thia finished as Darice picked up his pace and ran ahead. "You don't brush hands or anything like that, without permission. If you accidentally do so, you apologize immediately and profusely. Even then, there's a good chance you're about to be in a fight at best, arrested at worst."

Holy heaven . . .

Sumi fell silent as she realized how egregious her behavior had been. Granted, it was done in ignorance, but still.

Yet what sickened her most was that she knew Dancer would never see her punished for their kiss. His honor wouldn't let him. He'd take full responsibility for it during Disclosure.

And Dariana would demand a harsh sentence for that trespass.

"Does anyone ever lie during Disclosure?" Sumi asked, even though she knew Dancer would never do such a thing.

"No. If you're caught in a lie, it's an automatic death

sentence. And if you help conceal an indiscretion, it's a death sentence. Andarions are *very* serious about their lineages and oaths. Which is why they're notoriously monogamous and why they think long and hard before pledging themselves to another. They either marry very early or extremely late in life."

"Why is that?"

Thia fell back to whisper to her so that Darice wouldn't hear her. "Well, you know about that need to be . . ." she cleared her throat, "drained. Aside from that, it's said that once an Andarion tastes the flesh of another, they're insatiable. Male and female. So if they don't marry early, they marry older."

"How much older?"

"Eighty to ninety, at least."

Sumi was aghast at the age. "What?"

Thia laughed. "Don't be so shocked. They live a lot longer than humans, as a rule. It's why my yaya is seventy and looks almost as young as my stepmother. And she's still well within Andarion childbearing years. They can have children until they're over one hundred and fifty."

"No *minsid* way."

Thia nodded. "It's also why they seldom mate outside their species. There's an old legend that claims the rocky belt surrounding Andaria isn't from a moon that was hit by an asteroid and broke apart, but rather it's the remnants of the heart of the first Andarion who married a human. He was one of the greatest Andarion warriors ever born and she was a young human who tempted him with her fragility. He defied his lineage to bring her into his world and when she died birthing their firstborn, because she was a mere, weak human, his heart shattered into the pieces that will forever orbit our homeworld as a reminder that Andarions should remain with their own kind. Forever."

Sumi grimaced at a story that wrung her heart. "That is awful and beautiful."

"Andarions have their moments," Thia said with a smile. "Good and bad."

Groaning at all their talk and mumbling about human women, Darice ran ahead of them again with Illyse chasing after him.

Sumi was still trying not to hear the sounds of Dancer fighting on his own. She walked beside Thia while they kept their eyes on Darice.

"So is it true about Andarion passions? Are they really that hard to control?"

Thia shrugged. "I wouldn't know, as I've never been there."

Sumi arched a brow. Given that Thia was easily in her twenties, she was stunned by that revelation. She would have assumed a girl so beautiful would have been pursued heavily by any man who saw her. "Really?"

Thia flashed a sad smile at her. "Really. There's no one I hate bad enough to sacrifice them to my father's ungodly temper. I'm honestly terrified of ever bringing a male home who I've slept with. My dad's so good at reading people, I think he'd know immediately and then gut the poor man before he could cross the foyer."

Sumi couldn't imagine a protective father like that. But at least Thia had a fairly positive attitude about something that had to drive the poor girl crazy. "What about marriage?"

Thia shook her head. "I don't want to chance it."

"Meaning?"

"I don't want to be tied down like my mother was and forced to live with that kind of misery." The sadness in her gaze burned Sumi with its intensity. "I'm not a fool nor am I naive. I come with the blood of three royal houses, and am attached to almost a dozen more. I would never trust a man to love me and not see me for the political ties I can give him." She sighed. "Maybe one day I'll change my mind, but I doubt it. And luckily, my father would sooner gut someone than use me for a political marriage. That is the one thing I *never* fault him for."

"Your father sounds like a wonderful male."

Thia laughed. "He can be, so long as you don't annoy him. Or make any sudden, unexpected moves."

Darice came running back toward them. "Do you hear that?"

They fell silent to listen.

"Hear what?" Thia whispered.

"The fight's over."

He was right. There was no sound whatsoever.

Darice swallowed hard. "You think Dancer's all right?"

Sumi exchanged an apprehensive look with Thia. They both knew he'd been wounded and poisoned before the fight had even begun. While he was extremely strong, and skilled, those were bad odds for anyone.

Even an Andarion Tactical Assault Monkey.

CHAPTER 15

Hauk stood slowly as he surveyed the bodies for any sign of life. Pain suffused every inch of him. He hadn't felt this battered since his days as a League cadet. Back then, Kyr had taken it as a personal challenge to beat the shit out of every recruit assigned to him. The psycho bastard had viewed it as his divine right and duty to "toughen" them up for battle.

"If you can't take a beating, the only part of a League uniform you deserve to wear is the flag we'll wrap around your coffin when we bury your corpse."

The only thing that kept him from hating Kyr for that was that the bastard had been right. Though harsh, the things Hauk had learned in training, and from his older brothers, had kept him alive and sharp, no matter who or what came for him.

Ironic really. Neither he nor Nykyrian would be half the challenge for Kyr that they currently were had the bastard not trained them to be every bit as ruthless as he was. Phrixian, Andarion, human. Didn't matter. Cold was cold.

You steal someone's soul and sooner or later, you will pay for it.

And Kyr was feeling that bite now, in a major way.

Cautiously, Hauk searched all twenty-five bodies, making sure that none were breathing or wired with explosives. Same for their transports.

"Hiller? You there, copy?"

Hauk paused as he heard the deep voice on the short-range radios. Picking up the link closest to him, he answered with a guttural, "Yeah."

"Did you get him? I don't hear no more fighting."

"Yeah," he repeated.

"Fucking awesome. Don't forget to bag the head with the DNA sample. We get twice the payout for it. See you in a few."

Fucking awesome, indeed. Fury darkened his sight as he went into full-on rage mode. But that was fine. With the earwigs these bastards had, he could easily backtrace to the source and get a few needed answers. Whoever had hired them wouldn't be getting his head.

They would be getting one last visit.

As Hauk double-checked the ignitions to make sure they weren't biolocked, he heard the faintest of footsteps to his right. He pretended to ignore it while he got a bead on the man's location. The instant he had it, he jerked his blaster out and aimed.

"Don't!" His own weapon drawn, the man had him firmly sighted with a green laser dot hovering over Hauk's heart.

Hauk didn't flinch or move as he kept his dot between the man's eyes. "One twitch and I promise you'll be dead before I will."

That dot didn't waver from Hauk's heart. With his left hand held up, the man moved slowly forward. "Ditto."

Hauk scowled as he took in the man's ragged, unkempt condition. It was obvious that, unlike Sumi, he'd been out here on his own for a long time. His hair was ragged and trimmed to his shoulders, as if he cut it with his own knife. He wore it tied back from his face. He also had a scraggly beard. There was something vaguely familiar about him and the way he moved, but Hauk couldn't place it.

Around Darling's height, he was well muscled and held the blaster like a trained soldier, not a mercenary or civ. Likewise, he wasn't sweating or even perturbed by the fact that Hauk could kill him without flinching. This man was used to fighting for his life and had come to terms with his own mortality.

A slow smile of appreciation spread across Hauk's face. "So are we going to stand here all day, weapons drawn? I'm game if you are."

His humor caught the man off guard. He relaxed a tiny degree. Hauk watched his eyes carefully. They were always the window to say when someone was about to attack and when they were scared.

This man showed neither tendency. Rather, his dark gaze was wary and thoughtful. After a moment, he lowered his blaster, but not so much that he couldn't get a well-placed shot off if Hauk made a move he didn't like.

"I'm just here to scavenge before the others arrive. You do your thing, I do mine, and we part ways."

Hauk nodded. "You're Kirovarian?"

The blaster came right back up. "How do you know that?"

Hauk holstered his weapon. "Your accent. So what was your rank, soldier?"

He hesitated before he finally put his weapon away. "What kind of Andarion knows humans so well?"

"I was schooled with humans."

The man's eyes flared before he brought the weapon up and Hauk caught his arm before he could pull the trigger. He disarmed him. The man attacked.

Hauk deflected the blow and returned it. He dodged, twirled, and delivered a staggering fist to the man's jaw. Hauk head-butted him then flipped him to the ground.

The fall raised his shirt to betray an emblem Hauk knew better than he wanted to.

Shit.

He was a Ravin. No wonder the man was so skittish and unkempt.

Hauk immediately held his hands up and backed off. "I'm not here to hunt or kill you, friend."

The man glared at him. "You're League, aren't you? Isn't that why you're here?"

Hauk scratched his chin with the back of his hand. "Used to be, and was discharged years ago. If I wasn't, I'd have killed you already. These days, I'm Sentella, only." He gestured toward the weapons on the ground he couldn't carry. Weapons this man would need if he was to live out the week. "Walk with peace, brother. Take your supplies and go. I won't stop or track you."

He wiped at the blood on his lips. Suspicion hung heavy in his eyes before he pushed himself to his feet. His gaze never wavered from Hauk as he began searching the bodies for things he could use.

Ignoring him, Hauk took a trophy of his own from one of the fallen that he bagged in the container they'd brought for his head, then he returned to studying the airbee.

"I was captain first rank. Gyron Force."

That explained why he was still alive. Gyron Force was the elite of the elite for the Kirovarian armada and infantry. Less than one percent of one percent of their soldiers qualified to wear those uniforms.

"I'm Hauk."

"Bastien Cabarro." He licked at the blood on his lips as he narrowed his gaze on Hauk. "You really Sentella?"

Not sure why Bastien was asking, Hauk slid his hand toward his blaster again. Just in case. "Yeah."

"You guys really declare war on The League?"

Hauk relaxed a degree as he heard the hatred backing those words. "Definitely."

"Then can you get this fucking chip out of me?"

Hauk winced inwardly at the man's fate and his justified outrage over it. Ravins were the targets League cadets were assigned to kill for practice and rank. As Gyron Force, Bastien would be a most coveted prize by a cadet wanting to advance. He could only imagine how many had sought to take his life. It was a nightmare he wished on no one.

"Absolutely. How long have you been implanted?"

Bastien curled his lip. "Almost eight full *minsid* years."

Hauk let out a low whistle of appreciation that Bastien had lived so long. Average life span for a Ravin was six to eight weeks. Because they were tagged and hunted so viciously, they couldn't risk being in any civilian population. Relegated to hellholes like this one, many ended up taking their own lives just to stop their suffering. It was physically and psychologically grueling to be hunted like an animal.

"Damn long time to be on the run."

"What can I say? I'm a stubborn bastard, fueled by venom and vengeance." Sighing, Bastien finally relaxed as he approached Hauk. "So is that your family you're traveling with?"

This time, Hauk did draw his blaster and pinned it right between Bastien's eyes again. "What do you know of them?"

Bastien held his hands up. "Nothing. I saw your camp a few days ago. Being hunted, I make it a point to check out anyone who lands here. I figured you were on a hiking trip of some sort, so I left you alone and went away. Seems to be some kind of Andarion thing around here. But usually it's only two Andarions at a time and they leave after a few weeks. Though why you guys want to vacation here, I cannot imagine. You are one fucked-up species."

Snorting, Hauk holstered his blaster. If the man

only knew. . . . "Have you been *here* the whole eight years?"

"Most of them. Once I realized the magnetic field and radiation play havoc with tracking devices, I decided Shithole Central suited me fine enough."

Hauk snorted at that. "Doesn't seem to be playing with mine. They haven't had any problems tracking me."

"Ah . . . that's why they keep hitting you. Wondered about that." Bastien frowned. "So who wants *you* dead?"

"That's what I'm going to find out."

Crossing his arms over his chest, Bastien nodded. "I guess being Sentella, you have a lot of friends who want to play with you."

"Yeah, but I'd rather take my ball and go home."

Bastien laughed. "Why do I doubt that?"

"Probably because I'm about to take my ball and go shove it up the ass of whoever started this."

"Spoken like a true Andarion."

"Known a lot of us?"

"Just one. Nasty-tempered bastard, but damn good in a fight." He narrowed his gaze on Hauk. "Now that I think about it, he looks a lot like you."

"Yeah, well, we all look alike."

Bastien rolled his eyes. "Wouldn't know. He's the only Andarion I've been this close to, besides you. Come to think of it, his name's also Hauk. Only it's his last name."

Hauk narrowed his gaze on the ragged human. "Friend or foe?"

"Good friend, so if you plan to shit-talk him, you better be ready to draw again and shoot when you do so."

Hauk grinned at the man. If he, a human, knew a full-blooded Andarion named Hauk who looked like him, there was only one male it could possibly be. "I never shit-talk Fain behind his back. Only to his face. Otherwise, my brother would kick my ass."

Bastien went slack-jawed. His eyes registered recognition. "You Dancer?" he asked in total disbelief.

He inclined his head to him. "I'm Dancer."

"Well, I'll be damned. Small fucking universe. The way Fain talked about you, I thought you'd be the size and age of the kid you're with. Had no idea you were so close to his age and build." Bastien held his arm out to him. At a distance that let Hauk know he really was familiar with Andarions and their culture. "I owe Fain my life. You need a point or anchor, *any* time, I'm yours."

He shook his arm. "How do you know my brother?"

"He used to live in my neighborhood on Kirovar. We worked out at the same gym. I was the only one who'd spar with him. After awhile, we ended up as drinking buddies."

While it was true his brother had lived on Kirovar, this story didn't sound like Fain, who couldn't stand to be around people. Other than the drinking. For all he knew, Bastien was lying his ass off. "So you must know his first-mate Durden."

Grimacing, Bastien shook his head. "Never heard him mention a Durden. Didn't know he had *any* friends, to be honest. Not that he ever talked much, but when he did, you're the only one he ever really talked about."

Now that did sound like Fain. And he was right. Fain didn't branch out much. Omira had seen to that.

"So did I pass?" Bastien asked.

"Pass what?"

"Your test to see if I'm really a friend of Fain's. Not that I blame you. Don't trust strangers as a rule, either. But I do know Fain. I even know you have burn scars on your back from a childhood accident he blames himself for. And that his ex-wife was named Omira Antaxes."

Hauk studied Bastien carefully. They had to be tight for Fain to mention any of that to him. "He must have been drunker than hell to tell you that."

Bastien rubbed at his neck. "Yeah. It was on what would have been their tenth anniversary. He didn't handle it well. He even told me why they divorced, and I know that if I allow *anything* to happen to you, he'll hunt me down to the ends of the universe and gut me hard."

"That I believe he would." Hauk sat back as he started the airbee. "I'm headed up to bust ass. You joining or staying?"

Bastien grinned as he slung his leg over the airbee beside Hauk's. "Always ready for a good fight. Especially when a mighty War Hauk's involved." He powered on the engine. "And I'm harboring a serious hard-on for anyone who hunts others for a living. I'd much rather be the predator than the prey."

"Then welcome, brother." Hauk inclined his head to him before he gunned the accelerator. Though the signal from the radios was faint, he was able to trace it to the small skimmer shuttle they had docked a few ticks away.

Hauk landed the bike and turned it off.

Bastien pulled in beside him. Hauk removed the safeties and locks from his weapons while his new friend swung his dirty poncho over his shoulder and secured it so that the material wouldn't get in his way during the fight. Next, Bastien took inventory of his own weapons. Hauk secured his braids back from his face. He unwound his long brown scarf from around his neck so that he could cover his head and the lower part of his face. Then he pulled out a pair of opaque eye shields he normally used for climbing.

Now concealed, he took the container he'd scavenged from the assassins and waited for Bastien.

Once his new friend was ready, they crept toward the shuttle where four men waited for their comrades to return with Hauk's head.

"So what are you spending your money on?" a large, grimy man asked.

"Women," his muscular companion said with a snort. "Lots of women."

"Always looking for the next ex, eh?"

"Always."

Hauk met Bastien's gaze. "Cover me."

He scowled at him. "Want to fill me in on your plan?"

"Told you already. Bust ass." Hauk rose to his feet and walked calmly toward the group. A breeze stirred, whipping the end of his scarf out while he entered their camp.

Two of them rose with their hands on their blasters.

"Can we help you?" the largest one asked. From the way the others deferred to him, Hauk assumed he must be their leader. His was also the voice he'd heard on the link, asking for a status update.

Without a word, he tossed the container in his hand at the man. It landed at his feet, on its side.

"What's this?"

Hauk slid his gaze to each target in turn, noting where the men stood in relation to one another, and how best to take them down. "A gift."

Curious, he knelt and opened the bag, then cursed as he saw the assassin's head it contained. He scrambled for his blaster.

Hauk shot his three companions before closing the distance between them. He snatched the blaster from the man's hand and pulled it back as if he was going to hit him with the stock. "Who sent you," he ground out between clenched teeth.

"W-w-what?"

Dropping the blaster, Hauk grabbed his shirt and shook him hard. "Who. Sent. You?"

Bastien came in, weapon drawn to make sure there was no one else in hiding. "Damn, Hauk. You're a selfish bastard. I thought you were going to leave some for me."

Hauk ignored Bastien as he lowered the scarf to expose

his face. With one hand, he dragged the assassin, who was now kicking and screaming, toward the skimmer.

"I'm a Boldorian! My guild brothers will swarm all over you for this!"

Hauk snorted in contempt of the threat. "Let 'em take a fucking number. Now answer my question or I'm going to start eating pieces off your body, *human*." He pulled the knife from his belt and isolated the assassin's thumb, but not before his gaze fell to the man's forearm and a series of self-imposed marks that nauseated him even more than the man's stench. "We'll start with this, I think."

He screamed like a girl.

Grimacing, Bastien sucked his breath in audibly. "You know, friend, I'd tell the Andarion what he wants to know. They're not a patient race . . . and they're always, *always* hungry."

Sweat poured down the assassin's face as he gulped. "I-I-I don't know. I just have the ID code. That's all. I swear. You can see for yourself."

While Bastien kept the man covered, Hauk yanked the assassin's PD off his belt and turned it on. He cursed as he realized he didn't know the language it was written in.

"Cabarro? Can you read this?" He tossed it over.

Bastien took a second to look at it. "Yeah. It's the contract for your ass. Spill-kill. Bonus for your head. Damn, Hauk. If I could spend money, I'd be tempted to end you for this amount. Fain or no Fain."

Hauk shook his head, knowing Bastien wouldn't dare. "Does it say who wants me dead?"

"Nah. He's right. Just lists an anonymous ID for payment. If this armpit of the Nine Worlds had any reception, you might be able to backtrace it. But as it is . . ."

"See! I—" His words ended with a sharp blast to his chest.

Hauk stepped over his body.

Bastien handed him the PD. "You're one cold son of a bitch."

Hauk jerked the assassin's sleeve back to show the catalogue of kills he'd carved into his flesh as proud tribute for all the victims he'd made.

Half of them were for women and children.

"He deserved worse."

Bastien shot the body three more times.

Hauk arched a brow at his actions.

Shrugging, Bastien holstered his weapon. "He deserved worse."

"Spend a lot of time in the sun, do you?"

Bastien laughed as Hauk went inside the skimmer to see if there was anything he could use to get away from any others who might come for him.

Or better yet, if they could fly it out themselves. Unfortunately, it was low on fuel. And as he'd suspected, it was a preprogrammed skimmer used to take the assassins to and from their outer atmosphere spaceship. Which meant there were more of them waiting for this group to return. With time, he might be able to reprogram the skimmer for manual flight.

An alarm sounded.

Or not.

"What'd you do?" Bastien asked sardonically.

Sighing, Hauk shot the control panel that housed the signal. It went instantly silent. "Must have been wired to the mission leader's vitals. It's an alarm to the mother ship notifying the others that they're dead."

Bastien glared at the sky. "How many you think are up there?"

"Don't know. But they're down twenty-nine men."

"Survivors will be glad they don't have to split that wide a cut."

Hauk grunted. "Boldorians won't care about that. It's

now an honor quest for them to come get me. With reinforcements."

"Really?"

He nodded. "You scared yet?"

Bastien let out a false laugh. "I'm hunted by League assassins for fun and promotion, and you think these backwater pussies scare me? Really?"

Hauk clapped him on the back as a sign of brotherhood. "When we get that chip out of you, if you need a place, The Sentella's always looking for good people."

"I have some long overdue payback to shove up someone's ass first. After that? I just might accept your offer."

Hauk confiscated arms, ammunition, and a radio before pulling back. He paused long enough to check the tracking device's broadcast frequency.

"What are you doing?" Bastien asked with a frown.

"Reprogramming this to their frequency. They land, talk to each other, and I can peg them as fast as they peg me."

"You *are* Fain's brother."

"Taught him everything he knows."

Bastien arched a disbelieving brow.

Hauk grinned. "About electronics. He taught me fighting . . . usually by sitting on my ass until I got big enough to make it hurt when he tried."

"Ah." Bastien grabbed food and water. "So what's the plan now?"

"Pull back. Keep them after me and away from my family until reinforcements arrive." He pinned Bastien with a hard stare. "If I die, go out with a major body count."

"My kind of plan."

Hauk took a few minutes to siphon fuel from the two airbees on board the skimmer and add it to the ones they'd ridden in with.

"If you need a good defensive place to lead them to,

there's an old abandoned base not that far from here where I make my home."

"Bredeh's?"

Bastien furrowed his brow. "You know it?"

Hauk laughed at the bitter irony. "Yeah, I do. It's where I sent my family."

"Oh. Damn. Hope they don't find my porn."

Hauk arched a brow.

"I'm kidding. I have it all locked up."

Laughing again, he shook his head. "You have been alone far too long."

Bastien sobered. "Yeah, I have. It's good to be around people again."

"Not people, human."

"Not human, either, brother. Lost my humanity a long time ago when I got betrayed into this hell of a life." Bastien glanced back to where they'd left the majority of bodies. "The caves will give us some cover, but trap us in an attack."

"Yeah. We're in the middle of the great Oksanan desert. Not a lot here, period."

"Nothing but buzzards and raiders," Bastien agreed. "Look, I know you don't want to chance leading them to your family. But I'm thinking that we can use the old transmitter at the base to signal your girlfriend's transport back from the city."

Hauk went cold at those words. "What do you mean?"

"The blond who joined you? I couldn't really make out her features, but she came in locally, right?"

"You saw her arrive?"

Bastien nodded. "She was dropped off a little ways from your camp a few days ago. . . . You look like you had *no* idea."

That's because he hadn't. "What all did you see?"

Bastien shrugged nonchalantly. "It was a small transport. Looked like it came out of one of the cities here.

Didn't appear space-worthy. It lacked shielding and . . ." His voice trailed off as he met Hauk's gaze. "Why are you so pissed now?"

His breathing labored, Hauk felt sick. "Because I think I just handed kids off to my worst enemy."

And when he got his hands on Sumi, he was going to show her exactly what happened to people who ran afoul of an Andarion's wrath.

CHAPTER 16

"Can't we stop yet?" Darice whined as he intentionally dragged his feet in the sand.

Again.

And again Sumi shook her head. Even though it was late and she was exhausted herself, she didn't dare make camp right now. "We have to find someplace to sleep that's not out in the open."

"But I'm so tired."

"We all are, Darice," Thia snapped at him. "You're not alone in the misery. Now shut up already. You're only making it worse. For all of us."

Sumi yawned as she forced herself to continue on. That set off a round with the kids, who quickly followed her example, and made her long for their fierce protector to lead them to safety.

"I wish Dancer was here." Darice rubbed at his eyes. "He wouldn't be so mean to me."

Thia rolled her eyes. "Then why do you treat him so bad? Huh?"

"Because he makes me mad. I don't understand why he can't please my mom and make her accept him already."

When Thia opened her mouth to respond, Sumi shushed them. "Do you hear that?" she whispered.

Both Thia and Darice looked up with pale faces.

"Engines," they said in unison.

Sumi nodded. "We have to find cover. Run for the rocks." It was next to nothing, but it was better than being out in the open. Illyse rushed ahead to crouch down.

Pulling out her blaster, Sumi prepared to defend them as best she could.

They'd barely reached the rocks when two airbees came into view. She held her breath, hoping the riders wouldn't see them.

At first, she thought it was safe and they'd skim right by their location.

Until the airbees turned back.

Lining up the shot, Sumi was just about to fire on them when she recognized the black and brown Andarion desert clothes on the one rider. Hesitating, she looked through the scope to make sure she wasn't imagining things.

She wasn't. She'd know that massive, sexy male anywhere.

"Dancer," she breathed, lowering her weapon. She motioned for Thia and Darice to stay hidden with Illyse so that she could make sure he wasn't being forced to track them down. The rider with him could be anyone.

Friend or foe.

As soon as Dancer saw her, they landed the bikes.

Thank the gods he wasn't hurt. Weak with relief, she hadn't realized just how scared she'd been for him. How much his safety mattered to her.

Until he approached her with a stride that said he was out for her blood. This wasn't the Andarion who'd been so protective over the last few days.

This was the warrior who'd stormed a League prison and killed everyone who tried to stop him from saving the people he'd come to protect.

"What have you done with them?" he demanded in a deep, terrifying growl.

His furious tone stunned her and she wasn't quite sure what he was asking. "What? The kids?"

"Darice! Thia!" he shouted.

The moment they stood up, he ran straight to them and jerked them against his chest as if he'd been terrified for them. Her throat tightened at the sight of his protectiveness. He kissed each one on the head before he turned his angry glare back at her.

Why was he so furious? What had she done?

"What's going on, Uncle?" Thia asked. "Is everything all right?"

The rage on his face was tangible as he made sure to keep himself between her and the kids. "It is now." Hauk released them. He glanced over to Bastien, who was staring at Sumi as if viewing a ghost. "You two know each other?"

Sumi shook her head.

"Omira Hauk?" Bastien asked.

Hauk went cold. Those words definitely confirmed that Bastien knew Fain well enough to have seen the photo his brother kept of his ex-wife. And the panicked expression on Sumi's face told him she wasn't ignorant of that name, either.

Not by a long shot.

Just what the hell was going on?

Bastien scowled at Hauk. "What are you doing with your brother's ex-wife?"

Blood fire shot through him with a ferocity so raw, he wasn't sure how he kept from killing Sumi right where she stood. He'd put a lot of faith in a woman he barely knew.

And he was done with it.

Hauk gathered Thia and Darice and put them on the airbee he'd been riding. He locked gazes with Bastien. "Get them to the base. And you better not betray me."

Bastien scowled as if offended he would even suggest it. "I would *never.*"

"Good. 'Cause that blonde, whose ass you're ogling, happens to be the most precious and beloved daughter of Nemesis. And he has only one rule for dating her . . . don't."

The color washed straight out of Bastien's face. "Your father's Nemesis?" he asked Thia.

Thia sighed heavily. "On a good day, yes. On bad ones . . . let's just say you never want to be on the same planet with him."

Bastien locked gazes with Hauk. "Nothing, and I mean noth-thing, will happen to them."

"Good. Because if his daughter so much as stubs her toe on your watch, he will hunt you to the end of time, even if he has to come back from hell to do it."

"I don't take threats, Hauk. But this one . . . I consider a suggestion for my continued health and well-being. Thanks for the heads up." Clearing his throat, he inclined his head at Thia and Darice. "Follow me."

Hauk didn't move until they were gone. Only then did he turn back to Sumi. The fear in her eyes choked him, but he was through being her pawn. Through buying into whatever game she was playing.

He wanted answers and he was going to get them. Even if he had to kill her to get to the truth.

Sumi couldn't move as she saw the raw fury burning in those eerie Andarion eyes. *He's going to kill me.* She knew it. She could feel it with every part of her being.

It was just like facing Avin all over again.

But she refused to cower. It just wasn't in her. Ever defiant, she stood strong and waited for the coming storm his stance promised to bring.

Hauk paused in front of her. His massive size dwarfed her and made her feel small in comparison. "You are here to end me, aren't you?"

Sumi swallowed hard against the lump in her throat. "I'm not here to kill you. I was never sent here for that."

"Then why are you here? Really? Bastien told me he saw the transport you were in. The one that dropped you off so that you could reach my camp. You're not on the run. If you weren't sent here to kill me, then what do you want?"

Biting her lip, she blinked back tears as she saw the unadulterated hatred in his eyes. It shouldn't matter to her that he felt that way toward her.

But it did. Much more than it should have. It was like being kicked straight in the gut. She couldn't breathe as everything slammed into her. And she deeply regretted hurting him in any way.

Her thoughts whirling, she tried to decide what to say or do. What it would take to win back the trust that she'd shattered. Strange how her own life didn't matter to her anymore. Honestly, she couldn't remember the last time it had. Since the night she'd killed Avin while he was trying to murder her, there had been nothing left of it anyway. Just one unending nightmare in hell.

Maybe that was the way it should be. Maybe it was what she deserved for being so blind and stupid.

"Answer me!"

She jumped at the ferocity of his demand. "I know you hate me, Hauk. You have every right to. And I know you're going to protect what you love. It's what I've learned to expect from you." She pulled the knife from her sleeve sheath.

He stiffened, but didn't move as she approached him with it.

She flipped it in her hand and held it toward him, hilt first. "Take it."

He didn't budge. "Why?"

"So that you know I'm telling you the truth. Kyr sent

me here with orders to gain intel on you. To find something that would tie you to The Sentella and, more importantly, to the prison break on Brinear."

His eyes snapping fire, he took the knife from her hand.

"I found what he wanted," Sumi continued. "My first day here." She brushed at the tear that fled down her cheek. "It's in your pocket. I put it there when I kissed you so that I wouldn't be tempted to ever use it against you."

Hauk scowled at what she was telling him. Was it true? Did he dare believe a single word from her lying lips? "I don't understand."

She drew a ragged breath and the bitter pain in those hazel eyes made him ache for her. Though why he should feel such for an assassin who'd come to ruin him, he had no idea.

"My Kalea is all that matters to me. She doesn't deserve to grow up as a League soldier, in their brutal custody. Or worse, be trained as an assassin. You promised me you would save her. And I know Andarions stand by their oaths. Please don't back out on that, no matter your feelings toward me. I can face whatever Kyr does to me as punishment over failing this mission, so long as I know she'll be safe. I don't trust Kyr to keep his word and release her. I can't afford to be that stupid. But I do trust *you*, Dancer. I do."

Hauk narrowed his gaze as he heard the heart in her words. She definitely wasn't lying now.

And he would never see her innocent daughter harmed, but he had to know what she was talking about. "What evidence?"

She reached into his pocket and pulled out his small PD. Turning it on, she flipped to an old photo of him with his best friends. "Anyone who's seen footage of the five of you fighting in Sentella battlesuits can tell by this who makes up their High Command. You really should delete it."

He double-checked to make sure the file hadn't been copied or forwarded.

It hadn't.

"I don't understand."

Her hazel green eyes glistened with unshed tears. "As I said, I can't afford to trust Kyr. I know better. I've seen the cruelty he's capable of. What he relishes doing to others. He has no honor or decency. No love of anyone. And I'm not really sure I can trust you, but between the two of you, you seem the more honorable. I know how important family is to you. That you respect it and your oath, above all. Even when you shouldn't. Even when it's harmful to you." She swallowed hard. "Kill me if you must, if it'll make you feel better about your family's safety, but please save my little girl. She shouldn't have to pay for my mistakes."

Hauk wanted to hate her. He did. But for the first time, he understood Keris's insane addiction to drugs. That need to have the one thing you knew was lethal to your entire being. To put your life on the line to have one second of pleasure.

Sumi was his addiction. And he was willing to die to possess her.

Growling in his throat, he knew he should kill her where she stood. It would be the smartest thing to do. Yet he respected any mother who would offer up her own life to protect her child.

Anyone who could be that altruistic wasn't a monster. Like she said, Kyr wouldn't hesitate to cut his own family's throats if he thought it would advance his career.

Or make him feel better.

She still had a soul, and those damn tears weakened him even more as they fell unimpeded down her cheeks.

They made him feel like an ass for accusing her and making her sad. So what if she'd done it?

For some insane reason, none of that mattered.

And she was terrified of him now. There was no missing the fear in those hazel eyes as she stood bravely in front of him. Toe-to-toe. Waiting for her death at his hands.

Before he could stop himself, he offered the knife back to her.

She refused to take it. "There's something else you need to know about me."

His gut tightened even more at her dire tone. This he couldn't wait to hear. "What?"

"I'm Omira's younger sister."

His jaw went slack. Though to be honest, he'd suspected as much. Still, suspecting and hearing it confirmed were two vastly different things.

"Is that why you withheld your name when I asked?"

She nodded. "I knew you would hate me for it. And it's why Kyr assigned this to me. He knew I hated your brother, and thought my presence might unnerve you enough that you'd make a mistake he could use against you."

Now *that* he hadn't suspected from her. No one hated Fain. Not really. Even when he beat someone's ass, they eventually ended up liking him. "Why the hell would *you* hate my brother?"

"For what he did to my sister."

His scowled at her. What Fain had done to Omira? Really? Was Sumi insane?

She had to be. . . .

"What? Let the bitch live when he should have ripped her throat out?"

She shoved at him, but it didn't budge him. And that pissed her off. "Don't you dare insult my sister!"

He held his hands up in surrender as he continued to

stare at her with total stupefaction. "You and I obviously have two very different sides of this story. What do you think happened to their marriage?"

"Omira freaked out when she learned she was pregnant, and left him. She couldn't handle the fear of having a hybrid baby and being responsible for the hatred that would follow it all of its life."

Before he could stop himself, he laughed out loud at the most ridiculous lie he'd ever heard concocted. "Is that what she told you?"

"Yes," she said between clenched teeth.

He couldn't believe what a lying whore Omira had been. It disgusted him that she would tell such a myth to her family. "Do you know what Fain's wedding present was for your sister?"

She shook her head.

"He was sterilized."

Sumi froze at the last thing she'd expected to come out of his mouth. No. It wasn't possible. She couldn't breathe as she heard those three little words that carried a heavy significance. "What?"

"Yeah," Dancer said bitterly. "He knew going into the marriage how terrified she was of being pregnant by him. So, for her, he had a vasectomy before they ever slept together."

Her head spun over this little nugget. Omira had never said a word about *that* to her. "Are you sure?"

"Positive. I was the one who went with him for the surgery and I did my best to talk him out of it. He refused. The last thing he wanted was to hurt her. In any way. He told me that he didn't care about kids. That they could adopt later if she changed her mind."

No, no, no. None of this made sense. Dancer was wrong. He had to be.

There was no way Fain was sterile.

"But she was pregnant when she returned."

"Yeah," he breathed. "She was. By a *human* Fain almost beat to death when he came home early and found them in his bed together." Bitterness and hatred flared in his eyes. "Fain gave up his name. His family. His military rank and future. His fertility. And Omira paid him back by betraying him in a way no one should ever know."

Sumi sat down hard on the cold ground as those words hit her harder than a physical blow. Over and over, she played the events of Omira's return in her mind. Strangely, what Hauk said made sense.

Complete sense.

It explained why Omira had been so terrified. Why she'd locked herself in her room and had refused to come out for days. A month later, Omira had aborted the baby and told her that Fain had wanted the child while she didn't. That he would kill her if he learned what she'd done.

That had made sense to her at the time. But not Omira's continued fear after their divorce.

But this . . .

This answered a lot of questions Sumi had always had about it. And Dancer was right. It was a wonder Fain hadn't hunted her down for what she'd done to him.

Sumi would have.

She covered her lips with her hand as the true horror and tragedy of it all racked her. "How could she do that to him?"

"You're her sister. Ask *her*."

She looked up at him as tears fell down her cheeks. "I can't. She killed herself."

Hauk froze as those ragged words left her throat. He winced for all of them. Sumi, Omira, and Fain, who would be devastated by this news. Even though Omira had ripped out Fain's heart, he still loved her. Deeply. Still kept her ring and photo close at all times. He'd never gotten over her or her betrayal.

Before Hauk even realized what he was doing, he sank down and pulled Sumi into his arms. "I'm sorry, Sumi. I didn't know."

Sumi tried to hold back her sobs—as she'd done her whole life. But for some reason, they poured out of her and she couldn't stop them. Clinging to Hauk, she let her fear and grief run from the darkest corners of her soul where she kept them tightly leashed.

"I have no one in this world, Dancer. No one. I've been alone for so long. Omira and Fain were the only family I ever had. Fain promised he wouldn't leave me and he did. He never came back or called. He just left. And Omira was selfish, and a bitch at times. But she was all I had and she wasn't supposed to leave me, either. What is so wrong with me that no one wants to stay with me?"

Hauk clenched his eyes tight as he hated himself for insulting her sister to her. He had no right.

Well, he did. But he regretted hurting Sumi more.

"Shh, *kahrya mia*," he whispered while he rocked her. "You're not alone. There's nothing wrong with you."

She shook her head in denial. "P-please just promise me that you'll save my Kalea. I don't want her to grow up alone, like I did. To become what I am. She deserves so much better than this life."

He pressed his cheek against hers. "I swear on the blood of my ancestors that I will get her out of League custody and to a home where she's loved."

That made her cry even harder.

Shit. *What did I do?*

What was he supposed to do?

Andarion women didn't cry. Ever. They cursed. They insulted. They clawed. They attacked. That was what he was used to—covering his crotch, and letting them have at it until they were spent.

But this . . .

He was completely at a loss as to how to deal with her

tears. Worse was the pain they wrung inside him. He hurt for her. Literally. "Sumi, please. I don't know what to do to make this better."

She buried her hands in his hair and tightened her hold on him as she continued to sob as if the world was ending.

If that wasn't uncomfortable enough, his body was well aware of the fact that he held an incredibly beautiful woman in a most intimate embrace. That her hair smelled as sweet as spring flowers and that her breath fell against his neck, raising chills all over him.

His breathing ragged, he felt a burning hunger the likes of which he'd never known before. Gods, it was excruciating.

You're pledged.

Yeah, but that bitch didn't want him. Even if Dariana stood by her promise to see their unification met—which he seriously doubted—she had no intention of ever sharing a bed with him. She'd told him as much. *Don't even look at me. You make my flesh crawl, you hideous freak!*

And that had been one of his better encounters with Dariana. But Sumi didn't look at him like he was disgusting. He saw nothing but warmth and kindness in her eyes. Acceptance.

The kind he'd dreamed of having his whole life.

This is not the time for this. The woman's crying and upset.

But his body refused to listen. It was why Andarions didn't touch each other. Why they didn't dare. Because with that innocuous touch came a hunger so intense, it was hard to walk away from it.

Even when they knew they should.

Sumi looked up as she heard the change in Dancer's breathing. As she felt him swelling against her hip. The fervent hunger in his eyes seared her and it ignited the part of her that was already falling in love with the last being she could be with.

But neither her body nor her heart paid attention to her brain. How could they? Yes, he could be aggravating and terrifying, yet he was always gentle and concerned. Caring. And he would die to protect what he loved. He wasn't threatened by her abilities. He appreciated even her strange bossy quirks.

How could any woman not fall for such a male?

Wanting him with a desperation that bordered on madness, she lifted her lips to his and kissed him with all the emotions that were at war inside her.

He fisted his hands in her poncho as he pressed her tight to his chest and deepened their kiss. Heat poured through her. Unable to let him go, she slowly undid his shirt until she could touch that wealth of hard muscled flesh that was scarred by a past that made her own seem tepid.

Hauk gasped as he felt her warm hands on his skin. He shivered at the sensation of finally being touched by someone who wasn't trying to hurt or kill him. And when she moved from his lips to his throat to lave his skin, he thought he'd lose complete control of himself and come immediately. His entire being simmered with heat.

Even better, she didn't recoil in revulsion of his scars. Her lips didn't curl from disgust. There was nothing in her eyes but desire and hunger. She didn't see him as unworthy or lacking.

She saw *him*.

No female had ever given him such a gift. In her arms, he felt worthy and whole. There was no judgement. No bitter past that made her hate him. It was just the two of them.

And she wanted him.

Throwing his head back, he roared as unimaginable pleasure consumed him.

Sumi hesitated at a sound the likes of which she'd never

heard before. It was a wild, primal cry that quickly reminded her he wasn't human.

Something driven home when he looked at her and she realized his eyes were now completely red. The color of blood. More than that, they glowed in the darkness.

Was he still him or did Andarions morph into something else whenever they had sex?

"Dancer?"

He answered her with a tender, sweet kiss that belied the ferocity of that cry. Rising up on his knees, he held her against him with an ease that was even more terrifying than those glowing eyes. Yet his touch remained gentle. He left her lips so that he could nuzzle his face against the crook of her neck. Ever so tenderly, he scraped his fangs against her collarbone.

"Touch me, Sumi, please," he whispered in ragged need before he ran his tongue over her ear.

She wasn't sure what he meant until he led her hand to the bulge in his pants.

Hauk ground his teeth as she cupped and squeezed him in her tiny, delicate hand. All his life, he'd wondered what it would be like to have a female touch him intimately like this.

Now he finally knew.

It was sweeter than any dream he'd dared allow himself. Unlike his callused hand, hers was gentle and questing. It gave him nothing but bliss. And when she dipped her soft hand into his pants to touch his cock, he had to fight to hold himself back as he panted with desire for her. For a full minute, he couldn't see straight as she boldly stroked him and made him even harder. His body was both hot and cold. Fevered and chilled. He'd never known anything like this before. Every part of him was alive and far more sensitive than normal.

It was similar to what he felt in a good fight, and yet so much more intense.

So much sweeter.

Sumi smiled at the look on his face as he watched her while she ran her hand from the tip of his cock down the length of it to cup him in her hand. "I think you like this."

Biting his lip, he nodded bashfully. He lifted his head and pinned her with a needful stare that wrenched her heart. But not nearly as much as the next words out of his mouth. "Will you grant me the honor of touching you?"

It was only then she realized that he had yet to move his arms from around her body. She'd forgotten what Thia had told her about Andarions. That they had to be granted the right to touch their partners.

"I'm all yours, Dancer. I grant you full rights to my body."

Still, he hesitated as if a part of him was afraid she'd change her mind. Smiling, she pulled her poncho off and opened her shirt for him. Then she took his hand in hers and led it to her breast.

Hauk swallowed at how incredibly soft her skin was. How flawless. Amazed, he skimmed his fingers over the paleness of her large, full breast until he brushed his hand against her taut nipple. His throat went instantly dry. Dying for a taste, he dipped his head hesitantly, waiting for her to stab him for it, or slap him.

But she didn't. Instead, she cupped his cheeks in her gentle hands as he suckled the sweetness of her skin and breathed her scent in. Wanting to bathe in that precious scent, he nuzzled his face between her breasts while her hands played in his hair.

In the back of his mind was his common sense that told him he would pay for this with his life. But honestly, he didn't care.

He would die anyway, from something, eventually. And he could think of no better reason for it than being with Sumi.

Just once, he wanted to lie with someone who didn't look at him like he was a piece of shit. Someone whose touch was loving and sweet. Kind. Gentle.

If he had to die to have it, so be it. It was worth it.

No, *she* was worth it.

When he brushed his goatee over her nipple, she jumped and laughed.

"It tickles," she said, smiling at him. She ran her fingers along the arch of his brow.

Closing his eyes, he savored her touch before he reclaimed her mouth for another kiss. Sumi nipped at his lips then she pulled back and stood in front of him. He wasn't sure what to expect until she toed off her boots then slowly undid her pants.

He couldn't breathe as she slid them down her legs, baring herself completely to him. She was even more beautiful than he'd imagined.

Every part of her.

Sumi smiled at the famished look on his face as he stared up at her. He still hadn't moved. It was as if he feared doing anything to offend her.

Cupping his face, she straddled his legs and sat down on his lap. Then ever so slowly, she removed his shirt before she pressed herself flush to his chest.

He ran his hands down her back until he cupped her buttocks. His fingers dipped and probed, making her even hotter and wetter. Unable to stand it, she opened his pants wider and slid herself onto him.

Hauk shook all over as she sheathed him fully with her body, all the way to his hilt. Then ever so slowly, she began to ride him while she stared down into his eyes with a fevered passion that matched his own. He sucked his breath in sharply as the most unimaginable pleasure racked his entire being. All the times he'd tried to imagine this . . .

Yeah, he was an idiot. No wonder the guys had all laughed at him whenever he'd downplayed the pleasures of sex.

They were right. For this, he'd forgo anything.

Everything.

There was nothing he wouldn't do for the mere touch of Sumi's hand against his skin.

Even die.

Right then, she could ask him for the entire universe and he'd gladly give it to her. Damn it. He was hers and he knew it with every part of his being. She owned him. Completely.

And he would have it no other way.

Sumi couldn't get over the color of Dancer's eyes as he watched her make love to him. This was something her sister had never told her about Andarions. And it thrilled her that she was the first one who'd done this to Dancer.

No other female had ever touched this part of him. No one had made his eyes glow. And as she rode him, she noticed something else different about Andarion males. He was growing larger inside her.

"Dancer?"

He bit his lip before he answered. "It's all right, Sumi. We do that."

"Get bigger?"

He nodded. "I won't hurt you."

It definitely didn't hurt. Rather, it was incredible. He lifted his hips and drove himself even deeper into her body as he quickened their strokes. Breathless, she cupped his face in her hands and kissed him.

In a white-hot blinding wave of pleasure, she came. Crying out, she panted as she reveled in the warmth of him inside her body and surrounding her.

Hauk watched as Sumi bit her lip and spasmed around

him. A beautiful smile lit her entire face. She licked her lips and continued to ride him with the sweetest of rhythms.

Gods, it felt so good.

Relieved he'd pleased her, he finally let go and surrendered himself to his own release. He shook all over from the ferocity of it. Never had he felt the likes of this. It just didn't compare to what he'd known on his own.

His jaw quivering, he laid his head between her lush, pale breasts. Weak and spent, he cradled her against him.

"That was incredible," she breathed in his ear.

He smiled. "Yes, you were."

Sumi watched as his eyes slowly faded back to their normal color. "Did you know your eyes glow red when you're aroused?"

He pulled back with a frown—as if her words greatly concerned him. "What?"

She nodded. "They were as red as they could be the entire time you made love to me. Is that normal?"

"I guess . . . you broke me."

She made a face at him. "I broke you?"

"Maybe?"

Sumi rolled her eyes at his uncertainty. "Do all Andarion males do that?"

He snorted at her question. "I don't know. I've never slept with a male."

She playfully tugged at his hair. "You know what I mean. Don't Andarions talk about it? Have Andarion porn videos and such?"

Tracing the line of her lips, he shook his head. "We're not human, Sumi. Sex is a very sacred thing for us. It's a sharing of ourselves. Whenever you engage in it, you run the risk of combining bloodlines. We don't undertake that lightly. Our ancestry defines us. Binds us. While there are Andarions who rut like animals, they're scorned by the rest of us. And are usually blocked from unification."

"And yet you slept with me. Why?"

He sighed heavily. "I don't know."

Offended to the core of her being, she gasped. "You don't know? What do you mean, *you don't know*?"

Hauk hissed as she rose up from him and practically tore the skin off the most delicate part of his body. "Ow!"

She broke off into a language he didn't know as she yanked her clothes back on.

He reached to her. "Sumi . . ."

She jerked out of his reach. "Don't you dare take that tone to me now! How dare you!"

Rising to his feet, he pulled her to a stop. "Don't be angry at me. Do you not understand what I just did?"

She raked him with a scathing glare. "Yeah. You just acted like a typical *man*!"

"No, *mia*. To lie with you, I've condemned myself to death."

CHAPTER 17

Sumi froze in the middle of dressing to stare at him as a horrid fear went through her. "They won't *actually* kill you for this. Will they?"

There was no missing the sincerity in his gaze. "While another female might not, Dariana will certainly demand my life for it when she finds out."

She straightened to frown at him. "Then don't tell her."

"It's not that simple. I have no choice. To lie under Disclosure is also a death sentence."

"They'll never know. I won't tell."

His gaze sad, he sank his hands into her hair and held her in the tenderest of embraces. "Then I would damn my soul for the lie. I'm not a coward, Sumi. I knew what I was giving up for this moment with you. And I have no regrets . . . except for the part where I made you mad. I didn't mean to do that."

Tears choked her. "Then run with me, Dancer."

"What?" he asked in confusion.

"I'm serious. We can get Thia and Darice back to their parents and leave. I'm not my sister. I'm not afraid of having your children, and I would *never* betray my husband's trust. There is nothing more I would love than to hold your baby in my arms."

"Oh, *mia*," he breathed. "Nothing would give me greater pleasure than to be with you, but we can't. You are Omira's sister. If Fain ever sees you, the pain of his past would destroy him. I could never buy my happiness at the expense of my brother's agony." He pulled her against him and dipped his head down to rest it on her shoulder. "I will get your daughter back for you and see to it that you're both outside of Kyr's reach. But I can't run with you, Sumi. I can't do that to my family. My mother would never forgive me for dishonoring her."

She scoffed at his words. "Are you telling me that your mother would rather have you dead?"

"Yes. She would."

"Dancer," she chided, "I promise you, no mother would rather lose her child."

Lifting his head, he traced the line of her jaw with his thumb while a sad smile played at the edges of his lips. "That's *you* speaking. You don't know my mother. I promise you, she would much rather see me dead than be dishonored."

"Then tell them I raped you."

He arched an amused brow at that.

"I could have drugged you first. I did kiss you without your consent."

"And my lips thank you for that."

She hated that charming tone most of all. "This isn't funny."

"No. It's not." He picked her hand up and placed it against his heart that beat a fierce rhythm under her palm. His gaze burned into hers as he spoke in that deep, lilting accent that meant everything to her. "For one touch of your precious hand, I gladly consign myself to death."

She wanted to hate him for that. But how could she? No one had ever made her feel like this.

Cherished and beautiful. Like she mattered.

That was why she couldn't let him go.

"I will find a way to save you, Dancer. Mark my words."

"Then I wish you luck. Because honestly, I don't want to die. I would rather spend the rest of my life inside you, and making you smile."

It was only then she realized he was growing hard again and his eyes were starting to turn red. Blushing, she looked down at him.

He snorted and laughed. "It appears what they say is true."

"And that is?"

"Once an Andarion has tasted the flesh of another, we're insatiable." He dipped his head to gently lave and nuzzle her neck.

"What are you doing, Dancer?"

"They can only kill me once." He pulled her shirt off, over her head. Then he removed his boots and pants.

Her throat went dry at the sight of him fully naked. But the last thing she wanted was to add another scar or injury to him. "What about the men tracking you?"

His eyes were really glowing red now—even more luminescent than before. He wrapped her hair around his hand then brushed it against his face. "We have Illyse to warn us. And if they dare interrupt me right now, they'll wish to whatever god they worship that they'd been more considerate."

Sumi started to protest, but her mind went blank as he entered her again and found the perfect rhythm for her body.

Sumi came awake to the warm, luscious scent of Dancer's skin under her cheek. Sighing contentedly, she opened her eyes to find herself still cradled in the shelter of his arms. She ran her nail over his nipple, making it pucker instantly as chills spread over his chest.

He sucked his breath in sharply. "Keep doing that, *mia*, and we'll never make it to the base."

She kissed his chest. "What does *mia* mean again?"

"Little mouse."

Cocking her head, she pinned him with a suspicious glare. "You're sure that's not an insult?"

He gave her a playful pout. "Why would I insult you, *munatara*? You're one of the bravest females I've ever known."

"You keep sweet-talking me like that, War Hauk, and you might get lucky."

A slow smile curved his lips before he gave her a gentle kiss. His eyes glowing, he rolled her over, taking care not to put too much weight on her body. The one thing they'd discovered last night was exactly how heavy he really was. He could easily squash her with that heavy Andarion frame. He seriously weighed a ton.

But she didn't mind it in the least. If she had to die, she could think of no better way to go than in his arms.

She groaned in ecstasy as he entered her again and stared down at her with those glowing, beautiful eyes. "How can you still be *this* aroused?"

He thrust against her hips in a slow, steady rhythm that sent waves of pleasure through her. "Do you want me to stop?"

"Hardly." She bit her lip as she met him stroke for stroke. "No wonder Andarions keep such a tight leash on themselves. Otherwise you'd never leave your bedrooms."

He laughed harder at that than what was warranted.

"What's that about?"

He cupped her chin and kissed her. "Last year, when Darling had himself wired with explosives, and was ready to blow himself and half his capital city to hell, Caillen and Nyk said that all we needed to do to redirect him from vengeance was get him laid. I scoffed at them for the suggestion, and they laughed at my stupidity. As much as I hate to admit those bastards were right. They're right. I understand completely now. There is nothing sweeter than being inside you, *mu tara*. I would gladly give up any quest to stay here with you, like this."

She ran her hand over his prickly cheek as he thrust faster against her hips. "I meant what I said, Dancer. I would gladly carry your lineage forward."

"As would I with you. But the gods won't grant us that and we both know it."

Tears choked her as she wrapped her legs around his hips and wished she'd met him in a different time and place. If Fain was half the male and lover Dancer was, how could Omira have ever betrayed him with another? How could her sister have held so much in her hand and then callously thrown it all away?

Was she out of her mind?

"*Mia?*" He paused to wipe the tears from her cheeks. "Am I hurting you?"

She shook her head. "It's the future that hurts me."

"Don't think about it. Just look into my eyes and know that you hold a place inside me no one else has ever touched. It's reserved solely for you."

That made her cry harder.

Hauk let out a breath of heart-wrenching frustration.

She buried her hands in his hair and held him against her. "It's not you, baby. I'm a woman. Not an Andarion female. I have a hard time keeping tender emotions bottled inside me sometimes. The mere thought of losing you now . . ." She teased his lips with hers as she rolled him over so that she straddled him. "It's not fair that I've waited my whole life for you and now that I've finally found you, I have to let you go."

Hauk growled as she took control of their pleasure. If he could, he would stop time so that they'd never have to leave this place. How ironic really that in this desert that had destroyed his life when it'd taken Keris's, it had given him a new one with Sumi.

Only this one couldn't last and he knew it. All too

soon, he'd have to let her go and return for a death sentence.

How can I let her go?

But like he'd told Sumi, he didn't want to think about the future. He only wanted to live right here and now where it was just the two of them.

Two souls bound by something far deeper than just the physical.

She tensed ever so slightly. Smiling, he knew she was on the brink of coming for him. An instant later, she threw her head back and cried out.

Grateful he pleased her, Hauk ran his hands over her breasts as he watched the ecstasy play across her face. He loved the sight of her doing that. Of her finding pleasure in his touch and body. It made him insanely possessive of her. Protective. He never wanted her to look like this for any other male. Never wanted anyone to have this part of her.

She was his.

Grinding his teeth, he lifted his hips and buried himself deep inside her as he joined her release.

Like a seductive lorina, she draped herself over his chest and sighed contentedly while she ran her hand over the scars his mother had given him so long ago. Strange how they no longer mattered to him. Unlike an Andarion female, Sumi didn't mind his scars.

Only his fresh wounds and bruises. She'd spent hours last night, kissing and bandaging them. And he'd done the same for hers.

He closed his eyes and savored the warmth of her flesh against his. "We should probably wash and head for the base."

"Mmm."

"Sumi?"

"I heard you. I just want a minute more alone with you, like this."

He wanted a lot more than a mere minute. What he craved was a lifetime spent in her arms.

But that could never be and he knew it. So he held her for as long as he dared, then he picked her up and carried her to the small stream so that they could bathe.

When he went to dress, Sumi's light laughter made him pause. "What?"

She pressed her lips together into an adorable expression. "Since the moment I woke up in your tent, I've wanted to climb up that long, hard body of yours and do a pole dance. I was just thinking how glad I am that I finally had the chance to do it."

He blushed. "I don't know about that. You looked pretty scared to me when you woke up in my tent."

"Oh, I was a *lot* scared." She left the water to approach him slowly.

His breath caught at the sight of her naked body glistening in the morning light as she neared him. She was lithe and well muscled. Sculpted and sweet. And his mouth watered to taste more of her. But the sight of her battle scars and injuries made him want to hunt Kyr down, and beat him until he was hoarse from begging for mercy.

She raked a hungry smile over him. "Not quite as scared as I was last night when I saw the look on your face, but—"

"I'm sorry about that."

She shook her head. "Don't be. You had every right to want me dead. I should never have agreed to come here to hurt you."

"You weren't exactly given a choice. I know Kyr. The words *if it please Your Majesty* never leave his lips. Even when he's addressing royalty."

"Still—"

He stopped her words with a kiss. "Fain taught me early in my life to listen with my eyes and not my ears."

"I don't understand."

"Lips and tongues lie. But actions never do. No matter what words are spoken, actions betray the truth of everyone's heart. And your actions gave me no reason to doubt you. You've been honorable since I met you. That's what I should have put my faith in."

Sumi stared up at him in wonder. He was so gorgeous, even with those strange eyes that were fast becoming normal to her. She fingered his goatee, then mustache. "It's amazing to me how a race that is known for its rowdy brutality can hold such poetry and beauty."

That handsome lopsided grin of his made her stomach flutter. "We are a fierce breed."

"And the Warring Blood Clan of Hauk are the fiercest of all."

"That we are, *mu mia*." He let go of her to finish dressing.

Sumi bit her lip as he bent over to retrieve his pants. That male had the nicest butt she'd ever seen on any being. And all that lush, rippling flesh . . .

Damn.

Just damn. Sighing, she turned to dress and tried not to think about how much she wanted to go take another bite out of him.

Hauk paused with a frown as he pulled his shirt on. There was such a strange serenity to him now. For the first time in his life, he was at peace and he didn't know why. He was absolutely calm.

The bitter rage that had lived inside him and driven him to war for so long was quelled and silent. Sumi had lit a joy within him the likes of which he'd never known. His heart was light and all he wanted to do was make her smile. To give her the same happiness she gave him.

She hesitated as she caught him staring at her. "What?"

He grinned. "What, what?"

A thousand expressions, all adorable, played across her beautiful face. "Why are you staring at me like that?"

"I don't know what you're talking about." He gently pulled her against him and ran his hands through her pale hair before he braided it for her.

She tilted her head back to look up at him. "What are you doing?"

"Giving you the hair of an Andarion warrior."

Sumi furrowed her brow. It was such a strange thing for him to do. And again, it seemed incongruous that a male so fierce would play like this in a woman's hair. "Is that why League assassins braid their hair? Because they were founded by an Andarion?"

He continued to brush his hands through her hair and plait it. "Not just any Andarion, *mia*. The first Keris of the Warring Blood Clan of Hauk. Back then, an Andarion warrior had to earn the right to grow his or her hair long. It was kept short until Endurance. Then it was allowed to grow, but only so long as you were undefeated in battle. And no one ever defeated Keris. So when he started The League to fight against the human tyrant, all The League soldiers wore their hair long and braided to pay honor to him."

It made sense, and she'd wondered why assassins did that. Now she knew. "So why don't Andarions still wear their hair braided down their backs?"

"Too many humans took up the style."

"I'm serious, Dancer."

"As am I. We have a fierce loyalty to our homeworld that is only matched by the Phrixians. When so many offworlders began adopting our style, we changed it to the many shorter braids we now wear." He pulled a leather tie from his bracer and used it to secure her hair.

Then, he stooped down and dipped two of his fingers into the dark soil. Smiling at her, he drew a pattern around her eye and down her cheek and jawline. "Now you look like the fierce warrior you are, *munatara*." He placed a tender kiss to her other cheek before he moved away and gathered their things.

Curious, Sumi went to the water to see the beautiful swirling shape he'd drawn. "What does this signify, Dancer?"

He didn't answer as he slung the pack over his back and secured it. "We need to hurry to catch up to the others. Once I see you safely to them and make certain they were able to contact Nyk, I'll take one of the airbees and lead the assassins away from you."

She started to repeat her question, until her gaze fell to the Andarion short sword he'd put across his back. There on the hilt, emblazoned in gold, was the same symbol he'd drawn on her face. It was identical to what was also stamped into his bracers. They were the swirling wings of a hawk. In that moment, she knew what he wouldn't say.

He'd marked her as his.

Listen with your eyes. . . .

Tears choked her. Quickening her steps, she caught up to his long strides and took his hand. He gave a light squeeze before he called for Illyse to follow them. Hand in hand, they walked while she tried to learn some Andarion. Which proved to be an extremely complicated language. It dripped like a song from his lips with that deep, resonating voice of his.

But her human tongue stumbled over all the vowels and diphthongs.

When they stopped a few hours later to rest and feed Illyse, she saw the blood running down Dancer's leg.

"How can you walk on that without complaint?"

He glanced down and brushed at the blood then shrugged. "It's not so bad."

Rolling her eyes, she opened the pack and took out an antiseptic cloth. "I swear Andarions must have different pain receptors than humans." She pulled his pants leg up to see that it was starting to fester. She grimaced. "This is looking bad, sweetie."

He moved his leg so that he could see it. Then he made an adorable face at the wound. "I'll be fine."

She shook her head at his nonchalance then did her best to clean and rebandage it. "What would Syn say if he were here?"

"That I'm an idiot."

His unexpected dry retort made her laugh. "Does he call you that a lot?"

"A good bit of the time."

"And you're okay with that?"

"I call him worse things."

Sumi tried to imagine having friends like that. She'd never had many, and Avin had chased off the handful of people she'd once hung out with from work. In her mind, she'd already made up personalities for the men and women she'd seen in Dancer's module. Too bad she'd never know if they were accurate or not.

Unwilling to think about the future that awaited them, she gave him a light kiss. "All done."

Without complaint, he stood, then pulled her into his arms with her back to his chest. He wrapped his arms around her and buried his face in her neck. She could feel him growing hard against her hip.

Hauk closed his eyes and savored the sensation of holding her like this. It was a very human thing to do. Andarions didn't really touch in public.

Unless they were fighting, they were very circumspect.

And it made him wonder how Keris and Dariana had ever managed to be wingmen together. How they'd had a marriage without children.

All he wanted was to strip Sumi's clothes off and spend the rest of the day inside her. To hell with everything else in the universe.

If they were married . . .

Hauk tensed as he remembered a flashback from his childhood.

"Are you okay?"

He tried to call back what his mind was trying to tell him. But it was gone as fast as it'd come. Straightening, he released her and wiped his forearm across his face. "Yeah, I'm just . . . confused."

"By?"

"Nothing. It was a fleeting thought that left no impression." He picked up their pack and took her hand. Yet as they continued on, he couldn't stop his thoughts from pondering that one question—

Given as long as Keris and Dariana had been together, how had they managed to stay childless?

As they neared Aksel's old base, Hauk pulled Sumi to a stop. He had a bad, bad feeling in his gut. Something wasn't right.

"Dancer?"

Instead of answering, he turned a small circle and scanned the desert around them. There was nothing there.

Still the feeling persisted.

Sumi buried her hands in his hair and forced him to look at her. "You're scaring me. What's going on inside your head?"

He gave her a dry stare. "You don't scare."

"I do on occasion. Now, what is it?"

"Just the ghosts of the past haunting me." He glanced back to the base, a shoddy, broken-down husk of what it'd been the last time he'd seen it.

A lot had changed in eight years. Then, Kiara had been kidnapped by Aksel and brought here to die. Nykyrian had come on a suicide run to save her life. Hauk's mission had been to secure Kiara at any cost while Nyk played decoy for Aksel and his men.

Even now, he could see the anguished look on

Nykyrian's face right before they'd left to come here. *"If I don't get the chance, tell her I love her, that I've always loved her, and that I couldn't have been more thrilled about the baby."* Nykyrian's heartfelt words still ran a chill up his spine. His best friend had given him one hell of a bad day back then. He still owed Nyk a beating for that.

But this was an entirely different time. It was an entirely different enemy breathing down his neck, trying to kill him. One whose face and name he didn't know.

Shrugging the feeling away, he took Sumi's hand and led her toward the dilapidated building.

They'd only taken three steps when Sumi pulled him to a stop. He glanced at her with a frown.

She dropped and tugged at his arm for him to do the same. He obeyed without question.

Sumi narrowed her gaze on the shadow that stood in the doorway of the base. Wanting a better vantage point, she crawled along the ground to a small rise. She pulled her rifle from Hauk's shoulder and used the scope to survey the building.

"We have a problem," she whispered, handing the rifle for Hauk to use.

He looked through the scope, then cursed under his breath as he saw what had alarmed her.

"Incas?"

He shook his head. "Boldorians."

"How do you know?"

"The sheer number of them. Incas travel in smaller groups and they don't set traps. They're cowardly raiders."

"All right. . . . Let me get a closer look. See what I can recon."

He grabbed her arm as she started away. "I'll do it."

She smiled at his offer and patted his arm. "You're too big to hide, sweetie. You know that. This requires someone who can actually vanish into a shadow . . . not cast a big one."

"Sumi . . ."

She looked back at him expectantly.

Hauk hesitated as he stared into those hazel eyes that seared him. Funny, eight years ago, he'd thought Nykyrian was an idiot for not telling Kiara himself what he wanted her to know. For wasting their time together in silence.

Now he understood. It was hard to let someone that deep into your life. To admit out loud to them that they, alone, held a place inside you where only they could destroy you. And Sumi definitely held his heart and soul in her delicate hands. One harsh look or word from her lips could break him even worse than any enemy assault.

Just say it.

Tell her.

The words choked him. *You're not a coward.*

"I'll be right back."

Before he could speak, she was gone. Hauk couldn't breathe as he realized he'd let her go without telling her to be safe. And every minute that ticked by was sheer torture for him as he imagined all manner of atrocities befalling her.

Please come back.

If anyone harmed her, he would tear them apart and relish doing it. No one better lay a single finger on her body. They better not even cast an evil glare in her direction.

Desperate pain swelled inside him as his mind tortured him with horrid possibilities. The Andarion in him wanted to storm the complex right now, and burn it to the ground.

But the saner part of himself knew that if he did that, the Boldorians would kill every being he loved in that building before he got through the door.

She's a trained assassin, not a civ. Give her time for recon.

That was a lot easier said than done. He hated not

having an earwig to stay in touch with her. To not know what was going on.

Screw this shit. . . .

He was just about to go in anyway when he felt a hand on his leg. Rolling, he intended to cut his attacker's throat.

Until he looked into a pair of loving hazel eyes. He grabbed her into his arms and held her tight against him.

"Can't. Breathe."

He loosened his hold. A little.

Sumi laid her head down on his chest and smiled as warmth filled her. He might not say she was important to him, but this hug told her just how worried he'd been. "Still can't breathe."

He finally released her. "What did you find out?"

"It's uglier than hell. Definitely *your* kind of place. Filled with undesirables, who have way too much training and ammunition . . . and not enough soap." She handed him a small knapsack.

His jaw went slack as he opened it to find a bevy of electronics. "How'd you get this?"

She winked at him. "Assassin, remember? Took out two of their burliest in the back. Hope they weren't anyone's girlfriend. Anyway, that's what they had on them. I couldn't even begin to get a body count. There's at least twenty on the first floor. Sounded like more upstairs. They are trained. They are savage. And they're loaded for Andarion."

"You're right. Sounds like my kind of party. Let's fall back and plan the festivities."

"Yes, sir. Captain, sir. On your six, sir."

Hauk scowled at her use of a rank no one had called him by in years. It sounded so strange and yet, he adored the teasing light in her eyes. Before he could stop himself, he kissed her lips again, then crawled away from their spot to a safe area where they could tie up Illyse, and make plans.

Sumi followed Dancer back to the cliffs. They found a small cubby to use for cover. She sat quietly as he ran over the layout of the facility.

"No doubt they'd have them in or around Aksel's old office." He showed her where that would be on the second floor of the diagram he'd drawn on his e-tab.

"How long ago was your strike?"

"Eight years."

She widened her eyes. "Are you sure about the locations?"

"Yeah. I have scary recall for floor plans. It's why Darling and I work as a team. He can't remember shite without a diagram of it in front of his face."

But what really impressed her was the fact that even though he had a *ton* more experience with strikes and planning such events, he still listened to her suggestions and advice. Nor did he get angry or defensive when she asked questions such as the one about his recall. It said a lot about him that he didn't let his ego get in the way. He treated her like a partner.

And that meant everything to her. No one had ever held her opinions with much regard.

Sighing, he turned the tablet around. "There was a munitions dump here when Aksel ran the place. I'm thinking if it's still stocked and we raid it, it'll give us a lot of firepower."

"That's a *big* if."

"I know." He rubbed his thumb thoughtfully against his goatee.

"But I like the idea of making a timer to cut the power. What if we go in a standard League two-assassin team and take them out systematically? We can grab weapons as we find them. What do you think?"

Dancer considered it. "Another big if. We won't know the capacity of the weapons they're using or their charge levels. Been there, got my ass flambéed. Not looking for a repeat. However . . . I like your idea best, so far. We can combine that with the strikes I make with Darling. You said you saw the raid on the prison?"

She nodded. "But . . . you two were a little on the brazen side when you did that. And we don't have a Sentella-Tavali army backing us."

"Yeah, well, Darling and I aren't normally *that* suicidal. He was a little bended by the fact he thought they'd killed his wife, and he was out for blood vengeance. But that being said, our normal mode of attack is a subtler version. If you've studied my moves, then you'll know what I need for anchor."

"You're taking point?"

"Yeah. I know the layout."

Sumi hesitated. Point was the most dangerous position. It would leave him completely exposed.

Dancer met her gaze. "It makes the most sense. I draw. You sweep."

Tears filled her eyes. "I'm not sure I can let you do that."

Hauk froze as he heard the most precious words in the universe. While he loved his friends, they'd never been that reticent to put his ass on the line for a mission. "We do our part. We all go home."

Her lips quivered. "You better. I won't forgive you if you die on me."

He pulled her against him and held her tight. "I'm not going anywhere, *mia*. I have a promise to keep for you."

Her hot tears fell against his skin as she kept her arms wrapped around his neck. "I love you, Dancer," she whispered. "I really do. And I've never said that to anyone. Not even Kalea's father."

For a full minute, he couldn't speak as his heart shattered and was left jagged and bleeding by those words. There had been a time once when he'd dreamed of hearing a female say that to him. But that dream had died along with Keris.

Now . . .

He couldn't believe he'd actually found someone who could tolerate him.

"I love you, too, *munatara a la frah.*"

Sumi pulled back to stare up at him. She couldn't believe what she'd heard. Not until she saw the truth in his eyes. No one had ever looked at her like that.

Like she was the air he breathed.

"I am not going to let Dariana have you, Dancer. If I have to cut her fucking throat to keep you safe, I will. And I will relish her blood flowing over my hands."

A smile spread across his face, exposing his fangs. "Spoken like a true Andarion warrior." He lifted her hand to his lips and brushed a tender kiss across her palm. "I am, and will always be yours and yours alone, Sumi." He pressed his cheek to hers before he stepped away.

Fear for him ripped her apart as she watched him prepare for their attack. But she knew she'd have to let that go. In the coming hours, she couldn't allow any emotion to cloud her judgments or make her hesitate.

This was about battle, and Dancer needed an assassin at his back. Not an emotional woman distracting him.

They removed all color from their bodies except for the black and brown that would help hide them in the shadows.

Hauk frowned at her hair as he noted the pale color. That would definitely stand out. "I understand now why you wore the black wig."

Sumi nodded at his statement. "Hard to hide pale blond hair in the darkness."

He handed her his scarf to wrap around her hair to help conceal it. He'd already applied more dirt and a reddish clay to her skin for camouflage. Likewise, he wore some over the shiny areas of his face—across his forehead and along his cheekbones and chin. In true Andarion fashion, he'd applied it in a geometric pattern that was as beautiful as it was serviceable. And this time, she definitely saw the marks of his family in it.

Before he gave approval to her wardrobe, he shrugged his shirt off and put it on her.

She scowled at his actions. "What are you doing?"

"It's blast resistant. Your poncho isn't."

"That's great for me. Sucks for you, and I'm not walking in there with you unprotected."

He grinned at her anger as he pulled a Sentella coat out of his pack. "I won't be unprotected."

When she arched a curious brow as to why he hadn't given her the coat, he handed it to her. The instant he let go, the weight of it caused her to stumble forward. "Oh my God! What's it made of? Rock?"

He laughed. "It's what we wear into battle."

Well, that certainly explained the size of his build. That thing had to weigh a hundred pounds.

At least.

Winking at her, he shrugged it on then secured his braids back from his face.

She lightly ran her hand over the black swirling pattern that swung up from his eye and across his cheek. "It's the wings of a hawk, isn't it?"

He inclined his head to her. "A sparn hauk. It was what my family was named for."

The fiercest winged predator known in any world. They were said to be lethal whenever their nest was threatened. Territorial and vicious. But those rare few who'd domesticated them had claimed that no creature was more loyal or a better companion. None more intelligent.

"Is that why your Endurance is held here?" This was the sparn's native land.

"In part. But also because it was the Oksanans my family held back from enslaving our world. During Endurance, we're to climb the tallest mountain on Oksana to retrieve a single sparn feather or bone to remind ourselves of the sacrifice our family made for our homeworld. To show our young that they can achieve any goal and climb any obstacle. And that no matter how high they ascend, there will always be family with them to catch them should they fall."

But no one had caught him when he fell. He'd been left alone and then abandoned and ridiculed.

And she knew from Thia that Dancer hadn't made it to the top before Keris had died. Instead, Dancer had learned that his family would turn on him if he wasn't the son he was supposed to be.

In that moment, she realized it was why he fought the way he did. Like he was proving himself worthy to everyone.

Even himself.

She kissed his lips. "You are the strongest male I have ever known, Dancer. No one is more worthy of your noble lineage. You honor your family and your ancestors. And you are a treasure for Andaria. I know the first Dancer of the Warring Blood Clan of Hauk smiles whenever he looks down and sees the strength and beauty of his namesake."

Hauk couldn't breathe as those words echoed in his head. No one had ever made him feel like she did. Like he could do anything. Even fly. "I will not allow you to be harmed."

"Nor I you." She pulled out her knife and unwound the scarf from her head.

He didn't understand what she was doing until she cut it in half and secured it around his face and head. It was how Andarions battled. They never exposed their faces to their enemies.

When she was finished, he returned the favor to her. He tied Illyse to make sure she wasn't hurt. Then together, side by side, they headed to war.

CHAPTER 18

Hauk led the way into the building from the back part that had once served as crawl space access. As silent as the akuma demon he'd been dubbed by Nykyrian years ago, he opened the tile that led from the crawl space into the electrical room. He took a moment to make sure he was alone before he held his hand out to Sumi and pulled her up to squat beside him.

They froze at the sound of footsteps outside the room. Because the base didn't have full power, he hoped that meant that the security sensors wouldn't detect bodies that appeared out of nowhere. It was really weird to be on a mission without the support staff he normally relied on. Weird to not have the voices of Nyk, Darling, Jayne, and Syn in his ear as they made snotty comments about each other and their targets.

Instead, this was as old school as it got. No sound. Having to rely on the person with you to anticipate and know what you would need in the fight. He'd never been this reliant on any single person.

And she'd been sent here to ruin him.

I must be crazy to trust her.

Yet against all reason, he did. Mostly because he now

valued her life over his. He'd rather see her through this than come out on his own.

Yeah, I'm fucking crazy. Nyk and Darling were right. His sanity had hijacked his common sense long ago and they were off vacationing together on some remote planet.

The footsteps faded.

Hauk crept to the main generator. Sumi handed him the timer he'd constructed while they'd dressed and planned for the mission. He reprogrammed the gen's settings then added the timer. Once it was set, he snuck to the door to listen for the others.

The good thing about Aksel was that he'd been a paranoid son of a whore. Instead of electronic portals someone could remotely lock, he'd used old-fashioned hinge doors.

Waiting until Sumi was in position, he cracked open the door and took a minute to look down the hallway.

It was clear.

Careful to stay to the shadows, he headed for the first guards he visually detected. Sumi was right. They were savages, and packed with weapons. The kind of mercs who lived to kill and torture.

Hauk pulled the small wire in his leather bracer out and used it to garrote target one. He hauled the body into a storeroom while Sumi took out hers.

Bit by bit, assassin by assassin, they made their way to the weapons locker. Once inside, he uncovered his face and started silently opening crates and cabinets to search for weapons and ammo. Thankfully, it hadn't been depleted by scavengers. Bastien must have made an effort to keep it stockpiled.

Sumi had to bite back a laugh at the excited expression on Dancer's face as he saw the inventory in the room. He was like a little kid visiting a carnival for the first time.

She tsked at him then whispered, "And here I thought only I was capable of putting *that* look on your face."

His happiness melted into panic.

"Kidding, sweetie. Load up." While he pulled out heavy artillery, she focused on the smaller calibers. When she reached for grenades, she noticed the way Dancer tensed.

They locked gazes.

Hauk held his breath as a thousand bad memories went through him. The pod exploding and pinning him to the hot metal. Being trapped in the fire while circuitry exploded around him. The mountain blowing up in his face.

But that was the past. Sumi couldn't carry the heavier guns and ammo. He knew that. The grenades were her best defense.

"Load up, *mu mia*."

She tucked them into her clothes as he made sure everything was charged and that he had more cartridges for the smaller blasters.

He led her out of the room before he rigged the door to detonate should anyone else try to access it to rearm.

With luck, they might make it upstairs without being seen. So far they'd done a remarkable job of silently eliminating their enemies.

They took out five more as they swept the hallway. But just as they reached the stairs, a door opened behind them.

Hauk winced as he realized the man was too far away. He slung out his knife and caught him between the eyes.

But not before the man opened fire and set off the alarm.

Hauk laid down cover fire for Sumi as they were swarmed by assassins. "Get behind me."

She did, but only after she shot one blast that caught a man in the head and sent him to the ground. She fisted her hand in Hauk's munitions belt and drew him with her.

They turned the corner and all hell rained down on them.

He moved to shield Sumi. She pulled his two modified Andarion blasters from his holster and shot at their attackers from around his waist.

On autopilot now, he did what he did best.

Fought and killed.

Hauk paused to reload. "How many bastards are here? Are they cloned?"

"If they were, I'd like to think they'd have chosen better-smelling donors for the program." Sumi swapped weapons before lobbing her grenades. She pulled him with her as he covered them while they fell back toward the stairs.

He lost count of how many blasts hit him. They hurt, but so long as they landed on his coat, he was shielded. It was the one that went into his thigh that caused him to stumble.

As he started to fall, he found Sumi by his side, offering him her shoulder. She pulled him into a room, out of the line of fire.

Biting his lip, he cursed at the pain. "You should go before you get hurt."

She shook her head. "Not without you. . . ." She locked gazes with him. "Strong alone. Stronger together. Fear no death."

He smiled as she voiced The Sentella motto. "Not very League of you."

"Screw The League."

He pulled his scarf off and used it to put pressure on his thigh. "Let's finish this."

Sumi hesitated at the look in his eyes. As she stared at him, they turned that deep vibrant red that glowed. So sex wasn't the only thing that aroused him to such a level. Fighting did it, too.

Fascinating.

"Hauk!" a man shouted in the hallway outside.

He fell back from the door and braced himself against the wall. Sumi went low in the center of the room, behind a crate.

"What?" Dancer answered.

"Surrender or we're going to kill them all! Piece by piece, until their screams echo in your ears!"

Dancer laughed at the threat. "You do that and I will eat you, piece by fucking piece. The three of them are the *only* thing keeping you alive right now. Release them and we'll let you live. It's your choice on how you leave this place. On your feet or feetfirst. You have thirty seconds to decide."

Sumi made her way over to him. "Dancer?" she whispered.

When he turned toward her, she pointed at the ceiling, where there was a hole to the next floor.

Nodding, he handed her the climbing gear.

She shot the hook then shimmied up the knotted rope. But no sooner did she reach the top than they opened fire on the room. Shrapnel and debris went flying. Her heart stopped as she saw Dancer running for the rope.

Dancer came up and grimaced as he scraped his injured leg against the rusted beam.

She dropped two grenades down then rolled away as they detonated. The ceiling under her squealed in protest.

Shit. It was breaking and about to send them back into that room.

One minute, she was sure she'd die, and the next, Dancer caught her and rolled with her. She came to rest on top of him, between floors. It was tight and cramped. But there was no time to even thank him as they heard the men running after them.

Dancer kicked the tile out above him. Carefully, he lifted her off him before he went through first to clear the room. He returned to pull her through the small opening.

Once they were on the second floor, he headed for a set of stairs on their left. He stayed back to cover the hole they'd made in the floor so that she could go first.

When they got to the top of the stairs, Sumi paused. The room there was empty. "Um . . . Dancer?"

He let loose a string of profanity as he saw what had her concerned.

"I take it this is the office?"

Dancer nodded and whimpered. The door behind them crashed open. He seized the first one through and slammed him against the wall so hard, it dazed the man.

Sumi sucked her breath in sharply. "Ooo, buddy. Real bad timing for *you*."

Dancer grabbed the assassin in his mammoth fist and held him against the wall. "Where are they being held?"

Sumi started to make a sarcastic comment to Dancer that they probably should have asked that question before they came this far. But since she was as much to blame for that oversight as Dancer, she let it go.

Besides, he seemed to enjoy beating on the assassin.

"Downstairs . . . bay."

Dancer made an inhuman sound before he broke the man's neck. "Downstairs. Who does that?"

"Someone who hasn't read the Andarion manual on where to store hostages?"

He gave her a dry stare. "You're not funny." He leaned back and groaned. "Ugh . . . more stairs."

"You could take a shortcut and crash through the floors, but it'd probably hurt more."

"Don't remind me." Sighing, he tightened the bandage on his thigh. Then he opened the door and led her down the hallway.

They could hear the men on the floor below, searching for them.

He took a minute to evaluate his weapons. A strange smile quirked at his lips.

"What?"

"Just remembering an old mission. Years ago when Nyk and I were in The League together and we were at a battle on an outpost backwater place. We were under some seriously heavy fire and running low on ammo. When Kyr heard that, he swept his gaze over us and said, *'Yeah, well, I'm not running out of men. Forward!'* " He sighed. "We lost eighty percent of our unit that day."

"Sounds like Kyr."

They turned down the next hall and shots flew at them.

Cursing, Sumi fell back and grabbed her arm to see a lovely seared mark on her biceps. It throbbed and ached, giving her a new appreciation for Dancer's ability to walk with his thigh wound. Gah! It hurt!

Dancer killed the assassins who'd attacked them, then turned to see her arm bleeding. Cold, terrifying rage descended over his features.

His glowing eyes turned a darker shade of red.

Scared it was directed at her, she swallowed hard. "I'm fine. It's just a flesh wound."

A strange glint came into his eyes then. He held her against him so tight that she could hear the beating of his heart. He pressed his cheek to hers before he removed his coat and draped it over her.

She staggered from the weight of it.

"Fuck this shit," he growled in a deadly tone.

One minute, he was in the room with her, and the next he was gone.

Sumi couldn't breathe as she realized he'd just left her to finish off the rest by himself.

With no blast armor. No anchor or point.

No cover fire.

He's out of his Andarion mind!

She tried to run after him, but the coat weighed so much, she couldn't. In that moment, she wanted to beat him.

Her heart pounding, she heard the sound of battle. Determined to protect him even from his own stupidity, she dropped the coat and ran after him. She slowed as she saw the bodies he'd left in his wake. *Well, don't I feel worthless.*

Without her, he appeared to have had no problem getting through them all.

But what concerned her were the bloody footprints that were so large, they could only belong to one being. And there was a *lot* of blood.

Terrified for Dancer, she followed the footsteps, taking care to pay attention so that no one came up behind her. By the time she reached the bay, she was afraid of what she might find.

"Shoot him, Uncle Hauk! Blow his *minsid* head off!"

Sumi stayed in the shadows as she saw Thia being held by the man who had told Dancer to surrender. Her young face was battered and her lips bleeding. As her old memories surged, Sumi wanted blood. How dare they harm a girl Thia's age!

His hand perfectly steady, in spite of the blood on him, Dancer eyeballed the man. Dancer's lips and face were swollen and bleeding. "Kill her and you know what happens next. They'll be scooping your brains up with a ladle for weeks."

Darice was tied and gagged while Bastien lay in a heap near Dancer. He appeared dead.

Sumi turned her attention back to Thia and realized the man had target fixation as he watched Dancer. He had no idea that she was here.

Moving silently, she positioned herself so that she had a clear shot to the assassin's head.

Thia's gaze slid to her, but she gave no outward clue

to the men that she saw her. All the fear faded from her eyes as she knew instantly what Sumi was about to do.

With a single nod, Sumi held up three fingers to let the girl know when to expect the shot. When she got to her fist, Thia picked her feet up and dropped straight to the ground at the same time Sumi fired.

The man staggered back and Dancer unloaded on him. No one moved until he stopped shooting. Only then did Thia look up with tears in her eyes as Dancer ran to her.

Sumi went to Darice, who didn't move at all. He was completely frozen. "Darice? Are you in shock?"

He blinked slowly as he scanned the room full of bodies and then looked to his uncle. It appeared he couldn't comprehend what Dancer had done. He frowned at Sumi. "But he works in IT."

She laughed at Darice's confusion. "He doesn't work IT, sweetie." Ruffling his hair, she cut Darice loose and went to check on Bastien.

"Is he alive?" Dancer asked.

She glanced over her shoulder to see Dancer with Thia in his arms. "Yeah, but they beat him terribly."

Thia looked up at Dancer. "He refused to tell them anything about you or the base."

"Damn right," Bastien breathed, then groaned as he rolled himself over. Hissing, he grimaced. "Bastards hit like kindergarten girls. I think one of them even pulled my hair and said I had cooties."

Snorting, Dancer set Thia down beside her and Bastien. "I'm going to call for an evac." He placed every one of his weapons down beside them, except for his two prized Andarion blasters. He changed out their cartridges before he tucked them into his holsters. "Anything moves, shoot it with extreme prejudice."

Sumi dropped her gaze to his side and leg where he was bleeding profusely. "We need to tend those."

"Call first. I'll be back in a few."

"You're a stubborn beast, Dancer Hauk!" she called as he made his way to the door.

He turned back to grin at her. "You forgot to add sexy to that list."

"Nah, that might go to your big fat head!"

Laughing, he vanished into the hallway.

Darice still looked shell-shocked. "How did he move like that?"

Thia rolled her eyes. "Uncle Hauk *is* a war hero, Darice. One of the best of his breed."

Still lying on his back, Bastien turned his head toward Thia. "He's Akuma, isn't he?"

Thia gave him a blank stare. "Don't know what you're talking about."

"Yeah, you do. But that's all right. He told me he was Sentella. Only one being I've heard of who's almost seven feet tall and fights like that. Damn." He laughed bitterly. "And here I offered to help *him*." His maniacal laughter ended with a sharp groan.

Sumi moved to help him with his wounds as best she could. "Thank you, by the way."

Bastien scowled at her. "For what? Getting my ass kicked or bleeding on the floor?"

"Keeping them safe."

Bastien quirked his lips. "It's good to play hero again. Forgot how much I missed it." Sucking his breath in sharply as she touched the cut on his forehead, he growled at her. "Then again, this shit sucks! Gah, what was I thinking?"

But she could tell by the gleam in his eyes that much like Dancer, Bastien lived for the fight, too.

Hauk sighed at the sorry condition of the subspace equipment. It appeared to have been idle since Aksel died. The dust and extreme weather conditions had done a number on it.

But within a few minutes, he had it mostly working. At least he hoped he did.

Flipping it on, he set the coordinates for Nykyrian's link and pressed the record. "Hey, *drey*. I'm calling to let you know that we're fine, but taking heavy fire. I have a tracker in my back and am about to head out alone to keep my pursuers away from the kids." He paused to grimace as pain racked him. "I'm sending them to Canyon Point. Fain will know where that is. Be aware, we've picked up two others with us. A woman named Sumi and a man Fain knows. Bastien Cabarro. Don't shoot the friendlies, especially the woman. It'll piss me off, if you do. We will keep Thia safe, but I need . . ." He hissed again as he fought down the pain. "I need you guys. Don't drag your asses."

His breathing ragged, he sent the message and got up to rejoin the others. He shivered from the agony of his wounds, and blood loss. But he refused to go down. They needed him and he wasn't about to let them get hurt.

His entire body protesting, he limped back toward the bay. It'd take a couple of hours for that transmission to reach Nyk. A couple more for everyone to scramble. Half a day to get here.

In the meantime, he had a few more things to take care of.

Pacing the room, Sumi chewed her nail, debating whether or not she should go after Dancer to make sure he was all right. She was just about to leave and check on him when the door opened.

By the slowness of his movements, she could tell he was in a lot of pain. With a smile, he touched her chin then looked to Bastien. "Bas? Anything in this place you need?"

"Not really. Why?"

"We need to get going. Boldorians are pack bastards.

In case they put out a beacon during this last round, I think it best we vacate."

Bastien stood then fell back down. "Well, ain't this a bitch? Could have sworn I was further from the floor than this a second ago."

Dancer snorted. He held his hand out and pulled Bastien to his feet. They both grimaced in unison. He stepped away from Bastien. "Darice, help the man."

To her shock, Darice did so without complaint. He offered Bastien his shoulder and together, they headed for the door.

Dancer paused to check on Thia. "You okay, *kisa*?"

Her arms folded over her chest, she had a strange look in her eyes as she swept her gaze around the building. "Do you know where my mother died?"

Dancer winced at her question. "Don't, baby."

Tears welled in her eyes as she glanced up at him. "Kiara won't ever talk about it. My father, either. I just want to know if she suffered much."

Pulling her into his arms, Dancer cradled her head with his hand. "No, baby, she didn't." He hated to lie to her, but the truth would serve no purpose other than to make her feel worse. He placed a kiss to her forehead. "Aksel owns enough of your soul. Don't let him take any more from you. He's not worth one molecule of your tears."

She hugged him then. "Thank you. For everything."

He nodded. "Love you, Thee."

"You, too." She kissed his cheek before she followed after Darice and Bastien.

Sumi moved to help Dancer. "You look like you're about to fall over."

Draping his arm over her shoulders, he gave a light squeeze as they walked toward the door. "I'm fine."

She didn't believe it for a minute. "Your eyes are still as red as they can be."

He said nothing as they left the building. The kids and Bastien were at the airbees. There were four of them, but only three had enough fuel in them to go very far. And that was only after Bastien siphoned the tank on one of them to add to it.

Dancer handed Bastien a bag of additional weapons. "Did you get your things?"

"Yeah."

"Good." Dancer pulled out a small handheld control then pressed it. An instant later, the entire building blew apart.

Bastien gaped indignantly. "My porn! You Andarion bastard! You didn't tell me you were going to blow my shit up."

Dancer cut a dry stare toward him. "Be glad I let *you* get out first."

Sighing, Bastien rolled his eyes. "You *are* Fain's brother. Just like him . . . bastard. All right, so what are we doing?"

"I'm taking the four of you to the Point then coming back for Illyse. I'll be on the move until the others get here." He handed Bastien one of the trackers that was set to his TD. "Give this to Thia's father and they'll find me."

Sumi moved to stand in front of him. "I'm not leaving you. You're wounded."

"Let's argue about this later. We need to get out of here in case some of the Boldorians are around to see the explosion."

She wanted to argue, but knew he was right.

Sumi took the first airbee. Thia climbed on the back of hers. Bastien pulled himself on another and Hauk took the third. Darice went to sit behind his uncle. When he wrapped his arms around Dancer's waist, she noted the softening of Dancer's features. He patted Darice's arms then took off.

They followed him to a small oasis at the base of Mount Grenalyn. In spite of the desert climate, it was strangely lush and green, with a rapid stream that ran through it.

Dancer parked and helped Darice off as they joined him.

When he started to leave them, Sumi caught his arm and held him in place. "You are hurt and bleeding. If you think for one second that I'm going to stand here and watch you leave without those wounds being tended, you're . . . even more insane than I think you are. And I *will* follow you."

Laying his hand against her cheek, he stroked her chin with his thumb. "I refuse to endanger you."

"You know, Dancer. Heroic is one thing. Moronic is quite another." She turned his airbee off. "Now get your ass over there, soldier, and sit!" She pointed to where Thia was unpacking their things. "And let me see how bad you're hurt. Then we'll revisit this whole death quest you seem to have."

He shook his head at her. "You are so bossy. I'd eat anyone else who talked to me like this."

"Promises, promises. Now move!"

Hauk wanted to argue, but honestly, he couldn't muster the energy or drive. So he obeyed her orders, even though it wasn't in his nature to do such. Sighing, he slung his leg over the airbee and allowed her to lead him to a softer area near the water.

In the back of his mind, he knew Darice was watching and making mental notes for Dariana. Yet he no longer cared. Darice already thought him the lowest of the low. He'd tried over the years to salvage his nephew's opinion of him, and it was time to realize that he couldn't. Darice would think what he would. There was nothing Hauk could do about it.

Lying down, he stared up at the side of the mountain where he'd once dangled helplessly and almost fallen to his death. Come to think of it, Keris had landed just a few feet from where he currently lay.

But he didn't want to think about the past. It was too brutal a place to dwell.

Sumi sat down next to him and opened his shirt. She gasped at the sight of the wound across his ribs that stung like Tondarion fire scorpions. "Dancer!"

He didn't speak as she cleaned it and continued fussing at him over it. Sick as it sounded, he enjoyed her anger over his injuries. Rather he dragged his knuckle along her jaw and watched her with hooded eyes. She was so incredibly beautiful and even more so while wearing the painted pattern of his family on her face.

All he wanted was to go back to this morning and make love to her again. To taste her lips and nibble every inch of her body.

Strange, he knew he was in pain, but with her so close, he didn't care. The only thing that mattered to him was keeping her safe and protected. Making sure that no one ever hurt her.

His gaze fell to her arm and again, he felt the adrenaline surge that begged him to go back and slap the corpses of every assassin who had endangered her life.

Taking her hand, he kissed her knuckles.

Sumi tried not to let his actions soften her. But it was too late. Especially while he looked at her with that adoring expression.

It made her ache to kiss him.

Most of all, she wanted to choke him over the amount of damage he'd taken for them. Yet, it was hard to be angry at him when he looked at her like he was already tasting her. Hard to stay angry when he touched her with such gentleness.

Still red, those eyes followed every move she made.

She sat back and frowned at how many wounds lined his torso and arms. "You really need an MT, Dancer."

He squeezed her hand comfortingly. "I'll be all right."

She shook her head. "You're not invincible."

"Damn near."

She rolled her eyes at his arrogance. Though to be honest, it wasn't. He really could stand stronger and take more damage than anyone she'd ever heard of. Was it an Andarion thing? Or was he just *that* strong?

Her stomach tightened at all the injuries on him. "Didn't at least one of them miss when they shot at you?"

He laughed then grimaced. "Yeah, I always wanted to be that hero in a movie where no one can shoot straight except me. Never happens. I seem to always walk into the school of award-winning sharpshooters." He dropped his hand to the injury she had on her biceps. "You okay?"

"Told you. Flesh wound. Throbs, but I can handle it."

He smiled. "My tough *mia*."

Tears filled her eyes as she bandaged his ribs. Without thinking, she lay her head on his chest and carefully held him. He wrapped his arms around her and for several minutes neither of them moved as she listened to the strong beating of his heart underneath her cheek.

Sumi lifted her head as she realized he was sound asleep. She pulled her poncho out and made a pillow for him before she finished cleaning and dressing his wounds. Only then did she remember that they weren't alone.

Ah crap . . .

Terrified of what she'd inadvertently done, she went to check on Bastien first.

Like Dancer had first attempted, he brushed aside her help. "I've had worse from bar fights. Trust me. Beatings I can take."

"You sure?"

Bastien nodded. "Hand me a cloth and I'm fine."

She hesitated.

Glancing over to Dancer, he gave her a sardonic grin. "Sumi, I learned a long time ago, you don't touch or get touched by an Andarion's female. They get really hostile over it, and I'm not physically able to keep Hauk from killing me right now. So no offense, let's maintain at least a five-foot no-touch zone. 'Kay?"

She scoffed as she handed him the foil package that held an antiseptic cloth. "He wouldn't beat you, Bastien."

"Not gonna chance it. In case it's escaped your notice, your male is a huge motherfucker. And I've had enough ass beating to tide me over for at least a month. . . . Maybe longer."

Shaking her head at him, she went to check on Thia. She sat on the ground with her legs drawn up tight to her chest, and her head lying on her knees.

Sumi brushed her hair back from her face. "You okay, sweetie?"

She nodded. "I just want to go home."

"I know."

Thia lifted her head. "Thank you, by the way."

"I didn't do anything."

"Yes, you did. Uncle Hauk would never have taken a shot with me in that smelly bastard's arms. You saved both our lives today."

Sumi gave her arm a light squeeze and patted her hand. "I'm just glad you knew what I needed you to do. I think it's safe to say you saved yourself."

Thia didn't respond. Instead, she narrowed her gaze on Sumi's face. "You're beautiful wearing the paint of a War Hauk. Not that you're not beautiful anyway. But Andarion looks good on you."

Sumi hugged her before she went to the last being she wanted to deal with.

Darice had been eerily quiet as he sat off, away from the group. That could not be a good thing for the normally verbose teen.

"How are you doing, kiddo?"

He glanced at her face, sneered, then quickly looked away. "Fine."

"You need food or—"

"I'm fine!" he snapped.

"Okay."

As she started away, his low tone stopped her. "Sumi?"

She paused to look back at him.

Biting his lip in an adorable manner that was identical to the one Dancer used, he glanced to his uncle. "I know what you and Dancer did."

Her heart sank at his words. "I don't know what you're talking about."

"Yes, you do," he said in an accusing tone. "Everyone will know. You can't hide it. He's stralen now."

"Stralen?"

"His eyes."

She scowled, wondering how Darice knew something about that when Dancer hadn't. Or had Dancer known and just not told her? "What about them?"

"It's a very rare condition that only manifests when an Andarion male has sex with someone he's possessive over, and then any time he has a strong adrenaline rush after that. If his feelings for the one he's bonded to are exceedingly strong, it's permanent and never goes away. My mother told me that the only Andarion she's ever known to have it was my father. And his was bad, according to her."

Sumi was aghast at Darice's knowledge of something he shouldn't have been told about. "Your mother talked about that with you?"

He nodded. "She wanted me to understand how much my father loved her. How much she meant to him." He slid his gaze back to Dancer. "By those eyes, I know Dancer broke his pledge to my mother and slept with you."

"Darice . . ."

He held his hand up to stop her words. "It's okay, Sumi," he said grudgingly. "I might be young, but I understand why he did it. No one, not even Dancer, can fight the stralen when it strikes. It's the most powerful emotion any Andarion can ever feel, and they have no control over it when it hits them. It overrides everything about their normal personality. But be careful. My mother said that it can be so intense that it used to terrify her whenever my father had it. It produces an extreme form of jealousy that makes them highly possessive, even violent toward the one they love. Controlling and domineering. That's why she told me about it. It usually runs in families, through the father, and there's a good chance I could have it, too." Abashed, he glanced away from her. "It's why she used to sedate my father. She was trying to find some way to mitigate its effects so that he wouldn't hurt her."

Sumi gasped at what he was saying. Especially given some of the past verbal attacks he'd made against Dancer. They had been overly harsh, especially given this revelation. "You knew she drugged him?"

He nodded. "They weren't illegal drugs. She told me that she got them from a doctor. And my father didn't give her a choice. She said it was so bad that she couldn't even speak to her best friend without my father flying into a jealous rage over it. He even put Pera in the hospital just two weeks before he died." His look pierced her with its sincerity. "Even though she loved him, she was afraid for her life, Sumi. It's why she didn't have children with my father until after his death. She didn't want him to hurt them in a fit of anger."

Sumi felt ill at what he was describing. It'd been just that kind of nightmare that she'd barely survived with Avin. "Is that why she's refused your uncle's pledge all these years?"

"Yes. When she married my father, she didn't know he had the gene. And stralen is something only felt by the male and has no relation to or bearing on how the female feels toward him. Only how possessive he feels toward her. She said it's why she thought Fain's human wife had left him. That he probably had it, too, and had hurt her because of it."

Darice swallowed hard. "It must have been the stralen's rage that allowed Dancer to tear apart everyone in the base today. He was so scary, Sumi. I've never seen anyone behave like that. He was like a possessed monster they couldn't stop. It was terrifying."

"That wasn't the stralen, sweetie. Your uncle's been able to fight like that for a long time."

"Really?" he asked in disbelief.

She nodded. "I've seen him do it."

Darice fell silent for several heartbeats. When he spoke again, his voice was barely more than a whisper. "My mother will never accept him now."

"Your mother was never going to accept him, Darice."

"I know." He sighed heavily then locked gazes with her. "Are you going to run with him like Fain did with his wife?"

"No. Dancer won't do it."

"My mother will have him killed if he stays."

"He knows that."

There was no missing the sad agony in Darice's white eyes. It was obvious he was torn between loyalty to his mother and to his uncle. "Can't you talk sense into him?"

"I'm not sure anyone can talk sense into Dancer. He's a very stubborn beast. But I will try."

Darice inclined his head to her. "Thank you, Sumi. They were planning to ransom us back to our parents, and then kill us once they were paid."

She laughed at the mere thought. "I'd have loved to see how that went when they called Thia's father."

"About the same as when Dancer came through the door, I'm thinking."

"Probably so." Sumi jerked her chin toward the cuts on Darice's wrists. "Would you let me tend those?"

He looked down at them before he acquiesced.

She knelt in front of him and carefully cleaned and bandaged his wrists. "You must have fought the restraints like a boss."

"I fought them like an Andarion."

She squeezed his hand. "Your uncle and father would be proud."

He smiled at her. "Thank you." When she started to leave, he took her hand. "Be careful with Dancer, Sumi. I don't want him to hurt you."

Her heart hammering over those words, she inclined her head to him then went to check on Dancer. He was bleeding through the bandage on his ribs. She considered stitching it, but the damage was such that she feared he might have internal injuries. Honestly, she didn't know enough about their anatomy to do anything more than keep his wounds clean and hope that Syn got here soon. The last thing she wanted was to make something worse in her ignorance.

So she did the best she could. As she redressed it, Darice's words about Dancer's condition went through her mind. Could Dancer really be dangerous to her?

Over and over, she relived some of Avin's more choice rage-fits.

Listen with your eyes.

Dancer had done nothing to make her think he would hurt her. Ever. She hadn't known Keris and she didn't really know Dariana. And while her sister had been terrified of Fain, Sumi had never seen him act threateningly in any way toward Omira, and she'd stayed with them a good bit.

Fain's eyes had always been white when she'd seen

him. The only red was a very thin band around the outer edge of his iris, which was normal for his race.

I won't listen to rumor.

Until Dancer did something to make her second-guess his temper, she would keep faith with him.

But even as she had that thought, her old fears rose up to slap her hard. She'd talked herself into a four-year relationship she should have walked on within the first six months.

Please, Dancer, don't be deceiving me.

The last thing she wanted to do was kill him, too. But no one, not even Dancer, would ever put her through the misery that had been her relationship with Avin.

She would kill him first.

CHAPTER 19

Hauk grimaced in pain. Blinking his eyes open, he found himself still in the camp with the others.

Shit.

He hadn't meant to stay here. But what stunned him was the sound of laughter. Scowling, he turned to see Thia, Darice, and Sumi enraptured by a story Bastien was telling them.

"So then Fain claps the guy on his back and says, 'So sorry my common sense offends you. But look on the bright side. In terms of procrastination, we've had a remarkably productive day.'"

The laughter died on Sumi's face as her gaze met Hauk's. She got up immediately and rushed to his side. But the warmth returned to her features as she felt his forehead. "How you feel?"

"Like a guy who made a pass at Thia and Nyk saw it."

Shaking her head, she rolled her eyes at him. Then she sucked her breath in sharply before she gently touched his cheek just below his eye. "You have one heck of a shiner. Who was tall enough in that fight to hit your face?"

"He wasn't. But the board in the bastard's hands gave him reach."

Snorting at his humor, she pulled out a bottle of water and then helped him to sip it.

"How long have I been out?"

"A few hours."

He cursed. "I need to get going."

"No, you don't."

"Sumi . . ."

"Don't argue with me. I'm putting my foot down, Dancer. But if you attempt to leave, I'll be putting it up your ass."

He laughed then groaned.

Thia and Darice moved to stand behind her. She shoved at Darice. "Told you he wasn't dead."

"I knew from the snore he wasn't dead. I said he was dying."

Thia made a noise of discontent at Darice before she scowled at Hauk. "Why are your eyes still glowing red, Uncle Hauk?"

His gut drew tight over her question. Damn. They should have stopped that while he slept. The fact that they hadn't . . .

He was in deep Andarion shite. "I didn't know they were."

She nodded. "They're very odd. I never knew Andarion eyes did that."

That's because it was exceedingly rare for them to glow in the first place. To remain glowing—that only happened one in a hundred billion cases.

Lucky me. . . .

A tic started in Darice's jaw, but for once his nephew held his tongue.

Bastien brought over a small plate of food and something that appeared to be a root of some kind. "If you took the punches I did, I know it'll be hard to chew, but . . . that root will minimize the pain."

"Thanks." Hauk set the plate down beside Sumi.

"C'mon, guys," Bastien said. "Let's give them some quiet time."

Darice hesitated before he followed them back to the small fire.

Hauk winced as he tried to chew the meat. Bastien was right. Eating was rough. "I need to go back for Illyse."

"We already took care of it." She gestured to the fire where the lorina was curled up and sleeping. "Bastien said you owe him a good night of drinking for the scratches she gave him." She paused. "Can you really not tell that your eyes are glowing?"

He glanced over to make sure the others weren't paying any attention to them before he took her hand in his and led it to his swollen groin. When he spoke, his tone was so low that it was barely audible. "I can only tell how much I want to be inside you. Which, given the amount of pain I'm in everywhere else, is ridiculous. Gah, how can I be horny and dying at the same time? It's not right what you do to me, woman."

She blushed at his teasing. "Is that," she dropped her gaze to his groin, which made his cock twitch, "what causes it?"

Hauk hesitated before he answered her. "No, but it is what started it. It's tied to my adrenaline and vasopressin levels."

She narrowed her eyes accusingly. "You told me originally that you didn't know anything about it."

He wrapped a lock of her hair around his finger. "I didn't want to scare you."

"Why would it scare me?"

Hauk released her hair and swallowed his food. Why would it not? Even though it was a highly sought after trait, it terrified most females he knew of—and they were Andarions who knew and understood it.

His mother was the only exception to that. Once she found out the male Hauks carried the mutation, it'd pissed her off that she'd never been able to induce that kind of devotion from his father. Some of their fights over it while Hauk had lived in their house had been quite nuclear, which probably had a lot to do with his father's inability to feel that kind of love and devotion for her.

How could anyone love someone who constantly nagged at them and derided them for something they couldn't help?

He took another sip of water before he answered. "It's an exceedingly rare condition for the males of my breed. A genetic defect where we overproduce vasopressin once we fall in love with someone. Whenever an Andarion male has it, it's said that no other female will ever please him—that he can never stray from the one female who causes him to experience it. It's the ultimate in pair-bonding."

She drew her knees up to her chin and he saw the fear in her eyes as she watched him closely. But he had no idea why she'd feel such with him. "Does it do anything else?"

"Like?"

"Make you violent?"

His heart wrenched at her question as he finally understood the fear he saw in her gaze. How could she think that of him? "No, *mia*. It just makes us extremely loyal and protective of the one who makes us feel it."

"Violently so?"

That sent a wave of anger through him. Not at her, but at the bastard who'd put such terror in her kind heart. "I'm not your ex-boyfriend, Sumi. I would *never* strike you. Not for any reason. And it doesn't work that way. It drives us to protect our mate and our children—to the point of suicide. Like today when I saw you bleeding and I went after them with no regard for myself, because they had caused you harm. That rage is part of it, but it's never directed at the one we love. Only to the ones who threaten her. They're the ones we beat into the ground. Not our females."

"Really?"

"Really. It was that surge of fierce adrenaline and protectiveness that allowed my family to hold off the Oksanans when they attacked Andaria." Sinking his hand in her soft hair that fascinated him, he stared into her eyes so that she could see his sincerity. "I am yours alone, *mia*. You own a part of me no other will ever have. And this"—he pointed to his eyes–"is only for you." He glanced over to Darice and sighed. "And now he knows it, too. I can't hide this. Not that I want to."

Her hand trembling, she picked up a piece of meat and carefully fed it to him. "I love you, Dancer."

He nipped at her fingers. "And I, you."

Sumi felt terrible for having done this to him. She'd single-handedly ruined his life. *That was what Kyr sent you to do.*

That thought really didn't help her mood any. How simple it'd seemed when Kyr had first assigned this mission to her. Now . . .

How could she hurt someone who meant so much to her?

Her heart aching, she brushed the hair back from his face. "Did you get a message out to your friends?"

He winced as he tried to chew his food. "I sent one. I hope it got through. Won't know for another day or so."

Sumi dropped her gaze to his ribs, which were still bleeding terribly. Neither Thia nor Darice knew what to do for him. And she hated feeling useless. "Bastien said that he couldn't get anything from them about who hired them. Only that you really pissed them off by killing so many of their brethren."

"Told you my list of enemies was infinite."

"You're not funny."

He wrinkled his nose playfully at her. "I'm a little funny."

She growled at him.

Thia came up to them with Dancer's sleeping bag and an inflatable pillow. "We've all agreed, Uncle Hauk, if you try to leave, we're siccing Darice on you."

He gaped at her. "Why do you hate me so much?"

Laughing, Thia squeezed Sumi's shoulder before she returned to the fire.

While he finished eating, Sumi carefully laid the sleeping bag out and inflated his pillow. Then she helped him into it.

No longer caring what Darice thought, Hauk opened his arms for Sumi to join him. She accepted without complaint by curling up at his side, taking care not to hurt him. Closing his eyes, he savored the feeling of having her with him. Of knowing she was safe.

Sumi listened to his ragged breathing in her ear. "Are you all right?"

"No," he said between clenched teeth. "I'm in hell. Complete and utter."

Worried, she turned to look at him over her shoulder. "What's going on?"

He ran his finger down her cheek. "I've had the shit kicked out of me and I'm so horny that I swear I'm about to burst into flames from it. And because of one I can do nothing about the other."

Sumi snorted at his dire, angst-ridden tone. "You can't be serious." But she knew from the size of the bulge against her hip that he was.

"What color are my eyes?" Groaning, he put his arm over his face. "I never knew this sucked *so* much."

"What? Loving me?"

"Yes."

"I think I'm offended."

He nuzzled his face against her hair. "Better to be mentally offended than in physical agony."

"Is it really that bad?"

He lifted his arm to pin her with an irritated smirk.

Pouting at him, she laughed. "I'm sorry, sweetie."

"You should be. You're killing me."

She tsked at him. "Is there anything I can do?"

His answer was drier than the desert around them. "Geld me."

"Really? That's what you want?"

"No . . . maybe. Ah, hell, just stun me unconscious until the others get here."

She laughed at his playful misery. "You're such a baby."

"I defy you to feel like this and not whine. All in all, I'm being pretty damn fierce."

She lay back down and glanced over to see where everyone else was. Darice had already gone to sleep. With their backs to her and Dancer, Bastien and Thia were on the other side of the fire, talking to each other.

Making sure they were completely out of everyone's line of sight, she opened his pants underneath the blanket.

He peeked out from under his arm. "What are you doing?"

"Trying to help you," she whispered. "Shh!"

Hauk had to bite his lip to keep from crying out as she brushed her hand against his cock. And as she worked her magic on his body, the pleasure of her soothing touch overrode the pain, until the only thing he could feel was the pressure of her hand as she gently stroked him. He thought that was amazing until she slid down inside his sleeping bag and took him into her mouth.

Unimaginable tremors of pleasure racked him. His heart raced as he arched his back and shook all over. *Oh dear gods. . . .* How could anything feel this good?

Beat me any time if this is my reward.

He gently buried his hand in her hair as she teased and

licked him until he thought he'd die from ecstasy. And when he came a few seconds later, the love he felt for her completely overwhelmed him.

In that moment, he knew she owned him in a way no one ever would. For her alone, he'd do anything . . . kill anyone she asked him to.

Sumi didn't pull back until the last tremor he felt settled down into the most tranquil bliss he'd ever known. She slowly slid up his body until her head was even to his. He locked gazes with her as he ran his fingers through her pale hair to smooth it down. Her lips were shiny and swollen, her eyes dark and filled with a tenderness that stole his breath.

Laying his hand against her cheek, he traced her amazing lips with his thumb.

She frowned at him. "Your eyes are still red. I thought that would make them normal again."

He slid his finger along her brow line, delighting in the softness of her skin and the fire in her eyes as she stared at him. "Because you own me the way you do, they may never be white again." She had changed him completely.

Scowling, she reached for his water to take a drink. "I don't understand."

He bent his arm under his head as he tried to explain it. "It's not tied to sexual desire, Sumi. It's tied to my love for you. My need to protect you from all harm."

She took another drink then offered the bottle to him. "Will they really remain this way?"

"I honestly don't know. Keris's would come and go, depending on his drug use and emotions. He's the only Andarion I've ever known who had the condition. But I have heard that in extremely rare cases, it becomes permanent." He took a sip then asked the one thing that hung heaviest on his mind. "Do they repulse you?"

"Dancer," she chided. "Nothing about you repulses me.

I simply adore you and I think your eyes are absolutely beautiful. Red or white, makes no never mind to me. I could stare into them forever."

He tightened his arms around her before he nuzzled her neck. "Do I need to help you now?"

It took her a moment to realize what he meant. Afraid of offending him, she suppressed her smile. "No, sweetie. While I would love to climb on top of you for the rest of the night, I know you're hurt and I don't want to do anything to worsen your injuries. Being held by you, right now, is more than enough."

"Are you sure?"

"Positive."

He screwed his face up as if he couldn't quite believe her. "Humans are very strange."

She laughed. "It's not a human thing, love. It's a female thing."

"You're sure?"

"Positive." Sumi laced her fingers with his, amazed at how happy she was in this one moment of being with him. The only thing that could make it better would be to have her daughter with them.

But that was a dream that could never come true and she knew it. Closing her eyes, she tried not to think about the fact that his friends would be here very soon. Then he would go back to his life and she'd return to The League. She clenched her teeth at the thought of what Kyr would do to her for failing her mission.

Or worse, living the rest of her life without Dancer. It burned and hurt so deep that it was a physical ache.

How stupid, right? She'd lived years without him and now he felt as integral to her well-being as breathing.

Holding his hand to her face, she savored the warmth of his body pressing against hers. This was all she'd ever wanted. Someone who loved her. Someone who wouldn't hurt her or make her feel like crap when she was with them.

How cruel that having finally found him, she couldn't keep him.

I will die for you, Dancer.

Saddest part of all? She most likely would.

CHAPTER 20

"Not enough root in the universe, eh?"

Hauk groaned at Bastien's perky tone as he silently damned every person who'd had a hand in making him feel like this. "Be glad my weapons are too far to reach or I'd shoot you."

With a groan of his own, Bastien sat down beside him. "Not a morning person, are you?"

"Fuck you."

Bastien laughed. "You're not my type and I'm not quite that desperate." He flicked playfully at Hauk's ear. "Though I have to say that you are awfully pretty for a male. If I were ever tempted, it'd probably be by someone as cute as you."

Hauk bared his fangs to him at the same time Sumi came over with a plate for each of them.

"Our fierce protectors." Her eyes danced with mirth. "You two don't look like you could take on a sleeping lizard this morning."

Hauk mustered a lopsided grin for the only person who could amuse him in the current physical misery he was in. "I have to say that I definitely felt better last night."

She blushed profusely.

Then Hauk blushed, too, as he realized where her thoughts went. That hadn't been what he meant, but . . .

Darice came running up. "I saw a sparn this morning. Isn't this where they nest?"

Hauk hesitated, knowing what Darice was really asking him. "Dari—"

"Can't I go with Thia while we wait?"

He shook his head. "That's a bad idea. Thia's no better at climbing than you are. I wouldn't trust the two of you at an indoor gym alone."

Darice's face swelled up immediately. "We're so close! It's not fair that I can't get my Endurance feather!"

Sumi was stunned that for once, Darice didn't turn that into an insult for his uncle.

Dancer's expression was every bit as despondent that he was having to say no. With his brow furrowed, he rubbed at his ribs as if he was actually considering taking the climb with his nephew.

Don't you dare. . . .

But he was crazy enough that he might attempt it to make Darice happy. Especially since he'd failed on his own trip with Keris. This had the makings of a whole new disaster.

Afraid of what Dancer might do, she looked up at the cliff in front of them. "What kind of climb are we talking about? Can it be done in one day?"

Dancer hesitated before he answered. "The main approach is just over there." He pointed to her left. "It's twelve pitches to the summit. Mostly face climbing with some corners and headwalls. There're a couple of gendarmes where sparns nest so you shouldn't have to go all the way to the summit to get the feathers. The only hazard really is loose rock and I wouldn't trust any existing anchors that you might find along the way." He locked gazes with her. "It's easily done in a day, barring an accident. . . . What are you thinking?"

"That I take him."

They all stared at her.

"What?" she asked, offended by those astonished faces. "League trained, folks. Head of my class. Before that, I was a xenobotanist. Been on many vertical expeditions in some frightening places. I can climb a mountain . . . building . . . dead body . . ." She cast a playful grin to Dancer. "Surly Andarions . . . no problem."

Hauk's gut drew tight at her offer as memories tore through him. He despised this mountain and everything it reminded him of. The last thing he wanted was to lose another loved one to this hellhole.

"Please, Dancer?" Darice screwed his face up like he used to do as a small child whenever he'd ask for a ride on his shoulders. "Please! Please! Please! I'll do anything if you say yes! I'll even wash your boots. Sharpen your sword. Be your personal slave."

Damn, how he hated that pleading, adorable expression. He glanced to Sumi.

"You know I won't let anything happen to him."

Darice went down on his knees, crawling toward Hauk and begging as if he were in absolute agony. "Please, Uncle Dancer, please!"

Against his better judgement, he nodded. "But!" He held his hand up to his overly excited nephew. "You lip off to her and she's to bring you right back down here. You understand me, Darice?"

"I'll be good. I promise! I love you, Dancer!" Whooping in delight, he shot to his feet and ran off to get ready.

Hauk pushed himself up. His entire body protested, but he wasn't about to watch them leave without some guidance.

"You okay?"

He nodded at Sumi's concerned question. "I want to double-check the climbing gear."

"All right, Grandma."

"I also have the pitches diagrammed."

"That'll be helpful. Anything else?"

He pulled her against him and pressed his cheek to hers. "Don't get hurt."

Sumi held him close as she felt his fear. "I won't let anything happen to Darice."

"Not just him."

"I know." She kissed his cheek before she pulled back. "Thia? You going with us?"

The look of horror on her face was priceless and comical. "Oh hell no. Peeing off the side of a mountain, listening to Darice moan and complain . . . I'd rather bring a date home to meet my dad—that would at least be entertaining until I had to scrub the blood out of my clothes." She gestured toward Bastien. "Think I'll hang at base camp and watch over the two males who don't whine like babies."

Sumi laughed. "All right."

Hauk turned toward Thia. "Hey, Thee? What size shoe do you wear?"

"Eighteen."

He looked back at Sumi. "You?"

"Eighteen. Why?"

"You'll need climbing shoes, won't you?"

That would be helpful.

"I'll grab my pack," Thia said, heading for her tent. "Everything should fit."

"Thanks, sweetie." Sumi followed after her.

While Sumi and Darice changed, Hauk checked the ropes, anchors, biners, harnesses, cams, hexes, nuts, slings, belay devices, and packed them each a day sack.

When they returned, he took a moment to help them gear up and double-checked everything again.

Darice made a sound of supreme disgust. "Do I have to wear a full body harness? Really? Dancer, I'm not a baby."

"If you invert on the climb, you'll thank me."

He rolled his eyes. And again when Hauk made sure everything was fastened properly to his sling. "Gah, Dancer. Really? I've been climbing since I was three. Stop, already!"

"Don't get arrogant. I had a lot more hours than you in a harness when I fell over four hundred feet, and your father had even more. Humor me."

Darice froze to stare at him. "What really happened on that climb, Dancer?"

Sumi held her own breath as she waited for the answer.

Dancer's eyes darkened with sadness. "The anchors and belay failed."

"Who was lead?"

"Your father."

Tears filled Darice's eyes as he realized Keris was responsible for setting the anchors and belay. That he'd been at fault when they failed. "Is that why you cut the rope?"

Hauk winced as anger and pain mixed inside him. He was so sick of that accusation. Furious at the way his mother and father looked at him as if he'd murdered his own brother. "I didn't cut the rope, Darice. I didn't have my hands free to do it."

He scowled. "I don't understand."

Hauk clenched his teeth as old memories surged past the darkest place he tried to keep them relegated to. "We fell because your father hit me before I could finish tying in to the belay station. I slipped and the anchors failed until we were down to only one. I was inverted, attempting to right myself and hold on with one hand, while I was trying to steady Keris with the other." He held his hands up to show Darice the scars he had from the rope burns. "My knot was coming undone and the last anchor was slipping. We both knew what was about to happen. Even so, I didn't stop trying to hold on for both of us. Next thing

I knew, Keris pulled out his knife and sliced through the rope before I could stop him."

Darice fingered the scars on Hauk's hands. "You really didn't cut it."

"I would have died before I cut my brother loose."

Darice wrapped his hands around his uncle's scars. "You were my age."

"A few months older."

He swallowed hard as if it finally dawned on him just how horrific that event had been. Then, he threw himself into Hauk's arms. "I won't fall, Uncle Dancer."

Sumi's throat went tight as she saw the look on Dancer's face as he held Darice against him.

"I know you won't, Dare. And don't let Sumi fall, either."

Darice inclined his head to him. "I'll bring you back a feather."

Dancer ruffled his hair. "Deal." He handed Darice his climbing helmet.

Sumi offered Dancer a bittersweet smile as he met her gaze. "We'll be very safe. I just need to get him a feather and return, correct?"

He nodded. "Remember, the sparn will attack if she thinks you're going after her nest."

"Don't worry. You rest and we'll be back before you can even miss us."

Hauk scoffed at her words. "Not possible. I miss you already."

She made the most adorable expression before she kissed his cheek and buried her hand in his hair.

Hauk wanted to hold her like this forever.

Unfortunately, Thia came running, which caused Sumi to release him. She handed her bright pink helmet to Sumi, and a pair of sport sunglasses. "Good luck. Try not to strangle Darice."

Darice glared at her as he fastened his helmet on.

"Thanks, Thia. You'll take good care of the guys while I'm gone, right?" Sumi fastened her helmet before Hauk rechecked her harness and sling.

She sighed heavily, but said nothing about his paranoia.

"Absolutely. Be safe." Thia kissed her cheek then moved to stand beside Hauk.

Sumi inclined her head to them and clapped Darice on the arm. "Ready, champ?"

"I'm your belay slave, *mu tara. Acrena tu.*"

"He said *after you*," Thia translated.

"Thanks." She led the way to the approach.

Hauk watched as Sumi and Darice began the climb he'd taken with Keris so long ago. It helped his mental state that Sumi was completely calm and did appear extremely accomplished, and the two of them weren't going at each other's throats verbally. Still . . .

He had a bad feeling.

Thia put her arm around his waist while he watched them. "It'll be fine, Uncle Hauk. You'll see."

He smiled down at her, hoping she was right and he was wrong. And he refused to move until they were out of sight. Only then did he return to sit and watch them through the scope in Sumi's rifle.

While he watched, Thia went to gather rocks for her little brothers.

"So who was the first mother hen? You or Fain?"

He dropped the scope to glare at Bastien. "Meaning?"

"You two are so much alike. It's actually scary."

That's because they were always having to watch out for each other. Between their parents and Keris, the only affection he and Fain could count on was from themselves.

And as Sumi and Darice vanished completely from his sight, he heard a strange sound. "What was that?"

Bastien scratched at his chin. "What?"

"That sound?"

"I don't hear anything."

Thia stood. "I do. . . . Someone's coming."

Hauk moved to draw his blaster, but before he could, three darts went into his chest. The paralytic hit him instantly as he saw similar darts fly into Bastien, Thia, and Illyse.

Before he could ID their attackers, he passed out.

Sumi was impressed with Darice's skill as he climbed up to her. "Who taught you?"

"My mother mostly. But Dancer's been taking me for small climbs since I was little. Maybe once or twice a year. He's really good at it. He actually free climbs a lot with his friends."

She remembered seeing that from the photos. He and his friends appeared to enjoy it as a favorite pastime. With and without gear. "I'm surprised he'd ever climb again, after what happened."

"Dancer's very brave. He started climbing within a year of his fall."

The fact that he defended his uncle, and was so complimentary, stunned her. It was as if he finally saw the truth of Dancer's personality, and not the lies his mother had filled him with.

Tying in, Darice paused to look down. His eyes widened as he realized how high above the ground they were.

"You okay?"

For several heartbeats, he didn't speak.

"Darice? You still with me, hon?"

His eyes filled with tears.

"Darice!"

He blinked twice. "S-s-sorry. I just . . . I never thought about how far Uncle Dancer fell with my father." He swallowed hard and licked his lips as he twisted to stare down the sheer drop. "I've never been this high before. Mostly we've done indoor climbing."

"Don't look down, sweetie. And I've got you covered. I'm anchoring you in like a beast. I promise you won't fall far if you slip, and it will hold ten times your plummet weight."

He nodded as she double-checked his knot and belay. "My mother blames every bit of the fall on Dancer. She said my father was the best climber she'd ever seen."

Sumi took a quick drink of water before she prepared to climb ahead. "Don't think about it, Darice."

But he continued to fret as she moved forward.

All of a sudden, he lost his foothold and slipped. Falling only a few inches, he screamed out until he realized he was safe and firmly anchored.

"It's all right, sweetie. I told you that I have you." She paused for him to get his bearings.

Instead of resuming his stance, he clung to the wall in terror.

"Darice? You can do this. I know you can."

He shook his head forcefully. "No, I can't! I don't want to die!"

"You're not going to die, baby. I won't let you."

Tears flowed down his cheeks as he stared up at her. "Aren't you afraid?"

"I've had to scale glass buildings a lot higher than this. As has your uncle. And he's already fallen without an anchor. If he can manage to continue to climb after the fall he took when he was your age, you can, too."

Still, he didn't move. He continued to hug the wall.

"Do you want to go back down?"

His lips quivered before he wiped at his eyes. "You promise I won't die?"

"On my own life."

He drew a ragged breath before he returned to his belay position. "Sumi?"

"Yes?"

"Thank you."

"You're welcome, baby. Just breathe easy. I promise I won't let you fall."

He paused to meet her gaze. "I know why Dancer loves you. . . ." He smiled at her. "I love you, too."

Her own tears welled as those words touched her heart. "I love you, sweetie."

With a tenuous smile for her, he fed her slack to climb. Sumi watched as he grew more confident right before her eyes. It was incredible to see the boy taking these first steps into adulthood. No wonder Andarions did this for their young. She totally understood it now.

But it broke her heart that Dancer's journey had been ruined. That he hadn't been allowed to grow up slowly. Rather it'd been shoved down his throat.

Like hers.

Not wanting to think about it, she stayed focused on Darice and their climb until they finally reached a small nest. She let Darice take lead for the last forty feet so that he'd reach the nest first.

On top of the small gendarme that was barely large enough for the two of them, he stood, looking out on the world so far below. By the time she joined him there, he was as exuberant as anyone she'd ever seen.

"I am emperor of the climb!" he shouted, his voice echoing off the canyon walls. "Fear me, bitches!"

Sumi laughed. "Remember, we still have to get back down."

"Oh." He peered over the edge. When he looked back at her, he stroked his chin and spoke in a faux professor-like tone. "Perhaps I spoke prematurely."

Still laughing, she hugged him against her. "So where's this nest?"

He pointed to a small crevice that was thankfully empty, except for the remnants of a nest that contained a handful of white feathers and two small bones.

His expression ebullient, Darice picked them up and tucked them into his pouch. "We did it!"

"Yep. Ready to head down?"

He looked over the edge again and cringed. "I think I liked climbing up better."

Smiling, she tugged playfully at his ponytail that peeked out from under his helmet. "You'll be fine. Look how far you've come."

"We did, didn't we?" He reached into his pouch and pulled a feather out. Then he held it toward her. "This is for you. You're an Andarion now."

She touched her hand over her heart and lowered her head to him. "I'm very honored. Thank you, *mi tana*." She tucked the feather into her own pouch.

He smiled, until he looked down again. Suddenly, he turned a little green around his gills. "All right. Let's slowly get this over with."

Sumi had a bad feeling before they even reached the bottom. Something wasn't right. She could feel it in her gut. As soon as they were on the ground, she unhooked herself and removed her helmet.

Darice dropped his on the ground and unbuckled his harness. "Where is everyone?"

"Not sure."

He went running toward base camp to show off his feathers. Sumi had just started packing up their gear when she heard him screaming her name.

Pulling out her small blaster, she ran to him. He was kneeling over Thia.

"Dancer!" she called. "Bastien!"

No one answered.

Her heart pounding, she ran to Thia, who slowly blinked her eyes open.

"Stop yelling, Darice," Thia snapped as she sat up. "My head's killing me."

"What happened?" Sumi asked.

At first, Thia appeared confused. Then she gasped and looked around with wild panic. "We were attacked."

"Where are the guys?"

Wide-eyed, Thia panted as she tried to calm herself. "Oh my God, they must have been taken!"

Sumi flinched at the last words she wanted to hear. She quickly searched the area and found impressions in the ground where someone had dragged their unconscious bodies away from here to some kind of wheeled transport.

It vanished into the desert.

She heard a faint whine coming from where they'd slept. Hoping against odds it might be Dancer, she ran to find Illyse limping and sniffing at the blanket they'd slept on. Their gear was strewn about and the tracker for the device in Dancer's back was near the blanket. "Easy, girl," she said, stroking the lorina's fur to calm her.

The lorina licked her chin, then nuzzled her.

And with every heartbeat, Sumi became more and more furious. "Dancer!" she screamed out again, knowing it was useless.

Someone had taken him.

Fear, worry, and grief tangled inside her. But instead of reducing her to tears, it stoked a rage the likes of which she'd never felt before.

How dare they!

And with that fury came the training she'd mastered over these last three years. She wasn't a woman right now.

She was a feral assassin.

"You better not have harmed a single molecule on his body." If Dancer had so much as shed a single skin cell while in their custody, she was going to take it out of their entrails.

CHAPTER 21

Hauk winced as he woke up to a splitting headache. The light burned his eyes. Frowning, he found himself inside a steel cage with Bastien and two other men. He pressed the heel of his hand against his forehead while he sat up to get his bearings.

"Do you speak Universal?" the guy on his right asked.

Hauk nodded then scowled as he checked Bastien to make sure he was unconscious and not dead. Thankfully, he was still breathing.

"Good. Just do what they say and don't argue."

Hauk turned an are-you-serious sneer at the man that caused him to gasp and scamper to the other side of the cage where the other man stared at him as if he terrified him.

"What the hell are you?" the man who'd been talking to him asked.

"Pissed. Off." Hauk rose slowly into a feral crouch. While the human men could stand inside the cage, he couldn't.

This was bullshit!

Ready for war, he got up and went to the door to examine the biolock. He kicked it in anger.

A woman gasped then fired a blaster at him. He ducked the charge and hissed, exposing his fangs.

"Pheara! You gotta come see this. Fast!"

He wouldn't call the woman's gait hurried as she came around the side of a wheeled transport to eye him. An inch or two shorter than Sumi, she was well muscled with short, dyed red hair and the swagger of a woman used to fighting for what she wanted.

The instant her dark brown eyes focused on him, she froze. "What the hell are you?"

He ran his tongue over his fangs, emphasizing the fact that he wasn't human. "Let me out of here."

She shook her head. "I don't think so." She pressed a button on the cuff at her wrist. Pain shot through him instantly.

But he wasn't human. Instead of weakening him, it sent a charge of adrenaline through his body. Furious, he kicked at the door again, hard enough to bend part of it.

Both women backed up.

"What the hell?" Pheara breathed.

"He's an Andarion."

Hauk cut his glare to another woman who joined the first two. Tiny and petite, with short blond hair, she was dressed in animal skins.

"I thought he was human when we stunned him. No wonder it took so many darts to take him down."

"Yeah," the blond snorted. "You're lucky you got him down at all. They are a savage breed and don't react to stimuli the same way we do." She hit the cage with a prod that sent electricity through it.

The men whined and screamed as they tried to avoid touching the metal. Bastien came awake with a foul curse.

Hauk didn't flinch as he curled his lip at her and defied her to keep doing it.

"See." She balanced the pole on her shoulder and swept her gaze over the other two women. "And we have a problem. Andarions eat humans. Raw. Leave him in that cage and he'll devour the others."

The men behind him began begging for release while Bastien laughed.

Hauk ignored them. "Let me go and I'll leave here without any drama."

The blond tsked at him. "It doesn't work that way, cutie. You have too big a bounty on your head. Eat the others if you must. You're worth a lot more than they are."

Great. They were slavers as well as assassins. Just what he needed.

Hauk glared at the women. "I *will* get out of here, and when I do—"

"Don't make me kill you, Andarion. While you have one hell of a bounty on your head, I'm thinking there are a lot of people who'd pay a fortune to have an Andarion slave." She raked his body with a hungry smirk. "Now be a really good boy and I might send you off with a smile on your face."

He exposed his fangs to her. "You're really going to let me eat your heart?"

She scoffed.

Hauk grabbed the bars over his head and used his entire body weight to kick at the door again.

The other two women took three more steps back.

Eyes wide, Pheara gulped. "I don't think that's going to hold him, Telise."

"If he kicks it open, blast the shit out of him. Pricewise, given the scars and wounds already on him, it won't matter if he's banged up a bit more."

Roaring in frustration, Hauk pressed his face between the bars to glare at Telise. "When I get out of here, I'm going to feast on your organs."

She pressed the prod to his stomach and blasted him.

Hauk growled as a violent shock went through his entire body. But he refused to give her the satisfaction of seeing his pain. He stayed on his feet, glaring at her.

That succeeded in putting fear in the bitch's eyes.

Unsettled, she stepped back and turned toward her friends. She handed the prod to the smaller of the two. "If he gets out, open fire and call for backup."

Hauk fanged them again as he cursed himself for allowing the women to get the drop on them. "Hey!" he called to the two who eyed him like the vicious predator he was. "There was a woman with me. Where is she?"

Pheara cleared her throat. "We took her weapons and left her where she fell. Why? Is she yours?"

"My niece, and if any harm comes to her, I swear by every god who protects Andaria that I will rain down a hell on you so severe you will beg me for the mercy of death." He kicked the door again.

They backed up.

"I'm going for more guards." Pheara took off running, leaving the other woman to watch him with a bug-eyed stare that would be hysterical if he wasn't so enraged.

Wanting blood, he turned toward the men behind him. They were even more afraid of him than the women. He rolled his eyes at the typical human reaction to his kind.

Bastien shook his head at their fear. "Don't worry. We fed him earlier. He's not hungry. Right, Hauk?"

He glared sullenly at them all. "Feeling a bit peckish, suddenly."

That only frightened them more.

No wonder Fain couldn't stand living among humans for long. His brother constantly risked his life to live on Andarion outposts and colonies so that he wouldn't have to deal with humans wetting their pants in fear every time he cleared his throat.

Stupid bastards.

Returning to the door, Hauk eyed the woman with

menace. When he went to kick it again, Bastien stopped him.

"Why don't we try something a little less violent and more productive?"

Hauk eyed him irritably. "Blood. Mayhem. Violence. That's my go-to happy place."

"How 'bout we try to find a new one?"

"Such as?"

He plucked a wire out of his cuff. "Picking the lock."

"I'd rather kick it open."

"You would." Bastien snorted. "How 'bout we save it for beating on our captors?"

Ignoring him, Hauk kicked the door again. Suddenly, something sharp stabbed him. With a hiss, he looked down to see another dart in his arm.

Crap. Three more hit him.

Hauk glared at the women who joined the first one as his anger mounted. He fought against the drug with everything he had, but in the end, he blacked out.

Hauk came to, cursing life and everyone in it. Most of all, he cursed the irritated smirk on Bastien's face as he eyed him from where he lay on the ground beside him.

"Told you not to kick that door, didn't I?"

Hauk ignored his taunt. Pain pounded through his body with such ferocity that he knew they must have beaten him while he'd been unconscious. More than that, the drugs played havoc with his system.

His stomach lurched. He tried to move, only to discover he was in the middle of their camp, on his belly and hog-tied. Like Bastien. Someone had chained his hands to his feet behind his back.

Yeah, that didn't help his temper in the least. Growling, he tried to break free.

Bastien rolled his eyes. "Calm down, Hauk. All you're going to do is hurt yourself."

He glared at Bastien. "If you want to see exactly how angry someone can get, tell them to calm down when they're already pissed off!" Bellowing, he tried his best to break free.

"Is that helping? I just gotta know."

"When I get loose, Cabarro, your ass is the first one I'm kicking."

"Oh good. Hope you get out soon. Been awhile since I had a good ass-kicking." Bastien made a kissy face at him.

"Says the man who's so bruised, he looks like a two-year-old banana."

"Now that's just mean and hurtful."

"Telise! He's awake again."

She moved forward and kicked Hauk in the face.

"I wouldn't do that," Bastien warned. "Don't motivate the Andarion for murder. It ain't going to work out well for any of us. 'Specially me, since mine's the first ass he's planning to come after."

Hauk licked at the blood on his lips as he grimaced at the *harita* through his braids.

"Learned anything yet?" she asked him.

He spat the blood out of his mouth. "Other than those pants make your ass look fat?"

She kicked him hard in the ribs.

A blast of color shot within an inch of Telise's face. "Touch him again and the next one goes right between your eyes."

In spite of the pain, a slow smile spread across Hauk's face at the sound of the most beautiful voice in the universe.

Sumi.

Telise reached for her blaster.

Sumi let fly a shot straight into her shoulder. "Hands up or lose your head."

Telise glared at her. "You don't know who you're dealing with."

"Neither do you." Sumi held her hand up to show the brand on her wrist. "Unless you've got another League assassin in your camp, I suggest you free them or I *will* bathe in the blood of every whore here."

Hauk saw one of the others coming up behind Sumi. He opened his mouth to warn her, but before a single sound could come out, she spun and shot the woman, then caught another one he hadn't seen at all.

And her blaster wasn't set to stun.

Sumi now had both weapons drawn as she surveyed the women. "Anyone else want to die today?" she called out to them. "Please! I'm so in the mood for it." She turned back to Telise. "What about you, bitch?"

Glaring at her, Telise reached into her pocket. Instead of keys, she drew a dagger and moved for Hauk.

She was dead before she took more than a step.

When one of them started running for cover, an explosion rocked the camp and drove the woman to the ground.

Sumi tsked. "I have charges set all over this place. Enough to blow us all to the outer atmosphere. Don't push me, people. Now who wants to be my friend and free my male for me?"

Pheara came forward with the keys. She kept her hands out so that Sumi wouldn't mistake her intentions. "We weren't going to hurt him."

Sumi stalked forward. "Then why's he bleeding?"

She swallowed hard. "Telise did that. We . . . we had nothing to do with it. Just take him and go." She freed Dancer, then Bastien, and stepped back.

Hauk pushed himself to his feet and retrieved Telise's blaster from her body.

Sumi's gaze skimmed him from head to toe. "You okay, baby?"

He shot two of the women with a stun blast. "Better now."

"Bastien?"

He wiped at the blood on his wrists. "All good. At least until Hauk keeps his promise to beat my ass."

Sumi turned back to Pheara. "Where are our weapons?"

Pheara gestured toward Telise's tent. "In there."

"I'll get them," Bastien offered.

Moving so that her back was against Dancer's, Sumi kept her gaze on the women until Bastien came back and belted his holster around his hips.

He tossed Hauk's weapons to him.

"Before we leave, I want to do something." Hauk went to Pheara and jerked the keys from her hand. "Is this the biofeed bypass?"

"Yeah."

He met Sumi's curious gaze. "Round the women up and follow me."

"You heard him. *Haritas* on parade. Let's go." Sumi and Bastien followed him to a cage where two men were being held.

Dancer opened the door and released them before he made the six remaining women file inside it. He locked the door and tossed the keys to one of the men. "Happy birthday."

And with that, he draped his arm over Sumi's shoulders so that she could lead him while Bastien pulled up their rear.

"Where are the kids?" Hauk asked.

"Armed to their teeth and hiding with Illyse."

Hauk tightened his arm around her as his vision clouded. Never had he been prouder of her, or more grateful that he'd ignored his common sense and saved her. "Good."

Sumi smiled, grateful that she'd found them in one piece. But as they left camp, she noticed he wasn't completely with her. "Dancer?"

He tightened his grip on her before he kissed the top of her head. "I'm all right."

"You don't look good." She pressed the back of her hand against his cheek. "You're very clammy."

"They drugged him," Bastien said from behind them.

"With what?"

Bastien shrugged. "Really didn't get a chance to ask them what they were using, or for any other recipe, either. But I would assume something strong enough to take down a huge Andarion."

Hauk ignored him while he tugged her forward. "Thank you, by the way."

"For what?"

He gave her an unsteady smile. "I'm usually the one doing the rescuing. It's been a long time since anyone's pulled my ass out of the fire." His words slurred an instant before he sank to his knees.

"Dancer!" She knelt by his side as terror filled her. He was so cold. Like ice.

He held on to her, but didn't seem to be able to speak.

Bastien locked a frightened gaze with hers. "We need to get out of here before they give pursuit. You take one arm and I'll grab the other." He reached for Dancer.

Suddenly, a deep, growling male voice came out of nowhere. "Hands up or die."

CHAPTER 22

Sumi bit her lip in indecision. She saw the same desire to fight their latest attackers in Bastien's eyes that she held. But they didn't know who or what they were facing now.

Or how many.

A flash of color narrowly missed her face. She glanced around, but couldn't see anyone. They were using some kind of cloaking device.

This group of assassins was much higher-tech than the previous ones. But they were in for one hell of a fight if they tried to take Dancer from her.

Slowly, she held her hands up and put her body between Dancer and Bastien, and where the shot had originated. Hoping Bastien would follow her lead, she decided to play stupid to get the numbers and locations of their adversaries. "Look, we don't have much. But take whatever you want. Just be quick about it. We need to tend our friend. He's badly hurt."

Dancer and Bastien collapsed behind her and hit the deck hard.

With a gasp, she turned to help them.

Something flickered on the other side of Dancer.

Afraid of their intent, she launched herself at where

it'd come from and hit a solid wall of muscle. With everything she'd been taught, she attacked.

Until someone humongous and strong picked her up from behind and effortlessly stepped back with her.

"No!" she screamed, trying to break free of the man's hold. "He's unconscious. He's no threat to you. Please, just take our supplies and go!" Shrieking in anger, she picked all her weight off her feet. The man holding her didn't even flinch or stumble.

Damn, he was strong.

Bastien tried to fight, too, but he was slammed to the ground and cuffed so fast, it was terrifying. He growled threats and spewed profanity at them.

"Please!" Sumi begged, praying they weren't here to kill Dancer. "We just want to help our friend."

Another shimmer appeared next to Dancer as the soldier turned his cloaking device off to show an unmarked black battlesuit. He shrugged off his backpack and removed his helm to reveal an unbelievably handsome man with long dark hair tied back into a ponytail. His dark Ritadarion eyes were ringed with black eyeliner, but she knew that face from Dancer's photos and stories.

"Syn?"

He scowled at her. "I don't know you."

She looked over her shoulder. "Nykyrian? Are you the one holding me?"

Syn opened his pack. "How do you know us?"

"Dancer." Only then did the tight grip on her waver the slightest degree.

"Are you Sumi?" His was the voice that had originally threatened them when they stopped.

"Yes."

He released her immediately and decloaked. He gestured to Bastien, who was fighting against the cuffs that held him. "Is that one Bastien?"

"He is."

Another man, who was standing beside where Bastien lay on the ground, decloaked. Kneeling down, he uncuffed Bastien's hands. "Sorry about that."

Glaring his displeasure, Bastien cursed him and his parentage as he rubbed his wrists. Amused by the insults, the man pulled off his helmet. His short red hair held the royal harone of the Caronese emperor. Darling was only slightly taller than her and was a lot more attractive in real life than he'd been in Dancer's photos.

Nykyrian, however, was every bit as scary and intimidating as both Dancer and Thia had claimed. No wonder everyone was so terrified of facing Nemesis.

But he wasn't important to her at present. Sumi ran to Dancer so that she could kneel beside him and give Syn a rundown on his condition. "He said they drugged him with something while they held him. He was poisoned two days ago from a Partini blade and he has several injuries from other attacks."

Syn gaped in disbelief. "What the hell did you do to him?" His question offended her.

"I've kept him alive."

Nykyrian pulled his helmet off and held it under one arm. His white-blond hair was cut stylishly short. Unlike Dancer, he had green, human eyes and his face was covered with scars. "Where're my daughter and Darice?"

"They're hiding near camp, with Illyse. There's a cave just to the south of the climbing approach."

Inclining his head to her, Nykyrian spoke into a link that was attached to his ear. "Jayne? We've secured Hauk. The kids should be near the base camp that we found earlier. I'm leaving Syn and Darling here with Sumi and Bastien. I need you for support while I go after Thia. Everyone else, stay where you are at camp and make sure no one goes near my kid. If they do, make them bleed hard." He headed off at a dead run for a cloaked airbike.

Bastien continued to glare at Darling. "Are we good yet? Or do I have to don my ass-kicking boots?"

Darling glanced to her. "Don't know. Are we good?"

Before she could answer, Dancer blinked his eyes open. "Sumi?" he whispered hoarsely.

Leaning over him, she placed her hand on his cheek. "Right here, baby."

Darling and Syn exchanged a shocked, exaggerated gape as Syn pulled out a light and checked Dancer's eyes.

With a savage hiss, Dancer shoved the light away. "Put that away or I'm going to ram it someplace both you and Shahara will curse me for."

"Dancer," she chided. "Let him tend you."

He started to grimace then pressed his lips together. "I hate that damn light. It burns."

Now it was Darling's turn to pull Dancer's eyelid back to see his eye.

Dancer grimaced and punched at him.

Laughing, Darling took it in stride. "You look like hell, buddy."

"You ain't no beauty queen, either. Asshole."

Darling grinned in bitter amusement. "You better take a nicer tone. I walked out on my wife and son to be here for you to insult me."

Dancer frowned at him as he rubbed at his eye in a very adorable boyish fashion. "Zarya had the baby?"

"Last night. About half an hour before Nyk called to say you were in trouble."

Dancer scratched at his head. "Sorry."

"Don't be. About time I get to save *you,* and don't think I'm not holding your impeccably inconsiderate timing over your head for the rest of eternity. You will be paying for this, that I promise. By the way, Zarya wanted me to tell you that you better get back home and see your nephew or she'll hunt your hulking ass down and skin it."

And that reminded her . . .

Sumi touched Syn's hand to get his attention while he evaluated Dancer's condition. "Someone planted a tracking device in Dancer's back. We've had incas coming after him for days."

Nodding, he tilted Dancer's head toward him. "You with me, buddy?"

With an irritable grimace, he slapped at Syn. "I'm thirsty."

Syn pulled a bag out of his pack and handed it to Darling, who held it up while Syn prepared the IV.

When Syn stuck the needle in, Dancer hissed and started for him.

Sumi caught his fist. "Dancer, play nice with the doctor who might not want to help you if you clock him."

He calmed instantly and nuzzled his face against her knee. When she went to brush his braids from his cheek, he took her hand and laced her fingers with his.

Sumi tensed as she heard the sharp click of a blaster from behind her.

Syn didn't react at all. "Put it away, Jayne. She's a friendly."

"You sure?"

He gave her a droll stare. "I've never known Hauk to cuddle an enemy. You? I mean, he is weird and all, but he's usually consistent with his surly demeanor."

Jayne decloaked and moved forward to join them. "What happened to him?" She pulled her helmet off to show that, like Darling, her pictures didn't do her justice. She was extremely beautiful.

Syn sighed heavily. "He's got enough toxins in his system that if he were human he'd be dead ten times over. Thank the gods Andarions are tough bastards."

"Is he going to be okay?" Sumi breathed.

Syn finally met her gaze. The anger there dissipated into kindness. "Yeah. I think so. Unless something has happened to Thia, in which case, we'll be scraping up his guts as soon as Nyk returns."

Jayne continued to glare at her. "Who the hell are *you,* human?"

"Jaynie," Dancer said weakly. "Be nice to my girl or I'll turn her loose on your hide. Trust me, I think she can take you."

Jayne scoffed as she squatted down beside Hauk and touched his shoulder. "What happened to your eyes?"

A knowing smile curved Syn's lips. "I think Hauk got around to taking your advice, Jayne."

"What advice?"

Syn glanced at Sumi then laughed. "I'll tell you later."

Darling frowned as he finally looked over at Bastien, who'd opted to sit quietly and bleed while Syn tended Dancer. "Do I know you? You look really familiar."

Bastien stretched out on the ground. "Summit meeting. Years ago. I was with my father. You were with your uncle."

Recognition lit Darling's eyes. "You're the one who decked Nylan's son when he spat in my food."

"Don't remember that, particularly, but it sounds like something I'd do. Hate that rank bastard."

Darling shifted to study Bastien's ragged condition. "You're one of the Kirovarian princes."

"Was."

"Holy shit. I thought you were all dead." Darling met Jayne's gaze. "He's one of Nyk's paternal cousins, who was deposed about a decade ago."

Sumi gaped at something Bastien had failed to tell them. Now that Darling mentioned it, she saw that regal bearing. She'd attributed it to his military training, but now that she knew, it was obvious what it really signified.

How had a prince become a League Ravin? Even a deposed one.

Suddenly, Syn grabbed Sumi's wrist and shoved her sleeve back to expose her League brand. He drew his blaster faster than she could blink and held it to her jaw.

Dancer knocked it away. "Stop it!"

"She's a League assassin."

"Yeah, I know. Kyr sent her after me. Remind me to order him flowers and a thank-you card later."

Syn, Darling, and Jayne exchanged a scowl.

"You know?" Jayne asked.

Dancer sat up slowly.

"Whoa, buddy." Syn held him back. "You need to stay down until we get a lift here for you."

Hauk hesitated before he stretched out again, only this time, he put his head in Sumi's lap. "Jaynie? Darling? Don't let anyone hurt my *mia*. Or I'll take it out of both your asses."

Darling arched his brows. "Look, bud, I know you're drugged out of your mind, but you are aware that Sumi's human, right?"

Dancer shoved at Darling. "Don't insult my female by putting her in the same class as *you*."

Jayne arched a brow. "How much crap have you given him, Syn?"

"That ain't my drug, baby. That's called l-o-v-e."

Jayne scoffed. "Hauk? Love? Lorina shit."

"It's true. That's why his eyes are red," Darling said to her. "Can't hide or deny that."

Syn injected something into the IV.

Dancer shoved at him. "Why did you do that?"

"You need to rest."

Still, he fought it. He grabbed the front of Darling's battlesuit. "Keep Sumi safe for me. Don't let anyone harm her. Swear . . ." He passed out.

Sumi caught him against her and laid him down gently.

They all three stared at her as if she was a three-headed Gourish snake.

"What?"

Without answering her, Syn moved to check on Bastien.

Darling continued to hold Dancer's IV while he studied her with an unsettling intensity.

"Jayne?" Syn called. "On my twelve, babe."

She went over to him, leaving Sumi alone with Darling. "So what did you name your son?" she asked, trying to break the awkward tension.

"Cezar."

"Congratulations. I know Dancer will be thrilled to meet him."

Darling shook his head. "And he lets you call him Dancer, too . . . damn. He really must love you."

"It's a beautiful name," she said defensively.

He scoffed. "Says the woman who didn't have to go to school or into League training with it. Take it from someone named Darling, it's been a constant source of agony for him the whole of his life."

She hadn't thought about that. "I-I didn't mean to hurt him with it."

Darling covered her hand with his. "Trust me, given the way you say it, he doesn't mind. If he did, he'd stop you. Tolerance is *not* one of his virtues."

That was certainly true.

"Little Sumi?"

She went absolutely still as she heard the one voice she'd been dreading most. Her heart choking her, she slowly looked over her shoulder.

Time froze in that heartbeat as her gaze fell to Fain. Much older than the teen who'd once rocked her to sleep, he was still huge. Even bigger than Dancer.

Dressed in a Tavali battlesuit, he had his face painted similarly to the way Dancer had done hers. His Tavali mask hung loose around his neck and his braids were pulled back from his handsome face by a black band. His black gloves were tucked into his holster. Her gaze fell to his hand where he wore Omira's wedding band on his pinkie. Just like Dancer had said.

The pain on his face was searing. He stared at her as if she were a ghost whose sole purpose was to haunt him. As if he couldn't believe his eyes.

Darling looked back and forth between them. "You two know each other?"

Sumi licked her suddenly dry lips as she tried to think of how best to answer Darling's question.

"I was married to her older sister." Well, Fain took that ball out of play. He blinked as if finally getting a handle on the fact that she wasn't Omira and that she meant him no harm.

Funny, she'd been so angry at him for so long. Had hated his guts with such passion and blamed him for what Omira had done—when honestly, her sister had destroyed them all.

Sumi had stupidly thought that if she ever saw him again, she'd want to murder him on sight.

Now . . . that hatred was gone. Melted by a wave of feeling lost, abandoned, and heartbroken. She felt as if she was seven years old and, like Thia with her father, she just wanted to run into his arms and have him hold her the way he'd done when she was a girl. To tell her once more that everything would be okay and that he'd never let anyone hurt her.

Jayne smacked her hand against her own forehead. "That's why she looks so familiar. I knew I recognized her from somewhere. Stupid me. I was thinking bounty sheets, not Fain's wife."

Fain's gaze dropped to Dancer's head in Sumi's lap.

In that moment, Dancer blinked his eyes open as if he felt his brother's presence. Guilt and anguish marked his features as he realized how this must look to Fain.

Moving forward, Fain dropped to his knees next to Dancer. "Hey, *drey*. You still with me?"

Hauk couldn't breathe as he saw the raw agony in Fain's eyes that his being with Sumi had caused his brother. And he felt like total shit over it. Fain was the one being he would never have hurt for anything. "I'm sorry."

Fain scowled at him. "For what?"

He glanced at Sumi then back to Fain. "I never meant to hurt you."

Fain cupped Hauk's head in his hands. "Dancer . . . this doesn't hurt me." He gave him a sincere smile. "You deserve to be happy, *kiran*. It's all I've ever wanted for you." He dropped his hand to Dancer's then he took Sumi's into his other hand and joined them together. "Don't let my past darken or taint *your* future. I love both my *kisa* and *kiran*. I always have."

But even so, Hauk saw the ragged torment in Fain's eyes. And he knew how much this hurt him to see them have what Omira had denied him. If anyone deserved to be happy, it was Fain. His brother was the most noble and decent being he'd ever known.

Pain in the ass at times, but always loyal and caring.

Always there.

"I'd rather you hit me, *drey*."

Fain laughed. "You're too weak at the moment. Few days . . . I'll be happy to beat you down."

Hauk playfully slapped his brother's face. "You suck as a brother. I want my money back."

Fain snorted. "Could be worse. I'm stuck with *you*."

Syn returned to them. He let out an irritated sigh as he checked Hauk's IV. "How much do I have to give you to keep you unconscious? Damn Andarion metabolism. Stay down, beast!"

He fanged Syn then looked at Fain. "Kill him."

"I would, but his wife would tear me up. And no offense, she scares me. You really don't."

Ignoring them, Syn added more medicine to the IV as a skimmer appeared. A small team of medics ran off with lifts for Dancer and Bastien.

It was only then that Fain saw who was with them.

"Bas!" he said with a laugh. "And here I thought you were dead. Should have known better."

Bastien gave Fain a droll, offended stare as they placed him on the lift. "Your brother damn near finished what *you* started. Luckily, I'm like a cockroach. Hard to kill."

Shaking his head, Fain patted him on his arm. "It's good to see you again, *drey*. Thank you for fighting with my brother for me."

"Only for you, *drey*. Only for you."

The medics rushed Bastien into the skimmer.

After carefully laying Dancer's head on the ground, Sumi moved out of the way. She watched and hesitated as they all boarded the craft.

Fain turned back toward her as she stayed put while the others scrambled. "You coming?"

Afraid, she bit her lip, debating the sanity of going. If she left with them, she'd never be able to go back to The League. While she had no doubt that Dancer would save Kalea, she wasn't sure what awaited *her* at their hands.

She was a League agent. They were all enemies to The League. Dancer might love her, but none of the rest did.

Well . . . maybe Darice and Thia.

But Dariana would hate her guts, as would Dancer's parents. For that matter, if she went, she might cause him to lose his lineage.

Forever.

I'm not Omira. The last thing she wanted was to cause any harm to Dancer or to those he loved. Her presence with him would be nothing but misery and continued problems for him.

Excessive problems.

He was Andarion. She was human. Thia's story about their asteroid belt went through her head. She had no business with him.

And yet . . .

She couldn't stand the thought of not having him in her life. It hurt so much that it made it hard for her to breathe. It was like losing her daughter all over again.

Fain stepped down from the ramp and approached her. "What's wrong?"

Overwhelmed by it all, Sumi wrapped her arms around her chest as tears filled her eyes. She couldn't hurt Dancer the way Omira had ruined Fain. She couldn't. One look at that wedding band on Fain's hand and his Tavali uniform, and she knew just how wrong it would be to take away everything Dancer loved.

Even his name.

Clearing her throat, she glanced away, scared she might lose her conviction. "Dancer's where he belongs. I should be going."

Fain scowled at her. "Are you nuts? Do I have to toss you over my shoulder and carry you into the skimmer?"

She raked a horrified look over him. "You wouldn't dare."

"For my brother, there isn't anything I would *not* dare. I would defy the gods themselves to keep him happy and safe." He moved to stand right in front of her. "I saw his eyes, Sumi, and I know that wasn't from Dariana. And unless I need to keep Nykyrian from ripping Dancer's spine out through his nose, there's only one female who could have done that to him on this trip. The one he was clutching when I arrived. It would devastate him to wake up without you."

Those words choked her even more. But still, she didn't want to hurt him. Or cause him harm. How could she buy her happiness at the expense of his entire life and family? "I'm a threat to him."

"So am I," he said with a bitter laugh. "Every time he speaks to me, he runs the risk of losing everything he has." Fain glanced back toward the skimmer. "Dancer's never done anything the easy way. And he never will. It's part of the little bastard's charm." He held his hand out to her. "C'mon. I'll be with you the whole time. Nothing to fear. I will keep both of you safe."

In that moment, something inside her shattered and sent a wave of uncontrollable sobs through her.

She wanted to hate Fain so much. But this was the brother she remembered having. The brother who had meant so much to her.

Just like Dancer, Fain swung her up in his arms and carried her into the skimmer.

"Damn, Fain," Jayne snapped as she saw them. "What'd you do? Break another human? I swear we can't leave you alone for five seconds."

Fain shrugged. "I don't know. Human women look at me and burst into tears. I'm kind of used to it."

Another Tavali who looked a lot like Darling snorted at him. "I'd burst into tears too if I had to look at your ugly ass." He took her from Fain and set her down on a small bench seat. Kneeling in front of her, he handed her a handkerchief. "I'm Darling's brother, Ryn."

Sniffing back her tears, she took his handkerchief and wiped at her eyes. "Thank you."

He patted her knees then looked up at Fain. "How's the beast?"

"He looked pretty beat up. But I've seen him worse. Hell, for that matter, I'm sure *I've* beaten him worse. And that was for just wearing my boots without permission."

Snorting, Ryn stood and clapped a hand on Fain's shoulder. "Syn would sooner kill himself than let anything happen to him. You know that."

"I know. It's why I'm not freaking out and going on a killing rampage."

Still nervous and unsure, Sumi glanced around the small group of men standing in the main cargo area— Darling, Fain, Ryn—and of course Jayne. Syn must have taken Dancer and Bastien into the small infirmary somewhere else on the skimmer.

"Where're Nykyrian and the kids?" she asked them.

Darling pointed to the link in his ear. "They took the other skimmer and are already on board, waiting for us."

"The kids were all right?"

Darling pulled the link from his ear and held it toward her. Even without it being in her ear, she could hear Darice's and Thia's excited chattering as they told Nykyrian everything that had happened while they'd been with Dancer.

She smiled. "Thank you."

He inclined his head respectfully as he returned it to his ear.

Syn opened a door to their right. "Sumi? Get in here and let Hauk know that you're okay. I can't do anything with this unreasonable, surly bastard."

"He's not unreasonable. He's just fierce." She went into the small room where Bastien was now unconscious. But Dancer was fighting Syn as he tried to pull monitors off his body and get up from the lift.

It was actually rather comical to watch the two of them swat at each other like children, as they traded insults.

She tsked at him. "What are you doing, sweetie?"

Hauk calmed as soon as he heard her voice and saw

her whole and unscathed. While he trusted his friends, he also knew how protective they were. And given Jayne's actions to Zarya over what her men had done to Darling, he didn't want to chance a similar occurrence with Sumi. "I wanted to make sure you were all right."

Her eyes tender, she cupped his cheek and rubbed noses with him. "I will be, if you let Syn treat you without fighting him. Now be a good boy and I'll give you a reward later."

He grinned at her teasing. Holding her hand, he allowed Syn to put the monitors back on him. "By the way, Syn, Sumi has a League tag we need you to remove."

"Okay. You're not going to punch me for cutting into her to get to it, are you?"

"Don't you hurt her," he growled in earnest.

Syn rolled his eyes then looked to Sumi. "Gah, are all Andarions this ridiculous? Oh wait . . . Nyk and Kiara. Got it. Never mind." His gaze dropped down to Sumi's abdomen and he scowled. "Is that your blood on you?"

She glanced at it. "I was attacked by a tourah a couple of days ago, but it's a flesh wound. I'm fine."

"She's not fine. She also has a blast wound to her arm."

"Flesh wound," she repeated. "I'm really not hurt."

Hauk gave her a droll stare. "Now who's being unreasonable?"

"Still all you, baby."

Gods, how he loved her teasing. Only she could get away with being this flippant with him. *I am a sick bastard.*

Syn moved to put a mask over Hauk's face. "If he pulls this off," he said to Sumi, "beat him."

Hauk made an obscene Ritadarion gesture to Syn.

"Not on your best day, Andarion. I don't care how much you look like a woman." Syn tilted Hauk's head to one side so that he could examine the bruise above and below his eye.

Hauk focused on Sumi as his vision blurred. He didn't want to be unconscious until he was sure she was safe from the reach of Dariana and The League.

His mother.

There was no telling what any of them would do to her. It was his job to protect her, but as he felt the medicine kicking in again, he knew Syn wouldn't leave him awake much longer.

"*Mia?*"

She took his outstretched hand. "Right here."

Panic set in as he struggled against the drugs. He tried to take his mask off, but neither of them would accommodate him. "Stay safe." He wasn't sure if she understood those badly slurred words as everything turned black.

Syn scowled at Sumi. "Why the hell is he so afraid of letting you out of his sight? He has to know we're not going to hurt you."

"It's not you he's afraid of."

She looked past Syn to see Fain in the doorway.

"Then what?" Syn asked.

"She's a League assassin in the middle of a Sentella-Tavali-Andarion and Caronese strike force that is at war with them. By going after Dancer when she did, she endangered a member of the royal Andarion family, and the last heir of a family the Andarions view as a national treasure. Queen Cairistiona can legally demand her head for this. As can Dariana, and Dancer's mother."

Sumi went weak at his words. "What?"

Fain nodded. "When we get to the ship, avoid anyone wearing a red-and-black battlesuit or uniform. Those are members of the Andarion Queen's Guard."

Syn scoffed. "Nykyrian won't let them hurt her."

"He can talk to his mother about Thia, but he can't stop Dariana if she calls out for Sumi's blood. And given how much she hates Dancer, she's liable to do it just for spite.

That's what he's afraid of. If she evokes her right of death over Darice, there's nothing the queen can do. The law is the law. Sumi would have to die for endangering Darice's life."

Syn put his hand on Sumi's arm. "We won't let her touch you. Believe me, there's not a one of us who doesn't want a piece of that bitch's hide for what she's done to Hauk over the years."

Fain nodded. "He's right. Make sure you stay with one of our royal family members at all times—Caillen, Ryn, Darling, Maris, Nyk, Desideria, or Drake. They alone can keep you safe from her."

She felt the skimmer landing on board the mother ship. Fear gripped her. But she was an assassin and assassins never showed their fear.

To anyone.

With her head high, she would face this. Bracing herself, she mentally prepared for the worst that was waiting for her.

CHAPTER 23

Sumi thought she was braced for the worst, but nothing could have prepared her for what awaited them in the landing bay of the massive ship. She felt as if she'd walked into a war-zone planning committee. There were creatures everywhere in battlesuits from more countries and organizations than she could identify.

Yet the weirdest feeling was seeing Andarions and humans working side by side without issue. Occasionally, someone might pass an irritated look at another, but they did that to their own kind as much as they did it to others.

A large number of the gathered beings pinned curious stares on her, which made her extremely uncomfortable.

Fain stood beside her with his hand on her shoulder to let her know he was there to protect her. "Just breathe, *kisa*. I'm with you."

"What does *kisa* mean?"

"Little sister. *Kiran* means little brother."

The word warmed her. But that feeling was fleeting as she saw the massive swarm of beings there to escort Dancer from the skimmer to the infirmary.

Thia hadn't been joking. Their family *was* terrifying and huge.

"Sumi!"

She barely registered the call before she was practically bowled over by Darice. His entire face alight with joy, he seized her in a tight hug that left her breathless. Then he kissed her cheek and released her.

"We were so worried about you. Especially when Thia told me that Dancer and Bastien were down. We didn't know if you'd been hurt or what. . . . I'm so glad you're okay."

Shaking her head, Thia walked up behind him with a huge smile. "You must have performed an exorcism on Darice while you were on that mountain."

He snorted before he playfully shoved at Thia, like any pesky little brother. He turned back to Sumi and sobered. "While we waited in the caves, we made these for you and Dancer." He pulled a feathered necklace from his neck and placed it around hers. The other two matched perfectly. Each one had a single feather and bone.

Like father and son.

Darice bit his lip nervously as he showed her the one he'd made for Dancer. "You think he'll like it?"

"He'll love it, Darice. I can't wait to see his face when you give it to him. And I can't thank you enough for mine. It's absolutely beautiful, sweetie. Thank you for the honor." She kissed his cheek.

His eyes proud, he glanced from her to Fain, who tensed visibly.

For several heartbeats no one moved.

Darice fingered the feather around his neck before he finally spoke. "Did you slip and fall on your Endurance climb, Uncle Fain?"

Fain couldn't have looked more stunned had Darice slapped him. He stammered for several seconds before he finally answered. "Um . . . no. Keris knocked me down a couple of times, but I didn't slip on my own."

"Were you scared?"

Fain was still casting his gaze about as if this whole conversation was terrifying him, and he expected some-one to attack him for having it. "Not really. I was too pissed over being kicked in the head and face every time I got within striking range."

Darice glanced to Sumi. "I slipped at one point and thought I was dead, but then I didn't really fall. Sumi caught me and we climbed up and I stood by the nest. You could see everything for miles and miles. It was so awesome! I felt like I could do anything!"

Thia met Fain's stunned, bewildered gaze. "Told you. She performed an exorcism. Weird, huh? She took a brat up the side of the mountain and came down with a sentient being. Who knew it'd be that easy?"

Darice cut an irritated glare at her. "You don't under-stand. You didn't make the climb. It was life-changing."

Thia held her hands up in surrender. "I'm just grateful for your new attitude, *kiran*. You keep this up, and you'll be my all-time favorite camping buddy."

Fain offered his nephew a tentative smile. "You're sup-posed to have your hair braided now that you've made your ascent into adulthood." Hesitantly, he reached out.

Darice moved closer to him so that Fain could braid his hair.

If Sumi lived a thousand years, she'd never forget the sad yet proud look on Fain's face that his nephew was al-lowing Fain to touch him for the first time in Darice's life. Darice appeared unsure at first, but after a few minutes he relaxed and accepted Fain as family.

It touched her heart to see them like that.

Thia draped her arm over Sumi's shoulders. "Don't look now, but the others have noticed you. . . . Heads up."

Suddenly terrified, Sumi glanced past their small group to see the truth in those words. Syn had taken Dancer and Bastien to the infirmary and everyone who'd been focused on Dancer was now staring at them.

Or more to the point, *her*.

Never in her life had she wished herself invisible more.

A gorgeous, bearded male in a burgundy Phrixian battlesuit was the first to walk over to them. He had the same intense, predator lope that marked both Fain and Dancer.

His long black hair had a bright red stripe in it and was pulled back into a ponytail. "No one told me we were doing makeovers! Stand aside, Fain, you're not doing that right." Using his hip, he bumped Fain to the left and took over plaiting Darice's hair. Then he flashed a bright smile at Sumi. "I'm Mari, by the way. Nice to meet you."

Sumi returned his smile. So this was Safir and Kyr's brother. She could see the resemblance between him and Saf, but not so much with Kyr. Maybe because he and Saf still had a soul.

And Mari didn't appear crazy.

"Mari?"

He cocked an eyebrow at her. "What, love?"

"Your brother, Safir—"

"Is at home, being taken care of, even as we speak."

"He's no longer in Kyr's custody?"

Maris paused to meet her gaze. "He's safe."

"Thank the gods," she breathed.

Thia grinned at them. "By the way, Aunt Mari's the one who's going to be grumpiest with you from now on."

That made Sumi's heart stop. What had she done? "Why?"

Thia wrinkled her nose. "He's Uncle Hauk's late-night gaming partner."

Mari winked at her. "It's okay. Hauk is one male I don't mind sharing. Besides, my son and hubby will be delighted to have more undivided time with me."

Sumi started to respond when she realized they were now surrounded by numerous strangers who were eyeballing her with way too much interest. She knew some of them from Dancer's photos, but she didn't know all their names.

Fain placed a comforting hand on her shoulder as he took up the introductions. "You know Darling and Ryn already. The Kimmerian assassin between them is their brother Drake."

She shook arms with the man who looked almost identical to Darling, except he had dark hair instead of Darling's and Ryn's red hair.

They stepped aside for the next wave.

"Caillen whatever he's calling himself this week and his wife Desideria. They are two of the ones, along with any of Darling's family, I told you to stay near for a while."

Handsome and irritated, Caillen glared at Fain's introduction. "Nice meeting you, Sumi."

"You're the Exeterian prince and heir?" she asked, trying to keep them all straight in her mind.

Caillen nodded.

And as Sumi's gaze fell to Caillen's tiny, pregnant wife, she realized that she bore an amazing resemblance to the little girl Dancer had been holding. "You have a daughter?"

Desideria smiled proudly. "We do. Lillya."

"Dancer has a picture of him holding her that he carries."

Her smile widened. "It's adorable, isn't it? She thinks her uncle Hauk hung the very moons, he's so tall." She stepped aside for another Tavali to step forward. "This is my brother, Chayden. He flies a lot with Hauk and Ryn, and is an old friend of my husband's."

Chayden held his hand out to her. "Pleased to meet you."

"You're the one who dropped Dancer off on Oksana."

"I am."

She grinned. "I've heard you're quite the pilot. Nice meeting you, Chayden."

After that, the faces and names blended together until an extremely intense, frightening redheaded woman came up, holding a small boy in her arms. While all of them held the stances of trained soldiers and assassins, there was something particularly deadly about this one.

She eyed Sumi with suspicion. "I'm Shahara Dagan-Wade," she said before Fain had a chance. "Syn's wife."

Ah . . . now she understood why everyone was so terrified of crossing this woman. A famed bounty hunter for the Overseer, she'd hauled in some of the worst criminals in the Nine Worlds.

Alone.

"You're the one who shot Dancer for pretending to drop, I assume, this little guy." She tickled his belly.

A miniature copy of his father, Devyn laughed. "I'm this many years old." He held his hand out with all five fingers spread wide."

They both laughed at him while Shahara kissed his cheek. "This is our little Devyn Devil."

Sumi shook his tiny hand. "Pleased to meet you, Devyn."

He screwed his face up thoughtfully. "So are you my new Aunt Hauk?"

Unsure how to answer, she exchanged an uncomfortable stare with Shahara before her gaze went to Darice. For once, he didn't seem to mind that she was with his uncle.

She suspected part of it was that he was too thrilled to have Mari braiding his hair to match Dancer's and Fain's to be agitated over her relationship.

"There we go." Mari patted Darice on the shoulder and stepped back to admire his handiwork. "Like a true Andarion warrior."

Fain pulled out his sword so that Darice could use the blade as a mirror.

Slack-jawed, Sumi met Shahara's unamused gaze.

Shahara sighed. "They're like feral animals. You really can't home-train them. I've been trying to for years." She glanced back at Fain, who had a what'd-I-do expression as he noticed Shahara's censure. "I give up."

Thia let out a "heh" sound. "At least he didn't hand him a loaded blaster and tell him to check the perimeter at night."

"And was that so bad, daughter?"

Sumi turned to see Nykyrian standing directly behind them. Dang, he moved as silently as Dancer.

Thia patted her father on his cheek. "It's fine, Dad. Scarred for life. But fine."

Nykyrian wrapped his arms around her shoulders and held her back against his chest. There was no missing how much he loved and adored his daughter. How fiercely protective he was of her.

Nor did she miss the way Thia savored her father's loving embrace.

Syn stepped around Nykyrian and handed a small jar to Sumi before he took his son from his wife and squeezed him until Devyn protested.

Sumi lifted it to see a small electronic chip. "What's this?"

"Hauk's TD. I killed the signal, but can't peg where it came from. I can't even ID the chip's DOM or origin. Thought you might have better luck."

Nykyrian gaped at Syn's disclosure. "*You? You* couldn't trace it?"

"Yeah, I know. Right? It's really pissing me off that I got nothing. I'm sure Hauk can do something with it when he wakes up though."

Sumi studied it carefully. "It's not a League tag. Any ideas?"

Syn shook his head. "I hit a wall."

Mari took it next to study it. "Never seen one like this before."

"Looks Andarion."

They stared at Fain, who was peering over Mari's shoulder.

Fain took it from Mari's hand. "It's an older model, but I swear it's similar to what we used when I was in the infantry corps."

His jaw ticcing, Nykyrian narrowed his gaze. "You think it's Jullien who tagged him?"

Shrugging, Fain handed the chip back to Sumi. "I don't know. He's had a hard-on for Dancer since he saved you at school. And the last few years definitely haven't endeared my brother to him. . . . It's possible."

"And speaking of . . ." Syn handed Devyn back to Shahara. "I need to borrow our lovely new friend and remove her tracker before it's turned back on."

Darice stepped forward like a respectful guard. "Do you need me to go with you, Sumi?"

She hugged him. "I'll be fine, sweetie. Thank you for offering, though. It means a lot to me to have such a fierce and noble protector."

When she started to release him, he held on to her. *"Kimi asyado."*

She glanced to Thia for the translation, but it was Fain who explained it. "He says that he loves you tremendously."

Sumi tightened her arms around him. "I love you, too, baby." She placed a kiss on his cheek. When she pulled back, she saw the tears in his eyes.

"I'm an adult male now, Sumi. Not a baby."

"Yes, you are, Darice. And you're a strong, beautiful male. You honor your ancestors and all of Andaria."

Darice smiled happily.

"Damn," Darling breathed as he joined them. "Whatever she has, we need to bottle it in droves."

Nykyrian scowled at him. "What are you talking about?"

"First Hauk, now Darice. I've never seen anyone tame so many rowdy Andarions with nothing more than a smile. Just think, if we had that, we could rule them all."

Nykyrian pinned him with a wry stare. "I already rule them all."

"Oh yeah, there is that."

Syn gave his son one last squeeze before he turned to Sumi. "Come on, let's get you deactivated." He led her toward the infirmary.

Sumi hesitated. "Can I see Dancer before we do this?"

"Sure." He took her to a small room where Dancer was hooked up to several monitors.

Her heart wrenched at the sight of him like that. He was so strong and vibrant that, like his friends, it was easy for her to forget that he was a mortal being who could be brought down by something as simple as a well-placed small shot or infection. "Is he all right?"

"The compound they used to stun him isn't playing well with his system. He had something similar to an allergic reaction to it—which is more serious for an Andarion than a human. But he'll pull through. I'm only keeping him unconscious because I know he won't stay down if he's awake. The bastard thinks he's invincible."

He was right about that. "Andarion TAM."

Syn laughed. "He told you, huh?"

"Yes, he did."

"Well maybe now that he has *you,* he'll be less suicidal."

"Meaning?"

Syn pinned her with a grim expression. "Instead of having something to live for, he now has some*one* to live for."

Sumi wasn't sure of the difference. From what she'd seen, Dancer had lots of people he lived for already. "I still don't follow."

Syn moved to check one of the monitors. "Since the

day I met him, Hauk's fought the world with one foot already on the other side of eternity. Like he's fighting a ghost. He's had no real sense of self-worth. No regard for whether or not he returned from a mission. I know, 'cause I was like that, too. We all were. We fought because it's all we knew. But it's different when you have something to fight for. Someone to come back to. Someone you know will be destroyed if you don't make it."

That she understood. She'd been there as far back as she could remember—not really caring whether or not she made it through the day or the mission. And he was right. Now that she had Dancer, it made things much more complicated. Made her want to hold on when she'd already relegated herself to letting go.

Suddenly, the door behind them opened. Sumi turned to find a full unit of Andarion soldiers there.

Syn put himself between her and Dancer and them. "What's going on?"

"Stand down, Doctor. We're here for the woman."

"She's a patient of mine."

He disregarded Syn entirely. "She's under arrest."

Sumi's stomach shrank as she took a step back. "For what?"

They didn't answer as they pushed past Syn and seized her, then hauled her from the room.

CHAPTER 24

His blood begging for vengeance, Hauk forced himself to kneel before his queen in the center of her small, makeshift office that had been set up for her onboard the ship, even though what he really wanted to do was take the sword from across his back and use it to cut her head from her body. . . .

Mother of Nykyrian or not.

But he knew the eight guards standing between him and her would kill him before he could take more than a single angry step in her direction. He was good, but they were loaded for Andarion and would be as motivated to murder him as he was to execute his queen for arresting Sumi.

Cairistiona sat on the opposite side of a large desk, staring at him with an expression he couldn't even begin to read. Her long black hair was coiled in intricate braids around her impeccably beautiful face as she watched him with suspicious white-and-red eyes. In her youth, before her affair with Nykyrian's father, she had risen to the rank of prime commander for the Andarion armada.

Her lineage had always been one of the fairest skinned of all Andarions and her blood contained the only warriors who could give the War Hauks a run for their ferocity in battle. It was why his grandmother had sought to unite their blood after all these centuries. She firmly believed that they would birth legendary warriors who would guard Andaria for eternity.

And like his family, Cairistiona's wasn't known for its forgiveness or tolerance. Some of the worst blood feuds marring Andarion history had come from her lineage.

She ran her tongue over her right fang speculatively before she finally spoke. "Interesting . . . the last time I had a War Hauk kneeling before me, it was your father confessing how he'd dishonored me and broke his pledge to my lineage. Have you any idea how embarrassing that was for me?"

He glanced down to the burn scar on his arm as he remembered all the times he'd knelt before Dariana and had his pledge coldly and painfully refused in front of their families. "Yes, Majesty. I do, and I apologize deeply for any slight my parents have ever caused you."

Tilting her head, she drummed her claws against the desk as she continued to watch him. He had no way of knowing what thoughts were going through her mind . . . if she intended to punish him for his parents' transgression against her. As queen, she had full rank and privilege to do with him whatever she wanted. All Andarions were viewed as property and servants to their royal house, which was another thing that made his father's actions against Cairistiona so egregious.

And it might have a lot to do with why she'd refused to have Nykyrian present at this meeting.

She stopped drumming her claws. "Rise, Dancer of the Warring Blood Clan of Hauk, son of Endine and Ferral, and tell me why you've so brashly requested this audience."

Hauk stood slowly and made sure to keep his gaze averted from his queen. He might be best friends with her son, but it wasn't his place to look their queen in the eye. "I've come to beg our most sovereign crown to allow me to take the place of the human woman you hold, Sumi Antaxas. Whatever her crimes, I offer my life for hers and will gladly accept her punishment in her stead." His request was normally something a husband did for his wife, a father for his son, or a brother for a sister.

She narrowed her gaze on him. "And why would you beg me for the life of a *human*?"

He had to bite back his sarcasm that she'd disdain the human race so, especially given the fact that her sons were half human. Swallowing hard, he knew only one answer might sway the queen into granting his request for leniency. "She is my life, Majesty. I would not see her harmed."

Cairistiona rose and moved to stand before him. She took his chin in her hand. "Look at me."

He glanced at her eyes and then away.

"You're stralen?" she asked in a shocked tone.

He nodded.

She dropped her hand from his face. "For this human?"

"Yes, Majesty."

Sighing heavily, she paced around him. "We have a bit of a problem, War Hauk. It is your own family that called for her arrest."

That stunned him. While he'd figured they would be a problem once he landed, he hadn't anticipated them acting *this* fast. "Excuse me, Majesty?"

Cairistiona inclined her head to him. "I am well aware that the human female endangered the well-being of my granddaughter. I also know that she saved Princess Thia's life and guarded her with her own. At the behest of my granddaughter, I forgave the human for those actions against the crown. But it was the insistence of *your* mother and *your* pledged that I had to arrest her for endangering the lives of you and your nephew . . . the last of your most sacred blood clan."

He went cold with those words. "As the last of my blood clan, Majesty, I forgive her. She saved our lives, too. She doesn't deserve to be punished for risking her life to save ours. But if it is to be, then please allow me to take Sumi's place. I will gladly accept whatever punishment they demand of her."

"I'm afraid it's too late for that."

His heart stopped beating as fear invaded every part of his being. Andarion justice was swift and extremely brutal. Rarely did an Andarion survive it.

A human, even one as strong and resourceful as Sumi, would never make it through.

Cairistiona shook her head sadly. "Had it been any family save yours, I could have delayed my actions."

But because they were second only to the royal house, she was required to act and give them the justice they demanded.

Immediately.

"Your mother was insistent that the human give up her life for her crimes against your family. I had no choice."

Absolute horror filled him and in that moment, he hated Syn for keeping him unconscious. Had he been awake at the time Sumi was arrested, he could have stopped this.

Six hours later . . .

"I will gladly die for her, Majesty."

"It's too late for that, War Hauk," she said sadly. "The human Sumi Antaxas no longer exists."

Tears filled his eyes as he felt like someone had just kicked his teeth in. How could Sumi be gone so fast?

Damn you to hell, Syn!

He would kill that Ritadarion bastard first. And then he'd kill the rest of them for not protecting the one thing he'd asked them to. For decades, he'd put his life and limb on the line for all of them. Had never once hesitated to protect them, no matter the personal cost to himself. He'd never before asked them for anything. Ever.

And they'd paid him back by allowing his woman to be killed while he lay helpless to stop it.

Never had anything hurt like this betrayal. . . .

Against the law and tradition, he met Cairistiona's gaze as a single tear fled down his cheek. He couldn't breathe or think. All he wanted was to die, too.

How could he have allowed Sumi to be harmed? Gods, it was so unfair that she should die like this.

Because of him.

Cairistiona stopped by his side to brush his tear away with a kind touch that made him hate her even more. "Since you were a child, Dancer of the Warring Blood Clan of Hauk, you have been a great friend to my son. When no one else could spare a kind word to him, you, alone, befriended him and stood at his back to protect him at great personal risk and cost to yourself. You've been a blessed protector of my grandchildren and daughter-in-law, and have bled countless times for them all. For that alone, there is nothing I wouldn't do for you. And I mean that with every ounce of honor that flows through my eton Anatole blood." She smiled and patted his cheek. "Now, if you don't mind, I shall leave you with my daughter to discuss your futures."

Hauk frowned as she gathered her guards and exited the room. Nykyrian didn't have a sister.

Was the queen insane?

A slight, hooded woman entered the room as the last guard left. The door slid shut behind her. Her royal scarlet robes shimmered in the dim light as she approached him.

His scowl deepened as he watched her move. She had a slow, seductive gait he knew intimately.

No . . . it couldn't be.

"Sumi?"

She lowered the hood to show him the smiling face he craved most. One that had been painted with the scrolling marks of the royal Andarion blood clan. "Hi."

Still on his knees, he pulled her into his arms and held her close as relief flooded him. He absolutely shook with the weight of it.

"Can't. Breathe. Dancer!"

He loosened his hold as he kept his face pressed against her stomach and inhaled the sweetest scent he'd ever known. "Please tell me this isn't a dream."

"It's not a dream, sweetie." She brushed the braids back from his face before she cradled his head to her. "When your mother demanded my life, Nykyrian and Cairistiona said that the only way to save me would be if I were a member of the royal house. No one can demand the life of an eton Anatole. They said she could challenge me to the ring, but she couldn't require an actual death sentence."

He still couldn't believe what he was hearing. What Nykyrian and his mother had done for him . . . it went far beyond friendship.

Hauk took her bandaged hand into his. It was Andarion custom that whenever a child was adopted by a mother, the hand of both was cut and their blood combined to seal the union. Now that he thought about it, Cairistiona's left hand had been bandaged, too. "The queen adopted you?"

She nodded. "Is that okay?"

Rising to his feet, he kissed her with everything he had.

Until someone cleared his throat.

Hauk pulled back to find Nykyrian staring at him with an arched brow.

"That's my unmarried little sister you're mauling, Hauk. Want to put some distance between the two of you?"

Still furious, he narrowed his gaze on Nykyrian. "Don't

push me. I'm barely refraining from planting my foot up your ass for not telling me about this."

"Didn't have time. We had to move fast and pretend we didn't get your mother's last transmission—she's a tenacious one. You have Chayden to thank for that subversion, by the way. Never heard anyone fake static so well in my life. He's quite impressive."

Sumi touched her nose to Dancer's. "I was on my way to the infirmary to tell you about it when I met Syn in the hallway. He said that when you woke up and I wasn't there, all he could get out was that I'd been arrested before you started tearing everything out of your body and you stormed out to confront the queen."

"And he should still be in bed," Syn chided as he joined them.

Hauk pulled Nykyrian against him into a brotherly hug. "Thank you."

"Told you I'd keep her safe. You didn't really doubt me, did you?"

"Maybe a little."

Nykyrian clutched his hand in Hauk's braids. "You're such an asshole."

"Learned from the best."

Jerking at his hair, Nykyrian draped Hauk's arm over his shoulder and walked him back to his infirmary bed, where Nykyrian was less than gentle in removing Hauk's sword and tucking him in.

Nykyrian handed the sword to Sumi. "Can you please keep his sorry ass in there, this time?"

"I will do my best."

Syn was also a bit rough as he hooked up Hauk's monitors. "Don't make me do this again. The next set I'm shoving where the sun doesn't shine, buddy."

Hauk started to say something truly insulting, but the sound of an excited little voice made him bite his tongue.

"Uncle Hauk!" Devyn came running into the room and

jumped on the bed before he threw himself over Hauk's chest and hugged him tight.

This tiny being was the only reason he hadn't killed Syn yet. "Hey, Devy. How's my boy?"

Eyes wide, he gave Hauk a huge smile as he sat on his stomach. Right where he was injured.

Hauk ground his teeth and forced himself not to curse at the pain.

"Guess what? Guess what?" Devyn asked in an excited tone. "I grew a monkey, Uncle Hauk!"

Hauk frowned at the impossibility as he looked from Devyn to Syn, who was laughing about it. "A monkey?"

"E-e-e o-o-o ew ew," a monkey said drily as it joined them in the room and sat down on the bed next to them. "Not that I haven't been the sacred embryo's monkey from birth, but this is a little ridiculous. Don't you agree?"

Hauk was aghast as he recognized that acerbic tone. "Vik?"

The metallic monkey sighed so heavily, even his shoulders slumped. "Who else would the bonebag torture *this* badly? I would be more upset about it, but look." With a large, creepy smile, he held up his hands for Hauk to see. "Opposable thumbs!" He wiggled them for emphasis. "Lot to be said for these. Makes me want to look up my old girlfriend."

"Why?"

Vik wagged his eyebrows. "Cause now I can really turn her on."

Hauk made a sound of irritation at the bad pun before he explained it to Sumi. "His old girlfriend was a lamp who, and I am using *his* words, lit up his entire world."

She pressed her lips together. "Ah . . . okay."

Devyn grabbed Vik into a choke hold. "I planted monkey seeds in a garden and I grew him! So he's all mine!"

Vik stuck his tongue out like he was dying. "Help! I'm

being oppressed and licked by a toddler! Stop sliming me, Dev. I'm going to rust!"

Sighing, Syn picked up the monkey and set it on the floor. "See what happens when your significant other can't find a babysitter and refuses to let you go save your friend without her?"

Hauk scoffed at his annoyed protest. "You love every minute of it."

Syn picked up his son and cradled him to his chest. "Yeah, I do." He inclined his head to Sumi. "Hauk, you need to take a look at your transmitter I dug out of you. Fain thinks it's Andarion. I've tried to get a lead on it, but this is more your expertise than mine."

Sumi pulled it out of her pocket and handed him the small vial.

Hauk frowned as he held it up to the light to study the circuitry. "Yeah, it's Andarion. But this is old-school stuff . . . kind of thing I first played with as a kid."

"Jullien?"

He shook his head at Syn's suggestion. "Jullien could afford better than this. He wouldn't waste his time with something so primitive and old. I need it under a mag to see more of it."

Sighing, Vik climbed back up the bed and took it into his hand. He opened the vial and placed the chip in his palm then turned to the wall and projected an enlarged image of it. "How big do you want me to go?"

"Twenty. I need the serial."

"Got it," Vik said. "Want me to run it?"

Hauk arched a brow at the snotty mecha. "Nah. Why don't you sit there and stare at it for a while?"

Vik turned to face Syn. "Could you please remove his anal probe?"

Hauk grabbed the mecha by his neck. "How about I give *you* one?"

"Andarions. No sense of humor." Vik gasped as his body hit the bed while his head remained in Hauk's fist.

Ah, crap. Hauk cringed at something that was purely an accident.

"Oh my gods!" Vik snapped indignantly. "The Andarion beast broke me!"

Devyn started crying.

"It's okay, Dev. Daddy can fix it. Don't cry!" Syn handed his son to Sumi, who sucked her breath in sharply at the sensation of holding a child.

What did a person do with one? Terrified, she wrapped her arms tight around him, afraid he'd fall, while he continued to wail.

Syn quickly put Vik's head back on, then paused as he looked at her. "Never held a kid before?"

"No. His head won't pop off, too, will it?"

"God, I hope not. Shahara would kill us both."

Laughing, she handed a much calmer Devyn back to his father. He sniffed back his tears as he inspected Vik to make sure Syn really had repaired his toy.

"Now I know why Dancer looked so scared in some of the photos of him with babies."

Dancer laughed.

Darling stuck his head in the door. "Quick warning that we're coming into the main Andarion port. We'll be docked in about fifteen minutes."

"Hey!" Hauk called to Darling as he started to leave. "You got any photos of this kid of yours I've been waiting to meet?"

With a pride-filled grin, Darling returned to the room and moved to stand next to the bed. "Do you one better than that." He pulled out his PD and pressed it. Instantly, someone answered. "Hey Z, I've got an irritable beast who wants to say hi to you and Cezar." He handed it to Hauk.

Sumi tried not to feel jealous at the light that came into Dancer's eyes as he took the PD and smiled at the woman.

"Hey, beautiful. Where's my nephew?"

Darling's wife audibly gasped. "What's wrong with your eyes, Hauk? Are you okay?"

"Fine. Just want to meet this baby we saved."

She pulled her PD back so that he could see the sleeping infant who had a tiny hint of red hair on his head. "There he is. Sleeping like an angel."

Dancer grinned. "You done good, woman. He's beautiful. Thank the gods, he takes after his mother and not his dad."

She laughed. "I'm so glad you're okay. I was terrified when Darling told me you were under fire and had to call for help. That's so not like you."

"Sorry I took Darling from you two."

"Hey, no problem. So long as you send him back in one piece, we don't mind. And speaking of, Ture wants me to ask you about Maris."

"Tell him he wasn't even shot this time."

"Oh thank goodness," a man said from off camera. "I don't know what I was thinking when I said I wanted to marry a soldier. I must have been insane, delirious, or stupid."

Dancer laughed at Ture's high-pitched hysteria. "I'll make sure and send them both back to you as soon as we land."

"We love you, Hauk."

"Love you, too. Take care of each other and I'll be by soon to meet Cezar in person."

Darling turned it off and put it in his pocket. "So where are you recuperating?"

"I was thinking home."

"Alone?"

Dancer looked at Sumi. "I hope not."

Her heart stopped as she realized she hadn't thought this far ahead. Everything was moving too fast. But there was one thing she had to take care of ASAP. "I have to get to my daughter before Kyr finds out that I no longer have a transmitter. There's no telling what he'll do."

"I've already got Syn on locating her."

Darling frowned. "Whoa . . . What? What daughter?"

"Sumi has a little girl in League custody," Hauk explained. "I'm going after her and bringing her home."

Darling gaped at Sumi. "Was he planning to do this without us? Really?"

Dancer sent a piercing look to Darling. "You need to get home to your son and wife."

Darling shook his head in denial. "Strong alone. Stronger together."

She saw the reticence in Dancer's eyes, but he must have recognized the determination in Darling's. There was no way the Caronese emperor was planning to give in on Dancer's request and let him fight alone.

Dancer sighed heavily. "Zarya's going to kill me."

"Zarya would kill *me* if I let you go alone, buddy."

"And I'd help." Syn grinned. "Don't worry, Darling, I wasn't going to let you leave without telling you what Hauk was planning. I haven't found her daughter yet, but I will. I have the search running. I should have her location in a couple of hours."

Sumi's heart raced at the prospect. Could it be that easy? "Really?"

Darling placed a comforting hand on her arm. "We take care of our own, Sumi. It's what we do."

She nodded as tears choked her. Their kind of loyalty was rare indeed. Not to mention unexpected.

And it reminded her of something extremely important. "Speaking of . . . Mari's brother, Safir? Maris said that they knew—"

"That Kyr was using him for a punching dummy?" Syn

asked. "Yeah. His family took care of that as soon as they found out. Saf's at home on Phrixus now."

Hauk arched a puzzled brow. "How's that possible? He's a League assassin." The only way out for an assassin was death.

Nykyrian was the only one who'd ever been granted a release dispensation from The League, after many years of being hunted, because he was the Triosan and Andarion heir. While Sumi was now an adopted daughter, the Andarions were at war with The League. It was far less likely they would be so accommodating with her right now.

And there was no way Kyr would pardon his brother. Not after he already felt betrayed over Saf's participation in a Sentella escape.

Darling let out a sinister laugh. "What can I say? Kyr had no choice. Saf was an assassin with a herd of angry, high-ranking brothers, who have dared Kyr to come get him. They're all aching for a piece of his psycho ass over what he did to Saf."

"How did they get him away from The League?" Sumi asked. "Kyr was holding him deep in the bowels of his HQ."

Darling crossed his arms over his chest. "Not exactly sure. But it turns out that Madai will still take Maris's calls. Once Maris called about Saf, Madai told him that they were all furious over it. Torture to a Phrixian is a crime worse than murder. So united, Saf's brothers had already gone in and pulled him out. They told Kyr that if he wanted Saf, he'd have to challenge him on Phrixus. Which I doubt he'll do since Saf can wipe the floor with him and he knows it. In the meantime, Saf is now wanted by The League as a renegade. If he leaves Phrixian territory, they're going to be all over him."

"How's Saf dealing with that?" Dancer asked.

Syn snorted. "Better than you'd think. Turns out, he

really missed having sex. . . . Last we heard, he was making up for lost time."

Laughing, Darling nodded in agreement. "If we can ever blast him out of the Phrixian bordello where he's been holed up since his release, we're trying to lure him to work for The Sentella."

"He'd be a great addition," Dancer said.

Before Darling could respond, the door opened to show Nykyrian and Jayne.

Nykyrian's eyes flashed with anger. "Heads up, Hauk. Your parents, fave yaya, and Dariana are waiting in the bay for you."

Hauk cursed. He could already envision the shitstorm that was about to engulf them all.

Unless he gouged out his eyes before they all saw he was stralen.

It was a semi-tempting thought.

Nah, he'd rather fight.

Darling swept his gaze to Nyk, Jayne, and Syn before he inclined his head to Hauk. "Then we'll go out together. United. And dare them to say one ill word to you or Sumi."

Tears choked Sumi as her hand tightened on Dancer's. "So this is what it's like."

Dancer furrowed his brow. "What?"

"Having a family," she said in a tiny voice.

Darling hugged her. "I guess Hauk forgot to tell you that he doesn't come solo. We're a package deal."

She laughed. "Actually, he did warn me. Thia, too. I . . . just didn't expect all this. May the gods love all of you for it."

They felt the ship land and all the humor left her face and was replaced by a fear that made Hauk's gut tighten.

He took her hand into his and locked gazes with her. "No one and I mean no one is going to harm you, Sumi. They'll have to get through me first and no one gets through me."

"I can testify to that," Nykyrian said drily. "I'm still scraping the remains of the last fool who tried off the bottom of my boots."

When Syn moved to unlock the bed, Hauk stopped him. "I'll walk."

"You're . . ." His voice trailed off at the grisly look on Hauk's face. "Going to walk out of here. What was I thinking? Apparently, I'm an idiot." Syn unhooked the monitors. "I'll have the MT unit take Bastien to the local hospital." He spoke into his link to place the order.

Hauk stood and braced himself for the coming hell that was about to be unleashed.

CHAPTER 25

Sumi wasn't sure what to expect. She'd never been around this many Andarions in her life. It was one thing to see one or two or even a unit, but this . . .

Yeah. Anyone who attacked the Andarions was a flaming moron. Aside from the sheer size of them, they stood as if they were made of stone. Their combined ferocity alone could kill someone.

Nykyrian took her trembling hand and tucked it into the crook of his elbow. "Sumi Antaxas no longer exists. You're an eton Anatole now, *kisa*. Princess Sumi. Breathe and remember we'll gut anyone who glances askance at you. As will every Andarion wearing a red-and-black uniform. You are among family."

She offered him a grateful smile. "Thank you."

Darice went running down the ramp first and flew into the arms of a tall, fierce female. Unbelievably beautiful, Dariana appeared able to kick the snot out of anything. Male, beast . . . nuclear device.

And that was just with the power of her ferocious sneer.

Holy gods.

But the moment her son embraced her she stiffened and shoved him back. "What manner of human behavior is this?"

Hurt flickered across his face before Darice regained his composure. "Forgive me, *Matarra*."

She narrowed her gaze on his feather necklace that he'd been so proud of. Picking it up, she sneered even more. "Not very large, is it? What a puny trophy."

Darice deflated instantly.

Without a word of greeting to his parents, Dancer went straight to her. "Leave him be, Dariana. As a true Andarion warrior, he gave the largest feather he collected to his princess as a gift."

The hatred in her white eyes was searing. And when she saw the glowing red of Dancer's, she stepped back. "You have shamed me!" she snarled.

"Dancer!" his mother growled as she approached him and saw his eyes. "What have you done?"

Facing their obvious wrath and contempt, he didn't flinch. "I took my brother's child to Mount Grenalyn and have returned with his heir. Darice has honored his father and his lineages."

"And you have shamed yours! Again." His mother struck him across his abdomen. "How dare you!"

A red stain spread over his clothes from the wound his mother had opened.

Sumi knew she wasn't supposed to do anything. She needed to let him handle this. But she couldn't stand here and let him be assaulted. Not even by his own mother.

Furious, she released Nykyrian and rushed to Dancer's side so that she put herself between him and the females who wanted his life. "Leave him alone!"

"A human!" Dariana spat. "You shamed me with—"

"Bow to your princess!" Six Andarion guards came forward to protect Sumi.

It was only then that Dariana and his mother saw the markings on Sumi's face and recognized the style of her bloodred dress.

His mother gasped before she bowed low.

Dariana hesitated. With one last feral glare at Dancer that promised retribution, she obeyed.

Sumi lifted her chin defiantly, wanting a piece of both of them. She was supposed to do this later, but . . .

Tolerance wasn't part of her nature any more than it was Dancer's.

She curled her lip at Dariana. "Dancer has done nothing save honor his family and his noble, heroic lineage. He deserves better than to be tied to the inferior blood of Terisool. Dariana of the Blood Kin Terisool, I challenge you for the right to tie my superior lineage to his."

Dancer's jaw dropped, but he said nothing.

Dariana rose with an evil smirk. "I accept your challenge . . . *human*."

"*Princess,*" Sumi hissed in reminder, refusing to back down or blink as she stood toe-to-toe with the bitch. "And good. I look forward to ripping out your spine and beating you with it."

The desire to respond in kind burned bright in Dariana's eyes, but she knew better than to say anything nasty to a member of the royal family. Instead, she grabbed Darice's arm and hauled him away.

Only then did Dancer's grandmother and father approach as his mother straightened. His mother was much more subdued toward him than she'd been.

His grandmother and father bowed low in honor to Sumi.

Dancer met Sumi's gaze with pride gleaming brightly in his eyes. "Yaya, Matarra, and Da, allow me to present to you Princess Sumi of the Most Sovereign Blood Clan of eton Anatole."

A knowing smile lifted one corner of his grandmother's lips. "Is she the one you allowed the honor of touching you, Dancer?"

"She is, Yaya."

His grandmother inclined her head respectfully to

them both. "Then it is with your paran's sword that she will fight and defeat the lesser lineaged. My gift to you both and I hope she runs it straight through Dariana's treacherous gut." His grandmother placed her right hand over her heart. "It is my most privileged honor to meet you, Princess."

Sumi wasn't sure how to respond. "The honor is all mine, Ger Tarra War Hauk."

That seemed to be correct.

Laughing, his father clapped Dancer on the shoulder. "You *are* my son."

Sumi didn't miss the look of pain that flitted across his features over his father's praise.

His mother, however, wasn't quite so accepting. "What were you thinking, Dancer? This will be a scandal to your blood!"

"But no more so than what you did to Ferral, Endine." Cairistiona came forward to confront her. "Seems poetic, doesn't it? You stole a lineage and my daughter restores what should have been."

Still, his mother refused to back down. "You never wanted Ferral Hauk."

"And Dariana never wanted Dancer. Again, restoration." Cairistiona placed her hand on Dancer's shoulder and smiled tenderly at him. "I look forward to the day I officially welcome you to the Most Sovereign Blood Clan of eton Anatole. And speaking of . . ." She stepped back and held her hand out.

It was only then Sumi saw Fain, who approached them slowly. Like her and Cairistiona, he was dressed in the bloodred color that only a direct member of the royal family could wear.

"Endine, allow me to present my other son. I don't believe you've met him. Prince Fain of the Most Sovereign Blood Clan of eton Anatole."

Sumi's jaw went slack. As did Dancer's.

Endine, however, looked as if she'd swallowed her tongue and a round of bile.

Like any proud, doting mother, Cairistiona brushed her hand tenderly through Fain's braids. "It seems this fierce, decorated male had no lineage of his own. Given the selfless, noble service he has provided to my son and granddaughter over the years, I have offered him mine." She arched a brow at Endine. "Are you refusing to honor my son?"

Endine finally bowed to Fain. As did his father and grandmother.

But there was no satisfaction in Fain's eyes. Only bitter regret. Until he glanced to Dancer then he blanched.

Fain caught him as Dancer's knees buckled. He lowered him slowly to the ground. "Syn!"

Sumi held Dancer's head until Syn brought a stretcher for him.

Syn growled at Dancer as they put him on it. "Damn it, Hauk! Next time you storm a building to save a princess, don't do it alone."

Fain snorted. "Patience is not his virtue."

"Neither is common sense." Syn put the mask over Dancer's face as he called for a med lift for them.

Fear tore through her. Dancer was paler than she'd ever seen him. "Syn?"

"I won't let him die, Sumi. I'm the only bastard in existence who's even more stubborn than he is."

"Good. 'Cause I plan to hold you to that promise." But as she looked at Dancer's face, she knew it was going to be close.

Sumi paced the waiting room, wanting to beat Dancer's mother into the ground. The Andarion hadn't punched him in the stomach, she'd clawed him so hard, she'd almost gutted him.

"How could a mother do such?"

Cairistiona hugged her to her side. "Endine is very traditional. We're not all like that."

Sumi wasn't so sure. "You disinherited *your* son," she reminded the queen.

Cairistiona shook her head sadly. "No. I punished my baby for trying to kill his own brother, and for putting my grandson and daughter-in-law in harm's way. Jullien is still a prince and has all the money entitled to him. He's just barred from inheritance because of his actions. I didn't physically harm him. Rather, I kept Nykyrian from tearing out his guts over what he did to Kiara."

"Oh. Sorry."

"It's all right. Jullien chooses not to speak to me, but my heart will always be open to my child. No matter what he does. He will always be my baby."

"Sumi?"

She glanced up to see Syn coming out with the Andarion surgeon who'd been attending the War Hauk family since Dancer had been burned as a boy.

Dr. Duece inclined his head respectfully to her and Cairistiona. "Majesty. Princess. Dancer will be ready to leave in a few minutes. He will be more scarred, but he will heal."

She had to force herself not to roll her eyes at something she couldn't care less about. But then, to most Andarions, that would be a primary concern. "Thank you."

He bowed to her. "He should take it easy for a few days. And in a week, he can resume a normal schedule. I have given the orders to the human doctor who will be staying with him while he recovers."

Cairistiona inclined her head. "You have the deep appreciation of the royal house for your service."

While she and the doctor continued speaking, Syn gestured to Sumi. "I'll take you back to him."

He led her to the room where Dancer was sitting on a

stark white bed. A nurse had him signing an e-tab with orders.

Looking up, he smiled as he saw her in the doorway. "Hey, *mia*."

"Hi, sexy beast."

His smile widened enough to show off his fangs. "Careful, Maris might get jealous if he hears you using his nickname for me." He scooted off the bed and retrieved his coat.

Syn growled at him before he took the coat out of his hands. "You don't need to wear something this heavy. What are you thinking?"

"That you're worse than my yaya."

"Yeah, well, just wait until you see how many of us are crashed at your house. You're going to think yaya."

Dancer growled low in his throat. "Are you serious?"

"I know, you hate company. Deal with it. You're wounded. Both of you are hunted, and Sumi just challenged one of the most decorated Andarion soldiers in your armada to a death match. Until we get everything settled, you got the yaya contingency sitting on you. Congratulations, bud. Smile."

Baring his fangs, he draped his arm around Sumi's shoulders. "Fine. I just want to sleep in my own bed again." He led her to the entrance, where Fain waited with a transport.

Sumi wasn't sure what to expect. Eris, the capital city of Andaria, was extremely modern and crowded. Congested. There were over ten million Andarions who called it home.

"You okay?" Dancer asked as he noticed her discomfiture.

She bit her lip. "I've never been in a city so large. It's impressive." And terrifying.

Dancer pointed to the tallest building, which was

almost in the center of the city. It had a main spire that rose high against a huge moon. "That's the royal palace where your mother lives."

She blushed at his teasing reminder.

"The two buildings flanking it are government buildings. One is the ruling senate that reports to and advises the queen. The other is the courthouse." He pointed to a smaller building nestled in the center of a park. "That's Nykyrian's house. Not that he's here much. He mostly stays with his family in his father's Triosan palace."

"It's rare for anyone in Eris to own a house," Syn explained. "There're just so many Andarions and so little property left."

She looked at Dancer. "So you live in an apartment building?"

Sheepish, he glanced away.

Syn leaned forward. "See that huge round building on the coast?"

She nodded.

"That's where your boyfriend lives."

Her jaw went slack. "By yourself?"

He passed an irritated glare to Syn for ratting on him. "My paternal yaya you met earlier gave it to me after my paran died ten years ago. It was his wedding present to her and she couldn't stand living there without him. My father's the eldest of her children, so by rights, it should have been his. However, she refused to let my parents have it, because she hates my mother . . . so it went to me."

Fain cleared his throat. "Dancer was always her favorite. He looks the most like our paran."

He shoved at Fain.

In response, Fain arched a disbelieving brow. "If you weren't stitched, *kiran* . . ."

Unperturbed by the threat, Dancer sat back. "Fain actually has the guest house as his. He's not homeless or abandoned."

"But I rarely use it. Never wanted to chance running into family there."

After a few minutes, they pulled into a massive garage that led to its own landing bay where Dancer had three fighters and one small freighter docked. He also owned a sleek city transport and two airbikes.

She blinked at Dancer. "Someone likes his toys."

Syn let out an evil laugh. "Oh, just wait till you meet his house."

"Pardon?"

His only answer was another creepy laugh as he got out and led the way.

When they neared the door, Dancer pulled her to a stop. "Let me get you entered into the system so that you can come and go as you wish."

She didn't know what he meant until he stood her in the doorway to be scanned. "Biolocks on the thresholds?"

Dancer nodded. "And windows. Anyone who's unauthorized who tries to access the house gets stunned senseless."

That was impressive and painful.

"Then Dancer kills them," Fain said sardonically as he entered the house first.

"Good evening, Fain. I see you, Syn, and our new unnamed entry have decided to join Hauk. Are we having a party? Should I cue music and order food?"

Sumi turned to see an exquisitely beautiful Andarion female hologram in the foyer. Dressed in the deep burgundy color that marked the War Hauk clan and in a gown that showed off an unbelievably curvaceous body, she had her long black hair pulled back into a silken ponytail that fell to her waist. Her gown was so sheer, Sumi wasn't sure why Dancer bothered to clothe the hologram at all. A stab of vicious jealousy and a feeling of gross inadequacy went through her as she realized this must be Dancer's ideal of what a female should look like.

And it wasn't *her*—in any shape, form, and definitely not in fashion sense. Something that was corroborated by the uncomfortable looks both Syn and Fain passed to her and Dancer. Not to mention the oh-shit expression on Dancer's face as he no doubt rethought the hologram's wardrobe. "No party, Eleron. They're . . . uh, just here to watch over me."

Her face lit up immediately with joy as she saw him behind Fain. "Welcome home, Hauk. I've missed you terribly. Where have you been? You should have called and told me when to expect you back. Or at least left me a message."

Dancer looked even more nervous and uncomfortable as he cast a sheepish frown to Sumi. "Sorry, El. I was with Darice." He cleared his throat as he pulled Sumi closer. "Eleron, meet the new entry, Sumi, who will be staying with us and is to be considered another owner. Sumi, say hi to the house."

She gaped at him. "Are you serious?"

"No, *mu tara*. My name is Eleron, not Serious. As another owner, you may also call me El." She turned to face Hauk with an innocent stare. "Should I add her voice recognition to our protocols?"

"Yes. Give her full access."

"Done." She smiled at Dancer. "It's been rather busy and annoying this evening. You will find Shahara, Jayne, Desideria, Illyria, and Devyn in the pool area with an irritating mecha I don't like. May I feed it to the garbage disposal system?"

"Really rather you didn't. Devyn would also be very upset and would spend the rest of the night crying."

Eleron made a horrified face. "Oh, we can't have that. It's the only thing more agitating than the mecha. Very well. No leaking, loud children. . . . Nero, Caillen, Drake, and Chayden are in the gaming room, draining resources. They made the entire north quad lag. I repaired it by shutting down non-vitals elsewhere, but really wish they'd do something else. Darling and Maris are in the command room, talking to Zarya and Ture. Is there anything else I can do for you, love?"

"Prepare my bedroom."

"Should I warm your bed?"

Sumi arched a brow over that particular question.

Dancer blushed while Syn and Fain burst into laughter. "Yes, please, El."

She inclined her head respectfully. "Would you like a guest room prepared for Sumi?"

"No. She'll be staying with me in mine."

The computer gaped. "*Really*?" Her tone was filled with incredulity.

Dancer rubbed his hand over his face. "Thanks for the shock, El. You're making me so glad I came home."

"My pleasure to serve you in any way possible, love. But since you have a physical woman tonight, I assume you will be fine with my returning to noncorporeal form?"

Hauk cringed at the question. "Yes, that'll be fine."

Eleron made a kissy face at him before she vanished.

Laughing, Fain clapped him on the back. "Heading to the game room to drain more resources and make El scream. You know a lot about that, don't you, brother?"

"Shut up," he said between clenched teeth.

Syn flashed an equally wicked grin. "Pool for me."

Hauk glared at him. "I would say make yourselves at home, but you already have. I really need to yank access codes one day." He took Sumi's hand and led her through the living room that had a glass wall with a breathtaking view of the city.

She released his hand so that she could move closer to it and stare out at the brilliant lights that made it appear as if the stars had fallen to the ground. "This is amazing."

"Yeah. I used to love staying here when I was a kid. I would cry myself sick whenever my parents made me leave."

"I can see why." She paused as she saw the oil portrait over the fireplace. Gaping, she stared at it in awe. "Who is that?" she asked breathlessly.

"The first Dancer, and founder of the Warring Blood Clan of Hauk. My grandmother left it with the house when she moved out. Since I was named for him, she thought it only right that it should pass to me."

Sumi studied the image of the warrior whose handsome face was mostly shielded by the cowl of a dark burgundy cloak. He wore bracers similar to the ones Dancer had and held a winged sword with glowing red eyes that matched the one eye of his the artist had painted in. He stared out with a grim countenance and the bearing of a proud sentinel ready to defend his family, home, and planet.

"He was stralen?" As soon as she asked the question, she remembered that had been part of the legend.

"He was. It's said that he only lived ninety-two minutes after his wife was buried. That he so couldn't bear the thought of living without her, his heart exploded the minute he returned home to an empty house."

She passed a frown to Dancer. "Andarions have the most beautiful and horrific legends."

He shrugged nonchalantly. "That is the mark of our breed." He inclined his head to the portrait. "And that sword in his hands is what my yaya is giving to you to fight Dariana with."

"Really? It's still battle-worthy?"

"Oh yeah," he said with a sarcastic laugh. "Andarion hyriallium. There's no metal like it on any world. It never breaks, rusts, or dulls. His sword used to rest in the brackets beneath the portrait, and when we were little, we would dare each other to try to touch it without getting caught or cut."

She smiled at the image of him and Fain trying to climb up to it. "Why did she take the sword and leave the portrait?"

"She didn't want the sword to pass to my mother's or Dariana's guardianship. That is the sword of the War Hauk ancestors and of our mighty clan. It has never known defeat or disgrace. Only the greatest warrior of his or her generation is allowed to own it, and it must be passed by the clan matriarch when she deems it's been earned. For her to offer it to you is the greatest honor my yaya can bestow, especially since she will be doing so prior to our unification. Once it passes to you, you will become the custodian of the Hauk Warsword and you will be the one to decide which of our children or grandchildren is the most worthy to wield it."

Sumi was stunned by what he told her. "Why would she offer it to me?"

He trailed his finger down her cheek, sending chills over her. "She sees you as the only one who is worthy of it."

A little unexpected thrill went through her. "That has to piss off your mother."

He let out an evil laugh. "You have *no* idea. I'm sure Dariana is doing her own screaming about it, too. As my mother most likely told her as soon as she was free to do so."

She glanced at him then back to the portrait. "Why is so little of his face showing?"

"He was badly scarred during the battle against the Oksanans, and he lost his left eye. So when they painted his official portrait, he didn't want to shame our family with his deformity. He had them only preserve the part of his face that was unscathed by war."

So they'd always been strange about their appearances. How odd when other races viewed scars as manly and desirable. A testament of prowess and courage. "Why are Andarions so obsessed with beauty?"

"We're perfectionists by nature. While we honor our ancestors, our attention is primarily on our children and the future. We want to pass only the best on to them. Our belief is that we are caretakers for our progeny. Everything we have, we hold only for them."

"Which is why your yaya gave you this house before she died."

He nodded. "She also thought that Dariana would honor her pledge and we'd have more children to fill it."

Sumi turned to face him. "I'm a bit confused though. If everything is about the children, why was Dariana so mean to Darice? For that matter, your mother so vicious to you?"

"They're trying to make us the best and strongest males that they can. They, as females, are the guardians of our lineage. We, as males, are the carriers of the future. And if we're not worthy, they would rather we be removed from the lineage than have us taint it."

"You know, I can never be *that* mother."

He kissed her slowly. "I know, Sumi. You will be a far better mother than either of them. *Mu mia* shames all those who have come before her. And I live for the chance to return your daughter to you."

Sumi frowned at his word choice and what it implied. "*Our* daughter, you mean."

A strange look crossed his features. One that stabbed her hard until he spoke to explain it. "You would share your precious Kalea with me? Allow her to call me Father?"

Tears choked her at his earnest, bashful questions. It was as if he couldn't believe she'd allow him to claim

Kalea as his. "Of course I would. How could you doubt that, Dancer?"

He looked at her incredulously. "Andarion females rarely share their children with males other than the blood father. While the mother may adopt, the father cannot."

"Never?"

He shook his head. "Unless we are the blood father, we can only mentor the children of our females, and we have no rights to them. Fatherhood, blood or adopted, can only be bestowed on our males by the mother of the child."

Sumi struggled to breathe as she finally understood exactly what Thia had been trying to tell her about Darice and his insults for Dancer. It wasn't just that Dariana didn't want to marry Dancer, it was that even if she did, she would never allow Dancer to be called Father by Darice. Not unless she judged him worthy of fatherhood.

That was why Dancer had never been allowed to spend time with Darice. It had been another stab to him that he didn't deserve.

Blinking back her tears, she cupped Dancer's face in her hands. "In my heart, you are Kalea's only father. The only one I would trust to be there for her and to protect her. I don't ever want her to know she had any father, *but* you."

Hauk savored words he'd never thought to hear from any female. "You would accept children from me?"

Sumi winced at his question as she finally understood why Fain had sterilized himself for Omira. Their entire culture was built on the female accepting the male as fathers for their children. And since her sister had been afraid of an Andarion baby . . .

"You have to ask? I told you, Dancer, nothing would *ever* give me more happiness than to hold your child in my arms. I meant every word of that."

Hauk pulled her against his chest and held her close as love and happiness choked him. "I will tear this universe apart to find our daughter and bring her home." But even as he said those words, he was terrified of not being able to fulfill them.

Of losing Sumi forever. While she might be a daughter of Cairistiona's, she still had to get through Dariana. And Dariana was one of the best warriors in the Andarion military services. Worse, Andarions didn't fight the way humans did. Sumi would have to learn their tactics.

And the rules of their ring.

If she didn't, Dariana would kill her without mercy.

What have I done? He knew that Sumi was an incredible fighter. A trained assassin. But it wasn't the same. Andarions came out of the womb fighting.

Fear poured through him as he realized that no matter how much he might wish it, Sumi would never be able to defeat Dariana.

Their love was as doomed as Fain's and Omira's.

Humans and Andarions didn't mix. He knew that. *Look at Nykyrian's parents.* They truly did love and adore each other. Yet they'd never been able to stay together. They lived entirely separate lives.

His heart pounding, he held on to Sumi, knowing that death was going to come for them.

And there was nothing he could do to stop it.

CHAPTER 26

Sumi followed Dancer up the stark white spiral stairs that led to an upper floor. His bedroom was at the end of the hall and looked out over the sea.

Once more, she was stunned by the beauty. Looking down on the other side, she smiled as she saw in and around the giant pool area where a little girl and Devyn floated on rings, while their mothers pushed and pulled them.

She turned back toward Dancer. "Your bedroom is larger than my entire apartment was." Never mind the tiny room that had been her League quarters. His bed alone was bigger than that.

He didn't comment as he waved his hand over an ornate burgundy lighted panel. The wall opened and formed a desk.

Gaping at the handiness, she watched in fascination. "What have we here?"

He moved his hands about to show her a 3-D monitor. "I'm checking on Syn's search for Kalea."

She walked over to see the same strange letters that had been on his PD. "Is that Andarion?"

"Yes." He made several hand gestures and it changed

over to Universal for her. Then he opened another monitor. "This one is the search on my chip."

Wow . . . "Did you build this system?"

"Yeah."

She stared up at him in awe. "Dancer," she said breathlessly. "It's amazing! I had no idea you could do all this."

Sheepish, he shrugged. "I always liked electronics. I started wiring the house in my teens for my paran to help him when he became ill. He had a lot of mobility issues from all the years he'd been in the military. Since my yaya couldn't move him on her own, I did what I could for them to make their lives easier."

"No wonder your grandmother gave it to you. No one else would know how to work it all."

He smiled with that boyish grin that warmed and charmed her completely. It was such a strange incongruity to see the playful side of such a fierce soldier. "It's not that hard."

"Umm-hmmm." Then she couldn't help teasing him about something that really did irritate her. "By the way, was Eleron so scantily clothed while your yaya lived here?"

An extremely attractive blush crawled over his face. "That's normal Andarion fashion."

Yeah, right. "I'm sure it is."

His blush darkened. "I normally change it out when I know humans are coming over."

"And I hope you change it out whenever Darice visits."

That killed the humor in his eyes instantly.

Sumi wanted to kick herself as it occurred to her that Dariana had most likely never allowed Darice to visit him at home.

His gaze still sad, he pulled her to stand in front of him. "This is how you access a monitor." Taking her hand in his, he showed her the gesture. "You can either type like this . . ." He moved her hands to the desk. "Or use voice commands."

She leaned back in his arms to look up at him. "I knew you were intelligent, but damn. Dancer, this is . . . beyond."

"Mmm."

Sumi smiled as she realized he wasn't listening to her. Rather he was nuzzling her neck and staring down her cleavage while he held her against his body. "Dancer?"

Slowly, he opened her dress so that he could run his hand down the valley between her breasts. She felt him hardening against her hip.

"Eleron," he said in a tight tone, "shield the room and start my shower. Continue to run my searches and notify me when they're complete."

The house responded immediately.

He gently nipped at Sumi's ear, sending chills through her while he ran his hand over her breasts and then down her stomach. "I'm dying to be inside you, *munatara*. But I'm filthy." Growling in frustration, he pulled away then paused after a step to look back at her. "Care to shower with me?"

Was he joking? She lived to see that body naked. "Absolutely. After you."

He pulled her into a huge bathroom.

She gaped at the size of it, and the ornate fixtures. She doubted if a palace could be more grand. "I think we could fit a shuttle in here. . . . Maybe two."

He laughed in her ear.

But she wasn't kidding. The whole room glistened like a rare jewel. There was a massive marble tub up four steps, on a dais surrounded with columns that would easily hold four or five people. To her right were his-and-her vanities and a shower large enough for ten people. It had an etched glass door with a motion sensor that opened and closed it automatically.

Impressed and rather awed by it all, she watched as he peeled his clothes off and exposed his ripped, sexy body for her hungry view.

But her heart sank at the sight of his latest stomach wound his mother had given him on his arrival. "Should you get *that* wet?"

"I'll be careful." He slowly undressed her, making her all the hotter and needier.

The minute he uncovered her back and saw the glue Syn had used to seal shut the small incision he'd made to remove her tracking device, Dancer hesitated. "Are you scared to have that gone?"

She shook her head, knowing that what she'd done was a death sentence for them all. "I just don't want to get you or Syn in trouble for it. As soon as it was implanted, I came to terms with the fact that I was living on borrowed time. That I could die brutally at any moment."

He brushed his lips over the wound before he brushed her wet hair back from her neck so that he could nibble a heated trail along her collarbone and over her League tattoo. "I will keep you safe, Tarra War Hauk."

Tears choked her at the noble title. It was how his wife would be addressed by others. But that wasn't the only part of his noble words that touched her. "Ever the Andarion TAM."

"And never more so than I will be for you."

She sank her hand in his hair. "Just remember that when you're fighting now, Dancer, you are taking my heart into battle with you . . . every time you are struck, it is a blow straight to it. And if anything were to happen to you, you would take my heart with you, wherever you go, and I doubt I would last ninety-two minutes without you."

Hauk froze as he savored words he'd never expected to hear from anyone. All his life, he'd felt so worthless.

Despised. Undesirable. Because of the way Andarions dressed, his scars had always been plainly visible to others. Unless it was necessary or required, even his own mother had refused to appear in public with him.

You're an embarrassment to our lineage. I can't believe you're what I'm left with.

Those scars had even kept him out of his obligatory Andarion military service. They had been the primary reason he'd joined The League after leaving school.

But Sumi didn't see his flaws. In her eyes, there was only acceptance and love. He tightened his arms around her as he whispered in her ear. "You don't take my heart with you, *mia*. You are the only heart I have. And I wouldn't last two minutes without you in my life."

Sumi's eyes filled with tears over those words. She bit her lip as his hands slid over her body, delving and stroking as they went. For some reason, he removed her shoes last.

She gasped the moment her feet touched the tile floor. "Is it heated, too?"

He nodded. "My paran hated the cold."

His abilities astounded her. Was there anything he couldn't do?

Without another word, he led her into the shower that had jets in one corner and a bench with a handheld, adjustable showerhead in the other. But the neatest were the gentle drops that fell from the ceiling.

Looking up, she held her hands out to let them soak her. "It's like bathing in the rain."

"Eleron can make it heavier or lighter or even stop it. Whatever you prefer."

Wrapping her arms around herself, Sumi spun around like a kid in the backyard. "This is incredible."

Hauk smiled at her as she explored the shower. He loved the excitement on her face while he lathered his body and bathed.

"What does this do?" She fingered the manual controls.

"That button you're touching is for the aromatherapy. You press it and select which scent you want. You can also turn on the steam shower, foot massager, chromatherapy lighting, acupuncture massage jets." He moved his hand and a monitor appeared in the glass. "You can also browse online, or watch something. Listen to music."

"Oh my God! Why did you *ever* leave home?"

"Because you weren't here," he said simply.

Sobering instantly, Sumi savored those words as he reached around her and held her against his sleek, naked body. "I don't want to hurt you, Dancer."

"You're not."

She gasped as he slid his fingers inside her. Slowly, carefully, he nibbled his way from her shoulder to her breasts, taking his time to thoroughly tease one, then the other. Her head swimming, she buried her hand in his braids as he kissed his way down her stomach to her hip. He knelt between her legs then nudged them wider apart.

Her heart pounding, she locked gazes with him before he took her into his mouth. She cried out as pleasure tore through her entire body while he licked and teased her thoroughly. No one had ever touched her like this. As if her enjoyment mattered more than his did. "Ah, gah, Dancer!"

That only encouraged him to be bolder and more thorough.

When she came, he laughed deep in his throat as if he was proud of himself for it. Only then did he stand. With an ease that never ceased to amaze her, he took the full of her weight into his arms before he entered her.

Gasping, she wrapped her legs around his waist and thrust herself against him. She cried out in pleasure with every stroke. Nothing had ever felt better than to have his strength inside her. To be so thoroughly cherished by a male so sexy and strong. One who made her heart light to be near.

Scarred or not. Scary or not . . . he was perfection.

Hauk growled at how good it felt to be inside her again. And the fact that she was as eager for him as he was for her only added to his enjoyment. Most of all, he adored her cries of pleasure that echoed around them. The way she said his name while she rode him.

"I love you, Sumi," he whispered in her ear.

"*Kimi asyado,* Dancer."

He pulled back as she responded in Andarion. Those unexpected words, in his language, while she clutched at him, sent him over the edge. He came an instant later in a blinding wave of ecstasy. Throwing his head back, he roared with what she did to him.

How deeply she touched every part of his being.

Completely satiated, he slowly withdrew from her and quickly bathed again. "I think I could sleep for a week now." He waved his hand to turn everything off.

"Where are the towels?"

He gave her a lopsided grin. "Don't need them."

She didn't understand until he walked her through the small opening that blew their skin dry as they left the shower. "This is so strange. Neat. But strange."

"Wait till you explore the kitchen." He took her hand and led her to bed, which was nicely warm and toasty. "And I have a present for you tomorrow that I think you'll really enjoy. I'd show it to you tonight, but it's something that's best appreciated in the daylight."

Sumi took care not to hurt him as she snuggled up against his side. He was already growing hard again under her knee. She started to say something about it then noticed he'd fallen asleep.

Smiling at him, she brushed his damp hair back from his face and savored the scent of his skin. The feeling of his flesh against hers.

Just as she closed her eyes, she heard Eleron's voice in a low tone.

But she didn't quite register the words. "Repeat that, please."

"I have the results on the tracking chip. Would you care to review them?"

Reluctantly, she pulled herself away from Dancer to return to the desk so that she could see the monitor. "What are they?"

"The tracking device was originally assigned to Keris Hauk, lieutenant commander of the Andarion armada, as part of his service pack. It was deactivated upon his reported death."

Sumi's jaw fell. "Deactivated how?"

"It was assumed destroyed with his unrecovered body."

How weird was that? Especially since she knew for a fact that his body had been recovered and cremated. "When was it reactivated?"

"The signal returned to service three weeks ago."

Three weeks? That was right around the time Kyr had assigned her this mission. Could the two incidents be related or was it just a strange coincidence?

What were the odds?

"Can you tell when it was implanted?"

"Not a miracle computer, sorry. Perhaps you can persuade Hauk into upgrading my abilities?"

She ignored El's sarcasm. "Where was it originally activated from three weeks ago?"

"That requires a manual search, as it is locked from general access."

Crap. She had no idea how to do that. But if the chip came from Keris, there was only one person who could have had it.

Dariana.

Yeah, I have you now, bitch. And with this, she was going to bury her once and for all.

CHAPTER 27

"Fain?" Sumi asked as soon as she'd convinced Eleron
to show her to the gaming room.

Dancer's computer had a bit of an attitude about her.
If she didn't know better, she'd think it was jealous.

Fain looked up from the game he was playing against
Caillen and Darling. There was another man with them
she hadn't met. Tall and blond, he held an ethereal es-
sence to him. Even seated and dressed in dark green,
he had an aura about him that said he was every bit as
lethal, if not more so, than the rest of the males in the
room.

"I'm Nero," he said as if he heard her thoughts.

"Hi. Sumi."

In those few seconds, Fain had gone back to playing.
Grimacing, he twisted the small tablet in his hand to control his character.

"Fain," Nero said in a tone a parent usually reserved
for dealing with their errant children. "She really needs
your attention."

He sat back, but kept playing. "What's up?"

"I have information about the tracker that was embedded in Dancer."

The game forgotten, all four pairs of male eyes turned

to her then. Something punctuated by the quick deaths of their onscreen avatars.

She'd underestimated how scary it would be to have all their undivided attention on her. She swallowed nervously. "It was originally Keris's service chip."

Scowling, Fain shook his head. "It's not possible. I was there when he was cremated. It should have been destroyed with his body."

"Was it removed during autopsy?" Darling asked.

"I doubt it. They didn't do much of one. Some blood and tissue samples. Nothing really on the body itself."

Caillen took a drink of his ale. "You sure?"

His eyes haunted and filled with grief and pain, Fain nodded. "He hit the ground hard. Basically his organs disintegrated on impact. His bones shattered. It was grisly." A tic started in his jaw. "I still can't imagine how Dancer, as young as he was, kept it together enough to wrap up his body, and carry it through that desert to get him home. For that alone, he deserved a lot better homecoming than what he got. If anyone *ever* earned a fucking feather for their Ascension, it's him."

Darling flinched at what he described. "How the hell did Hauk survive his fall?"

Wincing, Fain grabbed Caillen's ale and took a drink before he answered. "Didn't fall as far or as hard. Only a few hundred feet. Keris took a six-*thousand*-foot free fall straight down to the bottom. Dancer was able to grab the wall and some vegetation and slow himself as he fell and he slammed into a ledge. Even so, he was busted up pretty good. Some broken ribs. Broken collarbone and arm. Some internal damage. It's a miracle he didn't die, too."

"What exactly happened?" Darling asked. "Hauk won't ever talk about it."

Fain growled deep in his throat. "Keris was a *minsid* idiot. He thought himself this invincible supersoldier and he was always pushing us to be like him. He hazed the shit out of us growing up. Our father thought it was funny and that we needed to be hardened. You know? We were such pusses in his eyes. And our mother yelled at us if we ever dared to complain about it. '*Suck it up*,'" he said in a nasal, mock feminine falsetto. "And the punk bastard loved explosives. He was always throwing shit at us, and laughing when it blew up in our faces."

Darling went pale. "Is that why Hauk hates explosives?"

"Probably. Keris started throwing crap at him in the crib, before he could even walk. He almost blew Dancer's hand off when he was only two. More than that, the sick bastard had gone in and wired the mountain for our Endurances. Every other time we put our hand or foot in a hole, it exploded on us, knocking us down. Reckless idiot. By the time I was finished with mine, I was ready to kill him. It pissed me off so badly that I never really spoke to him again after it. And he used even more with Dancer. Worse, when Keris fell and hit the ground, it detonated every charge he'd set. The entire mountainside blew up on Dancer and sent him flying. That's what caused *his* fall."

Darling covered his face with his hands. "Why didn't anyone ever tell me this before now? Have you any idea how many times we've mocked Hauk for his fear of explosives?"

Nero patted him on the back. "It's all right, Darling. Hauk never held it against you."

"Not helping. I still feel like an ass. Gah . . . why didn't I ever shut up about it?"

Fain let out a heavy sigh. "It's okay, Darling. Nero's right. If Dancer had really minded, you wouldn't be breathing. If he likes you, he takes most things in stride." He looked back to Sumi and continued their conversation. "Anyway, while Keris was never brother of the year, he wasn't so bad until Dariana got him hooked on experimental drugs. Those brought out the absolute worst in him."

She remembered Dancer and Darice talking about that. "What exactly did she give him?"

A sad, tormented light darkened his gaze. "Like Dancer, he was stralen. Though his came and went. Probably because he was so bipolar. Keris and Dari didn't sleep together until unification so she didn't know what she was getting herself into, in that regard."

"Dancer says it doesn't really do anything to his personality, other than make him hyperprotective . . . right?"

Fain snorted. "Yeah, and as long as he trusts you, that's not a problem at all."

Fear pierced her as she tried not to remember Avin's viciousness. "What do you mean?"

The expression on Fain's face was cold and pain-filled. "Dariana wasn't faithful to my brother. She lied under pledge, and when you're stralen, your senses are even higher than normal."

"Meaning?"

"Keris could tell whenever she'd screwed someone else, and it drove him into severe rage-mode."

Sumi covered her mouth with her hand as the horror of that washed through her. Poor Keris. No wonder it tore Fain up so much. It was one thing he could definitely relate to. "Why didn't she stop cheating on him?"

His gaze filled with agony, Fain twisted Omira's ring on his finger. "I don't know, Sumi. I've never understood infidelity. But I understand why it made Keris crazy and accusatory. Terrified he would kill her for it, Dariana started spiking his food with different things, trying to keep him calm and lower his adrenaline, vasopressin, and testosterone levels. It's why she never conceived a baby while he was alive. The drugs had him too messed up. Half the time, he couldn't even get an erection."

Nero sucked his breath in sharply.

Sumi frowned at him. "What?"

Nero winced. "Sorry. Involuntary reaction. You do not want to sexually frustrate an Andarion male."

"Why?"

Fain let out an evil laugh. "It causes a form of rabid insanity with us. Once we hit puberty, we need a regular chemical release."

"Which is why they're good at handling things themselves," Darling added with a snicker.

Fain threw his controller at him.

"What?" Darling asked innocently as he knocked the controller to the floor. "We all know the stories about you guys."

"Shut up, human."

Caillen, who obviously had as much self-preservation as Darice, looked over to Fain. "So here's my question. Can an Andarion go stralen with his hand?"

Fain slapped him with a sofa cushion so hard it sounded like he broke a bone. "No. Asshole. Gah! Humans! You disgust me!"

"Ow!" Caillen held his arm against his body. "Damn, Fain. What's in that cushion? A rock?"

"Wah, wah."

While they argued, Sumi fell silent as she considered what they'd just told her. "So Dancer isn't dangerous to me, right?"

Nero tsked at her. "Let that fear go, Sumi. Hauk isn't Avin or Darnell. As Fain said, so long as you don't cheat—which I know you won't—you'll have a long, happy marriage with him. It really is that simple. Andarions treasure their females in a way few races do. Their males are frighteningly loyal and giving."

She frowned at his use of her ex-boyfriends' names when she hadn't breathed a word of them. There was only one way Nero could know that. "You're Trisani?" They were an almost extinct race that was renowned for its extreme psychic abilities. Because of that, most of them had been enslaved or murdered by those who were afraid of them or who craved their powers.

He nodded.

"Then do you know about Keris's chip?"

"Sorry. My powers don't work that way. There are too many variables. But if we can tie that chip to Dariana, it will be a death sentence for her. Not just by Andarion law, but there's not a member of The Sentella who wouldn't hunt down and tear apart anyone who had a hand in implanting that on Hauk."

Fain, Caillen, and Darling lifted their drinks in salute to his words.

"Speak it, *drey,*" Darling said. "The only challenge will be getting to decide which of us has first dibs on the death blow."

As Sumi started back to Dancer's bedroom, Fain followed her to the living room and pulled her to a stop. She arched a curious brow at him. "Is something wrong?"

Her gaze dropped to his pinkie, where he kept Omira's ring. "I didn't want to ask around the others and wasn't sure when I'd have you alone again, but . . ."

"You want to know about Omira?"

He nodded. Then he spoke in a hurry. "I'm not trying to stalk her, or check up on her. I told her I wouldn't do that to her and I won't. It's just . . . having you here. I just wanted to know if she's finally happy. If she ever found someone she could love."

Those sincere words, combined with the earnest love on his face, wrung a sob from her. *Damn you, Omira.* How could her sister have hurt someone who loved her so much? Even after what her sister had done to him, he still cared. What had Omira been thinking?

His own tears gathered steam as he saw hers. "No, Sumi . . . she's okay, right?"

She couldn't look at him and that sweet, desperate childlike hope. How could she tell him what Omira had done? She couldn't think of a single way to break it to him.

All she could do was shake her head.

"Please don't tell me she's dead."

She pressed the back of her hand to her lips as her sobs came more forcefully. "I'm sorry, Fain."

He pulled her against him and held her close as she cried. She felt his hot tears on her neck as he let out his own anguished grief. "Did she suffer?"

"No. She died in her sleep." At least, that was what the doctors had told her. And she liked to believe them.

His arms tightened around her as his shoulders shook. She rubbed his back, wishing she could make it better for him, and knowing she couldn't. Nothing helped this kind of pain, and anyone who said that time dulled the loss of a loved one was a total idiot. Even now, she would sell her soul to have her sister with her again. If for no other reason than to beat her for being so selfish and stupid.

She wasn't sure how long they stood like that. But Fain finally pulled back. He wiped his tears and then hers.

"Whatever happened to her baby? Was it a boy or girl?"

Sumi winced as she remembered Omira terminating her pregnancy. She'd told her at the time that it would be an Andarion monster, but now she knew better. "She lost it," she whispered, not wanting to hurt him any worse.

Wrapping his arms around himself, he cleared his throat. "I know you probably hate me, Sumi, but I swear to the gods of all planets that I never wanted to hurt her or cause her any harm."

"I know." She patted his arm. "Dancer told me that she cheated on you."

He flinched and nodded. "I didn't react very well to the news. I probably could have done better had I at least suspected it. But it came out of the blue. Until I caught her, I had no idea she was sleeping with a human male, too."

"You didn't kill her, Fain. Or hit her. How bad could it have been?"

Fain glanced away from her. "Words are harsher than blows."

He was right about that. Though her experience said she'd rather be called names than deal with a busted jaw.

Licking her lips, she tried to let go of the past. To not let it overshadow what was in front of her now. "I'm sorry Omira wasn't the wife you deserved, Fain. And I'm really sorry that I allowed her bitterness to taint you in my eyes. Most of all, I'm glad I didn't kill you like Kyr wanted me to do."

He arched a brow at her. "Seriously?"

"You were the carrot he dangled to get me to go after Dancer." She playfully slapped at his arm. "Ha! Joke's on him now."

He snorted. "We're sick beings to find humor in that."

"Yeah, well, I accepted my weirdness a long time ago."

Shaking his head at her, he took her hand into his. "I'm glad to have you back as my sister again, Sumi. I've missed you."

"I missed you, too," she said with another sob. "More than you'll ever know."

He tightened his hold. "I'm here now, and I will *never* leave you on your own again."

She let out a bittersweet laugh as she saw the bandage on his hand that matched hers. "Oh yeah. I forgot that we were both adopted today. You are legally my brother now."

"Damn straight. And I should probably tell you that

Andarion custom demands I sleep in the same room as you while you're under the roof of an unrelated male."

The blood drained from her face. "What?"

He laughed. "That expression *is* priceless. But don't worry. Dancer would kick my ass if I stepped into his bedroom. And while I might be larger, he's a lot meaner . . . and he bites in a fight."

She rolled her eyes. "No, he doesn't. I've seen him fight."

"Not against me, you haven't. He bites the crap out of me." He held up his arm. "See."

"Oh my goodness," she gasped. There actually were several bite-mark scars on his forearm. "Why does he bite you?"

"I told you. He's mean."

She ruffled Fain's braids. "I know better. He loves you too much."

"Well, I wish he loved me a little less. Or that he'd find another chew toy." He gave her a light squeeze. "And speaking of, you should return before he wakes. My luck, he'd come storming naked out of his room to look for you and blind us all."

She rubbed noses with him. "Goodnight, Fain." But as she left, she saw the sadness descend over his face again. And in the back of her mind was the fear that she and Dancer would meet the same fate as Fain and Omira.

How could they be happy when so many others weren't? When so many others were out to end their lives?

Just as she reached the hallway, her gaze went to the portrait of the first Dancer. He seemed to be holding secrets along with his sword. Secrets that could end them all.

Trying not to think about it, she headed back to Dancer, hoping and praying that whatever happened, he didn't die because of her.

CHAPTER 28

Flat on his stomach, Hauk blinked his eyes open to find himself at home. In his own bed. At first, he thought everything had been a dream until he realized the warmth against his side wasn't a pillow and there was a long, shapely leg draped over his buttocks and a delicate hand buried in his hair. Best of all were the warm, naked breasts pressed flat against his arm.

A wave of peaceful contentment washed over him. He didn't want to move and disturb her in any way.

At least that was his thought until he felt her fingers slowly massaging his scalp.

"You awake?" he whispered.

"Yes. You?"

He rolled over slowly so that he could draw her into his arms. "If I'm not, don't wake me from this dream. I want to stay here forever."

She brushed her hand carefully over his bandages. "How do you feel?"

"Wonderful."

She snorted doubtfully as she plucked at the bandage over his abdomen. "I find that hard to believe."

"I would gladly take a thousand beatings if it meant I could wake up with you, like this."

"You're a sick Andarion, Dancer."

Smiling, he laced his fingers with hers. "Eleron, status on my searches."

"Wait!"

He frowned at Sumi's almost shrill tone. That was as close to hysteria as he ever wanted her to come. "What?"

She bit her lip. "I didn't want you to hear it from the computer. The search on your chip came back last night and . . ."

"And what?"

"It originally belonged to Keris."

Hauk couldn't breathe as that news slapped him hard. "How is that possible?"

"I don't know. Fain said—"

"You told Fain?"

She nodded. "You were asleep and I didn't want to wake you. He took it to Syn so that he could run diagnostics on it."

"He hasn't found anything other than the DOM," Eleron broke in. "He also pulled the autopsy files for Keris Hauk, as well as his full medical history."

Hauk was taken aback to see Eleron in his doorway. She normally didn't assume her Andarion form without asking him first. But at least she did take his last command to wear more human-like clothing. "Thanks, El."

"My pleasure." She continued to stare at them from the doorway.

Feeling a little awkward to have a computer voyeur, Hauk pulled his blanket higher. "Is there anything else, El?"

"No."

"You planning to stay there for a while?"

Eleron blinked innocently. "Do you not want to look at me?"

Sumi arched a brow over that comment.

"Uh . . . I would like a little privacy, El."

She actually cast a menacing glare to Sumi. "Very well. Let me know when you need me again."

Sumi cocked her head. "I don't think your girlfriend likes me very much."

"She's not my girlfriend."

"Does Eleron know that?"

He rolled his eyes. "I'm not that big a pervert, *mia*."

"Then why was she naked last night?"

"She was clothed. I swear that was normal Andarion wear." He placed his hand over his heart. "Really."

"Well, where I grew up, that's naked."

He slid his hand down her thigh. "Not as naked as this is." He dipped his head to nibble her hip. "Am I forgiven yet?"

"You're getting there."

Grinning, he nudged her legs farther apart.

"Hauk?" Eleron said as she appeared next to the bed again. "Maris prepared breakfast and has left it in the kitchen warmer for you. Would you like me to heat it to full temperature?" She frowned at the bed. "Hauk?"

He stuck his head out from under the sheet to glare at her. "I wanted privacy, El."

"But you have a house full of guests. . . . Desideria is currently bathing Illyra in their guest tub. Nykyrian, Syn, Darling, Chayden, Fain, Nero, Maris, Caillen, Shahara, Devyn, the mecha monkey I despise, and Jayne are in the conservatory. They were joined an hour ago by Ture, Terek, Zarya, and an infant I am told is named Cezar. Should I create a new profile for the child?"

"Yes," he said through gritted teeth.

"Done. Now should I prepare your shower and food?"

Sumi's stomach convulsed under his head as she laughed silently at his misery. "Privacy, El. Please."

"Is it not considered rude to leave guests waiting?"

"She's not going to give on this, sweetie."

Hauk growled in the back of his throat at the bitter

frustration that begged him to pull the plug on his entire home system. But unfortunately, Eleron was right. It was rude to leave them unattended. "Would you like to meet the rest of my family?" he asked Sumi.

She gently brushed the braids out of his eyes. "Sure."

Grimacing, he slowly got up and dressed, and cursed Eleron while he did so. By the time they'd left the bedroom, Eleron was waiting in the hallway.

"Yes, El?" he asked irritably.

"Two more just arrived. I have allowed them access to the living room and am holding them there for your review."

He frowned at that. No one else should be here. "Who is it?"

"Ger Tarra War Hauk and Tarra Fadima Wulfryn."

Hauk groaned out loud.

"Who?" Sumi asked.

"My yaya and evil cousin. I swear if Fadima squeezes my cheek, I will stab her."

She laughed at his disgruntled threat. "Does that a lot?"

He rolled his eyes. "Sadly, it's a step up from the days when she used to throw me on the ground, sit on me, and fart. If you ever wondered where Darice gets his finer manners, I swear Dimie swapped wombs with Dariana."

"Oh joy. I can't wait to meet *her*." Sumi's humor died as Hauk led her into the living room and she came under the scathing glare of an extremely tall, gorgeous Andarion who made her feel like the twisted underbelly of a *torna*.

"Dancer!" When Fadima took a step toward him, his grandmother pulled her back.

"Our princess, Fadima." She fell into a low bow.

Fadima followed suit. "Forgive me, Highness."

Uncomfortable, Sumi bit her lip and glanced at Dancer,

who seemed to be enjoying this a little too much. "Please, rise. It's fine."

Dancer squeezed her hand to let her know that she didn't need to be nervous. "To what do I owe this honor, Yaya?"

His grandmother pulled the black, rectangle case from her shoulder and knelt on the floor with it. Fadima knelt beside her while his grandmother unzipped it to expose his family's Warsword.

Sumi gasped at the weapon that was centuries old and in perfect condition. It looked as if it'd just been forged. Never had she seen anything more beautiful. And it was with the blade of that sword that Andaria had been saved.

The sacredness of it wasn't lost on her.

Solemnly, Dancer fell to his knees and motioned for Sumi to do the same. With great ceremony, his grandmother pulled out a pair of thick black leather gloves and placed them on her hands. Then she handed a similar pair to Sumi.

"The blade is sharper than any you've ever held, Highness," his grandmother explained. "For that reason, gloves should be worn at all times when you handle it, and especially when you fight with it."

Sumi bowed her head respectfully. "I will always take care."

His grandmother sat back while Sumi covered her hands. "My husband's honorable mother bestowed the great Warsword into my stewardship on the tenth year of our unification. Menser of the Warring Blood Clan of Hauk was one of the greatest heroes of his generation. A decorated warrior, he never knew defeat in battle. To the day he drew his last breath, I couldn't believe my fortune in having a husband so noble. He fed this great Warsword the blood of many enemies. But alas, she has remained famished for many years now as I waited for the right Andarion to again wield her in battle."

Her eyes were filled with sadness as she looked at her grandson. "You, Dancer of the Warring Blood Clan of Hauk, have more than earned the honor of wielding this great sword. I've wanted to bestow her on you since the day your paran died. It was wrong of me to withhold her from you because of the animosity I bear the Terisools. But I couldn't stomach the thought of placing this in the hands of that bitch who killed my firstborn grandson. Nor allowing any child she brewed in her venomous womb to touch it." She turned back to Sumi. "Forgive me, princess, that's not part of the ceremony."

Sumi smiled at her. "By all means, think nothing of it. Dariana has no friend in me."

Her white eyes shined like a child's. She lifted the sword and held it with two hands, by the blade. "For the first Dancer War Hauk it was forged by the first Great Chief and founder of the Most Sovereign Blood Clan of eton Anatole. Since the moment the Great Chief's blood and that of the War Hauk mixed upon this blade, it has been foretold that so long as a War Hauk has possession of our Warsword, Andaria will know no defeat. We will stand strong against all invaders. It is my deepest and most sacred honor that I now move her forward and place her in the hands of the next generation that will feed her well. Into your honorable hands, Sumi of the Most Sovereign Blood Clan of eton Anatole, I place the greatest heritage of the Warring Blood Clan of Hauk. I know that you, Dancer, and all the beautiful children you will have to carry our legacy on, will bring nothing but glory and honor to this noble weapon. May you feed her well and defend our nation as all the great War Hauks before you." She kissed the winged hilt before she carefully placed the sword in Sumi's hands.

Sumi bowed low. "Thank you, Ger—"

"Yaya," she said, breaking in.

She smiled. "Yaya. I will watch over and protect this great Warsword with every ounce of courage I possess."

His grandmother placed her hands over Sumi's. "I know you will, child. I am proud to welcome you into our family and pray that I live long enough to see your firstborn." She released her hands and looked over to Dancer. "Now, you may finally touch your paran's sword and return it to its nest. I promise there will be no spanking henceforth when you pull it down."

He kissed her cheek. *"Kimi asyado, Yaya."*

She patted his shoulder. "You were always my favorite."

"That's what I keep telling him. But he never believes it."

Laughing, Sumi turned toward Fain at the same time Fadima hissed and exposed her fangs.

She started to rise, but their grandmother grabbed her and held her fast.

Sumi gaped. For an elderly woman, the matriarch of the War Hauks still had a lot of fight and strength in her.

"He is now an eton Anatole," she said in Fadima's ear. "Any harm, and it will be from your hide recompense is taken."

Fadima's jaw went slack. "Seriously?"

His grandmother gave a curt nod. "Yes."

Fain made a little-kid gesture of sticking his thumbs in his ears and poking his tongue out at her. "You can't touch me." He sobered as he looked over at his brother. "Damn, to have had these wicked powers when we were young."

Laughing, Hauk returned the sword to its brackets. "I know, right?" He winked at Dimie. "And not that I'm not thrilled to have you over, coz, but why are you here?"

She inclined her head to Sumi, who was removing her gloves and returning them to the sword's case. "To train our princess on how to fight an Andarion female."

His grandmother rose to her feet. "I asked her to do this as a personal favor. Dariana sent over word this morning that she wants Sumi in the ring, day after tomorrow."

Hauk scowled. "Why so soon?"

"Dariana is with child and cannot legally fight after that date."

CHAPTER 29

Sumi gasped at the last thing she'd ever expected to hear. And by the look on Dancer's face, she knew he was equally as shocked. "Dariana's pregnant?"

"How?" Dancer growled at the same time Fain cursed under his breath.

Their grandmother sighed heavily. "It's Keris's child. Dariana had the DNA test run already because she knew I would require it. Apparently, she was artificially inseminated almost three months ago."

Sumi couldn't believe it.

Fadima curled her lip in distaste. "Darice confessed that she never intended unification. She was planning to tell you of her pregnancy during Disclosure and reject you again."

Sumi seethed with the news. Before his entire family. What a whore!

His jaw ticcing, Fain crossed his arms over his chest. "How does Darice know?"

Fadima answered. "Dariana went home in a fury after Sumi challenged her. So much so, that once Darice overheard her ranting to a friend about her intentions, he left immediately to stay with our yaya. He wants no part of Dariana's dishonorable conduct and is ashamed to call her mother. He will not go home until she does right by you."

Dancer looked as sick as Sumi felt. "I never meant to cause friction between mother and son."

"This isn't on you, *kiran*," Fain said. "For once, Darice is honoring his War Hauk lineage with his behavior. While he should normally back his mother, she is bleeding his father's family. No child should be forced to choose one lineage over another. And he knows that had she done the right thing, you would be his father now. She had no legitimate reason to deprive either of you of that relationship. That level of selfishness is *not* Andarion."

Fadima nodded in agreement. "He's right. Dariana has callously and wrongfully used Darice, and now this new baby, to secure a bloodline and title for herself and her progeny while denying you what is rightfully yours. Because your mother has refused repeatedly to act to protect you, Dariana has kept you with your hands tied for far too long."

"Wait," Sumi interrupted then, as she tried to understand what they were implying. "Are you saying that the bitch was planning to keep Dancer tied to her without unification? Forever?"

Angry, his grandmother nodded gravely. "That's how it appears."

Sumi cursed. "I can't wait to have her in front of me so that I can beat her down like she deserves."

His grandmother laughed as she stared proudly at Sumi. "Spoken like a true Andarion female. Dariana is hoping the knowledge of her condition will weaken your human resolve, and that you'll take mercy on her in the fight."

Yeah, right. "She couldn't be more wrong, and she seriously overestimates my love of others. I would never harm a child, and I won't be striking her stomach. The rest of her, however, is all mine and I plan to drag her around that arena by her hair until she begs me for mercy."

A sharp gasp drew their attention to the doorway, where a tiny woman with auburn hair and gold eyes stood with her infant daughter cradled to her shoulder. Her face was absolutely ashen. "Sorry," she said quickly. "I am human and forget how human I am compared to the family I married into. I didn't mean to offend you, but ow! The sheer harshness of that last statement hit me very unexpectedly."

Sumi turned her furious glower to what must be Nykyrian's wife. Yes, it was harsh, but she wasn't about to back down. Not for Dariana and all the years of cruelty she'd shoved down Dancer's throat. "You haven't seen the deep scars on Dancer's back that bitch has callously given him, for no other reason than to publicly hurt and humiliate him, when he's done nothing to deserve them. Her pregnancy will keep me from killing her, but it won't spare her my wroth."

Kiara blanched even more. "The claw marks? Is she the one who gave them to him?"

Sumi nodded.

A steel anger descended over Kiara's face. "Then I hope you beat the snot out of her."

Sumi liked this woman immediately. Thia was right. Her stepmother was a good woman.

Against Andarion custom, Dancer's grandmother pulled Sumi in for a tight hug, then she kissed each of her cheeks in turn. "I could not be prouder of you, *grastiya,* had I birthed you." Releasing Sumi, she smiled at Dancer. "You have done well for yourself, *prie yeyonon.* I cannot wait to paint our heritage on her beautiful face for you."

Dancer struck his heart with his right hand. "Thank you, Yaya. You greatly honor us both." His eyes were filled with mirth as he turned Sumi toward Kiara. "I should probably introduce you two. Kiara Quiakides, this is Sumi . . . eton Anatole."

Kiara smiled warmly in greeting. "And having blindly stumbled into this conversation at probably the worst possible time, I can see why my mother-in-law adopted you. You're just like her, and that's not a bad thing. I adore Cairistiona with my whole heart. And it is a pleasure to meet you, Sumi." She adjusted the baby in her arms until the little girl, who was dressed in a frilly pink tutu, was sitting up, staring at them. "And this is our daughter Zarina."

Sumi's jaw went slack at the sight of the adorable Andarion infant. She had a mass of black curls around her head, and her skin was the same caramel color of Dancer's. Thia was right, her white-and-red eyes were a little strange at first, but once she smiled and her dimples came out, they faded into the background. "She's absolutely beautiful."

"Would you like to hold her?"

Sumi hesitated as fear tightened her stomach. "I've never held a baby that size before. I would hate to hurt her."

Kiara laughed. "What was it Jayne said to me right after Adron was born . . . ? Oh yeah, don't panic if you drop it. They're remarkably hard to kill."

Sumi gasped at something that sounded just like the Jayne Dancer and Thia had told her about. "No, she didn't."

"Yes, yes, she did. You've got to love Jayne's take on things." Kiara gently placed Zarina into Sumi's arms and showed her how to support her back. "And speaking of babies, I haven't had a chance to thank you for bringing Thia back to us." Tears welled in Kiara's soft amber-gold eyes. "I would be devastated if anything ever happened to my oldest daughter. And I know if not for you and what you did, we'd be planning her funeral. Thank you so much." She kissed Sumi's cheek.

"I'm glad I was able to do it. Thia is a remarkable young woman. Scary, but remarkable."

Kiara laughed. "She is her father's daughter. And his shining pride and joy. Just like this one."

Sumi watched as Zarina wrapped her little hand around her finger. She saw the differences between a human baby hand and Zarina's tiny claws, but they were soft and almost gel-like. Nowhere near as sharp—yet—as a human infant's fingernails. And to think, Omira had been afraid of an Andarion baby clawing its way out of her stomach. Really, there was next to no difference between them from what Sumi could tell.

Squealing suddenly, Zarina leaned forward and started gumming Sumi's chin. She wrinkled her nose at the odd, wet sensation.

"Oh my goodness. Sorry. She's teething and has been latching on to everything around her."

"It's fine. Just unexpected."

But not nearly as much as Zarina sighing and then placing her tiny head on Sumi's shoulder before she wrapped her arms around her neck. She melted instantly. Closing her eyes, she savored the sweetness of that single action and the complete love and trust Zarina gave her.

What she wouldn't give to have a house full of such preciousness.

Hauk's gut wrenched at the look on Sumi's face as she held Zarina against her. He could tell she was thinking of her own daughter, and it made him sick that they hadn't been able to find Kalea yet. But what infuriated him was that she'd been deprived of holding her child at this age. Deprived of watching Kalea learn to walk and talk and do all the special things that marked the early years of a child's life.

Damn you, Kyr. And damn The League his own ancestor had set up.

By the gods, he wouldn't let her miss another year of her daughter's life. Not for anything.

Wishing he could go back and protect them both from The League's callous dictates, and her boyfriend who'd tried to kill them both, he drew Sumi into a hug and smiled down at them. He wanted to say something, but knew no words could ease the pain he saw in her eyes.

Nothing would, except the return of her daughter.

"She is a cute little toe-biter, isn't she?" Fain asked as he made faces at Zarina and got her smiling and squealing again.

Sumi laughed at his comment. "She is truly precious."

His grandmother smiled at them. "It's been a long, long time since I've been so close to a baby. Yours is especially strong and beautiful, Highness."

Kiara blushed. "Thank you, Ger Tarra War Hauk."

"Please, call me Corinne." She bowed respectfully. "Might I have the honor of touching your daughter, Highness?"

"Kiara, please. And yes. It would be my honor for you to touch her and honor her with the strength of the mighty War Hauk clan."

Sumi carefully handed her to Dancer's grandmother. A warm, loving smile lit her entire face.

"What a sweet, sweet thing you are, Princess," his grandmother said in a high falsetto. "I was never blessed with a daughter, only exquisite sons. But had I been so honored by the gods, I cannot imagine she would have been lovelier than you." She placed her hand on Fadima's cheek. "But the gods were kind and made it up to me with the strong, beautiful granddaughters who well complement my strong, handsome grandsons."

Her kindness brought tears to Sumi's eyes. No wonder Dancer loved his grandmother so.

Fadima inclined her head to her grandmother. "Thank you, Yaya."

"And as much as I hate to set this precious child aside, I fear we have serious business to attend."

"I understand. Thank you for honoring my daughter." Kiara took Zarina back. "Shahara and Desideria would also like to help Sumi train. Desideria is Qillaq, and Shahara is a Gondarion Seax. While they are human, they are some of the best fighters of our species."

Fadima grinned. "I gladly accept their aid. The Qills have tactics very similar to ours, and a Seax has special sword maneuvers Dariana won't see coming. I've trained with them before. They are quite accomplished . . . for humans." Her eyes danced with humor to let Sumi and Kiara know it wasn't a real dig at their species.

She turned to Dancer and reached out her hand.

Fury darkened his eyes as he visibly tensed.

But instead of pinching his cheek, she brushed her thumb against his temple.

"I am glad to see you well settled, cousin. Out of all our rowdy kin, you were always the one closest to my heart."

Dancer placed his hand over hers. "You shame me, Dimie."

"How so? I meant no insult."

He pulled her hand to place it over his heart. "The shame isn't in your actions, but mine. I spoke ill of you on your arrival. For that I sincerely apologize."

She laughed good-naturedly. "I am sure, given the way I've shown my affections toward you in the past, that whatever you said was highly warranted and fully deserved. No offense is taken by me." She touched her forehead to his. "And have no fear, even though the beauty of your face tempts me terribly, I won't pinch your cheeks."

He growled low in his throat. "I hate that so much."

Stepping back, Fadima winked at Sumi. "It's not just that he's so handsome that made me do that growing up.

His name means *of beautiful cheeks* in Andarion. It seemed fitting that I should pinch them to remind him."

Sumi smiled. "He didn't tell me that."

When his grandmother started to lead them to train, Dancer stopped them.

"Yaya, before you take her to the gym, may I show her to the conservatory? She hasn't been there yet, and I would like the pleasure of seeing her face the first time she views it."

Sumi was touched by his question and especially this much quieter and more tender part of her fierce warrior. Thia had been right. There were two very distinct sides to Dancer. The ferocious War Hauk who took mercy on no one—who went in with both blasters at max settings and wreaked all manner of havoc on his enemies—and the precious Dancer who tempered his actions and sarcasm for those he loved and cherished.

And then there was the lover and protector she knew. A whole other beast entirely, and yet it was comprised of those two very different facets of what he showed to the world. The only difference was that for her, he dropped those shields and she saw the raw vulnerability in his heart that no one else was ever privy to.

She, alone, was trusted with his true feelings. Only she knew what really hurt him. And she would never cause him harm.

Taking her arm, his grandmother led her down the long hallway. "The conservatory was always my favorite room. Dancer's paran had it built for me to celebrate the birth of his father. Unlike my husband, I grew up on a remote outpost where we had such vegetation that you could walk for days and not see another Andarion. When I came here to marry his paran, I missed my home terribly. So he created this room to simulate what I loved most . . . besides him and our sons." She stopped to open a door.

Dancer moved forward so that he was facing her.

Sumi sucked her breath in sharply the moment the door slid open to show the most amazing room she'd ever beheld. At least a thousand square feet, it was like walking into a perfectly groomed jungle and park, all in one. The botanist in her sang out loud at the sight.

"Oh my goodness!" She rushed to the first small pond that housed fish and aquatic plants she'd never seen before. Not even in catalogues. Even the columns of the room held pockets of herbs in them. There were birds and butterflies. Other small flying creatures she'd need to look up to identify.

This . . . this was her idea of heaven. Giddy, she ran around until she came to a corner where a long table was set and everyone had gathered this morning.

Suddenly horrified by her childish behavior, she pulled up short. "Sorry. I didn't realize anyone was here."

Dancer came up behind her. "Don't be embarrassed, *mia*. The expression on your face when that door opened will live forever in my heart. I'm so glad my home pleases you."

Unable to contain the joy and love that overwhelmed her, she pulled him into her arms and held him close. "Thank you for bringing me here. It's absolutely stunning!"

Hauk closed his eyes and buried his hand in her soft blond hair. His entire body craved her now. So much so that it was hard to not scoop her up in his arms and carry her back to their bedroom. He couldn't wait to get everyone out of his house so that he'd have unrestricted time with his brave little mouse.

"Is it just me," Caillen said. "Or does Hauk's hulking ass make her look so tiny that it's a wonder he doesn't snap her in half?"

With an irritable growl, Hauk pulled back to glare at him. In fact, everyone was glaring at him.

"What?" he asked innocently. "Like the rest of you weren't thinking the same thing. He's huge. She's not."

Syn yanked the muffin out of Caillen's hands. "Case it's escaped your notice, fat ass. You and Desideria have a larger height and weight ratio differential than Hauk and Sumi."

"Hell no, we don't . . . do we?"

"Yes, sweetie," Desideria said with a laugh as she adjusted her slumbering daughter in her lap. "I know you're nowhere near as tall as Hauk, but you're well over a foot taller than me and he's only a few inches taller than Sumi . . . and if you say anything about my weight, you'll be sleeping at one of your sisters' homes from now until the Qillaq moons explode."

Caillen rolled his eyes. "What is it with women and their weight? Gah! You're pregnant, Ria. You're not supposed to fit into your pre-pregnancy pants right now. Not that I care, one way or the other. . . . Woman, you are perfect in my eyes. I married a sexy, hot warrior, not a number on a scale. Or this mutant life form you're convinced inhabits your body until you put on your makeup. How many times do I have to say it before you actually believe me?"

Desideria passed a satisfied smirk to Shahara. "You asked me why I love your brother? That's a biggie right there. You trained him right."

Caillen grinned, then belched.

Groaning, Shahara rolled her eyes before she gave Desideria a long, hard stare. "You were saying?"

"He's a work in progress." Desideria handed her daughter to Caillen. "Try not to teach her any bad habits over the next hour." She got up. "And speaking of training, we have serious work to do to get Sumi ready for her match."

Shahara handed Devyn to Syn. "I'm not even going to say don't do it. I already know better. I don't know what's worse. What Devyn learns from you or from Vik."

Vik snorted. "I'm not the one who sits on the couch and scratches his—"

"Vik!" Syn snapped. "You know Eleron wants to feed you to the garbage disposal, right? You keep that up and I'll green-light her."

Laughing at them, Devyn bounced in his father's lap.

Shahara paused beside Dancer. "Are you staying with the guys or following us?"

"You. I want to make sure that Sumi knows what to expect. But before we go . . ." Dancer headed to the small brunette who quietly held the tiniest baby Sumi had ever seen. He kissed the woman's cheek before he knelt down next to her so that he could peer at the newborn. "Hey, Cezar, it's a pleasure meeting the little guy who made Daddy lose all of his mind. You almost got his ass whipped by two Andarions and a Phrixian."

An attractive reddish-brown-haired man sitting across from her and next to Maris laughed. Like Zarya, he cradled a baby boy in his lap, who was a few months older.

Dancer flashed a grin before he held his hand out toward Sumi. "Zarya Cruel," he inclined his head to the man who'd laughed, "Ture Xans-Sulle, meet my Sumi."

Good gracious. How many more people make up his family? It wasn't fair. She had no one for him to meet at all. He really did come with his own army of people.

Nervous all over again, she approached them slowly. "Hi."

Zarya handed her son off to Dancer so that she could stand and give her a hug. She patted Sumi on the back before she withdrew and held both of her hands in hers. "I know that look on your face. I had it less than a year ago, myself." She tilted her head to Ture. "As did my best friend when he joined us. But the good news is, we all love you because Hauk loves you. And if you need anything at all, we are your family now. All you have to do is call us and we're there."

Tears welled up in her eyes. "Thank you."

Like a proud father, Dancer brought Cezar over to them. He was so tiny he fit easily into Dancer's palm. "Would you like to hold him?"

She made a face at the thought. "He's awful little."

Zarya laughed. "I had the same reaction a few days ago when they handed him off to me for the first time. I'm still rather shocked someone thinks I'm a responsible parent."

Laughing, Dancer moved to stand behind Sumi before he placed Cezar in her arms.

Emotions overwhelmed her as she stared down at the tiny little newborn. While she'd enjoyed holding Zarina, this was entirely different. She glanced over to the baby in Ture's arms. "Are they really only a few months apart in age?"

Zarya nodded. "They are."

"I never realized babies grew so fast."

"Unbelievably fast," Maris said as he joined them with the infant Ture had been holding. "This is our son, Terek. He's five months old . . . just a few weeks older than Zarina."

Terek had a very serious look to him as he chewed his fist. His face was swallowed by his large, dark eyes.

"He's beautiful, Mari. I know you're proud of him." Tears swelled in her eyes as she looked down at Cezar and then at all the other babies in the room. Especially Lillya.

For the first time, she understood Thia's pain. Why it was so hard to be with them. This . . . this was what life should be like. A family that would defend and protect. Mothers and fathers who would trudge through hell itself to shield their children from any enemy.

She'd never once known that. Thia had been practically grown before she'd found it.

And Kalea . . .

She was out there alone. With no one to hold her and love her. No one to protect her from harm.

Her sobs burst as she thought about her daughter in the hands of people who couldn't care less about her. People who wouldn't hesitate to hurt her any way they could.

She handed Cezar back to his mother before she ran from the room, seeking refuge from the pain lacerating her heart. This was all she'd ever wanted in her life.

Safety. Love. A place to raise her daughter with people who cherished her as much as Sumi did.

Suddenly, she felt Dancer behind her. He wrapped his arms around her and held her tight while she expelled all the misery she kept bottled up.

Zarya looked around, baffled by what had just happened. "Did I say or do something wrong?"

Syn shook his head sadly. "Sumi has a daughter in League custody that we're trying to find and save."

Maris winced as he tightened his grip on Terek. "I didn't even think about that."

Syn clapped him on the back. "None of us did. We're proud of our babies and wanted to show them off."

"Yeah, but if we couldn't be with them . . ." Zarya choked on a sob of her own. "I didn't mean to hurt her. I'm so sorry."

Syn swept his gaze around every person there. Countless times, they'd gone to war with a single goal. Seldom had they been as united as they were when it came to their families. "We will get that baby back."

Maris nodded. "Saf still has contacts. It's time to call in every favor we can."

"We already have," Syn said with a dismal sigh, "but we haven't found out anything yet."

Maris snorted. "You have contacts, yes. But it's time to show off the reach that my birth family has."

* * *

Hauk held Sumi close until she finally drew a ragged breath.

"I'm so sorry I embarrassed you."

He tilted her chin up so that she could meet his sincere gaze. Wanting to comfort her, he kissed away her tears. "You did *not* embarrass me, *mia*. Very soon, our daughter will be playing right alongside their children. And she will be spoiled more than any daughter ever born. She will know nothing but our love. I swear that to you."

"*Our* daughter?" his grandmother asked, suddenly.

He glanced over his shoulder to his grandmother and cousin. "Sumi has agreed to honor me with fatherhood when we find her daughter."

She smiled at Sumi. "So I will have another great-granddaughter to spoil? How wonderful! Then let us be about this training so that we can cement your family, Dancer. I want to see you settled with a female who is worthy of your heart, and there is nothing more dear to mine than another child to love and spoil."

Hauk inclined his head, grateful that his grandmother was so kind and accepting. However, his mother would be another story. Far more traditional, she would never forgive him for being with a human. And he doubted if she would ever so much as look at Kalea.

Not that it mattered. He and Sumi would treasure her so that she would never miss having a grandmother's love.

Shahara and Desideria slowly joined them.

"Are we interrupting?"

Sumi sniffed back her tears at their kindness. "Sorry. I—"

"Shh," Shahara said. "Don't apologize. We all understand, and we're very sorry if we hurt you."

Sumi pulled her into a hug. "God, no. You've all been so wonderful that it's made it extra hard, I think. I'm not used to this."

Desideria laughed. "Believe me, we all know that feeling. My older sister tried to kill me and my husband before we married."

"What?" Sumi asked breathlessly.

Shahara nodded. "That was after she tried to frame them both for murder. Makes you appreciate your own family, eh?"

"Sadly . . . yes."

Taking her by the arm, Shahara patted her shoulder. "Just remember, family isn't perfect. It's just perfectly ours." She led the way to the gym that was down the hall. Fain stayed behind.

Sumi wasn't sure what to expect given the extravagance of the rest of the house. And the gym definitely didn't disappoint. Which made sense, given Dancer's physique. He probably spent more time in here than anywhere else.

At the moment, the room was open and airy like the conservatory, but there were VR monitors all over. There were three separate fighting areas. Two had mats, one was the solid floor. Every known weapon she'd ever seen or heard of was in racks that lined one wall. He had a firing range at one end. An archery range next to that, that was also equipped with targets for other throwing weapons. Different kinds of punching bags, dummies, and speed bags . . .

She couldn't even take it all in.

Sumi gave him a dead stare. "Is there any piece of exercise equipment you don't own?"

"How do you think I stay so sexy?" He winked at her.

She laughed at his teasing tone. Yet he was right. The male was lickably hot. And she could easily imagine him in here with his friends as they trained.

"We'll be using the Splatterdome," Fadima said as she began stripping her clothes off to expose the skintight workout suit underneath. "Or ring, as it's best known."

She grabbed a long staff and headed for the unpadded fighting area.

Sumi stripped down to her League undergarments. Dancer handed her a staff similar to the one his cousin had chosen. As she reached for it, Fain joined them.

"You need fuel to fight." Fain handed her sausage muffins.

"Thank you." Smiling, she took the small plate from his hand and ate the muffins while Dancer and his cousin explained the rules of her coming match.

Which basically had no rules other than kill your opponent honorably.

"You can never strike Dariana's back," Fadima warned. "Should you do so, the referees will wound you."

Her eyes widened. "How so?"

"Depends on where and how hard you strike her. It could be a small penalty where they merely tie one of your limbs down or a larger one that would result in your being stabbed." Fadima used her staff to illustrate the area on the back of her leg where they might cut her.

Yeah, okay. Sumi didn't like these rules. Andarions really didn't play.

"An accidental strike," Fadima continued, "such as she's turning, doesn't count." She hit her on the shoulder. She handed another staff to Dancer. "Let's show her, cousin."

Sumi almost choked on her muffin as the two of them went after each other like they were in a League death match or Andarion ring title fight. Fain handed her water while she watched them in awe.

Fadima made a strike at Dancer's head that would have been lethal had it contacted. Luckily, he caught it and ducked.

"Anything frontal is permitted," she explained. "The rule is your opponent must see the blow coming either dead on, or peripherally. Those are all legal blows."

She held her staff up in both hands horizontally. "This is a request for a small time-out, as in you've been injured and need the break or sprain set. It only gives you three minutes."

As she stepped away, Dancer feigned a strike to her shoulder. He looked at Sumi. "If you strike her once she's requested a break, you will forfeit your weapon."

He moved to Fadima's back. "Any hits when she's faced away from you are the ones you have to avoid."

Sumi swallowed her food. "I wouldn't make that strike anyway."

"Yes, but . . ."

"Dariana's a cheating bitch," Fadima finished for Dancer. "You have to be in control of your strikes and temper at all times so that she doesn't lure you into making something the ref will misconstrue as a back attack."

"Ah, gotcha." Sumi licked her fingers then moved to take the staff from Dancer. "Let's try this."

Hauk stepped away, even though it was the last thing he wanted to do. Every instinct inside him wanted to protect Sumi. It was a painful, demanding ache.

But to Sumi's credit, she was an incredible fighter. She met every one of Fadima's strikes. Her circular moves were flawless and she had good weight behind her jabs.

"Dang!" she said as she stepped back after striking Fadima's side. "Andarions are solid. Were you born with a staff in your hand?"

Fadima laughed and glanced to Hauk. "You have your male to blame for my skills. He was forever picking a fight with me. I had to learn to fight him off or stay bruised."

Hauk snorted. "The lies that drop from your tongue, cousin. I was the innocent victim. I'd be lying on the floor, playing in total harmony, and she'd run up my back, flip, and pin me in a hold."

"I did do that," Fadima admitted with a smile.

"And let's not forget," Fain added, "how many times

we'd be playing ball and she'd run in out of nowhere and throw us down."

"That was only after she'd kicked us in *our* balls."

Fadima laughed. "As I said, I take no offense to your thinking ill of me, cousin." She met Sumi's gaze. "But I never once defeated Fain in a fight. Until the Iron Hammer came along, he was the youngest Ring title holder in Andarion history, and never lost a single match in his entire career."

"Iron Hammer, what?" Sumi asked with a frown.

"Iron Hammer is a legendary Andarion prizefighter," Fadima explained. "He retired a couple of years ago, undefeated in all class weights and in both league divisions."

Dancer jerked his chin at his brother. "In his youth, Fain was every bit as famous. He was one of the most celebrated Ring prizefighters of his generation and would have gone on to be the undefeated champ of all three titles had he not . . ." His voice trailed off.

"Had he not married my sister." That knowledge made her even sicker. Omira had cost Fain so much.

Fadima held the staff up for a break.

Sumi stopped immediately.

Breathing heavily, she passed an impressed expression on to Dancer. "Your female is very well trained." She tossed the staff to Shahara. "I'll let you have a go and see what you think."

Sumi thought she was prepared until Shahara started for her. She came after her like a psychotic ten-armed windmill. In less than a minute, Shahara had her flat on her back.

Hauk growled as he saw Sumi fall.

Fain caught him. "It's training, *drey*. They have to do this."

He knew that, but still . . .

Sumi flipped to her feet with a stunned look on her face. "What did you do? That was incredible! Teach me!"

"And me," Fadima said as she took another staff. "I've never seen anyone move like that."

"Because you're both tall. While I am for a human, I've gone up against a lot of Phrixians, Andarions, Partinie, and other humongous races that dwarf me." She inclined her head to Desideria. "She's even better at those moves than I am. I've seen her face-plant Caillen in training, and even *I* have a hard time doing that. My brother is extremely accomplished."

Desideria snorted. "I don't think it's that, Shay."

"What do you mean?"

"You really underestimate how much your brother fears you. You threatened to turn him into a girl one time too many, growing up."

"Hmm . . . too bad I couldn't stop him from turning into an ill-mannered tourah."

Desideria laughed.

"But unfortunately, you won't be fighting with staves." Hauk went to the wall and pulled down the practice swords. He handed one to Sumi and one to Shahara.

Shahara screwed her face up. "I'm a knife fighter. I have basic sword skills, but nothing to brag about."

Desideria took it from her. "*This* is my forte. 'Qillaq' means sword-bearer."

Sumi glanced down at Desideria's distended belly. While she had no problem fighting Dariana, who had yet to show her pregnancy, fighting a woman who was well into her third trimester was another matter entirely. "Out of curiosity, when exactly are you due?"

"I still have a few more weeks to go."

Sumi stepped back. "Um, yeah . . . I don't think we should be doing this."

Desideria scoffed. "I am Qillaq. My great-grandmother gave birth *during* battle. She handed her daughter off then buried her enemies on the field. I promise, even though

I'm not quite as centered as I normally am, you won't hurt me or Vashe."

"Vashe?"

"The son I carry. Even he's eager for this. I can feel him tumbling at the mere prospect of the fight."

Sumi was stunned. "I'm still not sure about this."

That was her thought until Desideria started fighting. Her strikes and parries were as flawless as Shahara's moves with a staff.

"My Lord, I'd hate to face you when you're *not* pregnant."

Desideria laughed. "Told you. But . . ." She stepped back. "I am very winded now." She handed the sword to Fadima. "And I have to go to the bathroom. Vashe is dancing on top of my bladder."

"I have felt that pain. Every child I carried used mine for a trampoline." Fadima faced Sumi, "Do you need a break as well?"

"Good to go."

As they fought, Hauk caught the strange look on his grandmother's face.

He moved to stand beside her. "Is something wrong, Yaya?"

For several minutes, she didn't speak. Then, she touched his shoulder where his mother had sliced him open. "Tell me, Dancer. When your mother chastised you, what did you do to deserve it?"

He started to move away without answering, but she caught his arm.

"I am old, *tana*, I won't think ill of you for it. But no one has ever told me what it is you did that was so wrong she publicly scarred you over it."

Hauk flinched as he went back in his mind to that day that was forever carved not just into his flesh, but his memories.

At eighteen, he'd been as headstrong as Darice. Dariana's mourning period was coming to a close and his mother had scheduled their pledging.

"I won't do it, Matarra."

She'd growled in his face. "You *will* do this."

Hauk had been adamant. "I can't take her as my wife."

She'd backhanded him for his denial. "No one else wants you. Do you understand? You're revolting. Deformed. There are no other noble families willing to pledge to you. Not for any reason. And she is your brother's widow."

"She's my brother's murderer."

This time, she'd struck him so hard, she'd loosened his teeth. "Never say that out loud!"

He'd wiped away the blood on his lips as he glared at her. "I was there, Matarra. I saw him using the drugs she gave him. It's why she destroyed his body that I carried home, in honor."

"You're lying!"

"Why would I lie?"

"To protect yourself."

"From what? Disgrace? Humiliation? Contrary to what you and Dariana think, I didn't kill him, Matarra." All he'd wanted was for his mother to understand the truth. To stop looking at him like he was a piece of shit who should have died. "Too high to understand what he was doing, Keris took his own life. He cut the line and—"

Shrieking, she'd attacked him so viciously that he'd stumbled and fallen. She'd seized him by his throat and before he realized her intent, she clawed open his flesh from shoulder to pec. "You ever breathe a word of your lies to anyone and you can join that piece of human-loving filth in exile. I cannot believe the gods took my one, true son and left me with *you*. I wish to all that's holy that you'd never returned."

"Dancer?"

It took him a minute to realize his grandmother was calling him. Blinking, he looked down at her. "Yes, Yaya?"

"Why did she chastise you?"

He forced his emotions down and answered with the simplest, least painful explanation. "Because I let my brother die."

She sighed heavily. "I know there's more to it than that. One day, Dancer, I hope you'll trust me with the truth."

As she walked off, the door opened to show a very grim-faced Nykyrian and Syn. His gut shrank at what those expressions could mean.

"What?"

Syn glanced to Nykyrian before he answered. "It's time for our favorite How Screwed Are You report."

"Oh goody," Hauk said drily. "My day was already sucking. How nice of you to kick down more for me."

"Ever my pleasure."

Hauk ignored Syn and turned to face Nyk, who would actually answer his question. "So what's going on?"

"We have a traitor in our midst. And we will find them and choke them with their entrails. But in the meantime, Kyr knows that Sumi's defected."

Hauk felt his stomach slam into the ground. "What?"

Syn nodded. "But wait, there's more. He hasn't harmed her daughter yet. . . . Maris assures us that Kyr will do his best to leverage her for you and Sumi. Which is a very Kyr thing to do. So as long as he thinks there's a chance he can use her to get you two, she's safe. But we don't have long or one of you or all of you will be dead."

CHAPTER 30

Hauk took a moment more to watch Sumi as she sparred with the others. His *mia* was the strongest, most courageous female he'd ever known.

But this news would shatter her.

The thought of stealing that smile from her face shredded his gut. All he wanted was to make her happy. To protect her at all costs. Too many had worked to hurt her. And she'd cried enough for one day.

"Let's wait to tell Sumi. I want more information first."

Nykyrian clapped him on the back. "Understood. As parents, we get it. We know how we'd react."

Syn snorted. "Yeah. Pick a weapon and do something really stupid and suicidal."

Hauk passed a hard stare at his friend. "I may yet yield to that. The day is still young."

"Which is why we're all here. I've got your left leg. Nyk called your right."

"And I've got stun duty," Darling said as he joined them. "They think you're less likely to hurt me since I'm the newest father in the group . . . well, second to you."

Hauk laughed at Darling. "You're sick bastards."

Nyk slung his arm around Hauk's shoulders and gave him a rare hug. "But only for you, brother."

He glanced down at the scar on Nyk's arm from that long-ago pod crash. There was truly nothing he wouldn't do for this male.

Darling stiffened before he touched the link in his ear. "Go."

Hauk could vaguely hear Maris's voice on the other end.

"Be right there." Darling cut the link. "Maris has an update. He wants us in the comm room."

Hauk inclined his head. As he started for the door, Sumi paused her training.

"Is something wrong?"

Damn, she was too perceptive at times.

Not wanting to upset her, he gave her a light kiss. "We're hoping it's good news." Hopefully, it wouldn't be a lie.

"About Kalea?"

He nodded. "Keep training and I'll let you know as soon as we have something."

"Okay." She kissed his cheek. "Love you."

Those words never got old to him. "You, too, *mia*." He took a moment to watch her run back to his cousin and Shahara. Biting his lip, he felt his body harden instantly. No other female had ever done to him what she did. While he'd had attractive females turn him on, it was nothing compared to the hunger Sumi caused by doing nothing more than breathing.

Gah, this was unbearable.

And right now, he had other things to do besides strip off her clothes and taste that body that was driving him insane with lust.

As he headed for the door, his grandmother gave him a suspicious stare. "Can an old female be privy to this or is it a cock-only event?"

Hauk choked on her use of an old, less-than-proper term he hadn't heard since his grandfather had been alive and reminiscing with his father. "Feel free to join us, Yaya. You're always welcome wherever I am." He offered his arm to her.

She took one last look at Sumi and smiled. "Your female stands a better-than-good chance at beating Dariana. That *harita* doesn't know what she's up against."

"Having been hand-fed by you, Yaya, you should have known that no ordinary female would do for me. I require her to equal you in strength, prowess, and beauty."

An attractive blush stained her cheeks. "You flatter an old bird."

"I speak honestly and with candor. As you taught me."

"You speak with the guile learned from your paran. He was ever able to charm me. I would never have married anyone save him."

He heard the sadness in her voice. "I miss him, too."

Her eyes sad, she nodded. "He always loved you, Dancer. I know he was hard on you. Unkind at times even, but he was doing what he thought best to make you as strong as possible. He always said that you would be his heir to the Warsword."

Hauk looked away as she dredged up memories he'd rather not think about. Like his grandmother, his grandfather had remained angry at his father throughout his lifetime over the fact that his father had shamed Cairistiona and tied their line to his mother's lesser lineage. And his father had taken that anger out on all three of them, as if they were to blame for their father's mistake in not keeping it in his pants.

But that was a long time ago. And Hauk didn't want to think about how furious his grandfather would be to see a human under the roof of this house. Never mind the herd of them that Hauk had assembled as family. He could hear that old buzzard in his head—*the only good human is the one lying dead under my boot heel.*

Luckily, he didn't think that way. It'd been Andarions who had done him wrong throughout the majority of his life. Andarions who saw him as lacking. But then cruelty, unfortunately, was found in all sentient species.

Hauk's thoughts scattered as he entered his comm room to find Maris on a call with what appeared to be several members of his blood family.

What the hell? How had this happened?

They hadn't just disowned Maris, they'd put him under a death warrant. So much so, that Mari was still healing from a wound his younger brother Draygon had given him just a few months ago when Dray had all but killed him.

Yeah, hell had frozen over and then some.

Maris smiled as they joined him and the others in the room. He stepped back so that Hauk could join him for the video chat. "Hauk, I know you've met my brother Safir."

Yes, he had. Many times. But the last time he'd seen Safir, Saf had been in a League uniform with the long braid down his back that marked their top assassins. Now Saf's black hair was cut shoulder-length, and nasty bruises marred his face. Not to mention, his left arm was in a sling.

Hauk's gut tightened at the sight of his injuries. "Saf, please tell me we didn't cause that."

Saf let out a bitter laugh. "It's not on you, *drey*. I knew the minute I offered myself as a shield to Mari so that all of you could escape what I was getting into." He glanced down at his busted arm. "At least I thought I did. Still, I have no regrets. I'd rather be busted up than have to attend all of your funerals and face your families, knowing I chose my health over your lives."

Hauk could respect that, and it was why Saf was considered another member of their immediate family.

Like Saf, the other three men on the call were dressed in burgundy Phrixian battlesuits. One armada, and two army.

Maris indicated the tallest of them. "Allow me to introduce to you the prime commander of the Phrixian armada, Vadim Zahi." Unlike his brothers, he had light brown hair and silvery blue eyes. "Next to him is the prime commander of the Phrixian army, Valari Sadoq." With the exception of the cleft in his chin and the muscular build that would rival Hauk's, he was almost identical in looks to Maris. Same black hair and eyes, and that intense stare that said he could see straight through any bullshit. "And Madai Zhao, who is Val's second-in-command of the Phrixian ground forces." Now Madai could easily pass as Maris's twin. The only difference between them, again, was the larger build, and Madai's skin was closer to the color of Hauk's than Maris's paler complexion.

Maris stepped back to indicate Hauk. "Phrixian High Command, I present you to Dancer of the Warring Blood Clan of Hauk, one of the high commanders and founders of The Sentella. It's Hauk's daughter who's being held by Kyr."

The unified fury in the Phrixians' gazes was a thing of beauty and raw terror. They were out for blood, too.

Val clenched his teeth before he spoke. "We apologize for the cowardly actions that have been taken against your family, War Hauk. We assure you that no member of the Phrixian royal house will rest until this is rectified and your daughter is home safe."

Vadim nodded. "Our brother—the prince-heir—and father, the emperor, also wish for us to extend their regrets that they were unable to be here to speak with you themselves. They're en route to Andaria to meet with Queen Cairistiona. I'm sure as soon as they land, they will be in touch. But our father wanted us to contact you immediately to let you know that we do not condone such behavior, and that the Phrixian army and armada are at your full disposal."

Hauk scowled at everyone in the room. "I feel like I've stumbled into the middle of a conversation."

Safir let out an evil laugh. "When Kyr decided to use me as Maris's scapegoat, he forgot two things. One, we are Phrixian. You have a problem with someone, you fight it out. You don't tie them up and torture them. Two . . ." He grinned viciously. "I'm the baby. The rest of the family might hate Mari, but they adore me. I'm the favored son."

Madai shoved him. "You're an asshole."

"You're just jealous Mom and Dad love me more."

Hauk scowled at Safir's declaration. "I didn't think the Phrixians had a word for love."

Saf chuckled. "We don't. But if we did, they would love me best."

Maris rolled his eyes at his brothers. "Because of what Kyr did to Saf, the Phrixian emperor has already contacted and negotiated a treaty with the Andarion queen, and both the Exeterian and Triosan emperors. Once they get here, they will sign the treaties and become our allies in the war against The League."

Hauk was still confused as he stared at Maris. "So they're all talking to you again?"

Maris screwed his face up. "Kind of."

"What's *kind of*?"

Saf let out an irritable sigh as he cast an evil smirk at his brothers. "*Kind of* would be me. They're telling me what to say to him, even though he's standing right there in front of us. I agree, it's so fucked up. But they did this to me all the time when we were kids and they'd get crossed up, so I'm kind of used to it. However, I am not their universal translator, and I'm really tired of them treating me like it's my sole purpose in life."

Yeah, that sounded about right. As the youngest of his brothers, Hauk had been there a few times himself. But he did have one more question. "Does this mean the Phrixians are also signing a treaty with the Caronese?"

"Sort of," Maris said again. "It's more of an informal agreement not to kill or attack the Caronese, and especially their emperor."

Who was suspiciously missing from this meeting, Hauk realized, now that he looked around his gathered friends.

Saf rubbed nervously at his neck before he elaborated. "Our father is still upset at Darling, and Darling is still . . . shall we say, unforgiving of his treatment toward Maris. We're all thinking for the sake of peace that we keep the two of them out of the same room for a while."

Hauk couldn't agree more. "Probably a good idea."

Vadim slid a glare toward Maris. "But we are willing to fight with whomever we must to get your daughter back and see her kidnapper brought to justice for it. We're already mobilizing our forces and will be heading to neutral ground in a few hours so that we may attack wherever you need us."

Val nodded in agreement. "To hold a child to strike at the parents, and especially the mother, is the most shameful of all acts. We will not tolerate it or stand for it."

Nykyrian inclined his head to them. "As the Andarion heir, I want you to know that your assistance in freeing our princess will not be forgotten and it will be returned to your empire."

Vadim returned the bow. "It is our privilege, Highness. While the Phrixians and Andarions have not always been on the same side in war, we have always respected your breed as some of the fiercest and most loyal warriors in the Nine Worlds. It will be our honor to fight with you."

Safir stepped forward. "And Hauk, since we are now officially at war with The League, our father has given

Kyr an ultimatum. He is to surrender your daughter in five universal hours to either Andarion or Phrixian custody, or he will be viewed as a war criminal by our people."

That was a nice touch. "You think he will?"

"Honestly, I don't know. That creature isn't the brother I once knew. If he has any honor, he will let her go. But he might see it as a challenge to his authority and there's no telling what he'll do then. That being said, our father has recalled every Phrixian in League uniform. If they don't return immediately, they renounce all ties with Phrixus, and Maris can tell you firsthand what a joy that isn't. While we expect the handful of Phrixian assassins to stay with Kyr, the vast majority of the others will return home. And there are over two thousand of those. One of them is bound to know where he's keeping Kalea. Most likely, it's been Phrixians who've been guarding her. One way or another, we will have her location any time now."

"And we'll mobilize immediately," Val said. "We will do everything in our power to make sure no harm befalls the Andarion princess."

Hauk inclined his head to them. "Thank you, commanders. As my prince and heir said, it is an honor and debt that will not go unpaid or be forgotten."

As one, they gave Hauk a Phrixian salute, which he and Nykyrian returned before the screen went blank.

Hauk scowled at Maris. "What did you do?"

He shrugged nonchalantly. "Safir told you. He's the golden baby child. While my parents haven't hesitated to put him to the hazard to hone his battle skills, they've always been especially proud of his achievements. More so than anyone else's. I think a lot of it has to do with the fact that he was born the runt of the litter. And they basically left him to die at every turn. And at every turn, he defiantly survived. Once he started training, he excelled far beyond the rest of us. While Kyr made the decision to enter The League, Saf, as youngest, had no choice. That has been part of the Phrixian treaty with The League since they signed it, centuries ago. The youngest son of the ruling family has always been given to The League as a soldier. They fully expected Saf to take Kyr's place as head one day. But when Saf helped us escape, Kyr took him prisoner."

Hauk felt suddenly sick. "Are you telling me that Saf has been held and tortured for months now? Because of us?"

His gaze haunted, Maris nodded. "Kyr should have punished him and released him. Bastard. And he was smart enough not to tell a single soul about it. He knew what would happen if word got back to the family." He moved to stand beside Hauk. "By the way, Saf owes his life to Sumi, and it's a debt he won't ever forget."

"How so?"

"To cow her and make her fall in line, Kyr took her to see Saf. He wanted to show her how far he'd go if he was crossed, and what he'd do to her and her daughter. Sumi, before she went after you, sent this to my father." Mari played the voice message. While her voice was low and broken in places, there was no mistaking it as hers.

"Emperor Zatyr, I hope you will listen to this message and that it reaches you. I have been told that the Phrixians do not condone any form of torture. Please let that be correct. Um . . . Sir . . . Majesty, I know it's not my place, but I wanted you to know that your son, Safir Jari, is being held without trial and routinely tortured. Not interrogated, Majesty. Tortured. Horribly and brutally. For no other reason than the prime commander wants him to feel the weight of his anger. I don't even know if he'll live long enough for you to receive this or what the Phrixian stance really is on such things. But as his father, I thought you should know. I know no other way to help him. I hope you can. No one deserves what's being done to him. Thank you, sir. And if you would, please destroy this. It would mean my life if the prime commander ever knew I'd sent it to you."

Hauk gaped at Maris. "Why didn't he destroy it?"

"He kept it only so that he could find and thank the woman who sent it, and make sure she wasn't harmed for alerting him. And if you knew how my father felt about women, you'd *really* appreciate the gesture. When it comes to females on our world, we are not Andarion. They are only property and trophies to my people. A means to an end. My father is a misogynist on steroids. I'm still reeling that he's actually acknowledging Cairistiona as a ruling queen. Which tells you exactly how seriously he's taking this, and how badly Kyr tortured Saf."

Hauk winced over that. "We should have never left him behind."

Maris sighed. "We had no choice. I tried to drag him with us, but he chose to stay with Kyr, and that loyalty is what saved his life and his royal standing on Phrixus. And it's what has motivated my father to go to war and help you find your daughter. You don't repay loyalty and honor with betrayal."

Still, Hauk felt sick over what had happened to a good male and friend. "I never meant for him to be harmed."

"None of us did. But for your Sumi, he'd be dead now. Madai told me that Saf was barely breathing when they got to him. I don't know what Kyr did to him, but they said he wouldn't have made it two more hours. It had to be worse than even we're thinking. As soon as my father had the medical report on Saf, he declared war instantly."

Poor Safir. It was bad enough to be held and tortured. Yet for it to be family . . .

There was no way he'd ever be able to make this up to his friend.

Maris gave him a lopsided grin. "By the way, I finally found a way to pull Saf out of his brothel."

"How?" Hauk asked with a frown.

"Told him Kyr was holding an Andarion princess hostage and that she was *your* daughter. He immediately went to the others and they called to speak to you."

Hauk clapped him on the shoulder. "Thank you, Mari."

"Least I can do. I've not forgotten how many times you've been there for me. You saved my life and Ture's. We owe our sexy beast."

Hauk laughed.

"Oh," Mari hesitated. "For the record, I didn't tell Saf who left that message for our father."

"Why not?"

"They were plenty motivated to help Kalea without it. And I wanted you and Sumi to see their faces when they find out who he owes his life to. Phrixians may not have words for gratitude, but we do have the emotions. And there are some things that words can't convey. What's more, she also told me again the first time she found out who I was. Even though he'd been released by then and she knew Kyr was his brother, she was still trying to help him." Maris swallowed hard. "You've got a good woman, Hauk. There aren't many in her situation who'd risk it all like that for a stranger."

No, there weren't. And as Hauk thought about what she'd done for Saf, he choked up. If Kyr ever found out . . .

Hauk had never met anyone with her integrity and heart.

Overwhelmed by emotions he really wasn't used to, he left the others to run back to the gym.

Sumi was learning an Andarion sword attack when she saw Fadima step away and disengage from the fight. Her white eyes were focused on something behind her. Unsure of what to expect, Sumi turned to see Hauk stalking her with an intense expression on her face that she couldn't read.

Was he angry?

Before she could ascertain its source, he grabbed her and lifted her from her feet. He held her so that his head was even with her stomach. Dropping the sword, she looked down at him.

"Dancer?"

He didn't answer. He held her tighter.

Confused, she ran her hand through his braids as he walked her out of the ring and toward the glass wall that looked out onto the sea. Then he slowly slid her down his body until she stood in front of him. He whispered in her ear, but it was Andarion so she had no idea what he was saying.

"I don't understand. Did I do something wrong?"

He cupped her face in his hands and stared at her with a love she couldn't fathom. "You are and will forever be the Ger Tarra of my heart." He gave her the sweetest, tenderest kiss she'd ever known.

Closing her eyes, she breathed him in. His fangs scraped her lips ever so slightly before he deepened the kiss. Every hormone in her body went into overdrive.

"Should we leave you two to some private time?"

Horrified, she pulled back to see Fadima, Shahara, and Desideria staring at them.

Desideria grinned. "Who wants to take bets that we will have a little War Hauk in about thirty-six to forty weeks?"

Worse, the guys and Dancer's grandmother came in just in time to hear that last bit.

In that moment, she wanted a black hole to appear and suck her in.

Unabashed, Dancer kept her in the shelter of his arms as he faced them. "What?" he challenged.

Darling held his hands up and grinned widely. "All I'm saying is, given last night, I don't ever want to take crap from you about me and Zarya again." He pinned Dancer with a meaningful stare. "Know what I mean?"

The blush on Dancer's face said that he got it. But she had no idea what Darling was referring to.

And that wasn't the most important thing on her mind. "Do you have news?" she asked Dancer.

"Only that the Phrixians have declared war on The League and are on their way to sign a treaty with Cairistiona."

"Really?" She looked over to Maris. "What happens to you? Are you back in their family?"

He shook his head sadly. "For now, they're honoring the fact that I'm an Andarion ambassador. But the horrible, awful part is that I shall have to dispense of my snazzy Phrixian battlesuit, and be forced to wear drab to battle in. My people will take issue with me in their uniform since my ex-father decommissioned and disinherited me rather rudely." He tapped his bearded cheek as if something new occurred to him. "Wait!" He smiled at Nykyrian. "As an Andarion ambassador, am I privied to wear an Andarion warsuit?"

"Sure. Why?"

Maris clapped his hands together then used his hip to bump Darling's. "I finally get to wear bloodred into battle. And I look so smashing in red. Ooo, we must order those boots tonight. Only Andarions really know how to accessorize for war."

Darling laughed and shook his head.

Sumi frowned over that comment. "Does it really matter what you wear to fight in?"

"Oh honey, of course it does. When you're going to fight you have to be dressed to kill."

They all groaned at the bad pun.

"Speaking of," Dancer's grandmother interjected. "I have commissioned Sumi the suit of a War Hauk for her match with Dariana."

Hauk let out a sinister laugh at his grandmother's actions. "That'll piss her off."

"As was my intent."

Sumi sucked her breath in sharply as she passed an amused glance to Hauk. "Remind me to never get on your grandmother's bad side."

His yaya smiled at her. "You keep that light in Dancer's eyes and you'll never see the wrong side of my blade."

"Okay, then," Sumi said, stepping back. "Maybe I should go bathe the sweat off. I've heard that stralen heightens your senses. How you can stand to be near me right now after the way I've been sweating is beyond me."

He nuzzled her neck playfully. "It doesn't bother me at all."

"Glad to hear it, but it offends me."

Laughing, Hauk reluctantly released her, even though it was the last thing he wanted to do. However, he didn't need an audience for the serious hard-on he was developing already. One that would only get worse the closer he stood to her.

He shifted his weight, hoping to disguise it before he glanced over to his cousin. "Does she need to continue?"

Fadima shook her head. "Honestly? No. We don't want her sore for the match, and she's amazingly honed for a human. I think it's safe to say that Dariana will have met her equal for this." She smiled at Sumi. "I can show her more moves tomorrow that will help. The gods know, she picks them up faster than anyone I've ever seen."

That made him feel a lot better about it all. "Then have your shower, *mia*. We'll have a hearty lunch when you get out."

"Hearty?"

"Yes," Maris said with a laugh, "you are correct to shudder whenever an Andarion uses that word with food. And it should be interesting. My husband is a chef who owns the premiere restaurant in Perona. Can't wait to hear his review of whatever it is Hauk plans for lunch. It's always fun, as long as you're not the one who cooked it."

Shaking her head at them, Sumi left and went to Dancer's bedroom alone.

She hadn't been kidding about her stench. Yuck! It was the only thing she hated about working out.

But she was glad that Dancer didn't seem to mind. As she started to remove her shirt, she felt a sudden shift in the air.

Turning, she gasped as she saw the figure coming out of the shadows.

It was Kyr. And he wasn't pleased to see her.

CHAPTER 31

At the appearance of Kyr in her bedroom, Sumi felt the heat of a rage the likes of which she'd never experienced before. There was no fear inside her. Only a need to tear him into pieces.

He glared at her. "You didn't really think you could escape me, did you?"

Throwing her head back, she laughed at his question. "You're a fucking idiot. You know that? And I can't thank you enough for saving me the time and effort it would take to hunt you down." She went for him with everything she had. With the full of her weight, she caught him about the middle and flipped him to the ground. "Where's my daughter?"

He gave her a blow that sent pain throbbing through her skull. But she didn't care. She'd hurt later. Right now, all that mattered was beating him until he told her where Kalea was. She tried to pin him, but he rolled out from her hold and stood up. With a growl, he slammed her against the dresser.

Grimacing in pain, she used her legs to kick them both back. Unbalanced, Kyr released her. She spun on him with her fists, then landed a solid kick to the center of his chest. "Where is she, you bastard!"

"You want her? Surrender to me and I'll release her."

How stupid did he think she was? "I don't believe you!" There was no way he'd release the only leverage he had.

He came at her with his knife. Sumi pulled her shirt off and used it to wrap around his wrist as she rolled into his body, bit his forearm, and pulled the knife from his grasp.

Cursing, he punched her, then pulled another knife and caught her a glancing blow to her ribs. She stabbed him in the shoulder, burying the knife to the hilt. He kicked her back and stumbled.

"Sumi!" Dancer shouted from the locked door.

Kyr turned back toward the window.

Knowing if he left, she'd never see Kalea again, she ran at him and slammed him to the floor. She stabbed him again, but not before he cut her arm. Dazed, she scrambled to hold him as best she could. The slimy bastard escaped and kicked her hard in the head.

She was still holding on to Kyr's arm, slashing at him, when Dancer came crashing through the door.

With a furious shriek, Kyr punched her in the throat and broke free.

In spite of the throbbing pain, Sumi headed for the window, fully intending to give chase. Until she felt strong arms wrap around her. She moved to punch her attacker, but stopped as she saw Dancer's face.

Hauk had never felt a greater rage than the one that ignited inside him as he saw Sumi's battered face and the blood smeared all over his bedroom. "*Mia?*"

With the exception of Syn, his friends ran after Kyr.

"Let me go!" Sumi cried, trying to get free. "He's getting away! I have to stop him."

"Sumi!" Hauk barked harder than he meant to, but she was hysterical, and probably going into shock. "Baby, there's a difference between heroic and moronic." He used her words, hoping to get through to her. "You're naked and about to bleed out." He wrapped his shirt around her to cover her bruised and bleeding body. "You can't go after him. Look!"

She tilted her head down to see the blood flowing from a severe gash. Her legs buckled.

Hauk swung her up in his arms and carried her to the bed, then stepped back so that Syn could treat her. His heart shattered at the sight of her like this. He should have come into the room with her. He should never have left her alone.

Gods, she'd been assaulted in his own home, where she should have been safe.

His breathing ragged, he wanted Kyr's life with a ferocity that defied description.

Syn glanced at him over his shoulder. "Go, Hauk! I've got her."

"You sure?"

"Yeah. I'll call in a few."

Without hesitating, Hauk climbed up on the opposite side of the bed. Unable to speak, he pressed his cheek to hers and took a moment to hold her.

When he went to pull away, Sumi held him against her. "I stabbed him in his right lung before he escaped, and his shoulder. . . . I want to be the one who kills him. Bring him to me."

Nodding, he kissed her carefully on the lips and then ran after the others.

Sumi groaned as the full weight of her injuries bore down on her. For whatever reason, in a fight, she never really felt pain. It was only afterward that she regretted it.

And right now . . .

She really wished she'd killed him before he beat her to a pulp.

"Damn it," Syn growled as he tried to stop the bleeding, "you need a transfusion." He scanned the code on her wrist that The League had embedded with her brand mark that held her medical information. He frowned as he read it. "You're part Qillaq?"

"No."

He gave her a doubtful stare before he took a sample of her blood and ran some kind of test on it. "Um, yeah, you are." He glanced to the door where Dancer's grandmother stood, watching them. "Ger Tarra, could you please ask Desideria to come here as fast as she can." Then he tapped the mic in his ear. "Chayden, forget Kyr. Get your ass back here, double time." He kept pressure on her stomach wound. "You are so lucky we happen to have Qills on tap, girl. You've no idea how rare your blood type is. And no other race has it. Not even I can give blood to you, and Rits are basically as universal a donor as you can get. Even Nyk's taken my blood before."

Sumi could barely follow what he was telling her as her thoughts ran over the fight, and how she should have gone after Kyr.

Desideria came in huffing. "What's up?"

"Hold on." He tapped his mic again. "Chay, ETA?" He paused before he spoke again. "All right. Head on. I'm going to take some blood from your sister, but I can't take much. I really need you." He looked over to Desideria. "Can you hold this for a minute while I get set up?"

"Absolutely."

Syn showed her where to keep it compressed, then left.

Sumi began shaking uncontrollably.

"Oh, sweetie," Desideria gasped. "Don't die on us, okay? I've already lost one sister in my arms, I don't want to do it again. Just stay with me."

Sumi laughed bitterly. "Trust me, I'm too mad to die. I'm going to live, if for no other reason than to have the pleasure of choking the life out of Kyr myself."

Someone took her hand. Ignoring her body that protested the movement, Sumi tilted her head to see Dancer's grandmother on the bed, beside her.

She tenderly brushed Sumi's hair back from her forehead and offered her a kind smile. "You don't cry?"

"Not when I'm angry. And physical pain I can handle."

With an astonished expression, she swept her gaze around the room where Sumi and Kyr had all but destroyed it. "You put up quite a fight."

"And she seriously wounded Kyr," Syn said as he rejoined them. "He's leaving a hell of a blood trail the others are following, and she took out one of the prime commander's lungs."

His grandmother gaped. "It was the League prime commander you fought?"

Sumi nodded.

She lifted Sumi's hand to her lips and kissed her knuckles. "My great-grandchildren will be the fiercest of all their generation. No one will ever defeat them."

Sumi tightened her hand on Dancer's grandmother's then met Syn's gaze. "Get me on my feet, Doc. I want my daughter back, and that bastard is too close for me to yield."

"Um, yeah. You're not going anywhere for a little while. Just lie there and relax."

Sumi couldn't. At least not until Syn snuck something into her system. She fought against it as hard as possible, but in the end, she lost, and everything went black.

Hauk cursed as their trail turned cold. Neither electronic nor physical tracks remained.

Kyr had evaded them. Completely.

He bellowed with rage.

"*That* is the scariest effing thing I've ever heard or seen."

Hauk pinned his glare on Bastien as the human slowly approached him. "Where have you been?"

"Recovering. When I heard Kyr was on-planet, I really wanted a piece of him."

"Take a number." His breathing ragged, Hauk had never wanted to gut anyone more. It was all he could do to keep himself together as every fiber of his being begged for vengeance. "How did he get into my house?"

"He's an assassin," Nyk said coldly. "They're like cockroaches. They always find a way in."

Hauk arched a brow at those words.

Nyk shrugged. "I'm a cockroach. Yes. But that's okay, I know how we think and where to search."

"Yeah," Hauk said drily, "but he wasn't there. I already looked."

"So you're a cockroach, too?"

Hauk clenched his teeth. "My humor is currently out to lunch. Check back in a few days. If I have his heart in my fist, it'll return . . . as I eat it."

Maris tsked at Hauk. "Oh, sexy, there are two problems with that. One, my brother has no heart. Two, you don't need the indigestion. I've seen what you call food. Trust me. Not even your stomach could handle Kyr Tartar. But I do know something that will bring a smile to that beautiful face of yours."

While Hauk appreciated their attempts to lighten the mood, he didn't want to hear it right now. "I doubt it."

Maris rose on his tiptoes to whisper in Hauk's ear. "I know where Kalea is."

Hauk's breath caught in his throat as his heart stopped beating. "Don't play with me, Mari. I really might hurt you."

Maris handed him his PD. When Hauk couldn't read the Phrixian alphabet, Maris switched on the translator.

He had to read it twice to make sure he wasn't wrong. "Seriously?"

Maris nodded. "I've already got them prepping the ships. We're ready to fly out and bring her home."

Hauk picked him up and hugged him tight. "Gods, I love you, Mari!" He kissed his cheek.

Maris beamed. "Well, if I'd known this was all it'd take to get a hug and kiss from you, I'd have gotten you a woman years ago."

Laughing, Hauk clapped him on the back.

"Ow!" Maris whined as he stumbled.

Nyk and Darling inclined their heads to him.

"Let's go get your daughter," Darling said. "Jayne and Ryn are already doing preflights."

They hailed transports and rendezvoused at the main city port where Jayne had a battle cruiser ready. Hauk ran up the ramp and grabbed his unmarked black battlesuit. But before he started attaching the exoskeletal suit to his body, he paused to look at the men and women around him. Darling, Maris, Drake, Nyk, Shahara, Fain, Bastien, Caillen, Kasen, Nero—and Jayne and Ryn, who were piloting them.

Funny how he'd never thought twice about the fact that when they needed him he'd dropped whatever he was doing to run to their sides. Of course in his case, there was never anything that important to pull him away from. Gaming, maybe horsing around with his electronics. Nothing serious. But all of them had left their spouses and children to join him on this quest.

Never had he loved them more as he finally understood the sacrifices they were making to be here. The risk each of them took.

For him and Sumi.

And for their daughter.

"You okay?" Darling asked.

Hauk pulled him closer and pressed his forehead to Darling's. "Thank you."

"For what? Being family?" Darling shoved him away. "It's what we do. You know that."

"Just don't get me killed," Caillen said as he suited up. "My wife would follow me to hell and I'd never hear the end of it."

Hauk laughed. "You're not right, are you?"

Kasen sighed heavily. "No, he isn't. I blame Shahara totally. I tried to beat it out of him when we were young, but she always took the baby brother's side, instead of the sister's side."

Shaking his head, Hauk pinned a stare on Nyk. "How do you do it?"

"Do what?"

"Love such a tiny little woman who can't defend herself?"

Nykyrian cracked a very rare grin that exposed a set of dimples identical to Thia's. "Don't let her meek manner fool you. There's a lot of fire and courage in Kiara. You'd be amazed at how fierce she is. But I know what you're really asking. And the size of the person or their abilities doesn't matter. It's the size of the love you hold for them that keeps you up at night, terrified of losing them. In many ways, I'm grateful Kiara's not a warrior." He passed his stare to Shahara. "She doesn't put herself in harm's way. Since she's not trained to fight, she calls for help."

"What are you implying?" Shahara asked.

Caillen snorted. "That you can kick the shit out of us. And I have the boot prints on my ass to prove it."

She passed an irritated scowl to Nykyrian. "If I flushed him out the airlock, I trust the rest of you would back me in telling Desideria it was an accident, right?"

Kasen growled at her sister. "Now? Now, you agree with me that he needs killing? Where was this twenty years ago? You'd have saved us all a lot of time, money, and misery!"

Fain placed himself in front of Caillen. "It's all right, boy. I'll protect you."

Caillen postured at all of them. "Ha! Got my own Andarion bodyguard, bitches!"

Shahara looked at Kasen before the two of them charged. Fain drew himself up tight and covered his head while they ran past him to get Caillen.

"Hey!" Caillen snapped at Fain. "What kind of protective move is that shit?"

"Protecting my own ass, human. I don't know what I was thinking. Your sisters are terrifying. They can have you."

Caillen was playfully fighting them while they tickled him. Until Shahara swatted him hard across his butt.

"You're lucky I love you, boy."

Caillen kissed her cheek then ran behind her as Kasen lunged at him. "Help!"

Laughing, Shahara stepped between them. "All right, you two, we've got a real battle to prepare for."

"What is going on back here?" Jayne asked from the flight deck door. "I have never heard such in my life, and I have three kids at home."

"They started it," Darling said, pointing to the Dagan siblings.

"Of course they did. Do I have to separate you people?"

"Not people, human," Fain and Hauk said simultaneously.

"Not human, Andarions. I'm Hyshian. Learn the difference." Jayne sidled up to Hauk. She scowled at him before she tested his brow for a fever. "You look a little pale. You all right, buddy?"

Only because he was terrified for Sumi. "If this works out, I will be."

Nykyrian clapped him on the back. "They've sealed everything on Andaria. We're the only craft that'll be given flight clearance until Kyr's captured. We will get that bastard. You know that."

Hauk inclined his head to him. "If I forget to say it later, no matter the outcome, thank you all for being my family. For fighting with, and for me."

"Estra, mi dreystin," Nykyrian said, holding out his arm to him.

Smiling grimly, Hauk shook his arm. One by one, they each followed suit, and then they all dressed for battle.

It took almost three hours to reach Tarsa, the Gondarion capital city where both the Overseer of Justice and the main League HQ were located. A bustling major city, it was nowhere the size of Eris, but it would rival it for technology.

Even though she was no longer an active Seax for the Overseer, Shahara used her clearance to get them a landing permit. Hopefully, her code wouldn't be flagged by The League.

Preparing for the worst case any of them could imagine, they landed.

Ryn took a moment to lose his Tavali gear and suit up like the rest of them. All of their planets and allies had declared war on The League, and they couldn't afford to walk off the ship in enemy battlesuits. Only Drake wore his Kimmerian gear. The rest of them dressed in plain black battlesuits.

And since the Kimmerians were the only ones not currently at war with the Gondarion government, they let Drake take the lead. As soon as they reached the bottom of the ramp, they were greeted by Gondarion soldiers.

"Can I help you?" Drake asked the soldiers in a bored tone.

The guards pinned suspicious stares on them. "Why the armor? What's the reason for your visit?"

Drake shrugged. "We're here to plant petunias. Didn't you get the paperwork?"

The guard was less than impressed with Drake's imperious sarcasm. "Petunias don't grow here."

Bastien stepped forward. "We're here to petition the Overseer. You'll have to forgive my bodyguard, he's a little irritable, but I can't blame him. I'd be irritable, too, if I went a month without a bowel movement."

Drake laughed.

The guard, not so much. He eyed Bastien with extreme animosity. "And you are?"

"Bastien Cabarro. Prince and heir to the Kirovarian throne. I'm here to demand justice for my family, and to get sanctions against the bastard who wrongfully usurped my father's throne and slaughtered my entire family. And . . ." He looked down at the man's nameplate. "Officer Garox, I can either tell the Mistress of Justice that you were helpful to my family's quest or a major pain in my ass. Which I don't think Lady Alia would approve of since she was a close personal friend of my parents."

That totally reoriented the man's attitude. "Forgive me, Your Highness. We didn't mean to detain you. We just have to be careful these days."

"Believe me, I understand caution. My father nurtured the snake that slew him. Now, if you'll excuse me . . ." He swept past them with an arrogant royal saunter.

One that vanished as soon as Bastien walked outside the bay. He paused at the entrance and stayed at the door to watch the guards while Hauk and the rest filed out as if they were following and protecting Bastien. Once he and Nykyrian were sure they were cleared and not reported, they headed for the street.

Hauk paused by Bastien's side as his words haunted him. "Is that the matter you need to take care of before you join us in The Sentella?"

"Yeah." His eyes turned dark. Deadly. "They killed my brother and sister in front of me. And I want blood."

"I'm sorry, Bastien."

He pressed his lips together, but said nothing more about it. "Let's get that baby of yours home where she belongs."

Hauk understood why Bastien didn't want to talk about his family and their deaths. Some memories were too crippling, and he had his own share of them. But one thing he knew for a fact.

Bastien wouldn't be fighting alone.

After this, the Kirovarian prince had proven himself one of them.

Strong alone. Stronger together.

Nero brought them a commandeered transport so that they could stay off the street, and not attract undue notice. They made their way to a League orphanage near the Overseer's office building, in the center of the city. It was a drab, unremarkable building that was heavily fortified, and manned by League guards.

None of them spoke as Nero drove them to a side alley so that they could unload and prepare. They'd barely cleared the transport before a shadow flickered.

Every one of them leveled their blasters at it.

"Whoa! Good guy. Please, gods, don't shoot me. And if you do, kill my ass. I can't take any more physical therapy. I'm done with it."

Smiling, Hauk holstered his blaster and held his arm out to Safir. "You look like hell, buddy."

"And feel every *minsid* flame of it, too. I wish I could say I feel better than I look, but I really don't." After shaking Hauk's arm, Saf hugged Maris. "We have two of our own who are guards here. They're the ones who notified us of her location, after Valari put out a call for information on her whereabouts. The problem is, we know the room. But we're not sure which kid she is. They're not tagged with names." He looked at Hauk. "I'm hoping Daddy knows what she looks like."

Hauk shook his head. "They took her from her mother the minute she was born. Sumi was never allowed to see or touch her. She only knows her name because she bribed a nurse for it."

Shahara crossed her arms over her chest. "If I can get a cheek swab, I can run her DNA with Sumi's and verify it."

They all stared at her.

"What?" she asked defensively. "I'm married to a mad scientist doctor. You think I haven't picked up a few things from him after all these years?"

Caillen grinned. "Sister Shay for the win."

While they planned the extraction with Safir, Shahara called Syn to get Sumi's DNA downloaded to run against Kalea's.

Hauk thought over their ideas. "You know, Saf, it might be easier if Shahara and I can go in with your guys, and say that we were sent in to do a routine med check on the kids. That way we could run the DNA and they wouldn't know what we were about." It was also the best way to keep any innocents from being harmed.

Saf looked at the others. "Anyone got a better idea?"

They shook their heads.

"I like it," Nyk said. "Simple. Straightforward."

"Suicidal," Caillen mumbled.

Darling snorted. "All right. Suicide it is. Let's do this."

When Hauk took a step, Fain stopped him. "I'm going, too. Just in case."

He wanted to argue, but knew that tone of voice. It wouldn't be worth wasting time. And it was why he'd always adored his older brother.

So long as he lived, Fain would always be there for him.

Nyk signaled for everyone to dissipate and prepare for a hot evac.

Once Shahara was fully downloaded and had double-checked her medical kit, she gave a nod to Saf to lead them to the Phrixians who were guarding the facility as League soldiers.

Saf radioed them to meet by the back gate, away from cameras and other guards.

As soon as the Phrixian spies arrived, they saluted their prince, and explained the layout of the building.

Saf and Maris stayed at the gate to cover it while the two Phrixians led Shahara, Fain, and Hauk to the room where a dozen kids, ranging from ages three to six, were playing a game of chase and freeze. All in all, they appeared rather happy and normal. The only way to know they were League owned was the matching white uniforms they wore.

The Phrixians went in first to tell the instructor that they were there for a routine health screening. Either she didn't care or it wasn't unusual. Without looking up from her electronic reader, she told the kids to line up.

From the hallway, Hauk scanned the children as they fell into formation. His heart pounded as his gaze went to the girls. One of them was Sumi's beloved daughter.

No.

One of them was *their* beloved daughter.

I'm a father now. That reality hit him hard. It was something he'd never thought to have. A dream he'd given up on a long time ago. Because of Dariana's cruelty, he'd relegated himself to the role of uncle.

But one of those little faces would soon belong to him. . . .

I will never let any harm come to you.

Swallowing hard, he tried to figure out which one they should test first. There were only three girls—two blonds and one with dark hair and enormous silvery blue eyes. He leaned toward the fairer haired girls, but something about the brunette was familiar to him. He didn't know what, until they entered the room and the children screamed in terror, running for cover.

Except for the brunette. She folded her arms over her tiny chest and held herself with a defiance that sent a chill up his spine. He knew that tilt of chin and that fiery look that dared them to do their worst.

"Kalea?"

Staring up at him without fear, she narrowed her eyes and pursed her lips. "Who are you?"

It was so adorable, he smiled as Shahara stepped past him and knelt in front of the girl. "I'm here to do a little screening test on you, is that okay?"

With a suspicious glint in her eyes, she tilted her head. "What kind of test?"

Oh yeah, she had to be Sumi's blood. She was just like her mother and he was in love with her already.

Shahara held a swab in a gloved hand and showed her on her own cheek. "See. Doesn't hurt. And I have a big surprise for you afterwards."

"Is it a good surprise?"

"Better than good."

"It better be." The girl opened her mouth wide.

Shahara quickly pulled out a new swab and scraped it against Kalea's cheek. Rising to her feet, she placed it in a gold solution before she checked her chronometer. "Thirty seconds."

They were the longest of his life.

Kalea tugged at Shahara's leg. "What's my surprise?"

Suddenly, there were running feet in the hallway outside. Fain moved to check while Hauk looked around for an alternate exit.

"It's her," Shahara answered finally. "It's a complete match, and Sumi has a very unique signature. There's no doubt whatsoever."

Hauk wasn't prepared for the swell of protective love that filled him at that confirmation. For a moment, he couldn't breathe at all.

His throat tight, he fell to his knees in front of the tiny girl. His daughter. He wanted to grab her into a tight hug, but that might scare her, and that was the last thing he desired. "Are you afraid of me, Kalea?"

Arms akimbo, she widened her stance to eye him like a tough little mouse. "Am I supposed to be?"

"No. Are you?"

She twisted up her mouth and studied him carefully. "You look very strange. Are your eyes supposed to glow red like that?"

"They are."

"And your teeth? Are they supposed to be so long and sharp?"

"I'm Andarion. We all have those teeth."

"Dancer . . ." Fain said in warning. "We've got company. We need to go. Fast."

He held his hand up to his brother before he turned back to the girl. "I'm your father, Kalea, and I've come to take you home."

All the defiant fire went out of her as her jaw dropped. Her lips quivered. "I really have a daddy?"

He nodded.

Tears filled her eyes, making them glisten.

"You definitely have a father. And both your mother and I love you very much."

"I have a mommy, too?" she breathed in disbelief.

"Yes."

Tears rolled down her cheeks. "I hate this place, Daddy. Please take me home." She threw herself into his arms.

Closing his eyes, Hauk held her close to his chest. While he loved and adored every child his friends had, it was nothing compared to what went through him as those little arms encircled his neck and she placed her head on his shoulder. Not even what he felt for Darice compared to this.

She's my little girl. All he wanted was to hold on to her forever.

But he couldn't. They had to get her to safety first.

Kissing her cheek, he stood up with her. "Kalea, I'm going to hand you to the nice lady and she's going to take you to some men and get you to safety, okay?"

"What about you, Daddy?"

"Daddy's going to make sure you stay safe. Aunt Shahara is going to hold you for just a little bit. Okay?"

"Okay."

He handed her off to Shahara. "Fain, cover them out the back. I'll draw these bastards off you."

"You got it. Stay safe."

"You stay safer."

Fain inclined his head to him.

Hauk waited until they were clear before he opened the door where the instructor was gesturing to the Phrixian guards. As soon as the new arrivals saw him, they drew weapons. The Andarion in him wanted to start a war in the hallway, but there were too many children here. He wouldn't risk one of them getting hit in the cross fire.

So instead, he fell into the role of arrogant League officer. "Is there a problem?" he snarled at the approaching soldiers.

"By whose authority are you here?"

"The prime commander's," Hauk answered boldly. Technically, it wasn't a lie. He wouldn't be here if not for the rank smelly dog. "Would you like to call him and tell him that you're interfering? I've heard he's *real* forgiving of being questioned by lesser-ranking soldiers."

They started to accept that until one of them, unfortunately, used his brain to have a thought. "Why would he send an Andarion when we're at war with them?"

That was a good question. Luckily, Hauk was used to

thinking on his feet. "Some of us are still Leaguers." He didn't know of any offhand, but it was always a good bet that someone was stupid.

The soldier hesitated. "I don't know . . ."

"You three stay here and let us check this out." The soldier left the two Phrixians and one other guard.

Poor guy.

Hauk waited until the other guards were gone before he knocked the one unfortunate guard who'd been left behind unconscious. When the instructor started to sound an alarm, he drew on her. "Don't." He switched the setting from stun to kill to let her know he wasn't playing.

The Phrixians held their hands up as if they were afraid, too, and moved to shield her. Hauk ran backwards through the hallway, toward the exit. He was almost to the door when someone opened fire on him in the stairwell. He fired up at them and hit the door running.

Ah, great . . . There was a group of League soldiers in the yard who turned immediately toward him.

Shit. Why couldn't he ever catch a break during an escape? Just once?

They opened fire. And the moment they did, his friends came out to play and returned it with everything they had.

Grateful beyond belief, Hauk dodged the blasts that narrowly missed him and headed for the transport that was backed up to the gate. At a full run, he dove in headfirst and landed on top of Darling.

"Ah gah, Hauk! Lose some weight. You're crushing me, you fat bastard! I don't know how Sumi stands it."

Laughing at Darling's humor, he pinched his cheek. "Suck it up. You make a sweet cushion." He rolled to his feet, then frowned. "Where are the others?"

"We sent them on ahead with Kalea to get her out of the line of fire."

He sighed in relief as he saw Nyk, Maris, Fain, Darling,

Nero, and Drake, who'd stayed behind to cover him. They were the best and he'd never appreciated them more.

Nero drove them out at full throttle, under heavy pursuit. The transport went careening down the street, sending pedestrians and other vehicles in all directions.

"Nero!" Darling shouted. "Some of us aren't suicidal back here."

"Then strap your ass down. Or lose it." Nero jerked to the right.

This time, Darling landed on Hauk.

Hauk put him back on his feet. "Nuh-uh. You have to buy me dinner before you crawl on top of me, baby. No one gets a free ride on the Hauk train."

Maris laughed. "I'm learning all kinds of fun things about you today, Hauk."

Suddenly, the ride leveled out and slowed.

Darling blanched as they were hammered by League fire. "What are you doing, Nero?"

"Shh! I'm being stupid and I have to concentrate for it."

Hauk winced over what that really meant. "Is he giving himself brain damage?"

Darling cursed under his breath. "With all of us inside? Yeah."

Hauk clenched his teeth at the sacrifice Nero was making. "I can carry him out."

"I'll cover you both," Nyk offered.

The transport picked up speed again. Within five minutes, they were back at the port. Nero parked and opened the hatch. He got up and pressed his hand to his nose, which was pouring blood all over him.

Hauk helped him out and slung one arm over his shoulder to help him walk. No one in the hangar paid any attention to them at all. It was as if they weren't there. "You've cloaked us?"

Nero nodded.

Damn, that had to be killing Nero. Hauk tightened his grip on his friend. "Just remember, if you have to hurl, Darling's right there."

Offended, Darling twisted his face up in distaste. "Screw you, Hauk."

"Back at you, human. Besides, you handle it better than I do."

With an evil laugh, Darling nodded. "Okay, that's true, but still. I get tired of everybody doing that to me." He glared meaningfully at Maris.

Maris scoffed. "What's with that look? I only did it the one time. And at least it wasn't during your wedding vows . . . while being videoed and broadcast."

They hurried as fast as they could across the bay and headed to their ship.

"I can't hold it much longer," Nero breathed. "I think I'm about to pass out."

Hauk walked faster. "I've got you, *drey*. I won't let you fall."

His nose bleeding harder, Nero stumbled.

They were halfway to the ship when a voice rang out. "Halt!"

Nykyrian clapped him twice on the shoulder. A silent motion that said to run. Hauk swept Nero into his arms and ran while the others laid down cover fire for them. One blast landed in his thigh and almost sent him to the ground.

Catching his balance, he cursed and kept going. Like Sumi had said, if he went down, he was a lot harder to move than the others. And the last thing they needed was to carry both him and Nero out on their backs.

He ran on board first and placed Nero in the closest seat. Grinding his teeth against the pain in his leg, Hauk winced at the sight of the wound.

"Daddy!"

That one word and the excitement in that precious

high-pitched voice brought tears to his eyes as a wealth of emotion coursed through him. Before he could stand back up, a tiny form slammed into him and threw her arms around his neck.

"Daddy! I was getting so worried! But Aunt Shahara and Aunt Jaynie and . . . and Uncle Ryn and Uncle Caillen told me not to. You know, you gots a lot of brothers and sisters, Daddy."

He held her close to his chest. "That I do." He set her down in a seat and harnessed her in as Nykyrian, Fain, Maris, and Darling pulled up the rear while Shahara started tending to Nero.

"Burn it!" Darling pounded on the flight deck door to signal to Ryn and Jayne that everyone was on board and the ramp secured.

"Everyone hold your ass," Jayne said over the intercom. "We're having to blast our way out. They're sealing the doors, so everybody pray."

The ship lurched forward as she dropped anchor and hit full throttle.

Kalea's eyes widened.

Hauk buckled himself in beside her. "It's all right, baby. Daddy's right here. We're going to see Mommy."

He tried to hold her hand, but she was so tiny that she had to wrap her entire hand around his index finger. And as the ship shook, she buried her face against his arm and held tight. He rubbed her back, proud of the fact that she didn't cry like most children would. But she did squeal a lot. Something that was piercing to his Andarion hearing.

They should have named you Baby Harpie.

Hauk cringed as he heard the sound of metal on metal as they scraped through the hangar doors. Visions of being crushed in a blast shield went through his head. That would be bad enough, but Jayne and Ryn appeared to be in the middle of an argument while they escaped.

"Get your hands off that, woman!" Ryn snapped.

"Where'd you learn to fucking fly? At a shoe store?"

"Don't touch that!"

"You get your hands off!"

Gaping, Hauk met Nykyrian's stunned expression. "Oh my God, who let the two-year-olds fly us?"

They all pointed to Darling.

With an innocent expression, he held his hands out. "Ryn's a Tavali captain. He should know what he's doing. And Jayne's Jayne. She's never failed us before."

Suddenly, something hit the ship. Hard. The power drained instantly.

Ryn hissed over the intercom as Jayne went silent. "Oh . . . shit."

CHAPTER 32

"Attention all passengers," Ryn said over the intercom. "We seem to be experiencing some turbulence. Please, do not release your harnesses, and remember that if you kick the ass of the pilot right now, he won't be able to fly you out of this lovely mess."

"Passengers to pilot," Darling said drily. "Please note, every one of us here, except our new junior member, is licensed to fly, so we don't really need you and if you don't get us back into motion, there will be lots of Ryn ass-kicking to go round. Your two little brothers are back here and we don't like you much, anyway."

"Yeah!" Drake weighed in. "And one of your brothers is not only a pilot, but a licensed assassin and you're a Tavali. I get bonus pay if I deliver your head in a jar."

"Our father weeps at your merciless ways. A pox to both your nether regions." Ryn paused. "Oh hey, look! We got engines."

"Say, thank you, Jayne," Jayne said sarcastically.

"Thank you, Jayne," Ryn mumbled over the intercom. Then louder, "Nyk, open the back panel and cross the dampner crystal with shields for me."

Nykyrian's eyes widened. "That's a real bad idea, Ryn."

Hauk put Kalea's hand into Fain's. "Daddy will be right back, sweetie."

He unbuckled himself and went to the panel to access it. Curling his lip, he fought the urge to curse Ryn and Jayne for the damage that had been done during their escape.

"What are you doing, big guy?" Darling asked him.

"What I always do. Saving all our asses." Hauk hissed as he was shocked rewiring their power modules. Worse, life support was quickly bleeding out. Unless he restored it, they only had minutes before it was gone. He plugged it as best he could and then used an override code to fool the overheated generators back on. He tapped his link to Jayne. "One pulse on my mark. Three. Two. One."

She hit it and they went into hyperdrive.

"Go, Hauk, go!" Jayne shouted.

"Yeah. Don't cheer yet," he said under his breath as he kept working on everything that had shorted out. He cursed again at another shock.

His fingers turning black from it, he wanted to tell Jayne and Ryn where to shove this mess. Then he glanced to Kalea.

Snuggled up against Fain, she had her hands over her eyes and her fingers spread wide so that she could watch him through them. Damn, she was the cutest thing he'd ever seen.

She lifted one hand and waved at him.

Strange how in all the missions he'd run—in all the times he'd come through unbelievable odds and all the people he'd pulled to safety—he'd never felt as tall or as heroic as he did right then from that innocent sweet look on her tiny face.

That's my girl.

His throat tight, he returned to working on the ship until he had most of it going again. They were still lower on shields than he'd like, but . . .

"Jayne? I've given you guys the best I can without pulling over for parts. Can you radio for an escort?"

"We already have one. Saf and three of his brothers fell in about two minutes ago."

He breathed easier knowing that. "Good. We don't need to take a hit. Shields are minimum, but I had to put that power to the hyperdrive, dampners, and life support. Let me know when we come out and I can redirect it."

"You got it, Hauk."

He put the panel back in place and returned to his seat.

Kalea bit her lip. "Are you a superman, Daddy?"

"Yes, he is," Fain said. "He's saved the life of everyone in this ship at least once, and many of us, a lot more than that."

"Really?" she asked, eyes wide.

Fain nodded.

Hauk blushed as Kalea wrapped her arms around his biceps and hugged him tight.

After a few seconds, she tugged at his arm and made a face at him. "Daddy . . . I gots to go the bathroom now."

Horrified, he gaped at the mere prospect of something he'd never done before.

"Now, you can panic, Hauk," Nyk said with a rare laugh. "This one might not be housebroken."

"Does she have nappies?" Hauk looked at Kalea. "Do you have nappies?"

"No, Daddy! Kalea a big girl. But I gots to go bad." She twisted her legs together. "I can't wait!"

He looked at Shahara.

"Don't cut your eyes at me, big boy. I have a son. I know nothing about daughters."

Darling laughed. "You're crap out of luck, Andarion. We all got sons."

Maris nodded in agreement. "And I'm from an all-male family, too. I'm worthless with this aspect of child-rearing."

The flight deck door opened to show Jayne, who gave them all a withering stare. "Oh for goodness' sakes, you big bunch of nancies. I can't believe you're all cowed by a little baby girl's bladder." She paused on Nykyrian and Caillen. "And *you* need to learn, since your daughters will be potty training soon enough." She unfastened Kalea. "C'mon, sweetie. Aunt Jaynie will take you."

Kalea clapped before she scooted down to hold Jayne's hand and follow her to the head.

While they were gone, Hauk glared absolute murder at Nykyrian, who had the audacity to blink innocently at him.

"What is with that look?"

Hauk snarled at him. "I hate you, you *minsid* bastard."

"For what?"

"For cursing me. Damn you to hell, Nyk. I have a beautiful daughter and I hate you for it."

They all laughed at him.

"It's not funny. I hate all of you!"

Nyk shook his head. "Look on the bright side, Hauk. I have four boys who will gladly help you protect Kalea."

"Yeah, and my nightmare begins with those four little . . . things that they better keep away from my girl!"

Shahara laughed. "I'm so glad I have a son. I only have to worry about one penis. You guys have to worry about all the others."

Hauk glared at her and then to Caillen. "By the way, why didn't you volunteer? You have a daughter almost the same exact age."

"Yeah, but her mom does it. I tried once and dropped her in and got banned from potty duty for life. Desideria never got over it and neither did Lil. I set her back a full year in potty training. She still cries every time she sees a full-sized toilet."

Shahara covered her face and groaned. "You are so

worthless. I swear I should have let Kasen drown you when you were little."

"You see!" Kasen said. "I told you you'd regret saving him one day."

Kalea came running out to jump into Hauk's lap. She gave him a giant comical grin. Then laid her head down on his chest and hugged him.

Hauk was still floored by how easily she accepted him as her father. Most children were absolutely terrified and ran screaming from his presence. "Kalea? Why aren't you afraid of me?"

She sat back on his thigh and held her hand up. "Um . . . see, I told them all the time. I said my daddy would come. And he would take me home. I said that . . . I had the biggest daddy of any daddy. Of all daddies." She played with her ear. "And they said. They said I didn't have no daddy. That you would never come for me 'cause you don't exist." She held her arm up to show him a bruise where someone had pinched her. "They said I was lying. But I didn't lie. I said you would come. And you did! And my daddy's the biggest of all!" She looked over at Fain then back at Hauk several times. "Okay, almost biggest."

He cradled her against his chest. "I can't wait to put you in your mother's arms. But be warned. She might never let you go."

"That okay. Kalea don't mind. I'm just glad my daddy finally came like I knew you would."

Fain reached out and placed his hand on Hauk's forearm. "You have a beautiful daughter, Dancer."

Kalea gasped. "You a dancer, Daddy?"

Laughing, Hauk shook his head. "Afraid not. But . . ." He turned her around in his lap to see Nykyrian and pointed to him. "Uncle Nyk is married to your Aunt Kiara. And she is a very, very famous dancer."

"Really? Could she show me how?"

"Absolutely," Nykyrian said. "She loves to teach little girls how to dance. She has her own dance school."

Wide-eyed, she tilted her head back to look up at Hauk. "I can go dance school?"

"Lee-lee, you can have *anything* you want."

"Anything?" she repeated in disbelief.

"Anything."

"Can I touch your hair, Daddy?"

"Of course."

Biting her lip, she stood up. Hauk expected her to touch his braids. Instead, she raked her fingers through his goatee and mustache. Then she placed her hand against her own face. "Can I have one those?"

He laughed. "I can't do that, Lee-lee. They don't grow on girls."

"Oh." She pulled his lip up so that she could see his fangs. "Why are your teeth long? Do they hurt?"

"No. They're just like yours, only bigger. I'm an Andarion and we have longer teeth than humans."

"Will my teeth grow long?"

"No."

"Oh . . . Will my eyes glow red?"

"No, sweetie. You have beautiful eyes just like your mother's. They're human."

She pressed her hand against his. "Will I grow big like you, Daddy?"

"Probably not. But I don't know for sure."

When she opened her mouth to ask more, he looked over to Nykyrian. "How long do they do this?"

"Do what? Ask questions?"

"Yeah."

They all burst into laughter. Shahara patted him on the shoulder. "Sweetie, your days of having an uninterrupted conversation are over."

"What's 'conversation' mean, Daddy?"

Sighing, he pressed his head against hers and laughed, too.

Hauk paused as soon as he entered his house. His grandmother was there, waiting for their return.

"Ahh," she breathed with a smile as she saw the bundle in his arms. "Is this your Kalea?"

He nodded. "She fell asleep on the way home."

She brushed her hand through Kalea's soft, dark hair so that she could see her chubby cheeks and pert lips. "She's beautiful, Dancer."

"Thank you, Yaya. Is Sumi . . ."

"She's resting. Your doctor friend knocked her out and she hasn't awakened yet. He's still in the room with her." His grandmother rose up on her tiptoes to kiss his cheek. "Go and take the baby to her mother."

He'd only taken three steps before he was surrounded by Desideria, Kiara, Zarya, and Ture, who all wanted a look at his daughter. Since it was late, their kids were all put to bed.

His heart swelled with pride as they oohed and ahhed over her.

Desideria stroked her cheek tenderly. "Let me get her one of Lil's nightgowns. I'll be right back with it."

"Thank you."

"She's an angel," Kiara said, patting his back. "I know you're thrilled."

"I am. Thank you. She also wants dance lessons from you."

"Already?"

Nykyrian chuckled as he wrapped his arms around Kiara's waist. "She heard his name was Dancer and wants to be one, too. She also wants a goatee like her father."

Kiara laughed. "They're so much fun at this age. I hate how fast they outgrow it."

Ture brushed his hand over Kalea's head. "She's precious, Hauk. What a beauty!"

Desideria returned with a small handful of clothes. "I brought her underwear and a dress for tomorrow. I'm sure you don't want her in that League uniform."

He kissed her cheek. "Thank you so much."

"No problem." Desideria inclined her head to Kalea. "You need help dressing her for bed?"

He looked down at the tiny buttons on her clothes that seemed impossible for him to undo. "Yes. I have no idea how to dress a baby."

Desideria took her from his arms. She held her hand out for the clothes, which he returned to her.

Hauk said his good nights and then took them to his bedroom upstairs. While they'd been gone, the others had cleaned his room so that there was no sign of the brutal fight that had taken place.

Until he looked at Sumi. Rage flooded him as he again wanted to hunt Kyr down and rip out his throat.

"Hauk," Syn said in warning as he stopped him from approaching her. "It's not as bad as it looks. I mean . . . it is, but I gave her some Prinum to speed the healing and numb her pain."

Tears choked him. "How could I let her get hurt? In my own home?"

"It's not your fault." Syn glanced over to Kalea. "And you will have made her life when she wakes up and sees what you brought her."

His throat tight, he nodded, knowing Syn was right. He couldn't wait to see her face when she held her daughter for the first time.

"You okay?" Desideria asked him.

Hauk swallowed. "Yeah."

"All right. I'll be back in just a second." She took Kalea into the bathroom to dress her.

Syn cupped Hauk's face and forced him to meet his

gaze. "I know how pissed off you are. You have every right to be. There's not a one of us who wouldn't be out for blood after this. But I fixed Eleron while you were gone. Kyr cut through the system. I'm pretty sure he's locked out, but I'm better at hacking than securing. That's your job."

"Trust me, he'll never my break my system again."

Syn released him. "We'll get him, Hauk."

"I know. Just not soon enough to please me." He glanced past Syn as Desideria returned with a still-sleeping Kalea.

"She's all ready for bed."

His emotions overwhelmed him as he saw her in the white linen gown that was filled with pink ruffles. Desideria had even washed her hair and put matching booties on her feet. "Thank you, Des."

Desideria grimaced and put her hand over her stomach.

"You all right?"

Breathing in short gasps, she nodded. "Kicks like his father. He's been rolling around for hours." She patted his arm. "Good night, sweetie."

Syn paused by the bed. "She should sleep through the night. If she wakes up, let me know. I'm going to check on Shahara."

"Good night, Syn. Thank you."

"You don't have to thank us, brother. You know that."

Nodding, Hauk did the one thing he'd been dying to do since Sumi first told him about Kalea. He pulled the covers back from her and put Kalea in the bed by her side. Instinctively, Kalea snuggled in tight. Likewise, Sumi draped an arm around her and sighed as if she knew it was her baby with her.

Smiling as he blinked back tears, he pulled his office chair closer to the bed and propped his feet on the nightstand. "Don't worry, *mia*. I'm not letting you out of my sight again. And no one's ever going to hurt either of you during my watch."

Sumi sucked her breath in sharply as she came awake to a strange, stinging pain in her arm. It was asleep, she realized, and something was lying on it.

Yawning, she expected to find Dancer there.

Instead, it was a tiny little girl in a white, frilly gown. She frowned at the dark hair. "Lillya?"

The little girl opened her eyes and looked up at her.

It wasn't Desideria's daughter.

"Are you my mommy?"

Stunned, she couldn't breathe as her brain tried to make sense of this.

"Yes, Lee-lee," Dancer said from beside the bed. "That's your mommy."

Kalea threw herself against her. "Mommy! Mommy! Mommy!"

Sumi couldn't breathe as tears flowed and she sobbed in happiness and gratitude. Her baby was home! This was her daughter!

Closing her eyes, she savored the sensation of finally holding her baby against her.

Hauk caught Kalea and pulled her away. "Careful, baby. Mommy's been hurt." He turned on the intercom. "Syn! Run!"

Sumi looked down at the blood that had spread over her bandage. But honestly, she didn't care. She reached for her daughter. "Please, Dancer . . ."

He carefully returned Kalea to Sumi's uninjured side. "Don't jump on Mommy."

Kalea touched Sumi's stomach. "I'm sorry, Mommy. Kalea didn't mean to."

Completely unperturbed by it, Sumi wrapped her arms around her again and held her close as she finally rocked her. Never in her life had she been happier than she was right now. "I don't mind, at all." She looked up at Dancer and saw the warm tenderness in his eyes as he watched them. In that moment, she wanted to pull him into her arms and never let him go. He had no idea just how much this meant to her. How much *he* meant to her. "I love you so much! Were you injured?"

He shrugged with that Andarion nonchalance that would never allow him to admit to pain. "Blast to my thigh, but it's just a flesh wound."

"And you didn't bother to tell me last night?" Syn growled as he came in.

"I knew you wanted to see Shahara."

Syn rolled his eyes. "You haven't slept either, have you?"

"I'll sleep later."

Syn broke out into a round of Ritadarion that Sumi was glad she couldn't understand.

Kalea gasped as Syn lifted her shirt and she saw the sutures on her side. "Mommy! You're really hurt!"

"I'm okay, Kalea."

"That looks bad, Mommy."

Tears continued to flow down her face as she savored the little girl with her. "Right now, nothing can hurt me."

Kalea frowned at her. "Why?"

"'Cause I have you and your daddy with me. Everything's wonderful."

Kalea put her hands on Sumi's face and smiled a smile that made her weep even harder. "I have a very pretty mommy. And a pretty daddy."

Sumi laughed then groaned as Syn touched her wound. "Yes, you do, sweetie. He's the best ever."

"I wanted hair like Daddy . . . but . . . but Daddy said no."

Sumi frowned. "We can braid your hair like that, baby."

"That's not the hair she wanted." Dancer tapped his chin.

She laughed and moaned again. "Oh. Daddy's right. You can't have facial hair. We hope, anyway."

Kalca scratched her head. "But Aunt Mari has face hair. Why does she have it?"

Hauk laughed as he watched the two of them. His girls.

No, his family. It seemed so surreal to have them here in his home. He'd been alone for so long that it was hard to believe this was real.

Nothing would ever be the same and for that he was so grateful. While he'd been content and happy before, this was so much better.

And scarier.

Sumi brushed the hair back from Kalea's face. "Aunt Mari's a boy."

"But Aunt Mari's an aunt."

"You're not going to win this," Syn said with a laugh. "Trust me. I get my ass handed to me by Devyn every day. They wear you down with persistence and kid logic."

"Yeah," Hauk agreed. "I learned that the hard way, yesterday. In three hours of nonstop questions, she wore me out."

Kalea looked down at her clothes and frowned. She tugged at her nightgown. "Who dressed me like a princess?"

Hauk smiled at her. "Your Aunt Des."

"Is Aunt Des an aunt or is she a boy, too?"

"She's a girl," Sumi said, touching her nose, "and she has a daughter your age."

"Really!"

Hauk nodded. "You're wearing her daughter's clothes and she has another dress for you after you bathe."

Pulling away from Sumi, she opened her mouth wide and jumped on the bed. "Is it pretty, too?"

Hauk wasn't sure how to answer that. "Okay, sure."

Sumi laughed. "Daddies don't know about pretty dresses. But Aunt Des always has pretty things on her little girl, so I'm sure it's beautiful."

"When I meet them?"

Hauk reached for Kalea to pull her off the bed. "How about while Uncle Syn—"

"No!" Sumi growled the word out so ferociously that he released Kalea instantly and took a quick step back in fear of her. She'd never made that sound before.

She swallowed hard. "Sorry, Dancer. I've waited too long to have her with me. I'm not going to let her go. Not for anything."

He met her gaze and nodded. "I know the feeling, and I wasn't going to take her far. But I think I'll just leave her here with her mother before I lose a body part we both might miss."

Sumi held her hand out to him. He took it and she led it to her cheek. "I'm sorry I overreacted."

Syn shook his head. "Da—" He looked at Kalea and caught himself. "Dang, Hauk, here I thought I had the scariest wife. Now you done gone and upped me with one even more ferocious."

He rolled his eyes at Syn. "I don't know. Shahara's still frightening. After all, she did shoot me."

"Yeah, but yours just about ripped your arm off with her bare hands three seconds ago . . . and she's wounded. Never come between a mother and her baby. Hard lessons learned."

Hauk couldn't agree more. "Yeah. No kidding."

Kalea tilted her head at Sumi. "Are you scary, Mommy?"

Smiling sweetly, she brushed the hair back from Kalea's face. "Only if anyone ever tries to take you from me again. Or if they hurt you or your daddy. Then I will be terrifying. Grrr . . ." She made a frightening face that caused Kalea to laugh.

Syn moved away to wash his hands. "Don't pull that out again. I gave you Prinum, but that cut was deep. I can't believe you fought like that with it." He came back to the room, drying his hands. "Just rest today. If you leave the bed, have Hauk carry you."

Kalea frowned at the new bandage on Sumi's stomach. "How did you get hurt, Mommy?"

Hauk answered for her. "She fought a bad man while trying to find you, Lee-lee."

Eyes wide, she looked from him to her mother. "Really?"

She pressed her cheek to Kalea's. "I've been looking for you since you were taken from me. You're all I've thought about, night and day."

Jumping up and down on the bed, she clapped her hands. "Kalea loved!"

She had no idea.

Syn paused to smile at her. "Yes, you are, little girl. You have lots of people who will love you from now on."

"Yippee!" She jumped even harder.

Hauk caught her against him. "Honey, you're going to hurt your mom again."

"Oh. Sorry." Frowning, Kalea poked her finger against his arm. "You still got suit on, Daddy?"

"No. That's my arm."

Her eyes widened as she kept poking him. "Your arm is hard as your suit."

"I know, sweetie."

As Syn told Hauk to sit so that he could look at his injured leg, Desideria came in with her daughter. "See, Lil, there she is." She walked over to them and held Lillya so that she could reach Kalea. The two girls stared at each other for several seconds.

Finally, Lillya smiled. "Um, I'm Lil. We brought you a dolly to have so you can play with her from now on." She handed it to Kalea. "Mama said you don't have one and I have a lot so I wanted you to have one. You can have another one if you want, too, or if you don't like this one."

Kalea clung to Hauk. "Is it okay, Daddy?" she whispered loudly.

"It's fine, Lee-lee."

She was still hesitant as she reached for the doll. "Thank you." Then she started kicking her legs against him.

Desideria smiled before she wrinkled her nose at Hauk. "That means she wants you to put her down."

"Oh," he said. He looked back at Kalea. "You're short."

Kalea stared at him in confusion.

Laughing, Hauk rubbed noses with her before he set her down so that she could run over to Sumi and show her the toy. He took Lil from her mother and placed her on the floor to keep Desideria from bending over.

"Thank you, Hauk."

"Anytime."

Lillya ran to show Sumi and Kalea how to make the doll talk and change expressions.

Hauk sat down across the room so that Syn could stitch and wash his leg. He shuddered at the way the doll sounded as they played its voice track. "That is the creepiest thing."

"What?" Syn asked. "The baby doll?"

He nodded. "What is wrong with you people? I'm gonna have nightmares over that thing."

Desideria tossed an impudent look at him over her shoulder. "Your nightmare has only begun, handsome. Just wait until she puts it in a bag with only its head sticking out. That sends Caillen off every time. Apparently, his sisters tried to do that to him once, as a child." She moved to stand behind the girls. "Do you need anything, Sumi? I came to see if you wanted me to help dress or bathe Kalea."

"I got hair bows if you want," Lillya said. "They're

pretty in your hair. And we have little crowns. And . . .
and . . . and . . . other things, too!"

Sumi was torn. Part of her wanted to keep Kalea in
her arms, but the girl needed food and it was obvious
she'd rather play with Lillya than spend the day being
held by an overprotective mother.

"Kalea?" Lillya asked. "Would you like to go swimming?"

"In a pool?"

"Yes. Uncle Hauk has a really big one, with lots of toys
for us to play with. There's even a big sandbox and wag-
ons and all kinds of things."

Kalea nodded vigorously. Then she looked at Sumi.
"Mommy, may I?"

Sumi hesitated. "We don't have a suit for you, sweetie."

"I have just the thing," Desideria said. "I'll be right
back. Lillya?" She held her hand out.

Lil pouted. "Can I stay here, Mama? I like playing with
a girl and not them mean boys."

Sumi laughed. "It's okay. She can stay. We'll watch
her."

"All right. Two seconds, I'll be back."

Syn stood and glowered at Hauk. "I would tell you to
stay off the leg, but I know you won't listen. So rather than
waste my breath, I'm going to get something you can take
for the pain."

As soon as he was gone, Sumi motioned for Hauk to
come closer. He knelt on the floor next to her. Before he
realized what she intended, she kissed him with a passion that made his entire body sing. Worse, it made him
hornier than hell.

Growling, he deepened the kiss.

"Daddy hurting mommy!" Kalea started for them, but
Lillya stopped her.

"He's not hurting her. It's a kiss. My mommy and
daddy do it a lot."

"Really?"

Lillya nodded gravely as she flipped the doll over. "They smooch everywhere. All the time."

"Oh. It sounds painful."

"I know, but it's not." Lillya let out a trying sigh. "Mommies and daddies grunt and moan a lot . . . they make all kinds of noises, especially at night. And they pray a lot, too. Real loud. But they okay when they do it."

Gaping, Sumi pulled back from the kiss, horrified by what Lillya was actually talking about.

Hauk snorted as he caught her meaning, too. "Sound-proof the bedroom and add extra monitors to Kalea's room so that we can hear her and not the other way around. Oh, better yet! El?"

She appeared instantly. "Yes, Hauk?"

"I forgot to tell you last night that we have a new member in the household. Meet Kalea. Kalea, meet Eleron."

El stared at the girl, who stared at her. "What is *that*?"

Hauk gave his computer an irritated glare. "My daughter."

"And a lovely daughter she is. Hi, Kalea. I'm the house."

Kalea looked around, confused. "The house?"

Eleron nodded.

Hauk grinned at Sumi. "I can set El to babysit and watch over her like a mother hen. She'll even monitor her vitals. If her temp goes up one degree or her heart rate elevates, El will tell us."

Sumi bit her lip as she remembered Thia's words about her father's paranoia. She now understood it completely.

Eleron stiffened. "I will not change nappies."

Hauk rolled his eyes. "She's not in nappies."

"Oh. Good."

Sumi paused as she considered all that. "By the way, how did Kyr get past her yesterday?"

"He found a back door in. But I closed it last night. I

defy him to ever try again. Next time, it'll light him up like a supernova."

Desideria returned with an adorable pink swimdress that had butterflies sewn on. Their wings even flapped.

Kalea gasped as soon as she saw it. "It's so pretty! Can I really wear it?"

Desideria nodded. "Absolutely."

"I'll wait outside." Hauk went to stand in the hallway while they changed clothes on the girls.

"How is she doing?"

He turned to see his grandmother coming toward him. "She's delighted."

"And how are you?"

He wasn't sure how to respond to her question. He was at the pinnacle of heaven and at the same time, the lowest pit of hell. He'd never been happier, and he'd never had so much to lose. The mere thought of it was crippling.

His grandmother patted his arm. "I know that look. It's the same heart-stopping terror I had when your father told me that you and Keris had fallen down the mountain. And the joy in my heart when I learned you had lived . . . You've no idea how happy I was to know that you made it back to us."

Hauk frowned at her words. "I thought you hated me for it, like my mother did."

She shook her head. "I have *never* hated you, Dancer. Your mother denies a truth I was well aware of. She should have placed the blame for Keris's death where it belonged—on Dariana's shoulders. Not yours."

But she hadn't. To this day, she held him totally responsible.

His grandmother touched the scar his mother had given him that peeked out from beneath the short sleeve of his shirt. "Your Sumi will still have to fight for you tomorrow."

And they couldn't postpone it, because of the pregnancy.

"How can I let her go into that ring, wounded?"

"You have no choice, child. If she doesn't fight, she forfeits and you will continue to be tied to Dariana. She will birth another baby who will sneer at you and insult you. And she will force Sumi and Kalea out of your life. You know this."

Yes, he did.

Scowling, he stamped down the bitter pain that swelled inside him. Having been with a woman who cared for him, who loved him, and having held a child who accepted him without question, how could he go back to the life he'd lived? Ever?

Strange, he'd never realized what was missing from it. Other than companionship. But what he had now was so much better than anything he'd imagined on those lonely nights.

I can't go back.

He couldn't bear the thought of it. Yet how could he ask Sumi to risk her life for him when he wasn't worth it?

Dariana would never take mercy on her. She was out for blood, and all the hatred she bore him would be laid at Sumi's feet in that ring.

Why can't I fight in her place?

But their laws would never allow such. This was a challenge for the right to marry *him*. He couldn't interfere. Yet in his heart, he belonged fully to Sumi.

He always would.

The door behind him opened to show Kalea in her swimsuit.

"Look, Daddy, look! I'm a fairy princess!"

He ground his teeth as tears choked him at the sight of the love in those silvery eyes that stared up at him like he was some mythical hero. There was no judgment or reservation. Just total admiration and devotion.

Just like Sumi.

Smiling, he picked her up. "Yes, you do, Lee-lee." He held her toward his grandmother. "And this is your gre yaya."

She screwed her face up into an adorable pout. "What's a gre yaya?"

"Your great-grandmother."

Eyes wide, she sucked her breath in excitely. "I have a great-grandmama? Really?"

His yaya smiled. "Yes, little one. You do, indeed." She held her hands out.

Kalea hesitated before she leaned into his grandmother's arms and allowed her to take her. She touched his grandmother's cheek just below her eyes. "You have weird eyes like Daddy. But different."

"I do."

"Are you Anduran, too?"

His grandmother laughed again. "Andarion, and yes. Yes, I am."

"Am I Anduran?"

His grandmother tickled her belly. "You're not just Anduran, Kalea. You're an Anduran princess!"

"Hear that, Daddy? I'm a princess!"

"No, precious," he teased, brushing his hand through one of her pigtails. "You are the empress of my universe, and we need to get you back to Mommy or she'll be worried."

Hauk allowed his grandmother to enter the bedroom first and watched as she went to sit on the bed beside Sumi so that they and Desideria and Lillya could fuss over Kalea.

He tightened his lips to suppress their trembling. *Please, gods, don't give me this only to rip it all away tomorrow.* He would rather be gutted.

But in the back of his mind, he knew it couldn't last. While others were allowed to have happy lives, he'd never been allowed to experience such joy. Something always happened to steal it away.

Just like his Endurance. Other children, normal children, ascended without issue. He'd barely survived his. And it had left him scarred and bitter.

Abandoned.

You don't deserve happiness for what you did to my husband! I hope you live the rest of your life in utter misery! Even now, Dariana's angry curse haunted him.

Resigned to the hell he knew would come, he just hoped that this time the tragedy would take his own life. Because if it was theirs it demanded, he would follow them into the grave.

CHAPTER 33

Dancer carried Sumi to the part of the conservatory that housed the pool. His grandmother walked beside them with Kalea in her arms. While Sumi felt a little ridiculous about needing to keep her eyes on her daughter at all times, she couldn't help the physical pain that pierced her whenever she couldn't see her.

But what stunned her was the number of kids who were playing here. Kiara and Nykyrian had brought their entire brood over. All four boys and both daughters.

Thia came running as soon as she saw them and hugged Sumi. Her face brightened at the sight of Kalea in her great-grandmother's arms. "Oh my gosh! Is this the infamous Tara Kalea? You are a great beauty, aren't you?"

Frowning, Kalea hid behind her great-grandmother's shoulder and eyed her warily.

In total understanding, Thia smiled wider. "I'm your cousin, Thia."

Kalea stared at her as if she couldn't quite believe what she was hearing. "I have a cousin?"

"You have lots of them." Thia spread her arm wide to show not just her siblings, but Devyn, Terek, Lil, Cezar, and Jayne's two daughters and son. "See all those kids?"

She nodded.

"They're *all* your cousins."

"Even Lil?" Kalea breathed.

"Even Lil."

With a pair of round, excited eyes, she looked at Sumi. "Mommy? Can I play with my cousins?"

"Of course you can. Just stay so that I can see you and don't get close to the doors or windows."

Thia gave her a knowing stare. "I'll stay with her."

"Thank you, sweetie."

She inclined her head before she took Kalea off to meet Thia's brothers, who were playing with Devyn and Sway, and the rest of The Sentella clan.

Dancer set her right beside the pool and sand area where the kids were playing. It was only then that she realized how vigilant everyone was. And the fact that there were a large number of royal Andarion guards patrolling the premises.

It made her feel better to know she wasn't the only one who was overly cautious.

Dancer pulled a chair up beside her. "Would you like something to eat?"

"Sure. Where do I go?"

"I'll get it." He jerked his chin toward a long buffet table that had been set with all kinds of choices. "Just let me know what you like."

She gave him a hot once-over. "What I really want isn't on that table."

He blushed sweetly. "Might be messy, but I could arrange that."

She laughed at his dry sarcasm, though a part of her wasn't joking. She'd much rather munch on him.

With a sleeping Terek attached to his chest in a baby sling, Ture came toward her with a friendly smile. He tossed a towel over his shoulder. "I have some of everything, with a number of kids' dishes that are Maris tested and approved."

Sumi gave him a puzzled stare at the way he'd said that. "Maris approved?"

Ture nodded. "In spite of the sophisticated palate he claims to have, my baby has the taste buds of a five-year-old. And just because they're picky doesn't mean it can't be healthy. Do you want sweet or savory or both?"

"Um . . . both, I guess."

"All right. You two stay here and I'll be right back with food for you."

Dancer stood as Kiara came over with a very happy Zarina, and offered her his chair.

She smiled gratefully as she accepted it and balanced Zarina on her lap. "I hope the two of you don't mind, but I took the liberty of inviting my favorite local kids' store to the house with things for Kalea. They should be here in about an hour."

Sumi blushed. "That was extremely kind of you, but can we cancel it?"

"Why?"

She felt her face turn even hotter. "I'm sure Kyr's locked all my accounts. I don't have credits without them."

Dancer knelt beside her and took her hand in his. "*Mia,* you have all you need and more. There's nothing I would deny you or Kalea. Buy whatever it is she desires." He winked at Kiara. "Can you please call them back and say that Kalea wants to look like a fairy princess? They should bring things to make Her Fae Highness deliriously happy."

Sumi's lips trembled at his kindness. She still couldn't believe the male she'd been lucky enough to find. "You are too good to be true."

He snorted in denial. "Says the woman who has to fight a battle for me while wounded. Really don't think I'm *that* big of a prize."

She squeezed his hand. "You would be *very* wrong."

Hauk smiled, even though he cringed inside. But then, her last boyfriend had tried to kill her and Kalea. Compared to *that,* he was a definite step up. Sad, when he thought about it.

Kissing her hand, he rose. "I'll be right back." He motioned discreetly for Kiara to follow him.

Once they were alone, he leaned down to speak so that no one could overhear him. "Do you know anyone who could bring clothes for Sumi also?"

Adjusting Zarina on her shoulder, she smiled. "Way ahead of you, big guy. They'll be coming in two hours."

"Thank you, Kiara."

She patted his arm. "Anytime."

He started to leave then thought of something else. "Did you request more conservative clothes for Sumi? I'm not sure I want her in typical Andarion fashions, and she's thankfully more modest in her tastes."

She smiled. "Don't worry. That, too, is already done. Notice my hoo-has are never hanging out. No need in getting someone killed needlessly by a jealous assassin husband."

Hauk laughed. "Again, thank you."

"Is something wrong?" Nykyrian asked as he joined them.

Hauk gave him a dry stare. "We were just planning our afternoon tryst. Want to join us?"

Nyk let out a harumph. "Sarcasm like that could get you gutted."

"And I'm sure that when I die, it will be the result of just such a comment, at just such a time."

Kiara sighed at them both as she handed Zarina off to Nyk. "All is well. We were talking baby clothes and women's fashions." She pulled out her link and headed for a secluded corner.

Nyk raked a less-than-flattering stare over Hauk as he turned Zarina around to hold her back against his chest. "Women's fashions? So you really do wear frilly pink underwear, huh?"

Hauk groaned at something that had been a long-running joke between Nyk and Darling, that Darling had only recently told him about. It'd started back when they'd first become friends. Darling had been riddled with severe panic attacks, and to get him past them, Nyk would tell him that Hauk wore women's underpants. "I hate you."

Taking it in stride, Nykyrian pinned one of those stares on him that saw all the way to his soul. "Seriously, are you all right? You seem really distracted."

Yes and no. He was distracted, only in that he was hyperalert, waiting for Kyr or someone else to try and steal his happiness. "It's . . ." He let his voice trail off. "I'm fine."

Nyk studied him for a minute. "No, you're terrified. Though I've never seen that look on you before, unless explosives were involved."

"Shut up, asshole." He glanced down at Zarina, who was bouncing and laughing happily as she drooled all over Nykyrian's hand. "By the way, that frilly-dressed, drooling baby girl in your arms takes the badass right out of you."

Rolling his eyes, Nyk held his daughter tighter. "Seriously, I know what you're going through, Hauk. One minute, you're alone in your hole. Having a pretty good life. Content with things, for the most part. Lonely at times, but you're so accustomed to that, you don't really think about it anymore. You only have yourself to worry over, and whatever bullshit trouble your friends get into. Then out of the blue, this amazing woman blindsides you. She adds something to your life you didn't even know was missing. Next thing you know, she's got her bras hanging in your bathroom, you're eating dinner at a table in your house where you used to store parts, with silverware you didn't even know you had, and she's taken over your world completely. Worse, she has become your entire existence and you're now civilized in a way you never thought you could be. And instead of alcohol-induced brawls, you live just to see the way her eyes light up when you enter her line of sight. And the fear that she's going to be taken away is so consuming that you can't stop thinking about it. You see enemies everywhere. Every shadow. Every whisper of wind. And if that's not unnerving enough, you find out you have a kid who's even more dependent on you and who means every bit as much to you."

Nyk cradled Zarina against him. "Now, you stay with your gut in a knot, and you want to tether them to you to make sure no one can touch them, because you know exactly what your enemies would do if they ever laid hands on them."

Hauk hated just how true every bit of that was. "How do you cope?"

"That's the question, *drey*. When you find an answer, please let me know."

He shook his head.

"Honestly," Nyk continued. "The only thing that keeps me going is the memory of what it was like without them." He kissed the top of Zarina's head. "There are days when I feel like I'm barely hanging on to my sanity. When I wonder if I did the right thing by bringing them into my hostile world. Then I feel like a selfish asshole for it." He looked down at his daughter and smiled at her. "But truthfully, I can't imagine going back." He held Zarina up to Hauk's eye level. "If I have to lose sleep, I can't think of a better reason than this little face."

He gave Zarina a lopsided grin. "She is a cutie, even if she does keep springing leaks all over." And right now, she was going to town on Nykyrian's thumb.

Pain hit him so hard as he tried to think about what might happen to Sumi and Kalea. "I don't know if I can let her step into that ring tomorrow, Nyk. Dariana's a nasty bitch, and highly trained."

"From what I saw, Sumi's no slacker. Anyone who can take the chunk out of Kyr that she did is more than equal to the challenge. Kyr might be psychotic, but he's never been weak or unskilled." Nyk clapped him on the shoulder. "You know we won't let anything happen to your family. Not after everything you've done for ours. Breathe, Hauk. Have faith."

Ironic, coming from a male who'd been a devout atheist until Kiara had entered his life. She had changed so much about Nyk, and not in a bad way. She'd taken a savage beast and tamed him. Taught him humanity. While Nyk had always been loyal to his friends, he hadn't been long on compassion, and a discussion like this one would never have happened ten years ago.

Now . . .

Hauk glanced back at Sumi, who was sampling the food Ture had brought for her. Her long blond hair was plaited and fell over one shoulder while she smiled up at him and chatted. Overwhelming love and fear consumed him. "God help me, Nyk. I can't lose her."

Nykyrian glanced over to Kiara. "I know. But it'll be fine. We have your daughter, and we will find the traitor and deal with it. The entire Andarion army and armada are at your disposal. Not to mention The Sentella and Tavali . . . and now Phrixians."

Kiara came back to take Zarina, who was starting to fuss. "Daddy ignoring his baby girl?" she asked in a high-pitched tone. "Shame on him." She blew air against Zarina's cheek, which made the baby laugh before Kiara headed toward Sumi.

Nyk wiped his hand off on his pants leg. He started to say something, then he cursed.

Before Hauk could ask what was wrong, Nyk took off at a dead run. His heart stopped in fear of an unknown attacker, until he saw his friend rush to one of the columns where Adron was quickly climbing up, out of reach.

Nykyrian snatched his son down. "What are you doing?"

"Jayce said I couldn't make it to the top. I was showing him he was wrong."

Growling, Nykyrian tossed his son over his shoulder and held him upside down by the legs. "I swear on my life, I could lock you both in a padded room and you'd still find something dangerous to do."

Hauk laughed as he grabbed Adron from Nyk's hold and swung him around. "You making your dad crazy again?"

"Toss me, Uncle Hauk!"

He threw Adron into the air and caught him. As he started to do it again, he saw Kalea running to her mom . . . holding Jayce's hand.

"Look, Mommy! Jayce made me a flower crown like a princess. He says I'm the prettiest of all!"

Raw, unmitigated anger tore through him as he set Adron down and glared at Nykyrian, who was laughing over it.

Sumi jerked around at the sound of an inhuman cry. One second, Dancer was staring at Nykyrian. In the next, he'd pulled out a small stick and extended it into a staff.

Nykyrian did the same as the two of them went to war.

Literally. She hadn't even known they were armed. Gaping, she watched as they assaulted each other with seasoned ferocity and skill. It was impressive and terrifying.

"What's going on?" she asked Kiara.

Kiara let out an irritated sigh. "Who knows? They do that sometimes. One says something and the other draws a weapon or throws a punch. It looks serious, but they never really hurt each other. I've learned to ignore them and let it go."

But Kalea didn't. Screaming and sobbing, she ran at Nykyrian, who narrowly missed striking her.

That distraction cost Dancer, as Nykyrian's staff caught him on his chin and busted his lip.

"Don't you hurt my daddy!" She grabbed Nykyrian's leg and bit him hard enough to draw blood.

Dancer quickly pulled her back. "Lee-lee, it's fine. Daddy and Uncle Nyk were playing."

Still, she sobbed uncontrollably.

Dropping his staff, Dancer cradled her against his chest and wiped at the blood on her lips. "Shh, sweetie. It's all good. Really."

Nykyrian knelt down and placed his hand on her head. "We didn't mean to scare you, Kalea. It's how we play with each other."

Sniffling, she picked her head up from Dancer's shoulder to glare at Nykyrian. When she spoke, it was in short, staccato breaths as she struggled to calm down. "You weren't trying to kill my daddy?"

"No. I love your daddy. He's my little brother."

She continued to gasp for air as she looked up at Dancer. "Your lips are bleeding where he hit you, Daddy. Please, don't die!"

"It's just a busted lip. I'm not going to die. Really. I get them all the time." He wiped the tears from her face. "Don't cry, Lee-lee. We won't play fight anymore."

"Okay." She wiped at her nose before she scooted away from him.

Hauk frowned as he watched her return to Jayce and Adron, who led her to the sand to play. How weird that would upset her when she'd been so brave the day before. He met Nyk's apologetic stare. "Is that normal?"

Nyk shrugged. "My kids have never done that. But then they've grown up with us sparring against each other. And they've seen us both bleed a lot worse than your lip. Sorry about that, by the way."

"Don't be. I'm the one who started the fight and dropped his guard." A bad feeling went through him as his thoughts returned to Kalea's outburst. "You don't think they would have had her around death matches at that age, do you?"

He gave Hauk a droll stare. "It's The League. I wouldn't put anything past them."

Neither would he. But one thing was clear. There was no way Kalea would be able to attend the match tomorrow and watch her mother fight Dariana. Unlike Nyk, that bitch wouldn't be so kind or understanding if Kalea bit her.

Hauk glanced down at Nyk's leg. "You know you're bleeding. Right?"

"Yeah, I know. Your daughter has an amazing set of teeth." Clapping him on the back, Nyk went to Syn to have him stitch it.

Hauk licked at his busted lip as he went over to Sumi, whose brow was creased with worry.

"Did she draw Nykyrian's blood?"

He nodded. "She was scared."

"Is Nykyrian all right?" Kiara asked.

"Yeah. Hell, I've bit him worse than that in a fight."

Kiara let out an irritated noise. "I'm going to check on my husband and try not to think about how true that statement is."

He wiped another round of blood from his lip.

"Are *you* okay?" Sumi asked.

He nodded. "It caught a fang. Bleeds a lot worse than it hurts."

"Why did you go after Nykyrian like that?"

Cursing in Andarion, Dancer narrowed his gaze on Jayce as he picked a bouquet of flowers for Kalea to match the crown he'd made her. "That! Right there!" He jerked his chin at them. "Before I met you, Nyk cursed me to have a beautiful daughter. Bastard! I don't think I'll ever sleep again."

Sumi laughed at the anguished look in his eyes as he watched the children, who were being absolutely precious together. Jayce was taking care of Kalea as if she was his little sister. But it was more than that. "You really do think of her as yours, don't you?"

Hurt and fear mixed in his red eyes as he locked gazes with her. He swallowed hard. "I know she's your daughter, Sumi. I didn't mean to presume anything, or trespass. Sorry."

In that moment, she wanted to kick the snot out of Dariana for her cruelty to him over the years.

"Dancer," she chided as she realized the source of his fear. She reached out and took his hand into hers. "Sweetie, that's not what I meant. At all. I want you to think of her as yours. It means more to me than you'll ever know that you've accepted her so thoroughly."

He kissed her hand then rubbed it against his goatee as if he savored her touch as much as she relished his. He wasn't one to really talk about his feelings, but she saw them in what he did. She saw them every time he looked at her.

"My fierce warrior," she breathed.

That brought a smile to his lips. "My fierce Ger Tarra."

Eleron appeared by his side. "There is a group of two males and a female who are seeking you, Hauk. They say that they've brought clothing for your daughter."

"Bring them here, please."

"As you wish." Eleron vanished.

Clearing his throat, he left her to fetch Kalea.

Sumi choked on unexpected tears as she watched that sexy, loose-limbed gait. She would never get over the way he looked whenever he cradled Kalea. Their daughter was so tiny in his muscular arms and he was so gentle with her. So kind.

He rode her back to Sumi on his shoulder where she

squealed in delight. Then he flipped her over and sat her next to Sumi's side.

As the Andarion store clerks came in, Dancer left them with his grandmother, Desideria, Zarya, and Maris. They were quickly joined by Kiara, who made the introductions, and then Ture, who wanted to help pick out clothes.

Sumi had expected them to bring a small bag of clothing. Instead, they had four huge trunks to choose from.

Kalea and Lillya both gasped at all the fae and glitter items, and they tried on different shoes and accessories. There were even matching clothes for Kalea's doll.

"Mommy!" Kalea gasped as she saw one red dress that was ankle length with a poofy embroidered skirt and beaded neckline and matching sweater. It was, by far, the most beautiful gown she'd ever seen. "It's a princess dress. Can I have it? Please!"

Biting her lip, Sumi hesitated. She looked for a tag to see the price, but there wasn't one on it. "How much is it?" she asked the clerk.

He smiled warmly. "Gersen War Hauk had us remove all tags. He wants you and your daughter to buy what you like without worrying over the cost. He was quite explicit that we not dampen your happiness in any way, and that we outfit his daughter like a fae princess."

Kalea gave her the most adorable begging face.

"Then I guess you can have it, sweetie."

Kalea squealed as she hugged the dress to her and danced around the chairs.

Sumi pressed her lips together, enjoying the sight of her daughter's excitement while they picked out the rest of Kalea's wardrobe. She wished Dancer was here to see it, too. Especially since it was his kindness and generosity that made Kalea so thrilled and happy.

By the time they were done, Kalea had more clothes than Sumi could have dreamed of. She kept trying to say enough, but the other women, and Maris and Ture, came up with reasons and occasions that required more and more.

Giggling, Kalea rolled around on top of her new wardrobe like a happy little piglet.

Dancer finally rejoined them. He arched a brow at her actions. "What are you doing, Lee-lee?"

She sat up with a gasp. "Daddy! Look at what all I got!" She turned to show him the tulle wings on her back before she twitched and wiggled her bottom to make them flap. "They made me a fairy princess! And . . . and me and Lil got matching dresses, and me and Mommy got matching dresses, and me and my dolly got matching dresses, too!"

Picking her up, he rubbed noses with her. "So you like them?"

"I do!" She lifted her foot. "See my red shoes. Aren't they pretty! Aunt Mari said he has some the same color."

Dancer glanced over to Mari. "I think I've seen those shoes."

Maris winked at him. "Where should we stash all her new things?"

"The room that adjoins my bedroom. El can show you the way and open it for you."

Maris nodded then turned back to Sumi. "Don't worry. We'll get this all put away for you. Come, come, everyone. Let's tuck our girl into her new room."

"Can I go, too, Daddy?"

He looked at Sumi. "Are you okay with that?"

She nodded. "Don't be long, though, and stay with everyone."

"Okay!"

He set Kalea down so that she could take Lillya's hand and skip along with the rest to her new room. Then he knelt down by Sumi's side.

She cupped his cheek in her hand. "Thank you."

He inclined his head to her. "Did they please her?"

"You should have been here. She was deliriously happy." But there was a strange shadow haunting his eyes. "What's wrong?"

Dancer offered her a kind smile. "Nothing. I should keep an eye on Kalea. I'll be back in a few."

"He spoke to his mother," Fain said as soon as Dancer was gone. Sitting down next to her, he handed her a glass of juice.

Sumi tried to understand why a talk with his mother would hurt Dancer so much. And she didn't miss the fact that even though the female had birthed them both, Fain didn't claim her. "Why's he upset?"

"Both she and his father are planning to sit with Dariana's family tomorrow. And Dancer's furious and hurt about it."

Sumi snorted at their mother's stupidity. "He shouldn't let that upset him. I don't care where they sit."

Fain swallowed his drink before he sighed. "Easier said than done, Sumi. It's another slap in his face that he really didn't need. They know he loves you, and yet they're supporting a female who has done nothing but insult and humiliate him since he was a boy."

A furious tic beat a steady rhythm in his jaw as he watched the boys and Vik playing at war in their sandbox. "You've never seen an Andarion unification ceremony. The bride and groom are practically naked when they make their Disclosures. The male comes out and kneels so that the bride can *inspect* him."

A chill went down her spine at what he described. "Inspect him, how?"

"She walks around his body and looks him over. If he's acceptable, she nods to the priest to continue the proceedings. . . ." His voice trailed off as his tic picked up its rhythm. "Dancer was only eighteen the first time he went before Dariana, in good faith. You've seen his body. You know how scarred up he was, and those scars were still fresh, then. There he stood and knelt, just a kid, in front of his entire family and hers with his whole body visible for all to see—including the marks his mother had given him as chastisement. It was the last thing he wanted to do. He knew Dariana hated him, and that everyone would sneer over the condition of his body. Yet he went forward with it so that he wouldn't shame his parents. A decent female would have simply shaken her head no, and been done with him. Instead, Dariana sliced open his back, leaving him to bleed at the altar, and walked out in the middle of the ceremony."

Sumi ground her teeth as rage clouded her vision. "What did your parents do?"

"They left him, too." Fain set his drink aside. "Alone, he went and dressed, while his back bled, and returned home to find himself locked out."

Stunned at that, she gaped incredulously. "What?"

He nodded. "Because they were embarrassed that Dariana had denied his pledge, his parents refused him access to his own home. He didn't even have his wallet on him. All he had were the clothes on his back."

"Did he call you?"

"He was too ashamed. He didn't call anyone. The worst part was that his parents didn't tell anyone he was missing. They went on with their lives like nothing had happened. Almost a week went by before Nykyrian contacted me, asking if I'd seen him."

"Are you serious?"

Bitterness burned in his eyes as he nodded. "Nyk had been out on assignment and when he got back, he'd tried to call Dancer to congratulate him on unification. When he kept getting voicemail without Dancer returning it, he became concerned and learned what had happened. It took us a day and a half to find him."

"Where was he?"

"Comatose, in a hospital."

Her stomach lurched to the point she feared she'd be ill. "What?"

Fain took a deep breath before he continued. "The Enforcers had found him passed out on a bench, in the park where we used to play as kids. They'd said that he must have been there for several days before they saw him. Between exposure and Dariana's wounds, he was barely alive. Since he had no ID on him or credits, they had taken him to a charity ward and left him there to basically die."

Tears choked her. No wonder he loved Nykyrian so. And Fain. They were really the only family he'd had as a boy. "What'd you do?"

"We had him moved to a real hospital, and flew in the best doctor on Andaria. But I will never forget the look in his eyes when he finally woke up. It was worse than when Keris had died, or when he'd been burned. He looked devastated and broken. Defeated. And he was just a kid."

She knew that feeling of having everything in your world tragically taken. Of being lost and angry, and wondering why you were still alive when it was obvious no one gave a single shit about you. It broke her heart that they had put him through that. "What did he say about it?"

"Nothing. You know Dancer. He's never spoken about it to anyone. And he never went back to his parents' house. Not even for a single pair of shoes. He hasn't stepped foot in it since the day he left for that first unification."

"Where did he go?"

"Since Nyk was in The League and couldn't have visitors, he stayed with me until he had a job and a small apartment of his own. And every fucking year since then, his parents have demanded that he return to face Dariana again and again, and be put through the humiliation of public rejection."

And that cruelty, she understood least of all. "Why?"

"Penance for Keris's death, and the fact that his mother has been quite vocal about how no other female will have him because of his hideousness. As far as his parents are concerned, Dancer has basically been an orphan since Nyk pulled him out of that burning pod."

"Is that why you're so protective of him?"

Fain nodded. "My brother's a strong male. He's had to be to survive. And he's not the kind of male to let others see his pain . . . physical or emotional. Dancer holds everything in. But I know him better than anyone, and I've seen the longing he's had every time he's around his friends and their spouses, and children. All the times he's been sneered at by an Andarion female. It's why he built Eleron."

"I don't follow."

"He wanted to have a female who could look at him without curling her lip in distaste."

Sumi swallowed against the pain she felt over those words. "Andarion females are morons. Any woman—"

"Sees only an Andarion male. Trust me, Sumi. I know. While they might smile at first glance, the moment they see our eyes or teeth, they cringe and run. It's really hard on the ego, and much worse than how Andarion females behave. I, at least, have the memory of being sought after by eager females. Dancer never knew that. Not until you."

She still couldn't believe that, given how incredibly handsome he was. But then, she knew exactly how superficial and judgmental some people were. While she hated that Dancer had been forced to be alone for so long, she was more than grateful that she was the lucky one who'd won his heart.

"Why are you telling me this?" she asked Fain.

"I wanted you to understand exactly who you're fighting for tomorrow. How important you and Kalea are to him, and why his parents are fucking dipshits. And while they may sit with the enemy, we will be there for you."

She placed her hand over his and squeezed. "I love you, Fain."

"I hope, by that, you mean in a purely platonic kind of way," a voice growled from behind them.

Laughing, she turned toward Dancer, who eyed them suspiciously. "And how else would I mean that?"

"Good, 'cause I'd really hate to have to kill my brother."

Fain snorted. "And I'd really hate to die, especially since you still owe me money."

"I paid you back . . . didn't I?"

"Yeah, you did, but I like the doubt in that tone."

Dancer rolled his eyes before he faced her. "I have been sent by Her Fae Highness to retrieve her mother so that she can show you her room. She has very specific ideas on how she wants it decorated, and Mari and Ture aren't helping. They want you to knock out a portion of the roof and grow a tree or some weird shit like that."

She laughed at his baffled expression. "Oh joy. I can't wait."

"Hmm . . . and she wants her own Vik, too."

"Lovely. Let me go mitigate the damage before Eleron short-circuits."

He picked Sumi up and carried her toward the stairs.

Sighing, she laid her head down on his shoulder and buried her hand in his braids, while she savored the scent of his warm skin. Her other arm was wrapped around his back so that she could draw circles against his spine.

Hauk slowed as he relished the tenderness of being held like this. Gods, it was incredible.

"Is something wrong?"

He tightened his arms around her. "No, *mia*." He placed a kiss to her forehead as he carried her upstairs.

She trailed her hand from his hair to his jaw and then to his goatee that she fingered before she moved to trace his lips. "How can such a fierce, sexy beast be so incredibly sweet?"

"My enemies would beg to differ on the topic of my sweetness."

"Then I'm glad I'm not your enemy, for I would hate to miss seeing this side of you."

The redness of his eyes deepened before he dipped his head to kiss her.

Sumi moaned at the taste of him as he slowly lowered her legs and pulled her against him. She fisted her hands in his hair and shivered at the sensation of his fangs brushing against her tongue. He was always so careful not to hurt her.

His breathing ragged, he cupped her head in his hands and explored every inch of her mouth. Every hormone inside her fired as she ached to strip him naked.

"Mommy! Mommy! Mommy! You have to come see this."

Pulling back, she looked up to see Dancer pouting.

He placed a tender kiss on the tip of her nose. "Our daughter is summoning you, *munatara*." He stepped back and released her to Kalea's custody.

When she reached the door to Kalea's room, she glanced back to see Dancer watching them. Eleron appeared by his side and whispered something to him.

He tilted his head as anger sparked in his eyes. Without a word, he spun on his heels and headed back to the stairs with a furious stride.

Sumi had no idea what had just happened, but she could tell it wasn't good. She was dying to follow after him, but Kalea was insistent she join her.

CHAPTER 34

Hauk paced his comm room as he listened to the report from the senior officer in charge of the Bromese Sentella base. All of them in the room—Nykyrian, Nero, Bastien, Safir, Chayden, Fain, Madai, Darling, Jayne, Ryn, Caillen, and Drake—were silent.

"We lost over a hundred members in the attack. The central bay is down and we have almost a thousand wounded. For now, I've closed the base and have evaced everything we could move to the base on Altira."

"Is the Porturnum giving air support?" Ryn asked.

The commander nodded. "The Tavali have been a godsend to us, Ambassador. We'd have lost everyone had they not mobilized to our aid."

Ryn glanced to Fain and Chayden. "Do either of you know Venik personally?" Venik was the Porturnum leader, and a vicious pirate bastard.

But if you wore a Tavali uniform, there was nothing he wouldn't do for you.

Fain nodded. "I've known him for years. You?"

Chayden shook his head.

"Fain," Nykyrian said. "Can you contact him and convey our gratitude? Tell him we're in his debt. Send him a crate of the best Tondarion Fire you can find."

"Will do."

Madai met Saf's gaze before he spoke. "We will need to lead a retaliatory strike for this."

"No." Nero folded his arms over his chest. "Kyr did this to get back at us for taking Kalea from his custody. Another strike will only cost more innocent lives."

Madai scoffed. "I'm good with that. They're our enemies. The fewer of them who live, the better."

Fain nodded. "You don the uniform, you know the hazards."

"But they don't all wear them by choice," Saf reminded them. "And I was one of those."

Madai said something to him that caused Saf to cup his hand and gesture at him.

While Hauk had no idea what that meant, the murderous expression on Madai's face said it wasn't a gesture for health or well-being. He passed a quirked brow at Saf. "Should I ask?"

"No. It's not fit to be repeated. Even among you degenerates."

Nykyrian glanced to Hauk. By the look on his face, he knew Nyk was thinking the same thing he was. "We're going to have to destroy The League."

Hauk nodded. "Tear that motherfucker down."

"And Kyr will have to die." Darling spoke up for the first time.

Madai curled his lip. "*You* don't get to make that call, *arito.*"

Darling responded in Phrixian, which caused Saf to have to catch his brother before Madai attacked.

Safir spoke to Madai in Phrixian before he turned his attention back to the rest of them. "Darling's right. We all know it. This won't end until we bury our brother."

Sadness darkened Madai's face. "We are Phrixian and we will do what we must. But I would rather we take Kyr alive."

"We will try," Nykyrian said in true diplomatic mode.

Darling glanced at Nyk, then Hauk and Fain. "As much as I hate to admit it, Madai's right. We need to plan a strategic response to cripple them and make sure they don't hit us again without a strong sphincter clench."

Bastien stepped forward. "You'll need a war commander between your allied nations and the four main branches of the Tavali. Someone who can organize the logistics and make command-level decisions without running everything past your emperors, and waiting for their responses."

Nykyrian nodded. "Someone who was Gyron Force would make a damn good one."

Bastien shook his head. "I wasn't a commander, Commander. And I have something to take care of, first. Besides, I don't play well with others."

Caillen laughed. "I think that statement applies to everyone in this room."

Jayne snorted before she spoke. "You know who would be the best choice for this . . . Galene Batur."

"Who's he?" Madai asked.

"*She*," Jayne stressed the pronoun, "is the current prime commander of the Andarion armada."

Nykyrian considered it. "She's damn good. A little abrasive—"

Fain burst into laughter. "And hell is a just a hot tub. Have you actually met her?"

"Ignore him," Hauk said to Nykyrian. "He's still seething over the little prank she played on him in school."

"It wasn't a little prank and she's a nasty piece of work. Besides, the Phrixians won't follow a female war commander, and with the exception of Darling, the Caronese won't like it either."

"Her record is flawless," Jayne reminded him. "She's fierce and doesn't play games with anyone. She rose through the ranks the old fashioned way . . . she earned them."

"You're not seriously considering this?" Fain asked Nykyrian.

Nyk shrugged. "The Qillaq will have a hard time following a male into battle. And we can sct hcr up with a male liaison who can relay her orders to the nations that don't want to follow a female."

Madai narrowed his gaze. "And who are you proposing for that?"

Hauk laughed evilly. "I vote Fain. He's Tavali and has formal military training. Pretty much everyone loves him. . . . Except Galene."

Fain glared at him.

Hauk grinned at his seething brother. Galene was hell on earth, but he'd always liked her. She'd been extremely kind to him in school.

"I second it," Darling said with a laugh.

Jayne nodded. "Thirded."

Nyk inclined his head to them. "Then I'll talk to her about it."

"I hate all of you," Fain snarled. "Bastards."

A knock sounded on the door.

"Open," Hauk said.

It slid up to show Syn in the hallway. "Hate to interrupt, but I need to talk to Hauk for a minute, in private."

He left the others to join Syn outside. "What's up?"

"I wanted to run something past you before I pitched it to your better half."

Hauk frowned. "Yeah?"

He took a small vial from his pocket and handed it to Hauk. "I was able to pull a few favors and get that. It's stronger than Prinum and will completely heal Sumi for her fight tomorrow."

Impressive, but Hauk could tell by Syn's tone it wasn't quite as simple as it sounded. "What is it?"

"Experimental, which is why I'm asking before I say anything to Sumi and have you beat my ass for it. Right now, it's Compound X943. It's the latest in medical nano-tech from Gouran. There've only been very limited human trials so far, so we don't know what, if any, side effects it might have."

Hauk bit his lip. "What do you think?"

"I wouldn't have sent for it if I thought it would hurt her in any way. But there's always an unknown risk factor and I don't want to make that call without letting both of you know the gamble."

That was why he was so devoted to Syn. While the Rit could be a pain, he was always honest with his friends. "If it were Shahara?"

"I injected her with worse than that to get her pregnant."

Now there was something Hauk hadn't known. "Really?"

Syn nodded. "Believe me, I didn't want to. But she was so desperate for a baby, and no one, not even the questionable agencies, would let us adopt. It was my last resort, and is why Devyn will remain her only child."

Hauk still wasn't sure. On the one hand, he wanted Sumi to have every advantage against Dariana. On the other . . .

If this went wrong, he'd never forgive himself.

But in the end, it wasn't his decision to make. While her life meant more to him than anything else in the universe, it was still her life and not his. He would never substitute his reasoning over hers. "Let's go ask her what she wants to do."

He led Syn back upstairs where the women and Maris and Ture were still in Kalea's room. As soon as he opened the door, he froze at the sight of mother and daughter in matching tunics and leggings, while they were placing the same exact outfit on Kalea's doll.

Now that was adorable and hilarious.

And rather frightening.

Sumi looked up at him with a bright smile that wrenched his gut. She kissed Kalea's cheek and handed her off to his grandmother before she excused herself.

Hauk glanced over to the other clerks who'd come with clothes for Sumi. He'd forgotten about them. But luckily, they were packing to leave. "Sorry to disturb you."

She scoffed. "Baby, you never disturb me. I welcome your presence anytime." She gave him a quick kiss that made him ache for an empty house and open schedule. "What do you need?"

He inclined his head to Syn, who quickly explained the drug to her.

She frowned as she considered it. "What do you think?" she asked Hauk.

"I trust Syn completely, but it's up to you. I won't make this call."

She rubbed his arm. "Then let's do it. As long as we have enemies after us, I don't want to be down. I need all my fighting strength."

"All right. I'll get it ready. As soon as you're done here, we'll inject it."

She smiled at him. "Thank you, Syn."

"Don't thank me yet. Just remember, if you grow another head or other appendage, I did warn you it was experimental." He headed off.

Laughing, Sumi took Hauk's hand as Kiara showed the clerks out of the house. "Want to come see what I've picked out to wear? Give it your Andarion approval?"

He offered her a lopsided grin. "I'm sure I'll like whatever you've chosen. Besides," he leaned in to whisper in her ear, "I prefer you naked."

She tsked at him. "I don't think you'd let me leave the house like that. But I did pick out a dress very similar to Eleron's for dinner at the palace."

All the humor left him. "Excuse me?"

She laughed. "So you do care."

"Relax, Hauk," Shahara called from inside the room. "Her sedate taste in clothing makes mine look like a hooker's."

That made him feel a lot better. Shahara had always been very circumspect in her wardrobe choices.

"Daddy! Look!" Kalea came running up with her doll fully clothed. "We all match!"

Kneeling down, he smiled at her. "So you do."

"You need to get leggings and a shirt like ours! Then you can match us, too!"

"Um . . . yeah. I don't think I'd be so adorable in it."

"He'd also get beaten up by smelly boys," Maris said with a laugh.

Kalea arched her brow. "Really?"

"Probably." Hauk ruffled her hair. "And I'd be teased by your uncle, Fain, until I was forced to kill him."

"Oh. We can't have that. Never mind." She ran back to Lillya.

As he rose to his feet, Sumi tugged gently on his arm. "What's bothering you?"

"Besides the fact that I have to put the woman I love in a ring to fight for my worthless ass tomorrow?"

"Yeah. I can tell something else is on your mind."

Hauk hesitated before he answered. "One of our bases was attacked and destroyed."

Zarya, Desideria, and Shahara drew closer.

Maris joined them. "What happened?"

"League. What else? Kyr escaped and went after them." Just as Hauk started to tell Maris his family was downstairs, he felt a hush come over the room.

Looking toward the door, he saw Nyk with Madai, Safir, and two men he assumed must be Maris's father and the brother who was the heir to the Phrixian throne. Like Mari, they both had black hair and dark eyes.

For several seconds, no one moved or spoke as the emperor glared at his disinherited son. Not until Kalea whispered loudly to Hauk's grandmother. "Are they good men or bad men, Yaya?"

Nykyrian was the first to recover from the awkward silence. "Emperor Zatyr and Prince Zander wanted to meet the princess Safir and his brothers saved." He gestured to Hauk's grandmother first. "I present to Your Majesty and Highness the Ger Tarra of the Warring Blood Clan of Hauk, Corinne."

She rose and gave a slight bow. "It's an honor to meet your graces. I cannot thank you enough for coming to the aid of my grandson and his daughter."

Zatyr inclined his head to her. "The honor is ours, Ger Tarra."

Sumi picked up Kalea and brought her over to them.

Nykyrian indicated Hauk first. "And the Most Valorous, Dancer of the Warring Blood Clan of Hauk."

Hauk saluted them in turn. "Sire. Your Highness. I am forever in your debt for my daughter's life. It is a debt of blood I will forever honor."

They were both impressed that Hauk knew better than to thank them, since there was no word for that in Phrixian. To their people, everything was a matter of duty, honor, and blood debt.

Zatyr returned his salute. "It was our duty and honor to rectify the wrong done to your family by a member of ours. His behavior will not go unpunished, I assure you."

Inclining his head respectfully to the emperor, Hauk stepped back and placed his hand on Sumi's shoulder. "Allow me to present to you Her Royal Highness, Sumi of the Most Sovereign Blood Clan of eton Anatole, and our daughter, the Princess Kalea."

Sumi bowed low. "As Dancer said, Your Majesty, we are forever indebted to you and yours for your help in reclaiming our daughter."

Zatyr scowled. "What did you say?"

Sumi swallowed hard at his severe tone. Had she said something wrong? "We are forever indebted to you and yours."

He looked at Zander then Madai. "That is the voice, is it not?"

Before they could answer, Safir stepped forward to address her. "Highness? Are you the one who called my father about me?"

Sumi didn't know what to say. She glanced to Dancer to see what would be appropriate, but it was Maris who responded to them.

"She is, indeed."

Saf gaped at Maris. "You knew?"

He nodded. "It was also the first thing she said to me when I met her. She wanted to make sure you were freed."

All four of them went down on a knee to bow before Sumi, who panicked over that.

Maris placed his hand on Sumi's arm so that he could explain why they did such. "That is the greatest honor a Phrixian can bestow on another. And for them to do so before a woman is an extremely rare occurrence and distinction. What they do is a blood oath of service to you, and it acknowledges a family debt. It means that for the rest of your life, they will protect you and yours."

Sumi duplicated the gesture. "Majesty. Highnesses. You've already paid me back with interest." She tightened her hold on Kalea, who was watching them with wide eyes.

His expression stone, the emperor met her gaze. "I lost a son when he wasn't much older than your daughter, Highness. I had to stand back as my enemies took him from my home and do nothing to reclaim him."

He slid a furious glare to Maris, who was now every bit as pissed off. "When he returned years later, he wasn't the same child I had sent away. No longer obedient or respectful, he was angry and bitter. Filled with hatred for us all. And I was forced to lose him again, because of the choices he made against our culture and his family. There is no greater sadness than to say good-bye to a child, no matter the age. It is our honor to return your daughter to you before she was infected or corrupted by those who imprisoned her. It is our hope that she brings the same honor and pride to you that my Safir has brought to us. While all of my remaining sons are the best of our species, Safir has always shone above them. I would have been inconsolable had I lost him to such needless dishonor. And while you believe that the return of your daughter is equal to the sparing of my son, I respectfully disagree. All of Phrixus is in your debt for your service to my crown and our family." And with that, he rose and led his sons from the room.

Except for Safir, who remained. He drew Maris into a tight hug and said something in Phrixian to him.

Closing his eyes, Maris patted him on the back. "You were always your father's favorite."

"And you were always mine. I love you, big brother." Releasing Maris, Saf stepped back and turned to Ture. "I can't leave without seeing my favorite little nephew. How's it hanging, Big T?" He knelt down by Ture's side and peeked at the baby in Ture's lap. "And baby T . . . aren't you walking yet?"

Ture laughed. "He's still a few months away from that."

Saf tickled his nephew, who laughed in response. "Just wait, Terek, I'll have you cruising babes in no time."

Hauk snorted. "From what I hear, you need to cruise a few less."

Safir kissed Terek's head before he stood. "Just making up for lost time." He placed his uninjured arm over his chest and bowed to Sumi. "Thank you for what you did. Kyr would have killed me had you not called my father."

Sumi swallowed hard at the swell of emotions she felt

for Safir. He was a good man and she was glad to have helped him. "I just wish I could have called sooner."

Saf winked at her. "It's all good." He placed a hand on Kalea's head. "And you, little princess . . . returning you to your parents is my greatest accomplishment so far. I can't think of anything that will ever top this."

Frowning, Kalea reached out and touched his sling. "You have a boo-boo?"

"I do."

She leaned forward and kissed his arm. "Did I make it better?"

Saf laughed at her. "Yes, you did, princess." He bowed to her. "Thank you."

"Safir!"

He winced at his father's angry call before he glanced back to Maris.

Maris kissed his cheek. "You better go before he decides he likes Dray better."

Saf snorted. "I defy him to do that . . . especially after the way I kicked Dray's rank ass for what he did to you. Bastard's still limping from it. Trust me, he won't ever be after you again. I made sure of it." He hugged Maris. "Love you, Mare-Bear."

"Love you, too."

Saf inclined his head to them then left.

Hauk frowned at Maris. "I thought only Darling called you Mare-Bear."

Maris laughed. "What can I say? He taught Saf all kinds of bad habits."

Sumi set Kalea down so that she could return to playing. "In spite of what your father said, I can't imagine you angry and disrespectful, never mind bitter."

Maris passed a knowing look to Hauk. "You didn't meet me until better days. I'm not the same person I was when I was a commissioned officer in the Phrixian armada." He moved to take Ture's hand. "I like this Mari a lot better than that one. This model actually has a sense of humor and a most smashing wardrobe."

Ture cleared his throat.

Maris swung Ture's hand between them. "And the best hubby ever."

Sumi laughed. "Not that Ture isn't wonderful, but I think you'll find a room full of us who would argue for that title."

Desideria snorted. "You know what my mother always said? The first two years of marriage, you'll want to eat him up. After that, you'll wish you had."

They laughed.

Sumi looked at Shahara. "You agree?"

"At times, yes. Remember, I'm the one who lives with a mad scientist, who loves to experiment on things."

Zarya snorted. "Yes, but yours never wrapped himself up in explosives and threatened to blow up an entire city *and* his royal guard corps."

Hauk let out a low, teasing whistle. "And on that, I'm out. But before I go, I will say this. Yes, my brothers are extreme, but I like them that way. Besides, there aren't that many men in the universe who would kick down a League prison door, raid an assassin base camp, or start an intergalactic war to protect their spouses. Bat-shit crazy works for us."

Sumi wrinkled her nose at him. "And crazy looks good on you, baby."

"This is one of them times where they usually smooch and make noises," Lillya whispered loudly to Kalea.

Hauk groaned as he looked to Desideria, who was blushing profusely. "FYI, you and Cai *really* need to move your daughter's room farther down the hall."

"Apparently so. Gah, I'm going to kill my husband."

Zarya shifted Cezar in her lap. "Am I the only one who lives in stark-raving terror of the stories our children will one day tell about their parents?"

Hauk snorted. "Honestly? My fears are the stories about *them* that they won't dare allow us to know."

Hours later, Hauk lay naked in bed with Sumi in his arms. She'd fallen asleep on his chest. Her breath tickled his skin while he listened to her heart beating and fingered the small bruise on her arm from the shot Syn had given her. He'd tried to sleep, too, but that was an elusive bitch who had no use for him tonight.

In truth, he was afraid to close his eyes and lose his vigil. He had a bad feeling in his gut that nothing would shake. He had too much to lose now, and it was slowly making him crazy.

"El," he whispered. "Show me Kalea."

His monitor came on instantly to show her asleep in her bed in the next room. There were two Andarion guards stationed at the foot of her bed. They sat quietly playing a game of squerin. Meanwhile, two more were stationed outside her door, and another dozen patrolled his yard.

And still he was unsettled.

Sighing, he wrapped a strand of Sumi's pale hair around his finger and prayed for everything to work out tomorrow. For Syn's medicine to cure her, and for her to beat Dariana into the ground.

Actually, that wasn't true. He bore no ill will toward Dariana. Not really. He just wanted to be free of her treachery and schemes. Why she'd refused to move on and find another husband, he'd never understand.

But then, she hated him.

Shaking his head, he pushed Dariana out of his thoughts. He didn't want to dwell on that when he had such a beautiful woman on top of him. He lifted her hand to his lips and nibbled the soft skin on her palm. Nyk was right. She'd tamed the fury inside him that had driven him the whole of his life.

He had no desire to ever leave her arms. She and Kalea were an integral part of him now. The best part. Their smiles and love filled the ache that had been there for so long, he hadn't even paid attention to it anymore.

Sumi sighed in her sleep and rubbed her face against him. His body hardened instantly, causing him to smile. He should be well sated for at least a month or more, given how long they'd made love after dinner. But there was something about her that always left him hungry for her.

Closing his eyes, he tightened his arms around her and let the warmth of her silken body soothe him. Tomorrow would decide their fate.

Forever.

In that moment, he wanted to run with her. To leave behind everything and everyone. But that would put them in even more danger. They were at war with The League and Kyr. On Andaria, Sumi and Kalea were royalty. No one would dare touch them.

On any other planet, Sumi was a League fugitive with a death sentence, and Kalea was a weakness to be used against her. And while he'd fight to his last breath for them both, he knew he couldn't always be with them.

It has to be done.

He wanted to believe it would be fine. But deep in his gut that feeling of dread persisted.

Something was coming for them, and it would be lethal.

"How dare you!"

Darice didn't speak as his mother glared at him. He merely continued playing his game as if she wasn't there.

Until she snatched it from his hands and threw it on the ground. "I want you in the transport. Now!"

"No."

She backhanded him. "You will do as you're told!"

Darice wiped the blood from his lips before he stood

to glare at her. "I want no part of your schemes. You've lied to me, and you've hurt Dancer for too long. I will never again sleep under the same roof as you. Not until you make this right."

"You would side with a human-loving *giakon*?"

He slid his gaze to his mother's best friend, who stood silently, watching them. "Funny *you* should use that word to insult him."

His mother slapped him hard and shoved him back. "Careful what accusations fall from your lips, boy."

Curling his lip, Darice stiffened. "I'm not a boy anymore. I'm an adult. I can legally make my own choices."

"And I can disown you."

"Go ahead," he challenged her defiantly. "You might as well, since you can't use me to tie my uncle to you anymore. That is the only reason I was born, isn't it? And it's the only reason you're pregnant now."

Before she could answer, the door opened to admit his gre yaya.

She drew up short at the sight of her unexpected visitors. Her gaze went to Pera first and then to him and his mother. "Dariana . . . to what do I owe this honor?"

His mother turned her head to peer at his great-grandmother over her shoulder. "I came for my son. His place is with me and my family, not here with you."

She frowned at the sight of Darice's face. "You hit him?"

"He is my son. I'm allowed to discipline him when he needs it."

"And what has he done to warrant your wrath?"

Darice answered before his mother had the chance. "I've refused to leave with her."

"He chooses that deformed, hideous—"

Darice cut her off with a growl. "Dancer is a formidable warrior who has bled for me, and I will not have you dishonor him. *Ever* again."

"Agreed," his great-grandmother said. "He is my beloved grandson and when you speak of him, it will be with respect in your voice."

Dariana glared at them both. Then she turned back to Darice. "Fine. Stay here. But know that you will never again be welcomed into my home."

"I shall endeavor not to cry over *that* tragedy," he said sarcastically. "And I hope tomorrow that Sumi avenges Dancer, and you receive the full balance of the payback you've earned . . . Matarra."

By the look on her face, he knew she wanted to strike him again, but didn't dare do it in front of his father's grandmother. "You will regret this decision."

Darice scoffed. "The only thing I regret are all the times I let you use me to hurt my uncles."

She reached for his shoulder.

"Scar him in my home, Dariana, and Princess Sumi will be the least of your fears."

She turned on her heel and glared at his great-grandmother. "Tomorrow, after I beat that human whore into the ground, and remove her head from her shoulders, I assure you that all of you will regret this night. And this time, I won't simply reject Dancer's pledge. I will demand Restitution for what he's done, and turn your precious grandson into a granddaughter." She glared at Darice. "And you will spend the rest of your putrid life wishing you could take back your actions here."

CHAPTER 35

Hauk sat in Kalea's room, with his daughter in his lap, reading to her. He felt a sudden presence in the doorway. Looking up, his breath caught as he saw Sumi. He'd been banned from their room while his grandmother and Fadima had prepared her for the fight.

They had plaited her hair in true Andarion fashion and then coiled the pale, thin braids into an intricate style that wouldn't interfere with her peripheral vision. His grandmother had also commissioned for her a true Andarion fighting suit in the deep burgundy color of their family crest. The leather pants clung to her body and were tucked into a pair of buckled boots. Her cutaway suede coat fell to her ankles and exposed her holster. It was fastened diagonally with six buttons. Three burgundy leather stripes decorated the sleeves and matched the gloves that covered her hands. His family's Warsword was strapped across her back.

Best of all, his grandmother had painted her face not with the eton Anatole crest, but with theirs. His heart filled with pride at how good Andarion looked on her.

"You are exquisite, *mu tara*."

Kalea tilted her head back until she could see him. "Mommy looks like a fighting princess, Daddy."

"Your mother *is* a fighting princess. The best in the universe."

"Really?"

Hauk nodded as Sumi came forward and knelt on the floor beside them. "How do you feel?"

"Syn's a magician. I feel fine. Nothing hurts at all . . . except for having to leave the two of you."

"You're leaving?" Kalea's bottom lip quivered.

Hauk knew the feeling. He just wished he could do the same as their daughter.

Sumi brushed Kalea's hair back from her cheek and kissed it. "Just for a little while, sweetie. Your daddy will take good care of you, and I'll be back before you know."

"Okay."

Hauk took her hand and held it. "How can I let you do this?"

"We have no choice." She kissed him fiercely. "I won't be defeated. When this day ends, you will be mine. And no one will ever take you from me."

"I am already yours."

She kissed him again.

"Sumi?"

She pulled back at the sound of Nykyrian's voice. "I know. It's time."

Hauk had to force himself to stay in his chair and not go after them. This had to be done. He knew it. But every fiber of his being screamed out against letting her fight for him.

Don't get hurt. He could handle anything but losing her.

And still that bad feeling stayed in his gut. Holding Kalea tight, he prayed.

Sumi took a deep breath as Nykyrian, Fain, and Cairistiona led her into the arena. Fadima had gone over everything for her, a thousand times.

And still she felt unprepared for what was facing her.

There were three judges from the Andarion royal court to oversee the fight and to make sure the rules were followed. Dariana's family sat to the right of them. And sure enough, there were Dancer's parents with her people.

Her anger mounted that they would dare slight him so, but she forced it down. Something that was helped when she glanced to her side. Instead of being empty, it was filled with her new family. Kiara and Thia were next to Caillen, Desideria, and Chayden. Zarya and Ture were there, but Darling, Maris, Drake, and Ryn had stayed with Hauk so that they could try and keep him sane while she fought.

Shahara, Devyn, and Vik were seated in the front row while Syn walked in with her and her new adoptive family. After the injection he'd given her, he wanted to keep an eye on her vitals. Jayne had brought her husband, Hadrian, and their three children. Fadima and her sisters and grandmother took seats near Nykyrian's father, Nero, and Bastien.

"Sumi?"

She turned at the sound of Darice's voice. It was the first time she'd seen him since their return. "Hey, sweetie! What are you doing here?"

He lifted his chin. "I'm here to walk in with you . . . if you don't mind."

His loyalty touched her. "I would be honored, but I don't want to cause trouble between you and your mother."

"This is on my mother, Sumi. Not you. While I will always love her, I can't condone what she's done." He glanced to Fain. "We War Hauks must stand together, and since Dancer can't be here, I want to walk with you."

"Your uncle and father would be very proud of you. As am I." She hugged him against her.

A sharp whistle sounded, notifying them that it was time to begin.

Her family led her out to the center of the ring. Dariana, who strode into the arena like she owned it, walked behind her parents. She raked a sneer over Sumi's body that said she thought this match would be short and boring.

Sumi snorted at the arrogance. While royalty and family might terrify her, fighting didn't. Unlike Dariana, she'd cut her teeth on death matches a lot scarier than this. And with opponents who were much larger and far more skilled.

Bring it, bitch.

The head judge stood up to address them, while their families left their sides and took their seats. "Sumi of the Most Sovereign Blood Clan of eton Anatole has issued a challenge against Dariana of the Warring Blood Clan of Hauk, the daughter of the Rising House of Terisool, for the right to take over the pledge of Dancer of the Warring Blood Clan of Hauk. Is this correct, Princess?"

Sumi inclined her head to him. "It is."

"And do you accept the challenge and the outcome that the gods see fit?" he asked Dariana.

"I do."

"Then assume your positions and may the gods' will be done here today."

Sumi bowed to Dariana, who glared at Darice as Darice followed Fain from the arena and into the War Hauk section. She bowed to Sumi.

They approached the referee and covered their faces, then pulled their swords.

Dariana's eyes flared as she realized what was in Sumi's hands. "I will feast on your blood, human."

Sumi laughed. "Someone cue my fear pheromones."

The referee held his hand up then stepped back. "Begin!"

Dariana came at her with everything she had. Sumi met her strokes, but quickly realized one thing.

Andarion women were as strong as their men.

And Dariana hit like a sledgehammer.

"Hauk?"

He stopped rocking his sleeping daughter at the sound of Darling's voice in the doorway. "Yeah?"

"There's a Dr. Pera Duece here to see you. She said her father was the one who treated you at the hospital and she wants to check on you to see how you're doing."

Hauk frowned. "I thought that was tomorrow."

Darling shrugged. "Want me to tell her to go away? I can and will do that."

"Nah. It's fine." While he mostly saw the father, he'd been treated a few times by the daughter. She was a strange female, but he had no issue with her. Might as well get it over with.

He stood and placed Kalea in bed. "Will you watch her until I get back?" he asked Darling.

"Sure."

Hauk headed for the stairs. "El? Where's the doctor?"

"In your office, Hauk. Would you like me to have her move to another room?"

"It's fine." Yawning, he went in to find her reviewing his old trophies that lined the wall case.

Jerking around, she smiled at him. "Hope you don't mind my snooping. Are all these yours?"

"Most. So what can I do for you, Doctor?"

"I'm just here to do a quick health check for my dad. He's been worried about you." She pulled her bag from over her shoulder. "If you'll take a seat and remove your shirt, I'll be out of here in a few minutes."

"I thought your dad was coming tomorrow."

"Something came up. Since I was nearby, I told him I'd check in with you."

Hauk removed his shirt and took a seat while she pulled on a pair of exam gloves.

"So how have you been feeling? You look rather tired."

Because he had yet to sleep. But he didn't want to go into that with her. "Fine."

"Any pain?"

"Not really."

She moved to stand behind him. "That's a shame."

He frowned at her words. "Pardon?"

She answered by shooting him in the back with an injector.

Hauk cursed at the unexpected action, and tried to move away, but his head spun like crazy. One minute he was in the chair. The next, he was sprawling on the floor.

The doctor kicked him over. "I should have known better than to pay an assassin to kill you. If you want something done right, you have to do it yourself." She knelt by his side and shot him with something else while she covered his mouth with her hand. "Shh . . . just close your eyes and die like a good boy."

Sumi staggered back as Dariana shoved her whole weight against her sword. Her entire arm was numb from holding her ground. At this point, Sumi was short-swording and using her weapon more like a small staff. Which was working well since Dariana couldn't break through it to stab or cut her.

But it really wasn't helping Sumi to win the fight. How aggravating that Andarions didn't believe in a shield. They relied on their sword skills alone. And since the swords were shorter than human broadswords, yet longer than daggers, with large, ornate hilts, using them was more akin to axe fighting than actual sword fighting. It was a whole different style than anything Sumi had ever done, and it was using every muscle in her body to deflect and stay sharp.

Shrieking in frustration, Dariana finally made a strategic mistake. She lifted her sword to slice. Sumi twisted hers sideways so that when Dariana brought her blade down, it caught in the curved hilt of the Hauk Warsword. Faster than the Andarion could react, Sumi twisted Dariana's sword out of her hands and captured it.

She kicked Dariana's leg and knocked her down to one knee so that she could grab her throat and pin her.

Dariana tried to break free, but this was something Sumi had perfected in League training.

Sumi increased the pressure. "Yield!"

"Never!"

Sumi looked to the judges. "She's defeated. And while I'd hate to kill her and the child she carries, I leave that decision up to you."

The judges conferred for a few seconds before the head one spoke up. "She is defeated. Her claim on Dancer Hauk is cleared. The War Hauk heir is yours, Princess. The gods have ruled it so."

Sumi released Dariana, and saluted them before she twisted the sheath down to her side and placed the sword in it then returned it to rest on her back. Ecstatic beyond belief, she headed for Fain and Darice.

Darice's smile faded as he looked past her. Before she could turn, he jumped into the arena and shoved her back. The moment he did, a small knife buried itself into his shoulder.

"Darice!" Sumi grabbed him to her.

"No!" Dariana screamed as she realized she'd struck her son instead of Sumi.

Guards ran to arrest Dariana while Sumi lowered Darice to the ground. "Dare?"

He sucked his breath in sharply between his teeth. "How do you and Dancer stand it? This really hurts!"

She laughed as she realized it was just a flesh wound. While it wouldn't be comfortable, it wouldn't kill him. "You are ever my hero."

Syn ran over and quickly removed the knife so that he could stop the bleeding and seal it.

Dariana was shrieking in Andarion as royal guards removed her from the arena.

Sumi ignored her completely as she stayed focused on Darice. "I'm so sorry you were hurt."

"Better my shoulder than your throat." Biting his lip, he looked at Syn. "The scar won't be visible after it heals, will it?"

Syn rolled his eyes. "It'll barely be there. If anyone is close enough to you to see it, you better be pledged to them, kid."

Darice let out a relieved breath. "Thank the gods."

Sumi snorted. Andarions and their vanity.

As Syn finished tending Darice, his link buzzed. "Yeah?" The color faded from his face as he listened.

Dread tightened her stomach. By his expression, she knew it was bad. Had Kyr taken Kalea again? "What?"

His breathing ragged, Syn stared at her in disbelief. "Hauk's dead."

CHAPTER 36

Sumi's entire world came to an end with those two words. "Don't fuck with me, Syn. I mean it!"

By the look on his face, she knew he wasn't.

Her universe shattered as she struggled to breathe. Syn was calling orders to others that she couldn't understand. Not while her mind tried to get some kind of handle on what was happening. On how it'd happened.

Dancer couldn't be dead. He couldn't.

Not her huge, strong Andarion. It was a mistake. It had to be.

Syn and Nykyrian rushed for the doors. She ran after them. Nykyrian grabbed an airbike and waited for her to join him. She slung her leg over the back and put her arms around his waist. He flew them through the streets, back to Dancer's house, at a speed that was illegal on every known world. And still she couldn't focus.

Over and over, she saw Dancer in her mind. His large, intrepid nature that fought on, no matter what was thrown at him. He couldn't go down. Dancer wouldn't let himself. Not while he had Kalea to protect.

He's just wounded. That was it. Syn was mistaken. He had to be. There was no way her Andarion Tactical Assault Monkey would be dead. He was too strong for that.

Too intelligent.

As soon as they were parked, she ran from the bike into the house. She didn't have to ask Eleron where Dancer was. Darling's angry voice carried plainly through the house. She followed the shouts to the office, where Darling, Maris, Ryn, and Drake were gathered around Dancer, who lay shirtless on the floor.

"God damn you, Hauk!" Darling snarled as he attempted chest compressions on him. "You better breathe, you stubborn Andarion bastard! Don't you do this to me! *Get up!*"

Unable to cope with it, she froze in the doorway, hugging the door frame. Syn ran past her to kneel on the other side of Dancer's body, while Nykyrian brushed past her. Dancer was so pale. His eyes were half open and he wasn't breathing.

Tears filled her eyes and choked her. He really was dead.

How?

"What happened?" Syn snarled to Darling.

"I don't know. A fucking doctor came in. Said she wanted to check his injuries. I was watching Kalea for Hauk when Eleron told me his vitals were down. I handed her off to Nero and ran in here, and found him on the floor with no sign of the doctor. This is why I fucking hate medics! You can't trust *any* of them! I swear when I find that bitch, I'm going to blow her entire family into the upper stratosphere!"

As the others began arriving to witness the horror, Nykyrian pulled Darling away while he continued to snarl in anger and make more threats. Then Nyk handed the emperor off to Maris. He met her gaze.

Sumi couldn't move. She was frozen by grief and terror. Frozen by the agonizing fear of losing Dancer.

Forever.

You can't leave me. . . .

Like Darling, she wanted to curse everyone. She wanted to spill the guts of anyone who'd ever hurt or insulted Dancer.

Instead, she slowly approached him and knelt so that she could press her cheek to his. Brushing her hand along the stubble, she winced at how cold his skin was already. She buried her hands in his braids. "Don't leave me, Dancer," she whispered in his ear. "I need you here. Kalea needs you. Please don't break our hearts. You promised me you wouldn't leave me alone, again."

"Pull her back."

She started to protest until she realized Syn had pulled a defibrillator from his pack. Without protest, she allowed Fain to hold her while Syn worked on Dancer. Fain wrapped his arms around her and rocked her. He watched with a stoicism the bright tears in his eyes belied.

Silent tears fell down her own cheeks as she prayed and waited.

Nothing worked.

"Damn you, you fat, fucking bastard!" Syn shouted before he slammed his fists down on Dancer, in the center of his chest. "Get up!"

Dancer sucked his breath in sharply, then coughed. He glared at Syn. "What the hell are you doing? Damn it, stop hitting me! Gah, did you run over me or something?"

Sobbing, Sumi broke away from Fain and threw herself on top of Dancer. She rained kisses all over his face. "Don't you *ever* die on me again!"

"O . . . kay." Then he stiffened and groaned in pain. "Where's that bitch," he growled.

Pulling back slightly, Sumi frowned down at him. "Who?"

"Pera Duece."

"Who?" she repeated.

"My mother's girlfriend."

Every pair of eyes in the room went to the doorway, where Darice stood, watching them.

Dancer pushed himself up, even while Syn was trying to hold him down. "Stop!" he snapped at Syn, slapping at his hands.

The look on Syn's face said he was one heartbeat away from punching Dancer. "Three minutes ago, you were completely dead. You're the one who needs to stop. Don't make me slap you, 'cause I will!"

Dancer glared at him. "I'd like to see you try."

"How about I help him, then?" Nykyrian asked drily.

Dancer nodded slowly as he lay back down and allowed Syn to return to scanning his body. "Floor's looking mighty sweet." He glanced back to his nephew. "What were you saying about your mother?"

Looking away, Darice rubbed gently at his wounded shoulder. "She and Pera have been lovers since before she married my father."

Hauk was sure the stern scowl on Fain's face matched his as he met his brother's gaze. "Did you know this?"

Fain shook his head. "I don't think anyone did."

Hauk's frown deepened as he remembered what his brain had been trying to tell him on Oksana, outside of Aksel's base. It was a snatch of a childhood memory when he'd walked into Keris's house for a practice climbing session. Dariana and Pera had been in the living room, and they'd jumped apart guiltily, before Dariana had taken his head off over not knocking before he entered her home. Her extreme anger over it and the backhand she'd given him had been completely unwarranted.

Unless he'd walked in on them . . .

Darice kept rubbing his shoulder. "They made sure to keep a lid on it, because they knew what would happen to them if anyone ever found out. But I think my father knew. I'm pretty sure it's why he hated Pera, and went off into a rage every time he saw her."

And Keris had beaten her right before his death . . .

A bad, bad feeling went through Hauk. "How do you know this?" he asked Darice.

"I've suspected things for a long time. I knew Pera stayed over . . . a lot, especially at night. But I didn't know how far it went, not until you came back with Sumi. My mother has no idea how much her voice carries when she's angry. Nor how verbose she is when she rants."

Fain sighed heavily. "Is that why you went to your great-grandmother's to stay?"

Darice nodded. "And it's why I refused to sit with her family today." His lips trembled. "They killed my father . . . if he is my father."

"He's your father," Fain chided. "Your DNA was tested."

Shaking his head, Darice scoffed bitterly. "Pera's a doctor. She's . . ." His voice broke off before he continued. "That baby my mother's pregnant with isn't a War Hauk. Keris's sperm didn't take with it, so Pera used someone else's, and then fabricated the DNA results to keep my mother from having to marry another male, who would live in her home and find out about them. I think they might have done the same with me."

"Sweetie," Sumi said gently. "You look just like your uncles. You *are* a War Hauk."

"Maybe . . . but Pera and my mother have been scheming for years to shield my mother from having to sleep with a male. It's why Pera gave my mother drugs to keep Keris under control, and why my mother has never honored her pledge to Dancer."

Hauk met Sumi's gaze. "I'm hoping you won your match."

She gaped in mock anger. "You didn't just ask me that, did you? As if."

"Good." In spite of Syn's protests, Hauk rose to his feet. The room swam around him and for a minute, he thought he'd be sick. But he was through with these games.

Syn, Fain, Nyk, Ryn, Drake, Maris, and Darling formed a wall between him and the door.

Hauk glared at his family. "I'm ending this. Now."

"No," Fain said sternly. "You're going to let Syn treat you before you fall over."

Hauk shook his head. "This is my family they've threatened."

"And it's my brothers they abused. My brother they killed. I'm not letting them kill you, too."

"Dancer?" Sumi placed her right hand on his arm then cupped his face with her left. She forced him to look at her. "Remember what I told you? You are my life. I've already seen you dead once today. Don't make me do that again."

The tears in her eyes and voice weakened his resolve. And when one fell down her cheek, he was completely undone by it.

Nodding, he brushed her tear away. "For you, *mu tara*. I will be a good boy." He dipped his head down to whisper in her ear. "But only if you reward me for it later."

Sumi pressed her cheek to his and held him there as she savored the warmth of his body. Choking on a sob, she agreed. "Let Syn clear you of whatever she did to you. Vengeance can wait."

"Okay."

"Are we better now?" Syn asked sarcastically. "Can I finally take you to the hospital and flush the poison out before you collapse again?"

Dancer made a mocking face at him. "Next time, I'm going to collapse my fat ass on top of *you*."

Sumi rolled her eyes. "I wish all of you would stop saying that. Yes, Dancer's big as a house, but there's not a bit of fat on his body. And you all know it."

Holding her hand to his heart, Dancer rubbed noses

with her. "My fierce *mia*. Always defending me, even against myself."

She gave him a light kiss and stepped back as a medic team brought in a stretcher. "I'll see you at the hospital."

He inclined his head before he lay down and allowed Syn to begin treating him again. Even though the two of them slapped at each other like children, and argued the whole time.

Rolling her eyes at them, Sumi stepped to Darice and gave him a hug. "Don't frown so, sweetie. You *are* a War Hauk, and you are loved by both your uncles, and by me. And by your cousin."

He glanced up at her. "Is she here?"

She nodded. "Would you like to meet her?"

A slow smile broke across his face. "Very much."

Taking his hand, she led him upstairs to Kalea's room, where Nero sat, playing with her on the floor, under the watch of two guards.

"Mommy!" Kalea came running and launched herself into Sumi's arms. "You're back!"

She held her daughter tight. "I told you I would be."

"Did you win?"

"Of course I did." With Kalea on her hip, she turned toward Darice. "And this is another of your cousins. Darice Hauk. Dare, meet Kalea."

"Oh yaa!" she breathed happily, clapping. "Finally a cousin with my name." She launched herself at Darice with enough force that he staggered back.

"Wow, you're strong, Kalea."

She grinned at him as she wrapped her arms around his neck. "Just like my daddy, but not so big yet." Screwing her face up, she fisted her hands in his braided hair. "You got hair like my daddy, but not all of it." She touched his chin where he had a little bit of stubble. "Can you grow hair there, too? Or are you a girl-boy?"

Darice wasn't sure how to answer.

Sumi laughed at his confusion. "Darice is a male, and he's just at the age where his facial hair is starting to grow. In time, he'll be able to have a moustache and goatee like Daddy."

"Oh." Her eyes widened as she squealed in delight. Then she squeezed him tight and laid her head on his shoulder. "I love you, Darice, even if you don't have chin hair yet!"

If Sumi lived a thousand years, she would never forget the shocked, tender look on his face as he held Kalea. And she knew Kalea would have another very fierce protector in her cousin.

She met Nero's speculative gaze. "You're being re-markably quiet."

"Not sure what to say, other than yes, I'll watch her and make sure nothing happens while you're gone."

A chill went down her spine. "You shouldn't pry into people's thoughts, Nero."

"You shouldn't have thoughts around me you don't want me to know about."

"What thoughts?" Darice asked.

"None whatsoever." Nero went to take Kalea, but Darice kept her in his arms. He smiled at Darice. "Why don't I take the two of you to the hospital to be with Hauk? Knowing Syn, he won't release him until tomorrow. He'll want to run every test known to make sure he's fine." He paused to meet Sumi's gaze. "See you there in a few hours?"

She nodded. "Thank you."

"No problem."

After he left with the kids and guards, Sumi went to their bedroom to dig out their backpacks that someone had delivered after their return from Oksana. No one had bothered to unpack them. She paused as she found the violin case in Hauk's pack.

A smile tugged at the edges of her lips as she remembered how beautifully Dancer played. When this was over, she was going to make him serenade her.

And that steeled the determination in her to see this to the end, and to make sure no one ever threatened him again.

She rooted around until she located her League gear. It was time for her to go to work.

Sumi slowed as she felt someone following her. Turning into an alley, she fell into the shadows and waited.

Once the tall male walked past her corner, she grabbed him. She started to punch him then recognized the familiar form. "Bastien? What are you doing here?"

He offered her an unrepentant grin. "I figured you could use the backup."

"I'm an assassin. I work best alone."

"Even Nemesis has backup for these kinds of missions."

She glanced down to his stomach where he'd been marked a Ravin by The League. "I thought you hated the killing business."

"This isn't business. It's personal, and *that* I understand better than anyone."

She supposed he did. "You're planning to go after the one who killed your family?"

He nodded. "Once you're squared away, and I don't have to worry about the debt I owe the two of you. Hell, yes."

"You don't owe us anything."

"I disagree, and Hauk would never forgive me if I let something happen to you. Besides, I don't want someone who's done so much for me to lose what he loves most. So let's get this done."

She smiled at him and the kindness he denied having. "You're a good man, Bas."

"Not really. I just strive to not be a bad one . . . or on most days, a total dick."

Unsure what to say, she started back down the street to the apartment building she'd been headed for. Like her, Bastien wore a cowled coat with the hood up, concealing his face. Luckily, they were both tall for humans and dressed in Andarion clothing. As such, even though it was the middle of the afternoon, the Andarions on the street ignored them.

That was the first law of assassin training—to blend and not stand out.

Since the apartment lobby was guarded by private security, Sumi headed to the back of the building. With a link in her ear that kept her in contact with Bastien, she handed him her coat and then scaled the side of the building to reach the apartment that housed her target.

Sumi jimmied the electronic lock, deactivated the alarm, and slid herself into the back bedroom. In the late-afternoon shadows, she took a moment to get her bearings.

Pera was in the living room, on a call. "Listen to me. It's going to be all right. Don't panic and don't say anything. All they know is that you were so upset at having lost the bastard's pledge, that you overreacted. Keep telling them that. You're pregnant and your hormones are all over the place. They will believe you. I'll take care of everything else. Just breathe and stay calm." She hung up as Sumi skirted past her, unseen.

She didn't bother to decloak until she had Pera's link in her hand and the path to the door blocked. A strange calm permeated her as she watched the female who had planted the tracker in Dancer's back and set loose the assassins on him.

That knowledge was what had led Sumi here.

Once she'd had Pera's name and basic information from Darice, everything else had been easy to find in The

League database that she'd hacked. The contracts Pera had placed for Dancer's life. The deal she'd made with Kyr against the Hauks. And the one contract Sumi was sure no one knew about.

"Does Dariana know you put out a hit for her son?"

Gasping, Pera turned around and pinned her with a vicious glare. "I don't know what you're talking about, *human*."

"That would be 'agent' to you, bitch. Bet you never dreamed Kyr would want Dancer brought in for interrogation rather than death, huh?" Sumi moved closer to her. "That is why you went to The League before you paid for the private contracts, is it not?"

"I don't know what you're talking about."

Sumi snorted. "Don't worry. I'm not wired. I'm not recording this, in any way. I don't want witnesses, any more than you do."

"And why is that?"

"Because I'm here to kill you."

Now it was Pera's turn to laugh. "*You*? You're a human. What are you going to do? Make me choke to death on my own laughter?"

Sumi tsked at her disdain. "Had you been at the match today, instead of at Dancer's house trying to kill him, you'd have seen exactly what I plan to do to you."

Again, Pera scoffed. "You didn't do anything. You spared Dariana."

"For Darice only. I didn't want to kill his mother in front of him. But it's just you and me, now. And there're only two ways out of here. The window behind you and the door behind me." Sumi glanced meaningfully at the glass. "You might survive the window."

Pera held her arms out. "I'm completely defenseless. You're really going to kill me?"

Sumi's gaze went to the computer screen where Pera had been working. "You were about to post payment on a contract for Darice's life to have him brutally slaughtered. He's fourteen. A child. And you went after my male and attacked while his back was turned. What do you think?"

"I think you're human and weak."

"And you would be mistaken about both." Sumi pulled out her blaster and shot her. The blast went straight into the image and struck the wall behind her.

Shit! It was a hologram.

Furious, Sumi glanced around, trying to locate her target. "Pera!"

She heard a sharp click behind her. Turning, she dropped to the floor at the same time a blast of color went past her face, narrowly missing it.

Pera headed for the door. Sumi dove at her, knocking her into the wall. Backhanding her, Pera tried to kick her off. But Sumi returned the strike with a punch of her own. She grabbed Pera and fell to the floor, rolled with her and kicked her into the door frame.

When Pera moved to shoot her, Sumi beat her to it. This time, it wasn't a hologram. Cursing, Pera fell and tried to crawl away before she collapsed on the floor.

Careful to keep her blaster on Pera in case it was a trick, Sumi felt for her pulse.

There wasn't one.

She took another shot, just to make sure.

Once she knew for certain that Pera would never threaten anyone she loved again, Sumi went to the female's computer to cancel the contracts on Darice and Dancer.

Just as she sat down, she felt a whisper of wind. Jerking out her blaster, she aimed at the shadow that hadn't been there before. She started to fire, then recognized the tall, dark form that was barely discernable in the darkness.

It was Nykyrian.

She lowered her weapon as he gave her a respectful half smile.

He walked over to Pera's body. "Nice work."

"You, too."

He snorted as he double-checked Pera's vitals. "I should have known when you didn't get into the ambulance where you were headed."

She finished canceling the contracts, then pulled the hard drive. "No one threatens my family."

"Hence, why I'm here."

She heard sirens approaching. "Guess we weren't that quiet."

"I'll make sure the authorities know that it was self-defense. No one will question it." He jerked his chin to the HD in her hands. "What's that?"

Sumi gave it to him. "She had a contract she was posting on Darice. I figured there might be other incriminating things on here Syn can pull."

Nykyrian frowned. "Why would she put a hit on Darice?"

"I'm thinking he either knows more than he's told us, or she thought he knew more."

"I've never been able to stomach anyone who would go after a kid." Nykyrian slid the HD into his pocket. "How are you doing?"

"Been a heck of a day."

He hugged her with one arm. "That it has, *kisa*. That it has." He glanced down to Pera. "But how are you *feeling*?"

She considered what he was really asking her. "Normally, I'd be sick to my stomach. However, this time, I'm strangely okay about it."

With a knowing glint in his eyes, he nodded. "Ready to go check on Hauk?"

"That I am."

He took her out the way she'd entered, through the bedroom window.

Bastien was still waiting for her on the street. Along with Darling and Jayne.

He winked at her. "When I heard shots, I started to help, but saw the big guy here and decided the best place for me was making sure no one disturbed you two. Then the next thing I know, these two came up out of the shadows at me."

Darling shrugged. "Should have known Nyk would leave us so that he could have all the fun."

Hand on hip, Jayne nodded in agreement. "He's bad that way."

"Don't get all pouty with me." Nykyrian pointed to Sumi. "She beat me to the punch."

"Well, that's just not right," Jayne groused. She narrowed an irritated smirk at Sumi. "What? You think you're sleeping with Hauk, or something? You have all the rights to kill the person who killed him? Gah, the nerve of some bitches."

Sumi laughed at her teasing.

Maris tsked at her as he came out of the shadows behind them. "Jaynie . . . jealousy does not look good on you. It makes your butt look even fatter than your head."

Gasping, she lunged playfully at Maris. "I don't want to hear that from you! Do you even own a mirror at home? I bet you've put on twenty-five pounds since you've been with Ture . . . at least!"

Horrified over her words, Maris grabbed at his rear and turned his back to Darling. "Tell me the truth. *Is* my butt fat?"

Darling snorted. "I'm not looking at your ass, Mari. I don't want to go blind. But so long as Ture's happy, who cares what I think?"

Sumi shook her head at their good-natured barbs. She'd always wondered what it would be like to have lifelong friends, and Dancer was lucky to have all of them. No wonder he was so devoted to his family.

She looked over at Bastian and Nykyrian.

Now that they were side by side, she saw the family resemblance. Dancer had told her that Bastien's mother was the youngest sister of Nykyrian's father. And it was her death, along with the rest of his family's, that Bastien had vowed to avenge.

He thought to do it alone. But as she looked at the group who had shown up here to go after the female who'd threatened their brother, she somehow doubted that would happen. The one thing about The Sentella . . . they were a family, first and foremost.

And they always took care of their own.

Darling tapped the link in his ear to turn it on. "Yeah?" Cringing, he pulled it out and held it for all of them to hear Syn's ranting shout on the other end.

"So I see how it is. The lot of you go off, leave me with the big baby to tend, and hunt down the bitch without me. Thanks a lot, guys. Tell Nyk to pick up his link!"

Rubbing at his ear, Darling grimaced. "I think somebody wanted to come with us."

Nykyrian took the link and cut the transmission.

"Ooo," Darling said with a hiss. "Somebody's gonna get it later for that."

"Yeah," Jayne said, slinging her arm over his shoulders. "*You* are. It's your link."

Darling cursed. "Great. Just great."

"C'mon." Nykyrian jerked his chin toward the airbike he'd ridden. "Let's go help Syn hold the big baby down for treatment."

"Um, yeah," Darling said. "I—I got a migraine. I can't do Andarion babysitting right now. I'm still in therapy and having vicious flashbacks from the last time I tried." He looked up at the sky. "Why, Lord? Why? I'm a new father. I need to live, and raise my son!"

Jayne grabbed a handful of his suit and hauled him after her. "Don't worry, Darling. We have a secret weapon now that doesn't explode."

"And that is?"

She glanced back, over her shoulder. "Sumi. She's able to bring down a thundering TAM with nothing more than a quirked eyebrow."

Darling grinned. "Oh yeah, thank the gods, we now have the power." He let out an evil laugh. "Let's go make the most of it. Thinking I have payback to make."

Sumi paused just outside the doorway. Her heart hammering, she looked into the hospital room where Dancer sat in bed with Kalea snuggled against his chest while she read to him. Of course, she was too young to actually read, so she was making up stories for the pictures.

"And see this one here is the sweet kitty, Daddy. And he's saying that he don't want to go to bed. He's not tired. Not even a little."

"But what if it's past his bedtime?" Dancer asked with a smile.

"You're not listening, Daddy. See, little baby kittens know when they need sleep and when they don't."

Sumi smiled. "Luckily, it's not bedtime for little baby kittens."

"Mommy!" Kalea sat up and smiled. Then she stood on the bed and launched herself.

Gasping, Sumi caught her. "Careful, sweetie! You could get hurt."

"Sorry, Mommy."

Sumi sat down on the bed and took Dancer's hand. "Syn said that he thinks he got everything out?"

Dancer nodded. "He's paranoid, so I'm here until morning." He released a highly irritated breath. "I can't stand this crap. I'd rather be beat than locked in a hospital."

She fingered one of the braids at his temple. "I know, baby. But remember, if you're a good boy . . ."

He laughed at her promise. "I'm being *very* good. I only hit Syn once." Sobering, he brushed a portion of her face paint off and scowled at the bruise he uncovered. "That wasn't there earlier. What did you do?"

She glanced about innocently. "How do you mean?"

His eyes darkened with anger. "Someone hit you. Who?"

Kalea gasped. "Mommy got a boo-boo!"

Sumi rubbed at the tender bruise Pera had given her. She met Dancer's gaze. "It's fine. I just went and made sure you were safe."

"Pera?"

She nodded.

Hauk was stunned. He'd expected one of his friends to take care of her. But he should have known it would be his little mouse who did it. "You could have been hurt."

There was no denying the ferocity in her gaze, or the sincerity. "No one comes after what I love."

He reached out and touched Kalea's head, then Sumi's cheek. "I know the feeling. At least tell me you didn't go alone."

"I tried," she said with a laugh. "But the number of beings wanting a piece of her just kept growing and growing. It was the weirdest thing, honey."

He smiled. "Yeah. They're like space barnacles that way. No matter how hard you try, you just can't avoid them or scrape them off once they've latched onto your ass."

"See," Jayne said from the doorway. "I told you guys. He's totally whipped."

Hauk glanced past Sumi to see Jayne, Syn, Darling, Maris, Fain, Nyk, Nero, Bastien, and Caillen outside, laughing at him. He ran his finger along Sumi's jawbone. "Not whipped, Jayne. Tamed."

Crossing her arms over her chest, she led the others into his room. "Is there a difference?"

"Yeah, a big one. Whipped means I'm broken." He stared into Sumi's eyes as he considered everything she'd brought into his world. Everything she'd given him that he never had before, including a beautiful daughter he still needed to kill Nykyrian over. "But for the first time in my life, I feel whole."

More than that, he *was* finally whole. And best of all, he was finally accepted.

So no, he wasn't whipped. He'd been tamed by a fearless little mouse who had boldly stood up to the beast inside him, and found the heart that no one else had ever claimed.

The heart that no one else would ever own.

For the first time ever, the War Hauk was at peace.

But he would always be ready to war anytime, anywhere against anyone who came for, or at, his family.

EPILOGUE

Sumi cringed at the sight of herself in her wedding "dress." It was more like see-through wedding tissue paper. Gah, Fain hadn't been joking when he'd told her what Andarions wore for their unification ceremonies.

She covered her breasts with her hands and wished herself on another planet.

"I know," Kiara said with a laugh as she finished styling Sumi's hair. "I felt the same way when I went through my formal ceremony with Nykyrian . . . and given the brevity of the costumes I've had to wear onstage for dance performances, it takes a lot to make me blush."

Sumi could just imagine. She met Kiara's gaze in the mirror. "I can't go out there like this. I think I'll die of embarrassment on the spot."

"Yes, you can. Just think about Hauk and ignore everyone else."

Much easier said than done.

But if the red material were thicker, it would have been a beautiful gown. The halter neck fastened to a choker made of rows of a rare red Andarion gem she'd never heard of before. The sheer material clung to her body and another piece fell from the back of the choker and was attached to matching bands on her wrists. The eton Anatole crest was embroidered in a thin, fine gold thread through the gauzy red material.

With the help of Dancer's grandmother, Thia, and Cairistiona, Kiara had twined her braids into an intricate upswept hairdo that cascaded around a gold crown. And they'd painted the royal crest on her face.

They stepped back, pleased with their work.

Sumi, not so much. "I still feel like I need a blanket wrapped around me."

Cairistiona patted her on the arm. "As Kiara said, think only of the male you love and the fact that from this day forward, you two will always belong to each other. Forget everyone else in the room. This is between the two of you and it is sacred."

Sumi saw the sadness in her eyes as she spoke. Poor Cairistiona that she'd never been allowed to marry the one man she loved. While her heart would always belong to Nykyrian's father, her life and service would be forever tied to the Andarion nation.

Reaching out, she hugged the queen. "Thank you. For everything."

Cairistiona smiled. "It is my pleasure. I owe your male much for protecting both my sons. There is nothing I wouldn't do for him or you. And know that we'll guard and spoil Kalea blind until the morning, when you two emerge."

Laughing, she released her. "I know you will." Kalea was already looking forward to spending the night in a real palace as a real princess. She'd been telling everyone about it for days.

A light knock sounded on the door.

At the queen's nod, a guard opened it to admit Dancer's mother. Her stern features softened as she saw Sumi. While she still wasn't warm, she'd become much nicer to them both after she'd learned the truth about Dariana and her marriage with Keris.

And once she'd faced the fact that Dancer hadn't cut the rope that killed his brother. Not that it would have mattered. The drugs Pera had given Keris to take on Dancer's Endurance had been laced with a slow-acting poison that would have killed him before he returned with Dancer, anyway.

It was why Dariana had cremated the body and told them that Dancer had left Keris in the desert.

Guilt-ridden over how she'd treated Dancer, his mother had even testified against Dariana, during her trial and sentencing.

Clearing her throat, Endine stopped by Sumi's side and handed her a small box. "This is for you to give to Dancer tonight."

Sumi frowned as she took it from her hands and opened it to find a signet ring that bore the War Hauk crest.

"It is the ring that belonged to the first Dancer of the Warring Blood Clan of Hauk. And it is the wedding band that has been worn by the father of the direct line ever since. Ferral's time has passed and now the lineage and title will be carried by our youngest son and you . . . and by your children until they each marry. Then it is to go to the one who carries our title forward."

Sumi was confused. "I thought this wasn't conferred until the birth of our first child."

Endine squeezed her hand. "And it is so. For the two children you and Dancer already have that you plan to share lineage with, and for the one he just told me about that is to be born to you a few months hence."

Heat scalded her cheeks as his mother announced what they'd been waiting to tell the others until after their wedding.

Thia smiled knowingly and mouthed the words *fertile turtles* at her.

"Thank you, Ger Tarra."

"Matarra," Endine corrected. She placed a kiss on each of Sumi's cheeks. "It is my honor and privilege to welcome you to our lineage." Stepping back, she inclined her head respectfully to her mother-in-law and Cairistiona before she took her leave.

Kiara took the ring and slid it onto Sumi's thumb. "You give this to him when the two of you are alone."

"Thank you." Grateful for all of them, Sumi took a deep breath. "Okay. Let's do this. I'm almost ready to be naked in public."

"Just think of Hauk," Kiara said with a wink.

Fighting the urge to cover herself with her hands, she followed after them.

They led her out in a small procession and left her to stand before the decorated altar of the temple Dancer had been attending services in since his birth. It was here that he'd been first baptized and named as an infant. Here, he'd said good-bye to his family members who'd passed, and here Dariana had humiliated him every year since he was eighteen.

That thought brought a lump to her throat that tightened as she saw Dancer entering from the door to her left. His incredible body was bare except for an ornate burgundy loincloth. Avoiding her gaze, he moved to kneel on the gold cushion by her side.

It was only then that the full cruelty of Dariana's actions against him struck her.

The temple was filled with his family. And just as Fain had said, their disdain for his scars was plainly evident. Not even the priest would look at him.

His head held high, Dancer kept his gaze on the floor. But even so, she saw the pain and shame he felt at being so exposed before them all.

The priest cleared his throat. "Sumi of the Most Sovereign Blood Clan of eton Anatole, you have come before this altar and our gods to declare your allegiance to Dancer of the Warring Blood Clan of Hauk. To combine your two bloodlines and lineages into one. This is the most sacred action any Andarion can make and it is not one to be lightly undertaken. From this day forward, you will be joined and loyal to one another above all others. Do you both understand the solemnity of this event?"

"I do," Sumi said.

The priest looked to Dancer.

"I do."

Nodding, the priest moved to stand before Sumi. "Now, before these witnesses and our gods, have you, during your pledge time, allowed your body in any way to be tainted by the lineage of any male, other than your pledged?"

"No. I haven't."

The priest inclined his head in approval. "You understand that this disclosure is sacred, and to lie will endanger your immortal soul and result in your death?"

"I do, and I swear on my immortal soul that no male, save Dancer of the Warring Blood Clan of Hauk, has touched me. The gods themselves know this to be true."

He turned to Dancer. "And you, Dancer of the Warring Blood Clan of Hauk, have you violated your pledge oath to your lady and left any of your lineage with any other female?"

"No, Reverend Father, I have not."

"Have you kissed, or carnally touched, any female other than your pledged?"

"No."

The priest narrowed his eyes accusingly on Dancer. "You understand that this disclosure is sacred, and to lie will endanger your immortal soul and result in your death?"

"I do, Reverend Father."

She expected him to move on with the ceremony, but instead, the priest lifted Dancer's chin and forced him to meet his gaze. "You are stralen, and the last time you were here, you were not. So again, I ask you for the truth, under grave penalty. Have you lain with any female other than your pledged?"

Why was he badgering Dancer so? The priest was actually beginning to piss her off.

"I have been with no other female, Reverend Father. Princess Sumi is the lady of my heart and universe. She is the one I am stralen for, and she knows this."

The priest turned back to her. "And do you, Princess Sumi of the Most Sovereign Blood Clan of eton Anatole, accept the pledge and troth of Dancer of the Warring Blood Clan of Hauk? Are you willing to bind your sacred and royal lineage to his?"

For the first time, she saw real fear in Dancer's gaze as he returned to staring at the floor as if reliving every time Dariana had slashed open his back and left him here to bleed. How could he think for one instant that she would deny him?

Damn you, Dariana.

Sumi walked around his muscled body and paused in front of him. Smiling, she tilted his chin until he met her gaze. "You are the most handsome male I have ever seen, and there is no other I would ever accept."

Closing his eyes, he cupped her hand in his and held it to his cheek.

She moved to kneel on the cushion next to his while the priest blessed a long, silken cord that was made of burgundy and red braids that symbolized the joining of their two families.

He knotted one end around Dancer's wrist and then the other to hers. "Here, before these witnesses and members of your families, you have publicly declared your intention to combine your lineages. The gods are pleased, and so we will leave you to consummate your intentions."

His eyes filled with love, Dancer stood first and helped her to her feet. Side by side, they walked the path to the bedchamber that was behind the altar, that had been decorated for their unification.

As soon as the doors were closed, Dancer pulled her against his chest and held her tight. "I never thought I'd actually see the inside of this room."

She tsked at him. "You really looked like you thought I was going to deny you."

"I had a moment."

"And now?"

He led her to the bed. "Now, I want to finish this and claim you as mine. Forever."

Biting her lip, she followed his direction. Kneeling on the bed, they faced each other.

"Sumi, of the Most Sovereign Blood Clan of eton Anatole, will you grant me the honor of kissing your lips?"

"I will." She smiled up at him. "Dancer of the Warring Blood Clan of Hauk, will you grant me the honor of kissing yours?"

"Absolutely." He dipped his head to tease her mouth with his, taking care to touch no other part of her body. "And will you grant me the honor of seeing your unadorned beauty?"

She knew this was serious, but she couldn't help teasing him. "Uh, yeah. Pretty sure you and everyone in that temple have already done so."

Laughing, he bit his lip. "Is that a yes?"

"Yes."

Slowly, he removed her gown until she was exposed to him.

"May I have the honor of seeing yours?"

He nodded.

As she removed his loincloth, she couldn't resist copping a small feel.

He sucked his breath in sharply. "You're getting ahead of the ceremony."

"Sorry."

Hauk laughed at the unrepentant light in her eyes. "May I have the honor of touching you?"

"I am all yours, baby."

He cupped her breasts in his hands before he trailed one hand down to gently explore the part of her he was dying for.

Sumi shivered as he carefully dipped each of his fingers inside her. "And may I have the honor of touching you?"

His eyes glowing a brighter shade of red, he nodded.

Licking her lips, she slowly stroked him until he was primed for consummating the rest of their union.

His breathing ragged, he stared intently at her. "Do you grant me the honor of entering your body and fathering your progeny?"

She rubbed her nose against his. "Haven't you already done that, too?"

"You are in a mood." He nibbled her chin. "And you have to grant me permission or I can't finish this."

"Don't you dare leave me like this, Dancer War Hauk. You are more than welcome to fill me tonight and every night from now on."

Kissing her, he pulled her closer and slid inside. Sumi growled at how good he felt as he thrust himself against her. She held him close, unable to believe that he belonged to her and that she was his. In all of her wildest dreams, she'd never thought to have a male like him. Someone she could trust completely who would never seek to hurt her. Someone she would live for.

Hauk buried his face against Sumi's neck and inhaled the warm, sweet scent of her hair and skin. He still couldn't believe how lucky he was to have found her. How lucky he was that she'd agreed to share her life with

him. Strange how he'd given up on ever finding a female, on ever having a family of his own.

And then when he'd least expected it, she'd tumbled
into his world and sent it reeling.

Yes, Kyr was still out there and he was gunning for
both of them. There would always be enemies at the
gate. Always challenges for them both. But together,
they would face them all and nothing would ever get the
better of them.

Strong alone.

Stronger together.

Sumi tightened her grip on him before she cried out
his name.

Smiling, Dancer moved faster, heightening her pleasure. Funny, he'd always hated his name, until his *mia*.
Now there was no greater sound to him than to hear it
on her lips as she came for him.

He captured her lips as he felt his own release. His
senses reeling, he shook all over. Pulling back, he stared
down at her and cupped her face. He reveled in the sensation of her naked body against his. Of the love in her
eyes as she looked at him.

His heart swelling with happiness, he ran his hand
over her stomach where their child was already growing.
Then he kissed her belly and teased it with his tongue.
"I adore you, *mia*. And I will always be yours."

Sumi fingered his goatee as she savored those words.
"Good, because I have no intention of ever letting you go."

Sumi couldn't believe it was morning already. They'd
stayed up all night, talking about the future and making
love until she was amazed that she could still walk.

But then, she'd never get enough of her fierce warrior.

"I like this outfit much better," she said as she fastened a much more sedate gown on so that they could
complete their marriage.

He kissed her bare shoulder. "I still prefer you naked."

Cupping him where he was already hard again, she bit his chin. "I'm willing if you are."

He sucked his breath in sharply. "Don't tempt me. Let's finish this, and then you can chain me to your bed for the rest of my life."

She laughed as he opened the door and they returned to the altar.

Once again, their families were gathered. And this time, Kalea and Darice were waiting for them. Sumi held her hand out for them.

Kalea took it and knelt down between them. Darice followed suit.

The priest came forward and untied the cord that had bound her and Dancer all night. He paused to smile approvingly as he saw the ring on Dancer's hand. "While I may remove the temporary binding between you, remember that you have joined your lineages from now on, and you will protect your single lineage from any who would seek to divide it." He raised a small knife and laid it across Dancer's palm, drawing a small trail of blood. Then he did the same to Sumi. Taking their hands, he placed them together so that they could join blood.

The priest smiled at Kalea before he met Sumi's gaze. "Sumi, now and forevermore of the Warring Blood Clan of Hauk, do you agree to share the full parental and lineage rights of your daughter, Kalea, with your husband?"

"I do."

"And you agree that from this day forward she will be known solely as Kalea of the Warring Blood Clan of Hauk?"

Sumi nodded. "Kalea only has one father. Dancer of the Warring Blood Clan of Hauk."

The priest looked at Dancer. "And do you, Dancer of

the Warring Blood Clan of Hauk, accept the daughter of your wife as yours, and swear to protect her from this day forward as the progeny of your lineage?"

"I do."

Next, he cut Darice's hand and mixed his blood with Sumi's. He held their hands together. "Sumi, now and forevermore of the Warring Blood Clan of Hauk, do you agree to share the rights of your lineage with Darice and to claim him as your own child?"

This was the same ceremony Cairistiona had done for her. "I do."

"And will you agree to share the rights of your son, Darice, with your husband?"

"I will."

The priest met Darice's somber gaze. Everyone was well aware of the fact that once Dariana had been convicted of his father's murder, it'd relegated Darice to the status of a bastard. Even though Syn's DNA tests had proven Keris as his father, their laws no longer recognized Darice as a son of the War Hauk family. The only way to protect his standing and keep him from being disowned was to adopt him as theirs.

It was something both she and Dancer had agreed to immediately.

The priest took Darice's hand into his. Because he was an adult and not a minor child, he, unlike Kalea, had to publicly concur with his adoption. "And do you agree from this day forward to be known solely as Darice Hauk, son of Sumi and Dancer of the Warring Blood Clan of Hauk?"

Darice nodded. "Yes, Reverend Father."

The priest looked at Dancer as he pressed his hand to Darice's. "And do you, Dancer of the Warring Blood Clan of Hauk, accept the son of your wife as yours, and swear to protect him from this day forward as the progeny of your lineage?"

He smiled at Darice and laced his fingers with his. "I do, indeed."

Tears filled Sumi's eyes as she saw the bond between them. *This is my family. . . .*

No, this was part of her family. She glanced over her shoulder at all the others who were gathered there. It was both impressive and terrifying.

Even the little mechanical monkey that was holding on to Devyn and sobbing.

"I just love weddings," Vik sniffed.

Ignoring the mecha, the priest continued. "Then, before these witnesses and our gods, it is so. Rise and be acknowledged, House of the Warring Blood Clan of Hauk. For the four of you before me, and your future children, are the continuation of the two oldest lineages of Andaria. Know that your children will be honored and respected above all, and they will carry on the noblest and best of what it means to be Andarion. May the gods bless you with many, many sons and daughters."

But before she could stand, Hauk took Sumi's hand into his and led it to his cheek. Those red, glowing eyes seared her with his sincerity. "For you and our children, Sumi Hauk, I pledge that I will gladly die."

Sumi placed her other hand over his and shook her head. "We do not accept that pledge from you, mighty War Hauk. Our children and I expect you to *live* for us."

He smiled at her. "And that, *munatara a la frah*, I will always do."

TITLES BY
SHERRILYN KENYON

ENJOY
SHERRILYN KENYON
IN AUDIO!

The League series is available
on CD and for digital download.

BORN OF NIGHT
BORN OF FIRE
BORN OF ICE
BORN OF FURY

Don't miss the next audiobook in the series:

BORN OF DEFIANCE

Available May 2015

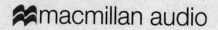